PARIS
Apartment for Rent

© 2012
PEGGY KOPMAN-OWENS

PARIS
APARTMENT FOR RENT

Cover Art
© Roger Kopman
KOPMANPHOTOS.com

First eBook Edition 2013
Aventura eBooks Ltd.
London, UK
First Paperback Edition 2015
First Hardcover Edition 2021
Independently Published

Audio Book
Narrated & Produced by
Steve Ember

This Reprint Edition 2023
PKOBOOKS LLC

Author Rights

The Author asserts the moral right to be identified as the author of this work.

This novel is entirely a work of fiction. Names, characters, businesses, places, events and incidents are either, the products of the author's imagination or used in a fictitious manner. Any resemblance to actual persons, living or dead, or actual events is purely coincidental.

Dedication:

The author at work on her first book.

"My mother, whose shadow appears in the photograph above, wrote stories and songs, becoming my inspiration. She taught that passion and patience are inseparable partners. From my father and mother, both musicians who loved to travel, I learned to embrace a world full of diversity and endless possibilities. I can never thank them enough for bestowing this lovingly unselfish gift of intellectual freedom."

꧁ꇸꇸ꧂
Acknowledgements:
꧁ꇸꇸ꧂

Michael D. Owens gives Paris new meaning by finding mysteries and surprises around every corner. His discoveries serve up feasts for our imaginations and romance for our hearts. Seeing Paris through his eyes, with his hand holding mine, has been the greatest adventure of a lifetime. This book, inspired by Michael, my lover - my friend, is also dedicated to him,

"Je t'aime, toujours."

Peg

&⊂℞℘∾
Contents:
&⊂℞℘∾

❧❦❧❦
Paris
❧❦❧❦

ᴥᴥ ᴥ

Chapter 1

ᴥᴥ ᴥ

T
his was Paris. He could learn to be patient, to keep his mouth shut, if that's what it took to stay here. People here did not surrender to artificial rules and regulations. They tolerated, ignored, or cursed them, but they never surrendered to them. Yes. French bureaucracy had its place, but that place was inside a government building, not inside their apartment buildings, where the villagers could make up their own rules.

The Épicier (grocer) had not yet opened his shop for the day. It was, after all, only 6:30 a.m. Just because a man advertised Open 6:30 a.m. to 9:00 p.m., it did not mean that he, actually, had to receive customers at such an early hour. Behind the metal security door, banging could be heard, as boxes were opened, then, roughly stacked. The occasional loud BANG only served to add to his anxiety. From somewhere behind the reverberating metal door, music played, and there was unintelligible conversation, but the source was not clear and could be coming from the radio.

It did not matter, Zack sighed. If the Épicier didn't want to face the world at 06:30, no one could force him to do so. Sleeping an extra fifteen minutes was his prerogative and his private revolution. Vive la France! Life here was about living the good life, not about watching the clock. Perhaps, the Épicier had remained in bed an extra thirty minutes to make love to his wife. Perhaps, her coffee had been too good to resist a second cup. It did not matter. It was the grocer's life – the grocer's rules.

Zack was learning to cast off ideas about how the world should work, and learning to embrace how it did work, or sometimes didn't. Coming to Paris was about leaving foolish expectations behind in the States, and experiencing a new way of living in France, a whole new way of thinking. He would adjust, even if it meant enduring an especially painful half hour of waiting for an épicerie to open because finding out about the apartment for rent was that important. On this particular morning, a vacant place in the 6th was so close to becoming his, he could already imagine himself living there, and nothing...nothing else mattered.

He watched from across the street, while two doors down someone on the third floor reached in front of the lace curtain and inserted an *Appartement Louer* sign.

"Rats!" He muttered.

Now, everyone would know where the hidden treasure was located. The sign in French was upside down. Zack translated it practically standing on his head.

Apartment for Rent.
Two Rooms.
28 square meters.
Third floor without elevator.
Inquire – Grocer 35 rue *********

The grocer's address had been handwritten and inserted as an afterthought, and although, nearly illegible, would not require a genius to figure out, (maybe someone acting like an ostrich).

Then, he heard them - two apartment hunters, walking towards him from behind. He turned to face them as they held a newspaper between them, reading aloud, and looking at addresses. "No, over there!" The woman said, loudly, not caring if her voice awakened the dead, and pointing to the wrong side of the street. They hurried past Zack, and then, turned the corner. Zack looked back at the closed épicerie. It would be only a matter of minutes, before the couple realized that they had turned in the wrong direction. He could still hear their voices a block away. Their accents? Yes. Yes, definitely, Americans, and they were probably as intent upon living in this neighborhood as he was.

Rats! Rats! Rats! Now, the world would know. They were probably texting messages to their four hundred closest friends. Soon, a crowd of apartment hunters would gather, ready to beat each other to death for this rare gem in the 6th Arrondissement. Zack thought Americans were the worst, always wanting to live where the great artists and writers had lived and worked in Paris. This part of Paris drew wannabes as the hives in the Luxembourg gardens drew real bees.

He had to take that *louer* sign out of the window, before they came back, but how? His imagination went wild and his heartbeats increased to rabbit-rapid speed. Looking over his shoulder to where the couple had disappeared, he decided that it was now or never. As if the angels of Saint-Germain-des-Prés had heard him, magically, the front door of the apartment building slowly opened. He made a mad dash across the street, and wedged past an older man with thick glasses, who mistakenly held the door open, thinking that Zack was "the nephew." Dropping a flurry of *"Excusez-moi's"* and *"Pardonez-moi's"* down the stairwell behind him Zack ran the stairs to arrive at the third floor, breathless.

With four doors, there was a one in four chance of knocking on the right one. Which one was it? Turned around, he wasn't certain which of the apartments faced the street outside, and so, stopped in mid knock on the closest one in order to gather his thoughts. Whatever he said, in the next thirty seconds, might very well determine if the people living in the surrounding apartments would think him acceptable. They must not think him a pervert, a rapist, a robber, just because he appeared so early, so unexpectedly, and so excitedly at their door.

(Breathe. Breathe. Breathe.) He told himself.

It worked, until the sound of shuffling feet below on the first floor startled him. He hung over the railing of the stairs, but could no longer see the old man, but then, came the sound of the front door slamming. The nephew must have arrived to collect his uncle. No doubt, the uncle was recounting the story of being nearly accosted on his own front stoop by another one of those foreigners, speaking very poor French.

Fear struck. What if the door was opening and not shutting? What if his competitors for the apartment were already closing in? What if they were approaching on the stairs below? What if? Panic was setting in. Was he no different from the other prospective tenants, who arrived in such frenzy, intoxicated by the prospect of living in Paris that they were willing to pay whatever it cost to share in the "joie de vivre?" The real estate agent would be accustomed to dealing with such people. How could he convince anyone that he was different? Perhaps, the agent had already warned the building's residents. "Beware! Take cover! An apartment is vacant in the building. They will be attacking at any hour of the day or night!"

Zack had no way of refuting that They were him, and all who might follow, and any one of them would be ready to throw down life savings for one year in Paris, not caring who lived next door. However, for the residents, forced to live next door to the outsider, the story was different. Outsiders represented a threat to the village. New arrivals always pushed up the rent, and threatened the stability of very delicately negotiated landlord-tenant agreements. Why should they be expected to pay more just because a crazy American was so willing to push up the rent?

Monsieur Épicier, their landlord, had told them that he both loved and hated Americans because they were both easy and hard to please. With their heads filled with stories of expatriate escapades in Paris, they could be enticed to pay an exorbitant amount of money with the mere drop of a name. A famous writer, musician, artist, or actor, who "might" have lived next door, bought bread down the street, or gardened on the roof drove them into a bidding war. It did not matter if the information was correct. It would take the American months to realize that his lease was based upon a lie, and by then, he would not care. He was living his Parisian life, and friends and family back home had already retold the lie so many times, it now seemed true. Hemingway had slept here... or was it there? Or there?

Their unrealistic expectations, however, drove Monsieur Épicier crazy. His apartments did not include such things as dishwashers, garbage disposals, and walk-in closets the size of a two-car garage. One prospective tenant had been so bold as to expect a parking spot right below his window! The grocer and his other tenants had laughed about that one for months.

An apartment in the 6th with one alcove bedroom, one bath, no closet, and an efficiency kitchen, but without an elevator or a parking spot, could easily rent for the equivalent of a three-bedroom, two-bath house in the United States. It was difficult for some foreign visitors to understand, and even harder for them to downsize their dreams in order to share a roof with Parisians. Only time could teach them, the luxury of living in Paris was not the apartment, but rather, the joy of being a few steps away from the heart of the city.

Zack, however, had read about finding the perfect apartment in the perfect Parisian neighborhood, knowing that it would be small by American standards. In preparation, nearly everything he owned had been placed in storage on Long Island. What remained consisted of two large boxes at his parents' home ready for shipment, once he settled upon an address. Electronics were being left behind, as nothing was compatible with French voltage. His laptop was adaptable, but he would be acquiring everything else in France. After all, as a real resident of France, he had a moral obligation to help the French economy.

Cooking at home was not in his plan. The French rarely entertained at home, except for family and the closest of friends. There were cafés, bistros, and brasseries on nearly every block, which served as meeting places for socializing. These were places, where people could observe and be observed; places for working out the details of their lives, and the politics of their neighborhoods. They were also sources of quick evening meals, boxed for reheating at home. Nearly every apartment came equipped with a microwave, but stovetops with ovens were luxuries of those with more money and more time. Zack did not plan to become one of them, as he had already lived in a place, where people barricaded themselves behind their front doors at night. He had grown up in a neighborhood of slam-clickers, a bedroom community on Long Island, where people – unlike their counterparts in Manhattan – came out only in the daylight.

He had become frustrated at an early age with the lack of curiosity, characteristic of so many of his high school friends, content to spend endless hours in cars on the weekends, looking for girls. He preferred taking the train into Manhattan to visit museums, art galleries, and when he was old enough, nightclubs. How else was a fellow suppose to know, if what one imagined, and what was real had anything in common?

He had come to Paris with that same kind of natural curiosity, eager to meet people, and despite his lack of proper language skills, determined not to hide. He planned on finding entertainment outside of his apartment in the evenings. With what he would save by not buying a television, he could afford a few more cups of coffee or glasses of wine. This trip was a work assignment, but in truth, he would have come with or without a job. Books about Paris had been piling up next to his bed for two years, prior to the job offer, and it was time to find out, if anything others had written about Paris was true. He was twenty-five years old, and if not now, when?

To downsize, he accepted that a small refrigerator, a coffee pot, and a microwave, in a small studio would be sufficient. He would survive, no matter what the Spartan conditions were by American standards. Parisians enjoyed life without unnecessary amenities, which only took up precious space. Here, good apartments in good neighborhoods, regardless of size, were gone within twenty-four hours of an advertisement appearing in the newspapers, or on the bulletin board of a café.

This one had appeared only a half-hour earlier in an expatriate newspaper, which Zack had purchased fresh off the press with his morning croissant. His fear was that the ad was a scam, a first reaction. Such things were not "un" common, a switch and bait operation to hook perspective renters into accepting poorer accommodation in a less desirable part of a city. The shrewd perpetrator, setting the hook, counted on visitors not knowing the Arrondissements.

Zack had prided himself on studying maps meticulously, and yet, he had already been tricked twice. On one of those occasions, he had arrived in the 6th, only to be redirected to the 18th, where the actual address was located. There was nothing wrong with living near Le Sacré Coeur, except its distance from where he wanted to be.

"The 18th Arrondissement," the last property owner had said, "is so perfect for artists, such as you. So close to Montmartre."

"Writer," Zack had corrected him.

"Writer?" the property owner had said, sneering. "Oh, then...you'll want the 10th, where the other communists live, or perhaps, the 12th."

What did communists, and writers, have in common - that they could be sneered at in the sentence? What did he mean by that? "No," Zack said. "I want the 6th."

"Bonne chance," was his response as he flipped his hand in the air and took off.

Yes. Good luck, Zack agreed. His mistake had been looking for an apartment without the help of an agent, and the results had been miserable. They played him for a sucker because he acted as one. If this apartment ad proved to be another scam, he would have to bite the bullet, and pay out the necessary agency fees to hire someone. It was obvious that taking a cheaper route was not paying off.

In fact, he had lost valuable time, and probably had lost out on potentially acceptable apartments due to nothing more than his stubbornness. He needed more than luck. He needed someone else's advice. However, in Paris, he knew no one.

Real estate agents made a fortune in fees to locate and lease apartments. Agents received the equivalent of one, two, or even three months rent in advance to negotiate a lease, and to cut through red tape to secure the proper documents required for a foreign resident. They also contracted the repairmen, who would overcharge to fix a leak, a short in the electrical, or to kill the mold growing in the ceiling. These costs were in addition to a security deposit paid directly to the actual property owner. An exchange of several thousands in Euros would take place, before a long-term tenant could expect to see a key in his hand.

The ideal situation was not to lease anything. Simply become the invited guest of someone, who had already navigated the murky waters of leasing, and then, not leave. But, he knew no one in Paris, and certainly, no stranger was going to make such an offer.

His employer in New York did not provide housing guidance for his overseas employees. The assumption was that anyone, who accepted a position in another country, would have the mental and financial wherewithal to set up house on his/her own. Zack didn't have the courage to call his boss's secretary, Molly, to tell her differently. It was too much to risk. What if his boss found out, and fired him (for stupidity), before he had a chance to write his first feature article? No. He would have to figure this out on his own...somehow.

In Paris, renters exceeded the inventory of good properties available, presenting a simple supply and demand situation. Despite the government's attempt to crack down on absentee landlords, this city continued to be a property owner's paradise. Landlords were free to charge whatever the market would bear. Zack's desire to live in one of the most sought-after areas of a city, which boasted of some of the world's most expensive real estate prices...well, that had been his choice, and if his choice exceeded commonsense, well...that too was his problem, and no one else's.

Yes. There were less expensive cities in France, but his heart was set on this neighborhood in Paris. And, yes, it did matter that it was here, where Gertrude Stein had lived, and where Hemingway had walked. Ok. Yes. He would admit it. He was an American, one of those

Americans.

After reading the ad in the paper, Zack had practically run all the way to the épicerie, hoping all the way, he might be the first to throw down his deposit and demand the key. L' Église de Saint-Germain-des-Prés was close, so too, many of the famous cafés and clubs, featured in his guidebooks. This apartment was too rare a treasure not to wait however long it took. How could Monsieur Épicier not appreciate his situation? How could he not open early, today of all days? How rude. How dispassionate not to know the pain, which his delay was causing this poor American boy.

On the Métro, he had made up his mind. His first and only question would be, "How much?" and if the amount were anything close to his budget, then, he would take the place sight unseen. He loved this neighborhood, having walked it every week since his arrival in Paris. He could agree to live in a pigeon coop on the roof, if it meant waking up on this very street every morning. Whatever was wrong with the place could be fixed, and everything was fixable for a price. Surely, the price of repairs would be less than the cost of staying in a hotel for another month.

In his daydream, he had already moved in to the place. There was also pressure on him from the States. It arrived every afternoon in the form of an email. It would start - "address?" His search had taken six long, very expensive weeks, and even though, his company had footed the bill for the first two weeks, his boss was now demanding a real address, unwilling to send his paychecks to a hotel room number. It was decided that this would be his last week in room 211.

Zack's boss in the States could not understand why this particular employee, unlike others sent to Europe, was having so much difficulty getting settled into his new surroundings. Others had done it, successfully, in less than a week. Zack danced around the question every time that it surfaced. Indecision had left Zack ensconced in the hotel so long he knew all of the hotel employees by their first names, and that familiarity was beginning to breed contempt. They had begun greeting him with "When do you check out?" instead of "Bonjour, Monsieur."

The answer would come from his checking account in the States, which had been squeezed down to its last dollar. His first month's salary had not yet been transferred to a French bank because according to its manager, he was "without residence," essentially – homeless. The bank executive had heard this same tale of woe too many times before. "I am searching for an apartment, but as yet, I have not found one." He would tell this uninitiated American, what he had told many other hopefuls, "Bonne chance!"

For the past three days, Zack had been withdrawing money from his savings, an account set aside for emergencies. A quick accounting had proved that his hotel bill for the last three days had justified the first, but hopefully, the last of those emergencies. If he didn't secure an apartment soon, he had no Plan B. The bank manager had been correct. He would need all the luck he could get.

A creak startled him, as the door of an apartment behind him was opened suddenly. He turned, speechless, his well-rehearsed introduction lost. One only had to take a glance through the opening to see the reason why. The thirty-something beauty at the door possessed that decidedly Parisian look of someone, who didn't need to work at all; a real estate agent, who had better properties in even better parts of Paris.

"Vous êtes ici à propos de l'appartement?" She asked, before Zack could open his mouth, or roll in his tongue. His eyes were having difficulty, taking in the vision of the magnificent floor to ceiling windows behind her because they perfectly framed the 18th century building across the street. It was a setting, deserving to be photographed for a postcard, but she was blocking the view. Then, he caught a better look at her, and his perspective and attitude changed, accordingly.

She asked, again, "Vous êtes ici à propos de l'appartement?"

This time, he was focused solely on her, and became nearly, as tongue-tied. "Oui," he managed to get out, worried that his French would be inadequate for the negotiation. However, his accent unmasked him.

"Oh, American," she said, dismissively.

Zack knew that tone, and upon seeing her expression, realized that the price on the apartment had just rocketed. There were Parisian prices, and then, there were stupid American prices. She had nailed him as falling into the latter category. He could not blame her for her quick assessment of him, a reflection of his fashion sense. He had dressed too quickly, choosing jeans over trousers, a sweatshirt, rather than a jacket. He was surprised that the woman had bothered to acknowledge him at all.

She had that look, which screamed 16th Arrondissement, where selling just one property, or simply renting three, could cover her expenses for an entire year. Her jewelry, suggested that she made more in one day, than he might make in a year. Her agent's fee for leasing this place, whatever it might be, would represent mere tip money. Later, over cocktails, she would confirm all of his suspicions, breaking a cardinal rule in France, which prohibited telling strangers your income.

Maybe she wanted to impress him, or perhaps, she wanted to discourage him. Whatever her motives, she accomplished both during apéritifs. Although, she had allowed him time to change clothes before dinner, a better appearance did not muster the courage he needed to make even a feeble pass. Her candor had paralyzed him, teaching him the first rule of courting French women. Lesson One: Let French women tell you what they want. It's really a time saver. Without hesitation, she had told him what to wear to dinner.

Claudine was single, rich, and available – just not available to Zack. She made no game of telling him, and although, her directness came as a jolt to his ego, he appreciated her brutal honesty. Unlike the women he had known, she did not play coy, try to manipulate the conversation, or expect him to pay for the honor of her company. With her last bite of poire belle Hélène, she had lifted her hand and called for "l'addition." She handed over her Carte Bleue, before Zack could fumble for his wallet. "Pour les deux," she said to the waiter. If there had been any doubt about her intentions, she had just cleared the air. This was business – strictly business.

It was a shame, Zack thought. A friend in Paris, one who could have taught him the ins and outs of civility, how to dress, how to act in an expensive restaurant, would have been nice. However, that desire was secondary to securing the apartment that he wanted, and in the neighborhood that he wanted. As they were saying goodnight, Claudine extended her hand to shake or kiss, (Which should he do?), rather than her cheek, and agreed to prepare a one-year lease with an option for two more years. He was elated, and yet, he had not stepped foot inside of the place!

Later, alone in bed, when he could not get the beautiful French woman, or the scent of her perfume out of his head, he wondered, "What had he said at dinner that had influenced her decision?" Did it have anything to do with him being a writer? Surely, that had not impressed her. Being a famous author might have, but internet blogger? No. There were enough of them in Paris already.

He sighed, content that his luck was changing. Somehow, he had passed her test. Somehow, he had become "acceptable." Perhaps, she, unlike the earlier landlord, did not believe that all foreign writers, who came to Paris, were communists, or belonged in the 10th. For this, he was grateful. The 10th was not an unpleasant place to live; it was simply, not the 6th. He fell asleep remembering every word that came out of her luscious red lips.

Claudine's instructions had been succinct. He was to meet her back at the apartment in the morning for the cursory inspection, after which he would hand her the deposit in cash, plus her agency fee. He would sign both the lease and inventory list. Every nail mark in the walls and every scratch in the hardwood floors had to be recorded, while both, he and the landlord's agent were in attendance, so that his deposit might one day be returned. If he did not show up on time, or refused to participate in the walk-through, the offer would be withdrawn.

The signed inventory had a double purpose, she explained. First, it established the condition of the apartment, when he moved in, and secondly, it permitted the landlord the right to sue for repairs, if Zack should damage anything. Anything, Claudine emphasized, could be something as simple as putting an additional nail in the wall, or repairing a scratch in the floor. Some flaws were there to give the place character. After she explained everything for the third time, (even though Zack had not asked her to do so), Zack agreed to meet her at 10:00 a.m.

Claudine, he was learning, was nothing – if not thorough.

Chapter 2

H e was at the apartment at 9:30 a.m., not taking a chance of missing Claudine's arrival. He stood in the pouring rain beneath the canopy of a flower shop across from the apartment building, and cursed the fact that the "Louer" sign, still remained in the third floor window. He wished that it would disappear, so that no one else might line up alongside of him, someone willing to double his offer.

Three different times, people walked past him, and twice, they had glanced up, making note of the sign. So far, no one had stopped, or tried to enter the building. He was holding his breath, hoping that they would not. If it continued to rain, perhaps, they would not look up. As the time on his watch approached 9:56 a.m., he held his breath and hoped.

One minute later, she approached from the corner beneath an orange umbrella. Although, he could not see her face, her distinctive style was already recognizable. Claudine wore a bracelet around her left ankle, which he could not avoid noticing, when she kept crossing and uncrossing her legs at dinner. Even in the rain, the diamonds on her ankle sparkled, signaling her arrival like a neon sign.

The four-inch heels were nearly as attractive, defining her thin ankles and muscular calves as trademarks of being not only a beautiful French woman, but also a true Parisian woman. Here, walking everyday served to preserve a woman's physical beauty, well into old age, making it difficult to determine the age of any woman. Claudine was no exception. She looked up and saw him waiting for her. He dropped his stare, and crossed the street to meet her at the front door of the apartment building.

"Vous êtes en avance," she said, then, remembered that Zack did not speak French, although, he struggled to speak something that sounded like a foreign language. "You are early. I have the contract here." She said, tapping the manila envelope, crushed up against her jacket to keep it dry. "Everything is prepared. Shall we go up?" she said, as she punched in the digicode on the front door.

Zack opened the door for her, enjoying that she smelled as good as she looked. Other than the postman, who passed them on their way in, they met no one in the hallways. The building seemed unusually quiet for 10:00 a.m. Perhaps, everyone had left for work. Perhaps, there were no retirees living here, no young families with crying babies. So far, so good, Zack thought, a quiet place to live.

Then, a whiff of something caused the first red flag to wave, as they passed a partially opened closet on their way up the second set of stairs, and a strange pungent odor filled his nostrils to the point of a major sneeze. He apologized as Claudine looked back over her shoulder to acknowledge, "Trash day. The désinfectant...you will become accustomed," she said, dismissively, waving the air in front of her face. "We hate bugs," she added, as if it were only a decidedly French preference.

Zack, trying too hard, felt compelled to comment, "Us, too." It struck him that he was attempting to speak for Americans everywhere. "Especially, cockroaches," he added. Her head snapped around to look at him as if he had uttered curse words, but she kept silent. Zack heard a loud "Ooops," in his head, a warning of "too much. Did you learn nothing at dinner? Let her do the talking."

Before the door had been unlocked, she explained that the appartement meublé (furnished apartment) did not include la cuisinière (stove), although, it had le micro-ondes (microwave). It had la douche (shower), but no la baignoire (bathtub). Amazingly, for such a small apartment, she pointed out, this apartment had its own la machine à laver (washing machine), which served double duty as le sèche-linge (clothes dryer). This was a luxury in Paris, she said, as if Zack should be grateful that the landlord was not charging more for this amenity.

There were hookups for television, telephone, and internet, but Zack would be responsible for setting up the service. Zack wanted to ask her "How do I...," but her manner was too intimidating, and he didn't want to come off as a total novice. Offending her, when she possessed all the power, was ill advised. Besides, his cockroach comment was still in the forefront. Listen. Don't talk. There would be plenty of time to ask questions, later, after the papers were signed, and the place was truly his.

Upon closer inspection, fifteen nail holes were found in the walls. Claudine used her cell phone keypad to type in specific locations as she took photos of each one. Evidently, the previous tenant had been quite a collector of art, covering his walls with paintings. It was understandable because the walls were covered in faded flowered wallpaper more suited to another century, not just another decade. Zack tried to imagine what he might buy to cover up the walls in the same way. What was large enough to disguise the more vivid, remaining pattern of missing artwork? His budget allowed for little more than cheap posters, and he had left that style of decorating behind, years earlier, when he left university.

Claudine had moved on, and was trying to draw his attention to the floors. Hard wood covered all except the bathroom floor, which had been updated with tile during its renovation twenty years earlier. The hardwood was, in fact, the best and least damaged surface in the apartment. It appeared to have been recently sanded and polished. However, Claudine counted exactly nine scratches. Six of them, Zack could not see, until he dropped down to his knees as she had done.

The kitchen and bathroom had been cleaned with products, smelling almost as pungent as the trash bins downstairs, although, neither room exuded quite the same odor. Claudine saw Zack's nose twitch, and explained that written instructions would be mailed on how to clean properly the apartment, along with a list of the appropriate cleaning products to purchase. He was never to mix up the ones designated for use in the bathroom with the ones specified for use in the kitchen. "Jamais!" she said, quite emphatically.

Did she speak from a bad experience with previous American tenants, who – being the sanitation barbarians that she imagined – insisted upon cleaning our homes with the same product! Incroyable!

She must have seen the smirk on his face, or read his mind because she curtly remarked that she could not understand how Americans could keep garbage in their kitchens, or trash in their bathrooms! He was to remove all rubbish everyday and place it in the cans provided on the ground floor, where it would be promptly removed by the sanitation workers, a group of people in Paris, hailed as heroes for their bravery.

He wanted to defend Americans against her generalized opinion of them, but she had launched into a second assault. Why would anyone want to park a car inside the same building, where he lives? "Don't the fumes kill people?" she asked, although, she was not expecting an answer, nor was willing to listen to one. Zack's learning curve was improving. The idea of an entire Long Island neighborhood, lined with homes and two and three-car garages, was beyond the comprehension of this life-long city dweller. Claudine did not even own a car.

In addition to the nail holes and scratches, Claudine discovered a cracked windowpane, and a strange hole about the size of a man's fist, punched into the back of the only closet in the apartment. She assured him both would be fixed before he moved in. "However, the nail holes and scratches will remain." The way she declared it, there would be no attempt to fix or hide any of these. To do so would change the count on her inventory, and somehow this act alone would void his lease. So be it, he thought. He could live with nail holes and scratches, careful not to add to or subtract from the total, which apparently was written in stone.

The apartment would be available for him to move-in in five days, she said.

"For you to move in…," stuck in his head. Yes! Definitely, he had heard her say it. This was going to become his apartment, and he was only seconds away from finalizing the deal. He could hardly believe it, and so, hurriedly reached into his pocket to find the cash, which would seal the deal and make his dream a reality.

Then, her phone rang. Actually, it played a song, which made him wonder how much could be determined about a person by her ringtone. Evidently, there was still much to learn about Claudine. In stark contrast, his four-year old cell phone still rang its factory setting, broadcasting not only his boring personality to the world, but his technical abilities. He made a note to change it, soon, if he could find the instruction manual, or an electronics store assistant, who was willing to help.

"Pardon," she whispered in Zack's direction, as she continued her conversation with the caller in French. Even with his bad translation skills, he could tell it was business, business far more interesting than conducting a walk-through with a potential renter. To give her some privacy, he wandered a few steps away into the sleeping alcove, which held a single bed hardly larger than the one he had slept in as a child. He lay down to confirm what he had suspected. His feet hung off the end. As he lay there, staring at the ceiling, it felt as though the walls were closing in around him. He popped up and looked for an alternative sleeping arrangement. Yes. He saw it. With some rearranging, the sofa could become his bed, and this little cave of a space – his office. Yes. He could make it work. However, there was a possible third option.

He was working out the design of an elevated platform bed, when he heard Claudine calling his name. "ZAHK?" Claudine hurriedly apologized in half-English, half-French sentences, explaining that she "doit quitter" (must leave) "tout de suite" (immediately). With that, she shoved the manila envelope and inventory list at his chest, and said, "Téléphonez-moi!"

She dashed out of the apartment, so quickly, that she caught her heel on the doorsill and started a free fall, headfirst, into the hallway. Fortunately, she reached out and caught herself on the banister of the stairwell, or she might have found herself "tout de suite" in the foyer three floors down. Ever the professional, and not to be detoured from her mission, she was already texting with her one free hand, as she got to her feet and headed down the stairs. Evidently, a bigger fish in the 16th was waiting to be hooked.

Zack called out, "Wait! Should I lock up?" But, the only thing he heard was the sound of the front door slamming shut. He looked around a moment, but since, he had no key, and there appeared to be no other way to lock the door from the outside, he was stymied. If he left, and anything was stolen, he might be held responsible. She had forced him to take the lease and the inventory, but yet, neither document had been signed, and more importantly, no money had changed hands. Was he technically the tenant, yet? He didn't know what to do. Should he stay, or should he go?

Then, he did something that felt unethical, if not illegal. He took the "Louer" sign out of the window and hid it on a shelf in the closet. For all intensive purposes, the place was now his. It was only a matter of paperwork. Right? If he left the sign in the window, someone might come in, damage the apartment, put an extra nail hole in the wall, or worse - fix a scratch on the floor. Then, what would he do? What would Claudine do? Start over? Draw up another lease? No. Taking the sign out of the window was the proper thing to do, the only sensible thing.

As he wandered around the apartment, conducting a private inventory of his own, he decided to send Claudine a text. She had already demonstrated that she could multi-task, texting, and falling at the same time. As he was composing, the sound of feet, shuffling outside his door became distracting. Was this the time to start meeting the neighbors? Or had the Épicier finally opened his shop and sent other prospective tenants? Rats!

"Bonjour," a sweet little voice called to him from the hallway. Then, a face just as sweet and innocent appeared in the doorway. "Avez-vous signé le bail?"

"Pardonez-moi," Zack answered. "Qu' avez-vous dit? Je parle Français not so..."

She interrupted him. "Oh. You are American, No?" She seemed already disappointed.

"American, yes," he answered, sticking out his hand for her to shake. "You live here?" He asked, hoping that she was not a competitor for the apartment. He was prepared to tell her that it was already rented. He had "Louer'ed" it, if that was a proper French verb. (He would look it up later in his French pocket dictionary.)

"Yes. Next door," she pointed. Zack visibly relaxed. "You signed the lease?" she asked, again, and looked nervously around him into the apartment, as she waited for his answer.

He clutched the papers against his chest, and answered, honestly, "No. Not yet, but I will," he announced proudly, feeling almost like her new neighbor. "Zack," he said.

But she did not accept his hand, instead, stared at it. Looking a bit relieved herself, she surprised him by saying, "Then, Zahhk, it is not too late."

"Too late for what?"

"Too late to leave... to run away," she said, not sure of her English.

Zack could tell from the look on her face, that she was quite serious. What did she know about the apartment that the thorough-to-a-fault Claudine had failed to mention? Zack studied her face, as her eyes surveyed the apartment from the doorway. It was such a timid, almost fearful look. She stared at the blank spots on the wall, where paintings had hung.

"Then, he is truly gone," she said, a statement rather than a question.

Her expression was difficult to read. Was it sadness, fear, or something else? Had her former lover lived here? Had he departed without telling her goodbye? Was it a love affair gone wrong, or was this the scene of something more sinister? Had a drug dealer lived here? A rapist? A murderer? What? If so, why hadn't he seen the blood? Then, he remembered how adamant Claudine had been about using the proper cleaning products, and how thoroughly cleaned the bathroom and kitchen smelled. Suddenly, the apartment did not seem quite so perfect.

er name was Mara, she announced, inviting him into her apartment. And thus, the ruse began. If Mara had not invited him in, Zack would have stayed outside her door to hear her story. Her warning to "run away" had already sucked him into the mystery that had begun when he saw her face. What was the pretty, young French woman so afraid of? The fact that she was young, pretty, and French, had nothing at all to do with it, he would later tell himself, but by then, it would be too late.

"Please!" she begged Zack. "Do not sign the lease."

"But, I need a place to live," he said, adamantly. "What's wrong with the apartment? Really, you must tell me. The agent wants these documents signed, today, and frankly, you haven't given me one reason not to sign them. I don't want to lose this place. This is a perfect location." He said, as Mara poured him a second glass of wine. "He had asked her twice already to explain. Each time, she had hesitated, instead, answering his questions with questions. Where did you live? How long will you stay? What's your dog's name?"

"My dog's name?" he had asked, "What does that have to do with anything?"

"Nothing," she answered, then, surprised him with, "And where did you go to school?"

The conversation felt more like a job interview, than a friendly conversation with a neighbor. Zack threw her short, quick answers, so that her focus might be redirected to Paris and the apartment he hoped to lease. "This is a perfect neighborhood, a perfect place to live," he said, hoping that she might return to the present, instead of his past.

"Yes. Perfect," she confirmed, sighing and looking down. "Perfect." She said, again, as if remembering something, which she wasn't quite ready to share. She had spent more than an hour quizzing Zack on his past, and so began telling him about every, single person in the building, as she had memorized their résumés during previous happy hours. She knew the intimate details of their lives, and it seemed important that she share them with him.

It was only noon, but his head already felt like it was well past happy hour. She rose to fill his glass, yet one more time. "No more," he said with some insistence, putting his hand over the top of his glass. "It's nice of you to tell me about the other residents in the building, but you really must tell me everything about the apartment. You appear to have mentioned everyone in this building, except the previous tenant." Zack asked. "Did you know..."

"Tito," Mara interrupted.

"Good," Zack answered. "Tell me more about...." At least, now, Zack had a name and someone to imagine. "Tito?" He asked, already picturing a drummer from Cuba, and not the late Yugoslavian leader.

"Yes. He was..." She said, sadly, struggling for the proper words in English.

("Hold the phone,") Zack thought, focusing in on the use of the word was. Was Tito dead?

"Tito was an entrepreneur de pompes funèbres. Do you know this work?" she asked, sweetly.

Zack did not want to appear ignorant. He was, after all, here to immerse himself in the language and culture. "Yes," he declared, "I do," not at all certain that he did. But, what did a simple white lie, handed so casually to a stranger, matter?

He did the quick translation in his head as she continued talking. He knew the word "entrepreneur" from reading it so often in financial pages, so he translated it to mean a young creative business person. The word "pompes" threw him, but so many French words were simply slightly different pronunciations of English words, and vice-versa. "Pompes" sounded like pumps. Pumps equaled pipes. So, by putting the three words together, he came up with the idea that the previous tenant had been an entrepreneur in the plumbing business. There! He said, silently, proud of himself. French was not so difficult.

Mara relaxed. "Then, it does not bother you that he lived in the apartment... before you?"

Zack, delighted that they were communicating so well, said, "Of course, not." He was thinking that, at least, the plumbing in his new apartment would not need to be repaired. In fact, he might have the best toilet in all of the 6th, along with the best water pressure. It also explained why there was a washing machine in such a small apartment. No doubt, Claudine, if she had stayed longer, would have explained all of this to him.

Whatever Mara's problem was with the previous next-door neighbor, it no longer concerned him. Tito was out. He was in.

Perhaps, the plumber had been a little too friendly. Perhaps, that was the reason she did not like him. Perhaps, he belonged to a union, and she did not. Perhaps, it was why she had spent so much time "interviewing" Zack. She did not want a similar problem with the new guy. Could he expect all of the tenants in the building to invite him in, offer him a glass of wine, and then, trash the other residents? Well, at least, now he was prepared for this new and interesting French custom.

However, at the moment, he was more concerned with what Claudine would think of him. She was waiting for his telephone call, and her fee. He had to go. Looking at his watch, he stood up, and prepared to say his goodbyes. Mara looked panicked by his intentions. They were not finished talking, she told him, and reached up to pull him back down on the sofa. All Zack could think was, "French women certainly aren't shy about what they want." Could she be making a pass at him, after spending the last fifteen minutes talking about her boyfriend? Ah, Paris. L'amour toujours!

"I want you to move in with me," she declared.

"Wow. Never saw that coming." Zack said in his head. "I'll be right next door." Zack offered aloud an alternative to moving in with a perfect stranger, who was becoming stranger by the minute. He was not sure where this conversation could possibly lead. Walking back his mistake for accepting her invitation to come in - so quickly, "I'm sure, once we get to know each other, that... I mean, you seem like a very nice girl."

"You do not understand," Mara pleaded. "I need you here." She pulled on him to return to the sofa.

"Whoa," Zack said, now, more than a little bit afraid of Mara. There were direct women, assertive women, and then, there were crazy women. Was Mara falling into the last category – quickly?

"You do not understand," she began, again. "I need you to become my cousin."

"Cousin?" Zack asked. Was this code? What exactly was the meaning of "cousin" in French? Now, more than ever, he wished that he had paid more attention in French class. At this particular moment, he could agree with her, wholeheartedly, when he said, "You're right. I do not understand,"

Mara began explaining that tenants were not allowed to sublet their apartments. It was prohibited in their leases. However, there was a small loophole, which stated that family members could share the same apartment. Zack sat down. Her apartment had been approved for two adult occupants and one child. If Zack would agree, to pretend to be her cousin, she would let him live in the apartment, alone, freeing her to move in with her boyfriend.

Mara was not yet twenty-one, single, and greatly attached to a man named Philippe. Although, she was old enough to marry, they chose not to, preferring to live together for a while. As Zack listened, he imagined that the not-getting-married part had been Phillipe's idea. Mara appeared to be very naïve and easily manipulated.

Her parents, she said, had not yet recovered from her decision to move away from their home in Verdun, and cohabitation with a man would push them over the top. Mara wanted to spare them the embarrassment, but also, to save herself from the confrontation, which was certain to follow – should they find out. She needed to keep her Paris address, if for no other reason than to provide the appearance of celibacy. Thus, the necessity for the ruse was born.

As Mara continued talking, outlining the conditions of her offer, and taking him through a familiar inventory spiel of her apartment's amenities, Zack found himself further sucked into the conspiracy. Her place was a mirror image of the apartment next door. However, her walls were not covered in flowered wallpaper. Instead, they were a pleasant shade of beige, and she had prudently chosen to punctuate the neutral palette with throw pillows, which could be easily changed or removed. She had chosen bright orange, and if Mara did not take the pillows with her, he would change them. Orange was his least favorite color.

Her bathroom had been updated in the past two years, (no doubt by the plumber next door). Perhaps, that was where the trouble with the next-door neighbor had started. Perhaps, the plumber had stayed too often, too long to work on the bathroom remodel. Perhaps, the boyfriend had objected. There was so much more to this story than she was saying, but he could wait until he and Mara knew each other better. Zack was delighted to learn that Mara would not be taking the full-size bed with her. Phillipe already had one. Phillipe had almost everything that Mara needed, and so, all of her furniture would stay.

But, it was what Mara said next that Zack found most seductive. If Zack understood her correctly, she was willing to let him have her apartment for three hundred Euros less per month, than the place next door. To have an extra €3600 in his pocket for the first year was a great incentive to continue listening, and he began calculating the additional savings on agency fees, if he took Mara's offer, rather than pay Claudine. Then, he remembered that Mara hadn't mentioned a deposit. Zack stared at Mara, even though she had stopped talking to await his answer.

Reasons for not accepting her attractive offer were running through his head, but none of them seemed that much of an obstacle, and this was itself, a red flag. There had to be a catch, other than the obvious one, of pretending to be the cousin of a perfect stranger. Did she not see it? Did she not notice that he was American and spoke very little French? Would not someone question that? Say... Oh, for instance, the landlord? One of her neighbors? Or, a relative? Surely, at sometime in the past, her parents had counted the number of cousins at the dinner table. Surely, they knew none of their relatives lived in New York.

But, then, seeing that he was wavering on his decision, she said the magic phrase. "I will give you one month FREE rent."

Wow! Had he heard her correctly? One-month free rent would almost make up for his extended stay in the hotel. Once his salary arrived in the French bank, he would be almost back to breaking even on the move. He ventured, "What about signing a lease? And deposits?"

"No bail," she answered. "I signed the lease and I paid the deposit," and then, she added, "and the taxes for last year."

"Taxes?" he asked.

"Yes. I will explain, later," she added, looking at her watch, and then, at the door as if she was expecting someone. "Please... tell me, yes, now!" She pleaded.

Then, Zack heard what Mara had heard – footsteps on the stairs. They both fell silent, as voices grew louder, and three people climbed the last set of stairs to the third floor. The group stopped at the apartment next door, and knocked on the unlocked door, which Zack had simply pulled shut. The man leading the parade attempted to use a key, but his effort only pushed the door open, fueling the urgency of Zack's decision.

It was now or never, his imagination, kicking into high gear, reminded him. Stop delaying the inevitable. Stop finding something wrong when there was nothing wrong. Stop being stubborn, fool! No doubt, the real estate agent, who was showing the apartment, had a similar manila envelope in his hand. No doubt, the people with him would be prepared to throw down their deposit. No doubt, if he waited much longer, Zack would lose out on yet another great apartment.

However, he had to give her a chance. She had bought him dinner. No woman had ever done that. Zack pulled his phone out of his pocket and checked for messages. There were none from Claudine, and she was his only link to the landlord. If these other people presented their signed copy of the lease first, which one would the landlord accept? The first one signed, of course, and he would be back to square one. First come – first served. Wasn't that how it was everywhere in the world? He wished for someone to ask for advice, someone other than Mara.

Mara scooted to the edge of her chair, leaned in towards Zack in anticipation of his answer, and could wait no longer, "Oui ou Non?" she insisted, still batting those endearing, large, innocent eyes.

Zack stood up, went to the door, and opened it slightly. He could hear bits and pieces of the conversation from next door. As the threesome exited to the hallway, Zack saw what he feared - a handshake. He looked over his shoulder at Mara, and with a sigh, whispered, "Oui!"

With that, Mara popped up off the sofa, and threw open the apartment door to confront the people in the hallway. She said in a strong, clear voice that had not surfaced in the previous hour and a half. "L'appartement n'est plus disponible" (The apartment is no longer available). Zack had no idea what she had said, and evidently, it had not been received well, as a heated argument ensued between Mara and the real estate agent, during which she wildly pointed to Zack several times. The sweet young French woman could fight a verbal battle like an experienced warrior. The transformation was amazing.

He sat bewildered on the sofa, and smiled each time his name was mentioned. In response, the faces outside in the hallway turned and glared at him, likewise bewildered. Moments later, the same faces filled with anger. Something Mara had said greatly upset them. Zack dropped his head, no longer brave enough to meet their stares. The question was quickly becoming – should he make a break for it? Was either one of these apartments worth this much trouble?

When the voices in the hallway grew louder, Zack looked up to see Mara throw her hand in the air like an orchestra conductor, finishing the last note of a performance. Applause did not follow, but rather, an intensely impenetrable silence, which proved as frightening as the noise moments earlier. It seemed that she had won the battle, for the group retreated down the stairs, defeated, and grumbling all the way. She stood at the top of the stairs, triumphantly, with arms crossed to stand guard, and she did not budget an inch, until she was certain that they were gone.

When the downstairs front door slammed shut, she returned to face Zack. "Maintenant, donnez–moi cette enveloppe!" (Now, give me that envelope!)" She demanded in a voice, which was deeper than any previously heard from her pretty, little mouth. Zack had no idea what had just happened. However, he was fairly certain that the place next door was no longer his.

⤖⟐⟐⤖
Chapter 4
⤖⟐⟐⤖

O ctober brought many festivals and conventions to Paris, but nothing caught Zack's attention quite like the classic car parade down Avenue des Champs-Elysées. He learned from those standing around him in the crowd, that a vintage car rally in May would bring still more beautiful old cars to Paris. However, on this particular October day, he was happy just to be alive, and outside. His mind needed a break from so much decision-making.

Seeing all of these great old vintage autos had been good medicine, bringing back memories of his old MG convertible, which he had left in the States. At this time of year, especially, he missed driving it. No season was better for driving with the top down than autumn, when the leaves were changing colors out on Long Island. Cold breeze, warm sweater, and nowhere to go, except anywhere the road led. That was his definition of a perfect October day in New York.

A friend was watching his prized possession, while he was overseas, and Zack hoped watching didn't mean - from behind the steering wheel. He had washed and waxed the car to perfection, before delivering it in pristine condition. The last thing that he wanted to see, on his return to the States in a year, was his car covered in salt or rust.

Zack continued to watch the parade, which included Alfa Romeo, Talbot, Porsche, and Bugatti, their drivers and passengers, costumed apropos for the particular year of their vehicle's manufacture. He was in writers' heaven, a place where it was easy to engage in fantasies of what Paris was like in the 1900's, 1920's, 1940's and so on. Each decade, represented by six or seven cars in the parade, seemed as fanciful as the previous one. He reverently made notes in the little notebook, which he carried in his shirt pocket. There was a feature article in all of this.

Some cars evoked memories of the war years, but defiantly, their

21st Century passengers partied with wild abandon, tooting horns and throwing back glasses of Champagne. Zack would write, later, that even during World War I and World War II – there had been people in Paris, who refused to give up. They, too, had partied in the face of death, destruction, and gas shortages. They hoarded champagne someone standing nearby explained. When they ran out of gasoline, they burned it in their automobiles!

Zack would have chosen to be one of these. "Me too!" the man chirped. "Me too," his companion repeated. Let the slippers (and the boots) be filled with bubbly! This was France. To do otherwise, would have been to surrender one's very soul. "Joie de vivre!" until "vous pourriez jouer" (you could play) no more, they added, laughing as they walked away to follow the parade.

Since his first Sunday in Paris, he had taken to the habit of walking from the Jardin du Luxembourg to the Champs-Elysées on Sundays. The journey took a few hours out of what was an already lazy day in the week, and forced immersion into crowds, which had haunted these two main areas of Paris since the time of Marie de Medici. Although, he walked a steady pace every day, sometimes five and six miles, Sundays were devoted to sauntering, and the opportunity to observe Parisians enjoying their leisure. They were filled with chance encounters such as this one, and he already regretted, turning down the revelers' invitation to join them for coffee.

He had an article to write and a deadline to meet. Every week a different topic presented itself. He didn't have to look far for it, and today was no different. He had already observed how Americans, mostly his family and friends back on Long Island, spent their Sundays with morning pilgrimages to places, where they were wedged into pews. In the afternoons, they made pilgrimages to places, where they were wedged into booths or recliners to enjoy another type of spiritual experience, cheering on their favorite football teams. In this, Americans and the French had something in common. Sports in both countries ruled Sundays.

However, Zack was surprised by the number of Parisian families, who preferred to gather in parks on blankets to spend the entire day, playing with their children. Fathers and mothers seemed content to watch their children, together, and to talk to one another. Imagine that, he would write, an American man spending a Sunday afternoon, actually talking to his wife and children, not for minutes, but for hours! It either said a lot about the quality of European televised sports, or about the quality of French marriage.

While embracing the absurdity of that thought, he spied what might have been the secret draw, something special, which made a few French husbands give up their Sunday afternoons in front of the television. Several men around him had suddenly glanced up. In the grass, not too far away, were topless young women sunbathing. One, especially well endowed, had chosen this moment to roll over. As Zack, too, was drawn in, puritanical voices in his head, still in residence from childhood, admonished, "Look at her! And on a Sunday! Has she no shame?" Yes. If he had any residual doubts about moving to Paris, on this particular Sunday afternoon, they were gone forever. He had never really cared for football, American style, or European, anyway.

He sat on the bench, and took in the every-changing ambiance of the park, for what was surely one of the last warm days of autumn. Only yesterday, he had pulled his scarf up close around his neck and zippered his jacket tight. The first of early seasonal winds had arrived from Scandinavia, the newspaper reported. "Un début de l' hiver!" Piercing the atmosphere with unsympathetic ferocity, it served as a warning that Paris was not immune to bitterly cold winters.

However, today the city had received a momentary reprieve, and no one in Paris was wasting it. The morning had dawned with the calm and warmth of a late summer day, and so, Zack sought out his favorite bench in the park to enjoy what might be the last of such pleasures. In his backpack a sandwich, a bottle of beer, and an extra notebook provided everything needed to complete his mission. He had come to the park to reconsider his decision. On the blank page in front of him were two columns: one with a plus and one with a minus.

Perhaps, he had made the wrong decision, telling Mara that he would move in with her. He had felt forced into saying, "Yes." It was so unlike him to cave like that, but how could he tell Mara? But, here in Paris - the world was tilting a bit on its axis, and the ground slipped a little under his feet. There seemed to be no control over which direction he would fall, and yet, he felt it was his fault. He had agreed to become "the cousin."

Telling Claudine, he would not sign her lease, should have been easy, but it wasn't. The pretty, young French woman, Mara, had complicated everything. With a simple, "Oui," he had become her co-conspirator. With his decision, he had made one woman his friend for life, and the other, his enemy. Claudine had been furious that he had wasted her time, keeping the documents an extra day, before returning them unsigned.

"Americans!" She had yelled, waving her hand in the air, as if he were an irritating insect, which needed to be swatted. With the other hand, she had grabbed the envelope from his hands, and thrown it down hard on her desk, announcing that his delay had caused the apartment to be lost; rented by another agent.

She had been the one to lose it, he wanted to remind her, – and because a wealthier client had enticed her to leave at the very moment he was ready to sign. If her greed had not gotten in the way, if she had stayed, Mara would have not emerged from her apartment in time to stop him. No, Zack wanted to shout back at Claudine, "This was your fault!" because, truthfully, the decision to leave had been entirely hers. He had planned on inviting her to lunch afterwards. Perhaps, it was that missed opportunity, which made him the most frustrated with her attitude.

But, he was not the kind of man to argue with beautiful women, even when he was angry with them. He had not thrown a fit, when she ran down the stairs, and into the arms of a wealthier client. He had not demanded that she stay to finish their business. He could not fight his nature, and he had never developed the kind of warrior skills, which Mara displayed, so impressively. In the end, Claudine's decision, to abandon him in favor of a bigger prize elsewhere, had cost him nothing...really...except perhaps, the embarrassment of Claudine's refusal to accept his lunch invitation. Maybe the unknown caller had done him a favor.

However, Zack's indecision had cost her a handsome fee, and since she needed someone to blame, the American was as good a target as any other. He wanted to put the blame back, where it belonged, but he was too much of a gentleman to do so. He listened until he could bear no more, and began fidgeting on one foot, then, the other. She gave him the look, which needed no translation. In response, he beat a hasty path out the door of her office, without revealing his decision to move in with Mara. It was probably best left that way. Claudine would have never understood his reasons for doing so. For Claudine, it was all about her.

Today, as he sat pondering his decision, he was more forgiving of the beautiful woman, whose only fault seemed to be that her career came first. There were a lot of successful women like Claudine in the world. How stupid had he been, choosing not to play by her rules? He tested the waters by sending her, yet, another message. So far, his apologetic texts had produced no response, and she refused to take his calls, but he had to try. Somehow, he felt responsible for every man, and every American, who had ever broken a promise to her.

How many had there been? Would she ever give another a moment of her time? Or had his foolish choice thrown them all under the bus? Her rant revealed that the other real estate agent had called her, complained, and they had fought. Perhaps, the other agent had an understanding with her. Get the stupid American to sign by noon, or my clients get the apartment. According to Mara, neither of them would earn the fee, as the apartment had been rented by a third party. How was he supposed to know this? There was so much to learn here; so much lost in translation. Lesson Two: Learn the language before you land.

Rationally, Mara's was the better offer. Financially, it made good sense. Claudine's offer, however, provided a legal recourse, if things went awry. There was nothing wrong, short of wallpaper, with Tito's apartment. Mara's apartment, however, had a bigger bathroom. Both were in a perfect location, and wasn't that what really mattered? Yes, but, shouldn't he be considering more than just that?

Mara had not told him how long he could stay. Not asking was a mistake. He could see that now. Claudine had offered him a lease, guaranteeing that he could live in Tito's apartment for at least a year, maybe three, if he decided to stay in Paris at the end of his work assignment. What guarantee had Mara provided? Would she throw him out, after his one free month? All it would take for him to be homeless, again, would be for Mara and her boyfriend to have a fight. Yes. He could picture that. She would show up on his doorstep, suitcase at her feet, and demand her place back. He would have no choice, but to become "without residence," again. And what impact would that have on his French bank account?

Yes. He decided. He had been stupid to say, "Oui. Had it been the wine? Or was it the thought of a full-size bed. He had always been swayed, too easily, by women, especially, young beautiful ones. His mother had warned him.

Then, he began thinking of the other residents in the building, which Mara had described to him, carefully, one by one. She demanded that he memorize their names and everything else about them, so that their stories would match. She did not want the truth revealed out of carelessness. Hers was a simple lie, but an important one. He had to get it right, she said, making it the only condition of their arrangement. Zack had agreed, without thinking about the difficulty of the task.

Her cousin, a total invention, was from America, New York - if he preferred, although the exact location was best kept undisclosed, in case someone in the building had relatives in New York. Zack tried to explain to Mara that New York City was really quite large, and there was no likelihood that he and anyone in the building knew any of the same people. Still, she was tentative, insisting that he remain vague about his exact origin. He agreed, as her explanation of "the rules" was getting tedious.

"Think of it," she said, "as if you are an actor in the theatre." She explained that her father had a brother, who left home, and was never heard of again. Zack would become this missing brother's son.

"Why is your cousin...I mean, why am I in Paris?" he asked.

Mara had answers for everything, but they seemed to be spontaneous ones, and not well thought out. She said her cousin had become curious about his French relatives, and had come to Paris to search for them, finding – serendipitously – Mara.

"How did you and your cousin meet?"

"You placed an inquiry in a French newspaper," she went on, saying that she had read it and answered. He thought this part of the lie to be the most dubious part of her story, but she seemed satisfied with it. Mara believed in chance, serendipity, and love at first sight. To her, finding a lost cousin in the want ads seemed perfectly reasonable. It also explained how Phillipe, a career gigolo, who claimed to Mara that he was turning over a new leaf, had come into her life. She was a sucker for good-looking, smooth-talking, dangerous men from the south of France. In that, there was another story to tell, but at another time, she insisted.

So, Zack had their story – the one of long-lost cousins. She never explained why she had happened upon the news item, or why she had been so willing to take in a perfect stranger, without vetting him with her family. Looking around her apartment, Zack saw no newspapers. Would any of her friends or neighbors buy the lie? Certainly, the university professor, living across the hall from her, would question the credibility of her newspaper story. No books, no magazines. Surely, the professor must have learned that this young woman was not much of a student, a reader.

According to Mara, sometimes late at night, Montague, the professor, would knock on her door, and they would share a nightcap (or two) together. Zack wondered if she and Montague had shared anything else, like her full-size bed. However, it was a lascivious thought, and he quickly put it out of his mind; wondering instead if Montague was the man's first or last name, and how he should address him.

Mara was a pretty girl, but she was not his type, Zack decided. Too silly. Too young. She was not nearly as sophisticated as Claudine, whose legs, and "you can't touch this" attitude had kept him awake for two nights. Not returning his phone calls or answering his texted messages had a familiar feel. Was this part of the attraction? Women, who played hard to get, had always intrigued him. Claudine was so hard to get, that if she kept a drawer full of blank restraining orders in her desk, it would not have surprised him. If she did, they were probably already filled out with American-sounding names.

Zack had let his mind wander as another of the topless beauties across the park, sat up, and rolled over. A mother pushing a baby stroller passed in front of his line of sight, bringing him back to the matter at hand. If he were going to move into Mara's apartment, he would have to do, as she had demanded. He would have to rehearse his role as her cousin. Move-in was tentatively scheduled for tomorrow. With that thought in mind, he pulled the notebook from his backpack, and began reading through his notes.

In France, the floor that Americans would call the first was referred to as the ground floor. The second floor became the first. The third floor became the second. And so the numbers followed accordingly. In Mara's building, the odd numbered apartments faced the street. The even numbers faced a courtyard, seen only by those tenants. Courtyard apartments went for a premium because they were quiet. They were, also for this reason, rarely available for rent.

Mara's apartment was on what Americans would call the third floor, but in France, it was numbered as the second. This made her apartment number 203, rather than 303. Apartment 201, the one now rented to someone other than Zack, was still a mystery. A great deal of pounding and dust had been coming from the place, Mara complained to him over the phone, but so far, no one had moved in.

Across the hall from Mara was apartment 204, and Montague, the professor. Next to Montague in the last apartment on this floor, 202, lived a middle-aged man, although Mara was not certain of his age. She said that he looked forty-five, but could be older. How could she make such a determination? She complained that he had made no effort to speak to her, came, and went from the building at every hour of the day or night, and so – Mara imagined that he was some sort of spy. His nationality was eastern...European, she said, which only reinforced her suspicions.

"They all come to Paris," she said, referring to spies, not eastern-Europeans.

Yes. Zack had to agree because in spy novels, they all seemed to find their ways to Paris. Why wouldn't they? Zack had.

The second floor was a mirror layout of the third floor. Apartment 101, below the still vacant 201, held a man and woman in their thirties with a seven-year old little boy. The Pollywogs, Mara had called them. She had first met them at the Luxembourg Gardens playing in the reflecting pool. The family name was Polish, and the best pronunciation that Mara could make of their surname was Pollywog, and so it stuck. Zack would use it, too, as his ability to pronounce Polish was no better than Mara's. She said the father was Ivan, and the mother, Berta. The little boy was named Bogdan, but the parents called him "Bog," and so, he became in Mara's world – Bog Pollywog.

Apartment 103, below Mara's apartment, was a woman, not as young as Mara. Her name was Gwendolyn. Mara did not know exactly what the woman did for a living, although, she left early every day, and rarely varied her routine. By her style, Mara judged that she held some sort of corporate job. Gwendolyn always wore suits, very conservative ones, Mara added, as if this indicated something about the woman's character. Then, she added with a sniff, "She's British." Apparently, the Thirty-Year War was not quite finished in this building.

Across the hall, in 104 was a proper French family, Mara said, proudly. Albert worked in a charcuterie (delicatessen) and his wife, Arness, in a Fromagerie (cheese shop). They were the two most popular people in the building, and were often invited to small dinners, as they could provide the best food at the best discount. They, also, had one child, a small boy of eight years, and his name was Sébastien, although Mara referred to him as "the little bastard!" Apparently, the child was not nearly as well liked as his parents because he had a decidedly mischievous streak. Twice, he had turned over the trash bins in the foyer, an unthinkable act of hostility inside the building, which Mara kept calling "the village."

In the last apartment on this floor, 102, was Madame Christy, a florist. Her shop, a third generation family business, was across the street. She left for work promptly at 6:00 a.m. each morning, except Sundays, when she opened later. Her morning commute took one minute. "She is in her fifties," Mara had whispered, as if it were a secret. Presently, she noted, everyone on the third floor was single.

Her friend, Montague was divorced. Mara was single, although, hoping for a ring – someday. Tito had been a bachelor, although, he had many girlfriends, who came and went at all hours. That left, only Monsieur Le Spy. Mara did not know anything about his private life, and could not say whether, or not, there once had been a Madame Le Spy. Zack suspected that there had not been, because the work of spying demanded a great deal of freedom, the kind most wives would not tolerate.

A soccer ball flew directly at him, and he stopped it with his feet, waiting for the small player, who had kicked it to come and request it back. He was a cute little fellow of about six years old, his socks so tall, and his legs so short, that his soccer shorts covered up any skin. He struggled with pulling up his soccer shorts as he rushed toward Zack.

Zack picked up the ball and held it up, and asked in French, "Le jeter? Ou le coup de pied?" (Throw it? Or kick it?)

"Le Jeter!" he insisted. Zack threw it about thirty feet away, and off the boy went.

When Zack got to know Bog and Sébastien, would they come to the park and play soccer with him and their fathers? It would be great to have some buddies to play sports with on the weekends. Maybe, hang out and drink beer. Did Ivan and Albert hang out together? If so, maybe he and the two of them could convince the spy in 102 to come out of his apartment long enough for a round of golf. Zack was allowing his imagination to run wild, again. Golf? Really? In Paris? Bocce, maybe, but not golf.

That left the first floor residents. Let's see, Zack muttered, flipping through the pages. He had tried to take fastidious notes, as it had seemed so important to Mara. Reading through the pages for the fourth time, he realized that knowing whom he might meet in the hallways was important to him as well. He could not expect to live in Paris for an entire year, and get by on "Bonjour" (Hello) and "À Bientôt!" (See you soon!). Eventually, someone would want to hear "the cousin story."

On the ground floor, the layout of apartments was different, adjusted for the space required by the foyer, the stairwell, and the trash closet. There were only three apartments, and instead of numbers, they displayed letters, and all were somewhat larger than the apartments on the other floors. Apartment A, which was positioned at the front of the building, and looked out onto the street with grand tall windows, belonged to the concierge of the building, who served as the building manager in all matters – other than leasing. Mme. Durand, a woman in her sixties, apparently having no known first name, ran a tight ship. Mara called her "La Capitaine, (The captain), and was known to salute her, behind her back, of course.

In the back of the building, in Apartment B, an older couple had made their home for thirty years. Marcel was a retired government worker, and his wife, Camille, had never worked, having lived comfortably on the generous salary, which the French government paid her husband. There were never two, more, patriotic French citizens in all of Paris, Mara said. On holidays, they decorated their door with the French flag and played military march music on their old phonograph. "Children of the resistance," Mara called them.

Mara warned Zack not to have any contact with the concierge, Mme. Durand, if he could avoid it. Mme. Durand was suspicious of everyone and everything. If anyone would "out" them, it would be her. Strangely, however, Mme, Durand and the man in Apartment C had a cordial relationship, which Mara had confirmed by overhearing their shared greetings, once, at the mailbox. Monsieur Le Postman had said, "Good day," and Mme. Durand had answered, "Yes. Isn't it?" Mara asked Zack, "What do you think this means?"

In Apartment C, lived Monsieur Le Postman. Mara had learned

from Mme. Durand, La Capitaine, the postman's first name was Henri, and he was not married. Mara also said that Mme. Durand had a crush on Monsieur Le Postman, but since he was much younger, she would never reveal her feelings to him.

"Did she tell you this?" Zack asked, thinking that Mara had a more vivid imagination than his.

"No," Mara had to admit, but she assumed that Mme. Durand had told her, in hopes that Mara would reveal to the man, that he had a secret admirer, and that it was Mme. Durand, thereby, avoiding any unnecessary public embarrassment. If Monsieur Le Postman was interested, he could pursue Mme. Durand on his own terms.

Zack interpreted this to mean that an older generation of French women still preferred men pursuing them, rather than the other way around. Was there a lesson in this? Should he give his attention to more mature women, and leave the younger ones alone? Perhaps, Benjamin Franklin was right; older women were by nature more grateful.

Reviewing the list of his future neighbors, it seemed that Zack had exceptional good luck. A plumber (albeit gone, but whose work remained), a professor available for late night think tanks, a butcher, a cheese-maker, a florist, a postman – all in the same building! His needs were practically covered. If the vacant apartment, next to Mara's, was occupied with a Chocolatier or a "vigneron" (wine maker), then, life here would be nearly perfect. With those thoughts in mind, he closed his notebook, and downed the last of his beer.

Yes. He had made the right decision, choosing this neighborhood. However, was his choice of apartments a mistake? Only time would tell.

❧ℭℜℌ❧
Chapter 5
❧ℭℜℌ❧

T his is your key. Do not lose it," Mara said, quite seriously. "It will cost thirty Euros to replace." The key was the length of Zack's palm, and looked to be two hundred years old, original to the door, if not the building. "Where would he carry it?" was his next question. Mara pulled a chain attached to her jean belt loop, and produced her own key. She wore it safely chained to her clothing, or around her neck, because it was too easy to lose. It wasn't the prettiest piece of jewelry, but carrying it this way, it would be less likely to forget. She suggested a place down the street, where chains were sold for this purpose.

Many Paris apartment dwellers proudly flaunted their original keys because a key this large had become a status symbol. It indicated that its owner was living at an historic address, and historic architecture held a place of respect and honor in French culture. Zack could see himself wearing the key only, if he were planning on becoming the poster-child for very large, latchkey kids, and so, for the time being, he zipped the key into his backpack.

Mara watched and shook her head. It would be only a matter of days, before her new cousin called for a replacement. She had warned him. Thirty Euros was thirty Euros, and she wasn't paying it out of her own pocket. She smiled at him, hiding her thoughts. He would learn the hard way. Perhaps, she should have put more in writing, as her boyfriend had suggested. Oh, well.

After today, it would be up to the American to figure out a lot of things on his own. Poor man, however, he was no longer her problem. She was moving in with Phillipe, and there were more, important things to do, than wet-nurse another American. Her two previous boyfriends had been American tourists, and although in Paris for a month, neither had lasted longer than a week in her bed.

With a cheery "Bonne chance!" Mara was gone.

Zack looked around the apartment, reminding himself, "My apartment!" Overjoyed, he was doing a bit of an Irish jig in the middle of the hardwood floors. Finally, he had done it, obtained a real Paris address. His boss in New York, and the French bank manager, would be happy. His parents would be relieved. Finally, they would have a place to forward his mail, send his bank statements, and visit – when they came to Paris, whenever that might be.

His mother's first words would be... is there a second bathroom? He would have to explain a few things to her about the size of a Paris apartment, including the unaffordable second bathroom. She was far more excited about coming to Paris, than his father, who thought the French were rude and arrogant, even though, he had never been to France, nor met a French citizen. His views had been formulated based upon American movies, mostly from the mid 20th century, and mostly about war.

His father was too young to remember World War I, a war in which half of the male population of France between the ages of fifteen and thirty had been killed. All he could remember was World War II, with its pissing contests between the American and the French military commanders over who should roll into Paris first, after the Germans fled. Zack had read enough history to know that the French were equals in fighting their enemies. The French Resistance movement, alone, had proven it.

Having made two previous trips to France, Zack had tried to convince his father to consider a kinder view of the French, but it had been a worthless cause. His mother, on the other hand, also influenced by the movies, imagined that all French people were like Maurice Chevalier, Louis Jordan, and Leslie Caron. She couldn't wait to meet all of them. Zack knew that both of his parents would be disappointed, but if they could keep an open mind, they also could be pleasantly surprised. The French were not so different from them, he attempted to say, but even he knew that it wasn't true.

The French were very different. Despite their own brand of prejudice, in actual practice, the French were tolerant of people, who looked and spoke differently. In Paris, that was about half of the population because the tourism industry supported the city and its citizens. International banking, the fashion industry, and the diplomatic corps brought people into the city from all over the world. No Parisian was foolish enough to kill all these golden geese, laying all of their lovely Euro filled eggs. Exhibiting tolerance made sense and cents.

Looking around the apartment, more closely this time, there were things missed in his initial walk through with Mara. For one, Mara's bathroom was not only much larger than the one next door; the shower stall was taller. The brown-tiled shower was wide enough for him to shampoo his hair without hitting his elbows on the surrounding glass. The nozzle was adjustable, accommodating his height. Another pleasant surprise? The bathroom did not smell from disinfectant, as did the one next door, but instead it was filled with scents of lavender.

Perhaps, Mara had committed the deadly sin of using the wrong cleaning product. To test his theory, he went into the kitchenette and sniffed. A different smell, but equally pleasant - lemons, greeted him there. Well, at least, Mara had used two differently scented products. Claudine would have approved of that.

He opened the small waist-high refrigerator and found that Mara had left him a bottle of white wine, considerately chilled for her American cousin, who probably never drank room temperature white wine. There was also a half-pint of cream for coffee, although, he took his black. There was nothing else, and the emptiness of the tiny refrigerator reminded him that he would have to shop for groceries, not that he intended to cook, but because he always got hungry in the middle of the night.

Groceries meant a trip to the neighborhood épicerie, to meet the man responsible for the "Louer" sign in the window of the apartment next door. Was Monsieur Épicier the apartment's owner? Zack hoped, first, that he would not run into Claudine there; then...that he might. Rats! He muttered, aloud. "Why can't I ever fall for an uncomplicated woman?"

He reached into the refrigerator and smelled the carton of cream, not that he intended to use it, but he had to smell it out of habit. He smelled everything edible before eating it. It was the last of his obsessive-compulsive disorders, leftover from childhood, when he could not determine what something was simply by looking at it.

His grandmother loved making casseroles from leftovers, often creating things – which for a child were unimaginable. One too many casseroles at Grandmother's house had taught him – Smell first, eat later or maybe never. Thankfully, Grandmother had a large dog, which would eat anything, and slept under the table. Poor old Rags had eaten a great many green-colored casseroles, probably, without ever knowing what was in them.

Zack put the carton of cream back inside, closed the refrigerator door, and began going through the small kitchen, compartment-by-compartment, and drawer by drawer. The kitchen appeared to contain everything a bachelor in Paris might need – wine opener, beer opener, bread knife, cheese knife, wine glasses, coffee filters, one coffee cup, two forks and two spoons, and two dinner plates. Yes. Everything. There was one saucepan and one skillet, but he could not imagine using them.

Whatever groceries had been in the apartment, Mara had already taken with her to her boyfriend's place. The same was true for anything extra in the apartment. Sheets, towels, pillows, etc. were gone along with sundries and cleaning products. Zack had been left with one set of bedding, one set of towels, and a completely empty closet and chest of drawers. He would have to be efficient about laundry, doing it at least once a week, if he was not to sleep on dirty sheets. Of course, he could buy new sheets and towels, but his budget had been so overblown, he decided keeping up with the laundry would be cheaper.

Since Mara's apartment did not have a washing/drying machine, like the apartment next door, he would have to locate a laverie (Laundromat) soon. The one near his hotel was too far to walk. His clothes had been piling up in the corner of his hotel room for over two weeks. Now, his dirty laundry was setting in the middle of Mara's bed, stuffed in a pillowcase borrowed from the hotel. It had grown too large to be ignored.

He felt bad that during six weeks of living in the hotel, he had failed to buy a laundry bag. He had every intention, of returning the pillowcase to the hotel, after it was washed. To assuage his guilt, he took a small notebook out of his pocket, and wrote down "Return pillowcase." It was third on his Guilt List, following "Write parents," and "Email Harrison." He was already a week past his deadline for the latest installment in his on-going Paris travel log.

He remembered how the sounds coming from next door had intrigued him on his way up the stairs. From inside his new apartment, the noise had grown even louder, producing a whirring sound, a little bit like a floor polisher, or a small airplane propeller. But, why? The floors were nearly new. It made no sense. The sound was so loud that, at times, he thought the machine making the noise might come straight through his wall. What could the new tenant be doing? With walls this thin, he would have to keep the volume down on a television or radio in Mara's apartment.

It certainly seemed that the new next-door neighbor was making some major changes, but Claudine had not indicated to Zack that changing anything was an option. Hadn't she emphasized, albeit threatened, that not even a tiny nail hole or an invisible scratch in the floor could be altered? "Was the flowered wallpaper now gone?" Perhaps, someone was sanding the walls, and not the floors. It was possible. He touched Mara's walls, and wondered if they could stand up to that sort of punishment.

He had wanted to peek inside the door, which had been left ajar about an inch, but he was not ready to meet others in the building, not just yet. His "cousin story" was not quite polished enough for a performance. Mara had made him promise to work on it, until it was perfect because not only his future, but also hers, depended upon it.

Before she left, he had promised her that he would. He had handed her the rent (in cash) for the second month, as she reconfirmed that his first month was, indeed, free. He had looked her straight in the eyes, and said, "Don't worry. I've got it down pat." She had looked into his eyes, hoping that he was not lying, and had smiled.

That was when she told him, they would probably not see each other for a while, "perhaps several weeks." She and Phillipe were taking a short vacation to visit his parents in Avignon, and then, "Well, who knows?" She had said it, casually, in that way that meant life was for living, not for planning. "Maybe, Italy."

Zack sat down in the middle of the floor. All had gone too easy. Easy - bothered him. Everything about renting an apartment in Paris was supposed to be difficult. Difficult, he understood. This felt wrong, but he couldn't put his finger on what was causing his anxiety. He was being ridiculous, borrowing trouble. There was no mystery here. Mara had been very upfront about everything in the apartment, and certainly, about everyone in the building. What didn't he know? What, indeed? The worry started to creep back into his subconscious.

What if an emergency arose? What should he say if someone wanted to know the rest of "the cousin story?" Whom was he supposed to ask for answers?

Stop it! Zack said, getting to his feet. He needed to go to the post office and pick up the rest of his mail, being forwarded to a temporary box number. He would give the post office this new address. He was tired of trekking back and forth across town, only to find an empty box. In six weeks, he had received six letters. The rent on the box was hardly worth the expense.

Mara had left him with a few tasks to perform. She had asked him to bundle up and forward her mail, once a week. If he saw anything unusual in the mail, a bill, an eviction notice, anything at all, he was to email her, immediately. She had given him a cell phone number, but with a caution - her voice messages rarely got to her as quickly as texted ones. No reason was given for why this happened. He had asked her, why she hadn't asked the postman downstairs to handle her mail, while she was gone.

"Because he doesn't know that I am leaving!" she had replied.

"Oh, yeah," Zack had answered in a way so casual that it made Mara very nervous. "But, won't your neighbors notice...after a while?"

"I will tell them, when the time is right. You must remember the things, I told you." She had chastised him. "You must."

"I will," Zack had said. "Besides..."

Mara had been forced to interrupt, certain that Zack was not paying attention. How was she to trust him, when he knew so little about France? "He makes no deliveries in this street. His route is elsewhere."

"Sure, sure," Zack had said, but in fact, he did not understand, nor was he interested in how mail routes were assigned in Paris. Mara, however, was off and running with multiple explanations. In the end, Zack promised, again, that he would take care of the mail, and the apartment, and then, they finally said their goodbyes, sealed with double kisses on the cheeks. Mara did not leave written instructions for how to care for the apartment. Claudine had indicated that tenants received a new tenant booklet of "Do and Do Not."

What was Mara not telling him to do? What about trash pickup day? What about recycling? What about curfews? Did someone lock the front door at midnight? How did the hot water heater work? How did the...? Was he just supposed to figure this all out for himself?

He had asked about connection and service fees for television, telephone, and internet service. Was he supposed to set up his own? Or could he use hers? She said that this had already been calculated into the rent that he would be paying her in cash. She told him the Wifi password, and he wrote it down in his notebook. It contained, among other things - thirteen numbers. For a seemingly silly girl, she had a good head for numbers. She had been able to calculate utilities and taxes down to the penny, and had explained the ins and outs of the French banking system in half the time that it had taken Claudine. Charging him three hundred Euros less per month, than Claudine had wanted – this still seemed too good a deal.

Which was it? He wondered. Was Mara charging him too little? Or had Claudine quoted him too much? Perhaps, Claudine had included a nice fat monthly fee for herself, on top of her one time agency fee. Perhaps, that was Monsieur Épicier's share. Or perhaps, they split it. He wanted to believe that Mara had been the honest one because, at the moment, he was growing irritated with Claudine. She still had not answered his messages.

And then, he thought about how odd Mara had acted on the first day they met. It was as if she had been waiting for him to show up at the "Appartement Louer" door. If it hadn't been him, would it have been the next unsuspecting man...or woman? Would any random person have done just as well, recruited to become her "cousin?" Why had she been so desperate to fill that role? Who had put pressure on her to do that? Was it really "the boyfriend?"

He remembered how Mara had been so intense that first day. When she disappeared with the lease in the envelope, he had panicked. "Pourquoi?" (Why?) He had asked as she was going out the door, clutching it tightly in her hand.

"Wait here!" she had insisted, giving him no excuse.

He had done as he was told, first, waiting patiently on the sofa, afraid to invade her privacy by looking around. He had thought, perhaps, Mara was showing the lease to the other tenants, showing them the price that their landlord was planning on charging him; the amount that they might be expected to pay in the future. Yes. He had convinced himself - that was probably it. After all, the front door had not slammed, so Mara had to be still in the building somewhere.

As the minutes ticked by, he had grown bored waiting for her. The apartment was going to be his soon, so he had gotten up and carefully, opened and closed drawers, cabinets, and the only closet in the place. Things had tumbled out. Stuffing them back in and, carefully, closing the doors, he could not imagine how she was going to box up her possessions and move in two days, but that was what she had proposed.

Perhaps, "the boyfriend" would help. Perhaps, he had a truck. Zack had calculated the final hotel bill in his head, as he wandered into the bathroom to look through her medicine cabinet. He was there, in the bathroom, when she returned. Hearing her coming in the front door, he had flushed to cover his indiscretions. "Sorry," he had said, coming out. "Hope you don't mind..."

Mara smiled, "No. Is fine," she chirped, as she handed him back the manila envelope. "You give to agent tomorrow." Her instructions had been in her abbreviated English.

"Not today?" Zack had asked, a bit confused as to why tomorrow would be better than today.

It didn't take much to imagine how angry Claudine would be, and suddenly, Mara's idea was the better one. There was no reason to rush returning a lease, especially one - which he wasn't going to sign. Logic told him to drop it in the mail to avoid a confrontation all together. However, as mad as he imagined Claudine would be, about him backing out of their agreement, he still wanted to see her again. There was something about her, which he couldn't get past. What was it?

In the park, recalling all of this, Zack was even more confused. Tomorrow would be the official moving day. He looked again at his notes. Mara was sleeping in the apartment tonight, as Philippe's brother was in the city, and she did not sleep with Philippe, when visitors stayed the night.

He would be spending his last night in a hotel. Tomorrow, everything would change because his new life as an official resident of Paris would begin. Perusing his notes, he wondered. Was that enough time? How was he to remember, "Who was who?" until he actually saw their faces? It would have been so much better if Mara had provided better descriptions. Who was tall? Who was short? Who was thin? Who was fat? Did any have a moustache? (Perhaps, the concierge, Mme. Durand, the one Mara called La Capitaine?)

Well, tomorrow, he would know. A stranger moving in would cause some concern, and a few tenants would find excuses to watch from their windows, or if bold enough, to knock on his door - offer a glass of wine – as Mara had done.

Tomorrow, he would become "the cousin."

It was done. He had said, "Oui."

Y ou have six days to finish three weeks work,"
Harrison said. Zack began to apologize, but was interrupted.
"I know it is Paris. I know you're supposed to be immersing
yourself in the culture," Harrison continued, "but do you have
to do it on my dime? You're not the only one with deadlines and
bosses, you know?"

Zack apologized, again, and this time Harrison permitted it, before
continuing his tirade, because his message appeared to have had
gotten through. Guilt'ing Zack into compliance had taken up at least
ten minutes of the phone call. Zack coughed, hoping it might inject a
pause in his boss's listing of what he had not accomplished. Zack
stopped apologizing. It wasn't making any difference. He knew Harrison
had to talk until he was talked out. Then, and only then, Zack might
have a chance to defend his actions.

The first three weeks in the new apartment had gone smoothly. No
one in the building had talked to him for more than a "Bonjour," or a
"Bon Nuit," although, he was prepared to tell his story. He had
rehearsed it at least a dozen times. In fact, he felt that he could recite it
in his sleep. Oddly, it had been disappointing that no one had
challenged him, not on the stairs, not at the mailbox, or when
emptying his garbage, (which he did unfailingly every day).

Claudine would have been so proud of him for remembering. He
would do this for the sake of every American, who rented an apartment
in Paris. Claudine would be... (Aw, let it go, Zack. She's gone.) For her,
he had made a point of buying two different kinds of cleaning products,
although, deciding which to use where had been too much of a
challenge. French labels were beyond his comprehension. Mara had
come to his rescue, and answered his email, which had asked – where
do you buy? And how do you use...? Now, his apartment smelled of
lavender and lemons.

Zack heard silence at the end of the line. Harrison had finally quit talking. "Well?" he said. Yikes. He had failed to hear the question. "Well, what?" he ventured, knowing that it was the worst thing he could have said.

"So? That's your answer?" Harrison huffed. "I should have known." With that, he hung up, leaving Zack to wonder, "What was what?" How was he to find out, without admitting that he, mentally, had gone on vacation?

He dialed Harrison's secretary, Molly, and pled innocence. "My phone has been giving me a lot of trouble over here. Harrison's voice kept breaking up, so badly, there at the end of his call..." (Listened) "Oh. Ok. Ok. I see. Ok. Yeah. Thanks, Molly. You're the best." (Listened) "No. No. I don't have to talk to him, again. No. No. You don't have to put him on the ..." (Listened) "Hello, Harrison? Yes. My phone has been giving me a lot of trouble over here."

Zack's mistake cost him another fifteen minutes of being reprimanded for taking "Que cera-cera," a little too seriously. His boss repeated the last ten minutes of his earlier call, and finished it with five minutes of demands. "Two days!" Harrison said. "I want to see everything finished – edited – everything in two days!" Zack did what he did best. He promised. "This is not rocket science!" Harrison yelled, punctuating his anger, before hanging up.

It wasn't really Zack's fault he had failed to meet his deadlines. He had been sick, suffering through a terrible cold for the past three weeks, spending most of it in bed. It might have been the flu. He couldn't be certain, but whatever it had been, it had really knocked him down. Sneezing, coughing, and wheezing had made him feel so light-headed, so miserable that he didn't want to eat. For him, that was a true sign of being sick, as he could always eat. After two weeks of this, he stumbled out of bed, out of the building, and found a pharmacy.

Unfortunately, filling his pockets and his body with over-the-counter medicines hadn't worked. He spent another week in bed, medicated into a dazed stupor. A second trip back to the pharmacy produced a more satisfactory result. The pharmacist told Zack that he was suffering, not from a cold, not a flu bug, but rather, from an allergy. After one injection, two pills, and another twelve-hour nap, he woke up feeling great. Vive la France!

That left the real question: What was causing his allergy? It had started shortly after he had moved into the new apartment. Was it the cleaning products or the trash bins downstairs? What? He began searching drawers and cabinets for mold. Discovering none, he was thwarted in his search, but comforted in the knowledge that he, now, knew the pharmacist by his first name. Here was a lesson learned. If there were further occurrences, he would know where to turn.

In France, le pharmacien (pharmacist) could diagnose and treat many things, as witnessed by the long line of people in the store, bearing all sorts of maladies. Zack had never seen so many rashes, bites, and swollen limbs, or been so subjected to such bone-rattling coughs outside of an emergency room. Lesson Three: Don't enter a pharmacy unless your life depends upon it. In France, walking into a drugstore simply to buy condoms or chewing gum was risking one's life. His allergy paled in comparison to the guy with the Black Plague on aisle three.

So this week, the third of his four "free" weeks in his new apartment was really his first to enjoy the new life he had imagined. The pounding next door had stopped, gratefully, two days after he moved in. Since then, it had been very quiet in the building, almost too quiet. Occasionally, there were footsteps on the stairs, but they were respectful ones, not clomping, not stomping, not even stiletto heels, clicking their way down three flights of stairs. Didn't anyone go out to eat in this building? Didn't anyone drag grocery bags up and down? Laundry? Didn't anyone care that a stranger was living under the same roof?

It was remarkable that in twenty-one days, he had overheard only two conversations and those came through his partially opened door. His French was simply not good enough, yet, to catch every word. He heard the number deux zéro un (201), and knew that his neighbors were discussing the vacant apartment – or perhaps, discussing the person, who had moved in. But, he couldn't be certain because it did not appear that anyone had moved in.

Coming back from the pharmacy, he had checked the mailboxes on the ground floor. His name appeared next to Mara's for apartment number 203. The name space for apartment 201 remained blank. Not everyone wanted his or her name on a mailbox for privacy reasons. Perhaps, the next-door neighbor had decided to continue collecting his mail at the post office.

Twice, in the middle of the night, Zack had heard muffled laughter. He could not tell the exact location, as it had traveled into his apartment through the airshaft. It could have been from Gwendolyn's apartment below, or from the holiday apartment in the attic, which Mara told him was rented only during the three months of summer. It was too tiny for a permanent residence, and yet, tourists loved the idea of staying in an attic crawl space in Paris. "They pay big money," she had said, "More for one week, than I pay for four!"

Perhaps, she had been mistaken about the attic only being available to summer visitors; or perhaps, the owner had decided the deal was too good to pass up the other nine months. All Zack knew was that he had seen no one come or go past his floor. The attic space was only accessible from the third floor and a different set of stairs, hidden behind a door. Tourists would have to drag their luggage up three flights of stairs, and right past his door. That, he would have heard.

Yet, there was the mystery of strange laughter, and his failure to locate its source. The return airshaft from the ground floor to the attic passed through his apartment's main room. Maybe it came from next door? Of course, he had felt feverish off and on, and maybe, he had hallucinated the laughter. A radio? A television?

Forget it, he told himself. Today, he would flee from these four walls, although, in his solitary confinement, he had come to love the place as if it were his own. Each day, tucked under the covers to sweat out his enemy, he had come to cherish the space. He had studied every little crack and flaw, embracing them, and re-counting the nail holes and the scratches. This was a safeguard, in case Mara was as much of a stickler for detail as Claudine had been.

Today, Claudine was the reason that he was braving the cold outside (and the allergy inside) to reenter the world. His conscience bothered him. He needed to apologize to her and if she would not accept an email version or a voicemail plea, then, he would deliver it in person. What could she do? Slam the door in his face? Ok, yes, maybe, but he had to try. He felt terrible for the way he had handled things with her.

On the Métro ride to the 16th, he observed the changing style of the passengers as they got on and off the train. As they came closer to his final stop in the NAP (Neuilly-Auteuil-Passy) area of Paris, the riders' dress reflected higher price tags. This area of Paris catered to the well-to-do. An address here signaled that one had succeeded in obtaining the right amount of money to meet all of one's needs, not only for living in Paris, but pretty much anywhere else in the world. Claudine not only worked here, she lived here – a confession at dinner, which Zack thought she, probably, regretted telling him.

He got off the Métro at Église d'Auteuil and walked to Claudine's office, but once he saw the sign over the door, he could not enter. Instead, he wandered off to a nearby café and called her. Again, she refused to answer. So, be it! He said, ordering a second cup of coffee. It was almost noon, and he could see the front door of the agency. Soon, she would go out in search of lunch, and if he saw her, he would follow. He had the scenario all worked out in his head.

He would pretend to be in the area doing what? Ok. So maybe he hadn't worked out all of the details, just yet. Shopping? Yes, that was it! But, he would need proof. Then, he saw it. Someone had tossed a shopping bag in the trashcan outside the door of the café. He got up, quickly, retrieved it, and made the waiter nervous about his intentions. Zack shook the department store size paper bag with handles, to make certain that nothing had clung to it, and that there was nothing too disgusting inside. It was in good shape, relatively clean. Carrying something inside it, he would look more believable.

He looked around for anything to put in the shopping bag. Another café customer had finished eating, planning to leave his newspaper behind. "Perfect!" Zack muttered, reaching over the table that was standing between him and the treasure. He grabbed the paper, just as the waiter arrived to clear the table.

To the waiter, he looked a bit too desperate, perhaps, even a little crazy. So, Zack sat down to finish his coffee, and made a display of pulling money out of his pocket, so that the waiter would see he was able to pay. He was not a street person, salvaging treasures from the trash. As he rearranged the newspaper inside the bag, a glimpse of something in the window glass caught his eye, and he looked up in time to see the familiar reflection. Claudine was passing the café, and she was as beautiful, if not more beautiful, than he had remembered. Could it be that in a month, she had improved?

This vision of her loveliness only served to instill greater trepidation. Could he... should he... go after her? She had made it poignantly clear that she wanted nothing to do with him. Why was he so insistent upon having his heart stepped on in public? Why couldn't he accept his rejection in private - like a man?

He tossed his money on the table and stepped outside to follow at a safe distance, until he could stage his "accidentally bumped into you" scene. He watched her enter a small shop a few doors away, and waited. Mostly likely, she would come back to her office the same way. He rehearsed the scene, again. He would start walking towards her, and pretend not to see her. That way, she would have to acknowledge him, making it appear to be less of a stalking.

Could he do it? Should he do it? He tried to calm down. (Breathe. Breathe. Breathe.) He momentarily closed his eyes, only to be caught off guard by the sound of two other people, coming out of the shop. Then, there she was, head down, putting away her pocket change. It was now or never, and so, he began walking towards her.

They were about to meet head on, when finally she looked up, stared him directly in the face, and made no expression whatsoever. Zack could not tell, if she did not remember him, or was refusing to acknowledge him. He dared to speak, "Oh, Pardon," as he pretended to bump into her, his head was turned towards the shop window. Then, the surprised, "Claudine!" he uttered, having practiced it all morning. "What a nice surprise."

Claudine stared at him for a moment, knowing that she should remember him, but not able to come up with his name. Which client? What property? Her mind was scrolling down a long list, but came up with a blank space - "Fill in name here." Then, it clicked. "Ah," she said, attempting to cover her omission. "The American, who cannot make a decision."

Zip! Ouch! Her arrow had reached its target. Zack tried to cover his embarrassment with a laugh, "Yes. That would be me."

"Still at the hotel?" she asked, only mildly interested, and only, if he was still looking for an apartment. It was, after all, her business that was of most interest to her, and as much of pain as the American had been, he was still a potential client.

"No," Zack said, proudly. "I found a place on my own." (Lie, Lie, Lie.) Mara had found him, (his conscience prudently reminded him.)

"In the 6th?" she asked. She had to.

"Yes. As a matter of fact," he answered. (Careful, Zack! Do not give her the address. Do not tell her that it is in the same building.)

"You are a very lucky man," Claudine said, this time, duly impressed.

"Yes. I am," Zack said.

"I have to go," Claudine said, dismissively, pointing in the direction of her office, where a blue car had just pulled to the curb. "My next appointment is here."

Zack looked over and saw a man, getting out of the blue car. He didn't know him, but he didn't like him because the stranger was stealing minutes away from this precious encounter with Claudine. Had the client been late, perhaps, Claudine would have agreed to the offer of dinner, which Zack had planned for days. "Oh, what the heck..." Zack murmured. "Would you like to go to dinner, again? This time, my treat."

"No, Thank you," she answered without dropping a beat. Starting across the street, she waved to the man, waiting in front of her locked office.

"Ok, then. Another time..." His voice trailed off. She had left him on the curb, talking to no one. He watched as Claudine unlocked the office door, and the impeccably dressed man followed her inside. He was worthy of her time, Zack was not. Claudine had made that very clear. His name had not even been important enough to remember.

Zack walked slowly in the opposite direction, as he dared not walk past the agency, for fear that Claudine might see and label him a stalker. He threw the shopping bag in the first trashcan that he passed. His idea had been a bust. "It was a stupid idea, anyway," he muttered. Mara had warned him that Claudine was trouble, and that he should stay away from her. Her exact words were, "I know this type of woman, nothing but trouble."

He should have listened.

❧☙❧☙❧

Chapter 7

❧☙❧☙❧

T he mystery was starting to trouble Zack. The evidence was circumstantial, but little things were starting to add up, and he could no longer ignore the possibility that something – criminal was afoot in the building, but what? It had started the day after Zack moved into Mara's apartment.

A man had followed Zack up the stairs to the third floor, and then, waited for Zack to go inside his apartment, before knocking on the apartment next door. Zack put his ear to the door, wondering if the apartment was no longer vacant. But, then, he heard a workman inside say something to the man in the hallway. Through his keyhole, Zack saw the visitor turn around and go back down the stairs already talking on his cell phone, and seeming very upset.

Then, a week later, another man showed up at the vacant apartment, but by this time, the noise inside had stopped, and there was no workman to answer the door. Through the keyhole, Zack studied the man, who knocked once, and then, again. When no one answered, he reacted in a similarly frustrated state, best demonstrated by the last loud thump of his fist on the door. This one muttered something unintelligible, before departing. Evidently, the former tenant had failed to tell his friends and his enemies that he was moving. This seemed odd.

When it happened a third time, it was very late at night, and the loud knock could be heard over the sound of Zack's computer streaming music. It startled him, and at first, he mistook the knock for someone at his door. Dropping down to his knees, he expected to see pant legs, but instead, observed the visitor at Tito's door. It was a dangerous decision to make, but he opened the door, to say once and for all - "He's gone. Maybe you should tell his friends."

The man stared blankly at Zack, and Zack, quickly, corrected himself, "Il est parti." He wondered, waiting for the stranger to answer, if he should have said, "Moved," but if he had, the stranger might have tried to engage him in conversation by asking, "Moved where?" And, Zack was not prepared to have that conversation in French or English.

The stranger continued to stare at Zack, absorbing the fact that he was an American, and debating whether, or not a foreigner could be trusted with an important message. Zack noticed that the man held a brown paper bag in his other hand, which earlier had been hidden from view. The stranger saw that Zack's focus was on the bag, and moved it slowly behind him, trying to make the act seem casual. It only made Zack more suspicious, and the stranger, shrewdly, read the look on Zack's face. No, he would not leave any messages with the stranger.

"Merci," he said abruptly, as he hurried down the stairs and out the front door.

Yes. Something illegal was going on. What had just transpired was not a late night delivery of plumbing supplies. Was Tito, the missing neighbor, into drugs? Was, what Zack witnessed, a missed delivery? Had someone forgotten to tell the dealer that Tito was gone? "He's gone," had seemed like news to the man. What about the two visitors before him? Did they all know each other? It was late, too late to figure this out.

Zack locked his door, and this time, he bolted it and checked it twice. The digicode on the front door evidently had been compromised, and was worthless, having been given out too many times to friends of Tito. Who was to say when the next one would show up? He thought that someone should mention these strange visits to the concierge, but Mara had warned him to stay away from Mme. Durand. But under these circumstances, wasn't it warranted? Wasn't Mme. Durand supposed to be keeping strangers out of the building? What was her purpose, if not to act as hall monitor?

Mara had never told Zack, exactly, what had happened to Tito. He had asked her, twice, but to no avail. She said the first time, "I do not know." That was probably the truth. The second time, she said that Tito had mentioned that he might be going away. Zack wondered, had Tito meant prison? Certainly, circumstantial evidence was pointing that direction. It would have been nice, however, if he had sent change of address cards to all of his closest friends. He looked through the keyhole, before checking the lock on the door, again. He turned off the computer and sat staring out the window. The street below was quiet, too quiet.

What was he supposed to make of Mme. Durand, the concierge? Mara had said, "Keep your distance." However, she had been coming out of her apartment, just as he had entered the building. It had been too late to do as Mara had asked. The sixty-something woman looked Zack up and down, twice, before making the statement, meant to be a question. "Le cousin," she said, stopping Zack in his tracks. All he could think was, "Is this it? Was this when "the cousin story" needed to be recited? Was he prepared? The stage fright was reminiscent of dreaded book reports in front of his grade school mates.

"Oui," Zack cleared his throat, timidly, prepared to continue.

"Hmmmmph!" Mme. Durand sniffed, then, turned around without a further word, and without looking back, slammed her door.

He was surprised and relieved, but also, a bit disappointed that she did not find him interesting enough to invite in for his telling of the cousin story. Later, Zack would wonder, had Mara other cousins visit from time to time? Should he assume that he was not the first? This felt wrong, but then, he was living in a different culture. What seemed wrong to him in New York might be completely acceptable here in France. Who was he to say?

Mara had said Mme. Durand was a nosy, busybody type, who gossiped. If that were true, wouldn't she have stuck around to ask more questions? Perhaps, Mara had already told the concierge, "My cousin is here from America. He does not speak French." Perhaps, that was it. Sure. It was something that simple. Mme. Durand did not speak English well enough to converse. At any rate, the unexpected encounter had come with a reprieve.

Then, Zack remembered the conversations, which he had overheard in the hallway and at the mailbox. He had nodded a hello to his neighbors in passing, but he had not stopped to engage them in conversation, and they had made no attempt to stop him. In each instance, they had fallen silent, not taking up their conversations, until he was too far away to hear them. Then, and only then, they had whispered. Was this not odd?

Of course, the French, normally, did not converse at the volume level that Americans did. They kept their voices down in restaurants, and even, on the streets. Speaking loudly was considered both disrespectful, and unsophisticated, according to the forewarning in his guidebooks. So, if his neighbors whispered behind his back, were they being suspicious, or simply being respectful? He couldn't decide. He really wished that he had paid more attention in French class. Understanding the language was so much more important, now, that there was a mystery to solve.

The people, whom he had overhead in the hallway on the second floor, were identified from his notes as Berta Polywog (with the Polish accent) and Arness (from the cheese shop). Berta was a sturdy woman, not fat, but strong from the ankles up. She had platinum blond hair, wildly spiked and lacquered, and brilliantly green eyes, which she batted constantly. Trouble with her contacts, Zack thought. Berta appeared to be in her mid thirties.

By contrast, Arness was a thin woman, taller than Berta, and exhibited no outstanding features. Zack could not even remember the color of her eyes, two minutes after seeing them up close. Arness was the kind of woman, who could blend into a crowd easily, especially, in France, where the majority of the women had brunette hair. She, too, looked to be in her thirties. She was as common as Berta was unusual. Together, they made an interesting set of bookends.

Another day, when he came down the stairs to check his mail, he observed the older man, whom he assumed by age was Marcel, and a second man, who by uniform was, obviously, Monsieur Le Postman. They both stopped talking, when they heard his footsteps on the stairs, and turned to stare at him as he reached the first floor landing. They never took their eyes off him, as they parted in the lobby entrance to make room for him to open his mailbox. He could still feel their stares on the back of his head, and their breaths on his neck, as they closed in behind him.

They were particularly interested in seeing for themselves what kind of mail was waiting for their new neighbor. As he turned around, each man took a step back to give him more room. It felt odd. Marcel attempted a smile, but the postman did not make any effort, preferring instead to raise one eyebrow. As Zack passed, they said nothing, and when he reached the first floor landing, he heard down below the conversation resume. A third voice had joined the others, which confirmed that Mme. Durand had been spying from her keyhole. This time, the conversation included the words "le cousin."

Could they all be involved in some sort of conspiracy? Or were their actions normal, given that a foreigner had moved into an apartment reserved for permanent residents? He imagined that the same could be said of New York apartment dwellers. If he had been the only French citizen, who had just moved in, everyone would be queuing up to trade rumors about him. This was not so different. There, they would ask, "Does the new guy speak English?" rather than, "L' étranger, il parle Français?"

Zack? In this building, this neighborhood? Of course, he would be the subject of rumors. He was not like the others, the attic people, and those holiday renters, who came and went in the summer, and were to be ignored. Yes. Like them, he was a foreigner, but he was also Mara's cousin, and that made a difference, didn't it? He would be living in Mara's apartment for at least a year. They would have to deal with him at some point in time. Was it too much to ask? When would they invite him in for a drink, to share gossip as Mara had done? Wasn't that the way things happened here? Truthfully, he was getting a little lonely. Wasn't there a statute of limitations on being the new kid on the block?

Then, one day, it happened. Mme. Christy was returning home from her flower shop across the street, and he happened to be at the front door on his way out. She smiled. He smiled. It was that simple. She stopped to ask, "You are the cousin?"

And, he answered. "Yes. I am the cousin," thinking that was the end of the exchange.

"You are going out?" she continued in English.

"For some groceries," he said, grateful that French was not required.

"And you stay out? Or you come back?" she inquired.

He answered, "Yes. I will be back soon." And there it was - his first real conversation with a neighbor. It felt good. It felt comfortable, remarkably easy.

She surprised him further, by asking, "After you come back, you come to my apartment for a drink. No?"

Wow. Never saw it coming. French women. Even the older ones? "I..." he stuttered, not sure what was an appropriate response. But, what the heck. This was Paris. "Yes. I will come by later. Seven o'clock good for you?" Zack asked, wondering if he should have suggested the hour, or should have waited for her to suggest it. The proper protocol for accepting drink invitations with beautiful, older women had not been covered in any of his guidebooks.

"D'accord!" (Agreed), she said, "Seven o'clock it is," and then, she smiled, again. With that, she passed Zack, who was happily, holding the door open for her.

All the way to the Épicier, Zack tried to think of what he would say to Mme. Christy during cocktails. Her English was good, and that was a relief. At least, he would be able to enjoy a conversation that contained more than elementary French sentences. He was hungry for an adult conversation, as he had been speaking French, at the level of a child, for the last two months.

On his way to the grocery store, he passed the window of her flower shop across the street, and stopped to admire the beautiful arrangements. Perhaps, he could discuss those – as a conversation starter, but he knew nothing about flowers, other than the names of a few common ones – roses, daisies, lilacs. Maybe she would be willing to educate him about the flower business, but who would want to talk about their work, after working all day? No, they should discuss something more interesting, but what? Politics, religion, and sex were out. His mother had taught him that.

He needed material for his next article. Perhaps, he could ask her for her help with that. At the épicerie, he picked up various vegetables and smelled them, before putting them back, and thought about Mme. Christy. Would it be considered rude to ask her where she was born? Where she went to college? Why she was alone? Why any beautiful woman her age was alone in Paris? He smelled a melon, then, remembered how Mme. Christy had smelled, remembered how - as she had passed him, the slightest bit of breeze had carried her perfume in his direction. She had smelled good in that way so many French women smelled good, sweet, and delicious.

Maybe he could ask her what scent she wore or where she bought it. Would that be flattering? Would that engage her in conversation? Was the fragrance industry in France a possible topic for a travel article? He became distracted with his daydreams while checking out at the grocery store. Perfume - that was a safe topic, wasn't it? He decided to test his idea. He leaned in towards the cashier, and asked, "What is your scent?" She leaned back away from him, before answering, "Savon" (soap).

Rats! Maybe the brand of a woman's perfume was off limits.

French culture was such a maze of faux pas and excusez-moi moments. "Pardon," he said to the cashier, as he lowered his head to begin bagging his groceries. He hoped that the customers behind him didn't think him a fool. As he turned to look back at them, they were talking to the cashier in French about something, which didn't sound like it was the price of eggs. "Asking a woman what perfume she wore!" (Was that it?) "...and in public!" (Yes. He understood that part.) His listening skills were terrible. He really needed to sign up for those French lessons, if he was going to continue living France.

Mme. Christy's apartment, 102, was down one flight of stairs. Descending the stairs, he noticed that there was no light coming from beneath the door of the vacant apartment, although a thin swatch of light shone brightly from beneath Montague's door. At exactly seven o'clock, Zack reached up to knock, but a ferocious bout of sneezing began. He searched desperately for the handkerchief, which he had forgotten. A trip back to his apartment, a good double nostril blow, and he was back in front of Mme. Christy's door, this time, fully prepared.

He had showered, dressed in his most presentable clothes, and put on the last of the cologne, which he had purchased in the States. Like some wines, too poorly produced to sit on the shelf long, his cologne had taken on a decidedly vinegary odor. Perhaps, wearing old cologne had not been a good choice. Perhaps, this was what had caused the volcanic explosion from his nose.

A second dose of cologne had been a last minute decision, as he didn't have anything else in the apartment that was scented, other than cleaning products. He wanted to wear something (other than lavender and lemons), especially, after smelling her earlier. She might be expecting it. A quick check of his how to survive in France book had convinced him. It said, annually, more French men than French women purchased cologne, and it was not bought as gifts, but rather, for themselves. Yes. In a country like this, Mme. Christy would expect him to smell good.

A nervous attempt to appear acceptable, if not sophisticated, had caused the battle between his cologne and his scented deodorant, a fact made painfully clear as he raised his arm to knock. Immediately, putting his arm down, he regretted his choice. Tomorrow, he would shop for a proper male cologne, and buy an unscented deodorant. Tonight, he would keep his arms down, and remain a respectful distance away from Mme. Christy, for fear of offending her nose, if not her sense of propriety.

Mme. Christy allowed him to knock twice, before she opened the door. He made a mental note. Lesson Four: Proper French women allow male visitors to knock twice. She was smiling as she opened the door, and that immediately put him at ease. Hers was a beautiful smile. Dressed in casual slacks and sweater; and with her hair, which had been tightly twisted onto the top of her head earlier, now down, she looked younger. Mara had remarked that Mme. Christy was in her fifties, and Mara's tone had made the florist seem a hundred and fifty. But, this woman, greeting Zack at the door, could have passed, easily, for a woman forty, and forty wasn't old in anyone's book.

Zack thought Mara had not seen Mme. Christy quite like this. She was the epitome of understated beauty, casually dressed, but with elegant style. She had a slim figure with curves in all the right places. Her nails were manicured (something which intrigued him); each nail perfectly polished in bright pink. Had she found time to do this, since arriving home? How did she manage to stay so clean in working in a flower shop? Did she have employees, who did the dirty work?

Her skin was perfect, her eyes made up, and her lips embellished by the slightest stroke of lipstick. "What would you prefer to drink?" she asked, closing the door behind them, and pointing to spot on the sofa. "I have red and white wines, beer, tequila...," she continued, as she turned on a jazz radio station.

Zack's thoughts stopped at tequila. Tequila, really? In France? Then, she stopped talking, and suddenly, he was aware that she was waiting for his answer. "You choose," he said. "I will have what the lady is having." He thought it sounded charming, in that 1950's Hollywood musical sort of way, but instead, it brought a momentary blank stare.

A moment later, she said, "Yes. Ok. I am having an aperitif." She moved to the little kitchenette in the corner of the room. "Then, you would like one, also?" she asked, unsure if she had understood him correctly.

"Oui," Zack said. His answer was a mistake, as Mme. Christy misinterpreted it as a cue that he preferred to speak in French. She began rattling off something in French, so fast that Zack panicked. He caught about every fifth word - something about his apartment, about Paris, about his job? He heard "Margarita." What was she asking him?

"Did he prefer a Margarita?"

Fortunately, she looked up and recognized the expression on his face. She had seen it many times on the faces of her foreign customers. "You are still learning French. No?" she said, a statement of fact, as much as it was a question. "Eez OK," she began. "I speak English."

"Thank you," Zack said, relieved. "I know I should take more lessons. I plan to in the spring," he lied, accepting the glass of Kir, which she was now holding out to him. "I promise, I will."

With that settled, glass in hand she sat down on the other end of the sofa. "Do you like Kir?" she began, after watching Zack take a sip. Zack had to begin the conversation by admitting his ignorance about Kir. She was eager to explain it was a drink made from white wine and Crème de Cassis. She launched into the reasons why the French believed in drinking an alcoholic beverage before dinner. From there, she went to great lengths to explain how it aided in digestion, and Zack learned quickly that Mme. Christy was knowledgeable about health, diets, and gourmet cooking. He thought any one of these topics might become a good subject for them to discuss. It might inspire an interesting article for his boss, who was still waiting for this week's installment.

Suddenly, she changed the topic. "So do you like Mara's apartment?" she asked.

Zack was happy that she was so ready to ask questions, and that he had become so comfortable in her presence so quickly. It didn't appear that he would have to use any of the questions, which he had rehearsed on the walk home. Her friendliness would lead them through the evening, eliminating the need to disguise his real reason for being there. Maybe, he could get through the evening without revealing too much about his arrangement with Mara.

Then, she smiled, waiting for his answer, "Do you like living in this neighborhood?" And there it was. The question he had been waiting for someone to ask. Why had he chosen the 6th Arrondissement? With that, he was off and running, unable to stop himself from talking. It seemed that he had been dying for a chance to talk in English. He told her of his dreams for becoming a famous writer in Paris. He told her stories about Hemingway and Stein, as if she knew nothing about the famous Americans, who had shared her neighborhood before him.

In the morning, all he would be able to remember was that her first name was Madeleine, and she had served him something called Kir. After that, his memories got fuzzy, quickly. Through the fog in his head, he remembered that he had an article to write. After several cups of very strong black coffee, Zack knocked out a 1000-word article on the history of aperitifs.

Most of the information he got from the bartender at the bistro down the street, and from the internet, and although, he did not give the bartender full credit in his article, he did properly cite his sources. Perhaps, the bistro's business would increase, compensating the man in an indirect manner. Amazingly, Harrison emailed back, within two hours of receiving Zack's article, saying that he loved it! The undeserved praise warranted a second visit to Mme. Christy's; plus, he wanted to know "exactly" what had happened last night at her apartment.

His first thought was of flowers, it was not appropriate to give a florist flowers from someone else's shop. Then, he thought – wine, but she was such an expert on such things that whatever he chose, it would not be good enough. Then, he thought – chocolates. What woman does not like chocolates? The bartender, who he returned to thank for his help on the article, suggested a Chocolatier about three blocks away. Zack made what he thought was a proper size selection, since it was only for one person, and the price of anything else would require credit approval from his new French bank manager. Chocolates were expensive! Who knew?

He walked home, wondering what the French gave out to trick-or-treaters at Halloween. Certainly, it wasn't what he had in his little shopping bag. "Is there anything more expensive to eat in France than chocolates?" he joked to the cashier at the Chocolatier. She answered, "Oui, truffes." Could he live long enough to understand the French? Chocolates, exorbitantly expensive, were possibly – maybe - understandable. But, mushrooms?

Back at the apartment, he looked out of his window and watched for Mme. Christy to lock up her flower shop across the street. It was a great view of her shop, and so, he watched much of the afternoon, as the display in the window changed several times, and people came and went. It was a bit like watching a foreign film without the sound, but also without the benefit of subtitles. Twice, Mme. Christy had stepped outside to complete a conversation with her customers, giving him a chance to study her. She glanced up from across the street, and once, Zack thought that she might have seen him in the window. He waved, just in case, but she did not wave back.

At precisely seven o'clock, he knocked on apartment 102. "Moment," she said, before coming to the door and unlocking it. She cracked the door only slightly, then, seeing Zack, opened it only a bit further. He could see that she was still in her street clothes with her hair up, and it was a bit disappointing, because she did not look at all like the woman he remembered from the night before. This Madeleine looked tired, and grumpy.

She said, slowly, tentatively, "Oui?"

Zack held out his little gift, and said, "For you." She looked down at what was in his hands, and suddenly, the grumpy look was gone, replaced by her beautiful smile. He extended his hand, so that she did not have to come out into the hallway, in order to accept the famous logo box.

"Merci!" she said, accepting his gift. "You are becoming very French, I see." She laughed.

Zack was thrilled. He had gotten something right. Lesson Five: Chocolates are a perfect thank you gift, after someone invites you over for cocktails.

It was obvious that, tonight, she would not be inviting Zack in, not that he expected it. His body language, moving a step further away, indicated that he understood, but to be certain that there was no misunderstanding, Zack added, "I'll see you tomorrow." With that, Zack returned to his apartment.

She was relieved to see that he knew not to invite himself in. As he climbed the stairs, she left her door open a moment longer to watch him from the slit in the doorway. Listening for the sound of him locking his door, she turned around to someone else in the room, and said, "Rendez-vous. Je vous ai dit. Il aura aucun problème" (You see. I told you. He will be no problem.)

everal days had gone by, and Mme. Christy had not invited Zack back to her apartment for cocktails. This was a disappointment to Zack, but his disappointment was soon replaced by an unexpected invitation from another neighbor, Professor Montague. They had not met once in the time that Zack had been living in Mara's apartment, and that seemed odd. Since the professor and Mara had become late night drinking buddies, Zack hoped that the professor might drop by for an occasional nightcap, and that he might be willing to discuss Mara. Zack still had many unanswered questions about his host. Like for instance, why she didn't answer her emails regularly? It had taken three days to receive a response to his last one. He only needed a simple answer. What should I do with your packages?

Mara had been clear about her regular mail, but not about what to do with anything too large to fit into her mailbox. The postman had brought six packages in six weeks to Zack's door, thinking that it was still Mara's door, and he had left them on the doorstep. Zack had stacked them next to the bathroom, behind the small armoire, which was the only spot he could find to fit them, without them being in his way. The stack of six stood almost as tall as the armoire.

Shouldn't he ask one of the other residents what to do? But, that would be violating his agreement with Mara by sharing his concerns with perfect strangers. What did they do, when they received packages for their neighbors? He had begun noticing that nearly everyone in the apartment building regularly received packages. Online shopping, perhaps? Everyone shopped on the internet these days – even in France. It was hard to ignore the home-shopping television shows late at night, when nothing else was being broadcast.

And this was how he and the professor met. A postman, but not Monsieur Le Postman, delivered two packages at the same time, one to the professor's apartment, and one to Mara's. Zack heard the heavy footsteps coming up the stairs, and the noise outside the door, as did the professor. The two men opened their doors at the same time, and Zack's first view of the professor was of a large derrière. He was bent over and picking up a box, which had been wrapped in brown paper. The label on his was hand-scrawled, exactly like the one on the box, lying at Zack's feet.

As Montague stood up, he realized that Zack had been watching him, and so, felt compelled to say, "Books," before disappearing into his apartment, and soundly locking his door.

When Zack picked up Mara's package, he wondered, aloud, "Books?" It was not heavy enough to be books, not even paperbacks. He had moved enough times since college to know how heavy books could be, especially, a package of them this large. No. She had probably ordered something off late night television. Perhaps, everything ordered from late night television came from the same shipping company – thus, the look-alike packaging.

He shook this box, something that he had not done with the others. It rattled ever so slightly. Vitamins? Diet pills? Or... Then, it struck him. What if the box held something more lethal, more illegal than diet pills? What if Mara had been receiving drugs for her neighbor, Tito? What if the professor had been doing the same?

Illegal drugs? His imagination was off and running. What ... if Mara had been involved with Tito? And, what if Mara had killed Tito, and or had him killed? What ...if Zack had been set up by Mara to take the fall? Stop it! Zack said, this time, aloud. "Stop it!"

He tossed the box on top of the last one behind the armoire. This time, the stack was partially visible, and that bothered him. He picked up a dirty shirt from the chair by the bed and tossed it on top of the box, hiding it from view, for the moment. Ok. If there was anything illegal in there, at least it might be a bit harder for the police to find it. Police? What was he thinking?

Rats! Why didn't Mara answer her email? He searched the apartment for his notebook, for the page where he had written down her cell phone number. It took a few minutes to locate. He dialed and waited, but the voice recording was not good news. "This number is no longer in service."

Near midnight, there was a knock at the door. Zack looked

through the keyhole and could see only trouser'ed knees. Should he open it? No. Too much had happened recently to make him feel comfortable opening his door to anyone. "Oui? Qui est là?" (Yes. Who is there?)

"C'est moi, Montague." (It is me, Montague.)

Zack debated a moment, before opening the door to the man, who had lived across the hall for nearly two months without introducing himself. Why now? Why at nearly midnight did Montague think this was the right moment? Then, Zack saw the bottle in the man's hand.

"A drink?" Montague offered, holding up the bottle.

Mara had drank often late at night with Montague. Perhaps, the man was lonely, missing his late night drinking companion. Zack cracked the door open a few inches and studied his neighbor's face, finding nothing ominous there, only deep lines and wrinkles. It seemed obvious that Montague had lived a hard life, and his face was a road map to be followed, if Zack were willing to listen. "Ok," Zack said, opening the door wide enough for entry.

Montague entered Zack's apartment with the ease of someone, who knew the territory. He made his way over to what must have been his favorite spot on the sofa. Unfortunately, it was also now Zack's, but Zack relinquished it to his guest. Montague looked around for glasses, helpless in finding any. Zack had made just enough changes to throw him off his game. Zack saw his difficulty, and went to the kitchen to retrieve the only two wine glasses that Mara had left him. They were sitting on the shelf next to the refrigerator.

Montague smiled. "Ah," he said. "Better than..." (He mimed drinking directly from the bottle).

Zack laughed. "Yes, better."

Montague poured as Zack watched, not knowing what it was that they were drinking, but then, Montague held the bottle out for Zack to examine, as if Zack might have a clue about wine. He had none, but masked his lack of education by pretending to read something on the label, and then, remarking, "Ah!" Montague seemed pleased, and that was enough for the two men to take a drink, before fumbling for a conversation starter.

Montague sat back and looked around the apartment, as if he were searching for something new to admire in a place that he knew so well. It was still Mara's apartment in almost every way, except that Zack had tried to make it appear more masculine by removing the orange pillows, and replacing them with blue ones. Montague picked one up from the sofa and pretended to be admiring it. "I like," he said. "More like us," he said, "men."

Zack smiled. "Yes," he answered. "More like us."

They drank a while longer in silence, awkward silence. Then, when Montague drank a bit more, poured a bit more, he launched into what must have been his purpose in visiting. "So… you are the cousin."

Ok, the voice in Zack's said, this is where it begins. He tried to remember exactly how to start the cousin story. "Yes," he said, "I am the cousin… from New York." He recited every passage perfectly, as practiced, and Montague listened without interrupting. It took all of six minutes, during which time Montague's eyes followed Zack's lips, as if English were still a challenge to comprehend. It seemed to Zack, because the professor had not interrupted, that he had understood most of it.

When Zack was finished, and happily expecting some sort of acknowledgement, Montague refilled their glasses a third time, and said, "So… you are the cousin."

Oh, rats! Zack thought. I have to tell it, again!

But, in fact, the professor was simply acknowledging that Zack was, indeed, the cousin. They drank together for another twenty minutes. Zack knew, asking someone what they did for a living in France, was considered rude; the equivalent of asking, "How much do you earn?" Jobs and salaries were so regulated by the government, that to know the job a man did was to know his income. So, Zack had prefaced his question, softening the crudeness of the intrusion, by telling Montague, first, what he did for a living. "I'm a writer," he announced, proudly.

Montague nodded in a way that implied approval.

Zack, then, asked, almost as a punctuation mark to his revelation, "And what exactly do you do?" Any interview had the potential of becoming a new magazine story.

Montague studied Zack's face for a moment, before answering. "I teach botany."

"Hmmm," Zack uttered. His mind fixated on a florist and a botanist in the same building, thinking that it must make for interesting conversations at the mailbox. He asked, "So do you know

Mme. Christy very well?" Properly gassed up, Montague might prove to be as much of a gossip as Mara had been. After all, they drank together. They must have gossiped together. Zack was hoping.

"Yes. I know her very well," Montague answered, then, smiled slyly. "A beautiful woman. No?" The young American had an eye for the women, did he?

"A beautiful woman. Yes." Zack answered, then, held up his glass in a salute to Montague. (You old fox...you.)

Then, Zack asked something, which he shouldn't have, and the conversation came to a very abrupt ending. "It seems like everyone in this building buys a lot of books."

The room drew in around Zack, as Montague stood up, bottle in hand. "I must go home now. It is late." With that, he went to the door, let himself out, and did not bother to say, à Bientôt, or au Revoir. Zack was taken aback by his guest's sudden rudeness. The visit had been going so well up until...

Even through the haze of three glasses of wine, Zack could see his mistake. Lesson Six: Don't be a busybody. Talking about other peoples' mail was being too nosey, and nobody likes snoops. Ok. Got it.

Montague had visited on a Monday night. On Tuesday night, Ivan and Berta Polywog dropped by with a small gift of bread and pastries. On Wednesday night, Albert and Arness dropped off a basket of meats and cheese. On Thursday night, Gwendolyn, the Brit, brought a basket of scones, double-Devonshire cream, and fresh berries. Marcel and Camille dropped by on Friday morning, after returning from the market, because they thought Zack might like some apples and pears.

Zack had been given more food in one week, than he had purchased in the previous month. By the weekend, he did not know quite where to store everything. Even Mme. Durand, the concierge, had managed to make it up the stairs to leave a little gift at Mara's door. It was a potted plant, a cactus, purchased from Mme. Christy's shop across the street. The only other residents, who had not put in an appearance, or left a welcome basket, were Monsieur Le Postman and Monsieur Le Spy.

None of those, who had shown up, had stayed more than a cursory five minutes, enough time to introduce themselves, look Zack over once or twice at the door, and then, leave. Zack found this all very suspicious, but he wanted to believe that he was now accepted. Mme.

Christy, Madeleine, must have been chosen by committee to extend an invitation to the newest resident. She must have been given the task of interviewing him, and then, had delivered her judgment. It seemed obvious, given the cache of goodies, that she had told the others, "The American cousin is ok. I have checked him out. He is not dangerous."

Professor Montague, then, was recruited to second her opinion by making a cursory midnight visit. That had to be it. Between Madeleine and Montague, Zack had passed muster. Lesson Seven: Be patient. Eventually, you will win over the French. It takes time. He ate well all weekend, giving thanks that his neighbors had found him – acceptable, if not completely civilized.

❧℘℘℘
Chapter 9
❧℘℘℘

A few weeks went by, and courtesies were now routinely exchanged with everyone in the building. There were Bonjours in passing in the hallways and Au revoirs at the mailboxes. Zack believed that his French skills were improving, or if they were not, that at least his neighbors were making concerted efforts to understand his poor attempts. They helped him with pronunciations, correcting him when necessary, and offering suggestions – when it was, amusingly obvious, that he was searching for the proper word.

Little Bog Polywog liked the American very much, and he, more than any other of the residents, tried to make friends with Zack. However, Zack found Bog's ability to switch back and forth between three languages, more than challenging. It also made Zack laugh. Based upon their son's endorsement of their newest neighbor, Ivan and Berta Polywog invited Zack to walk with the family through the Luxembourg Gardens.

It was a beautiful, sunny, but cool Sunday morning in late November. He loved the idea of being included, and since it was the week of Thanksgiving back in the States, he brought food to be shared. It wasn't exactly turkey and dressing, but as the three adults sat and ate, watching the young boy play with his sailboat, there was a sense of family. Ivan asked Zack about America and about the Thanksgiving holiday. In an equal exchange, Berta told him about Poland, and about some of the holiday traditions, which they missed. It seemed to Zack that this Polish immigrant family were the friendliest of all of his new neighbors, and the least complicated.

Albert, Arness, and young Sébastien had also invited Zack for an afternoon in the gardens, but the day chosen was cursed by bad weather, causing them to retreat from the cold and relentless rain. They returned home without sharing a meal, but that was Zack's preference. Their young son was mischievous, and had spent his time in the park bullying other children, twice, making it necessary for Albert to intervene. Other parents argued with Albert about his son's manners. Albert and Arness seemed blinded by their love for the child, defending him, when commonsense was against them doing so.

Zack did not like the child, and therefore, it made his time with Albert and Arness awkward. He did not want to offend them, not only because they had offered him discounts on meats and cheeses at their shops, but also because they were now his neighbors. Neighbors should overlook each other's foibles; perhaps, even their ill-mannered children. Right?

He convinced himself. Yes. That was right. One should give his neighbors a wider berth in which to live their lives, more room than say – a stranger? One should ignore things, which seem strange, noises in the middle of the night, laughter coming up or down airshafts, packages, which look mysteriously all the same, being delivered on the same day each week.

Then, Zack saw something that he could not overlook. The noise in the hallway had brought him to his knees once again, to look through his keyhole. And there it was! It had confirmed his suspicions. Montague was coming out of the vacant apartment next door, the apartment which no one else in the building spoke about, the one which was no longer for rent. There was no Louer sign in the window. However, Zack had not been certain, that no one went in, and no one came out, at least, not until now.

So who did live there? Zack was dying to find out. He did not like the idea of challenging Montague, but his curious had to be sated. He grabbed his hat and scarf, and pretended to be leaving, just as Montague reached his door. "Oh, hello," Zack said, cheerfully, surprising the professor. "Were you visiting the new neighbor?" he asked, and then, waited.

Montague appeared to be sweating. His face and hands were dirty. He, also, looked terribly guilty. However, Zack could not imagine why.

"New neighbor?" Montague asked, his English faltering in its delivery. Had Zack seen him coming out of the vacant apartment? "No. Old neighbor. I was downstairs... I mean..." (catching a glance at his dirty hands) "...across the street, helping Mme. Christy. A truck brought new flowers. Sometimes, I help her." He waited to see if Zack would dispute his claim.

Zack thought, ("Ok. You want me to believe that? I'll let it go."), but what he said was, "You like to help beautiful women? You are a smart man. Maybe someday, a beautiful woman will help you. No?" He punctuated his words with a laugh.

Montague laughed, nervously. "Yes. I like to help beautiful women." With that, he turned and hurried into his apartment, relieved that the American had not seen him leave the vacant apartment.

Zack felt obligated to leave the building, if for no other reason than to make his lie into the truth. He walked around the block until he was so cold that he had to stop at a café for coffee to warm up. He was surprised to find Gwendolyn sitting there, alone, having coffee. She looked up from her newspaper, and he nodded a hello. To his surprise, she invited him to sit with her. "Sometimes," she began as an excuse for the invitation, "I do not enjoy sitting alone."

"Yes," Zack said. "I understand. It's nice to have company."

They talked for over an hour about much of nothing. He found her very kind, soft-spoken, and intelligent. She explained that she had been transferred to Paris three years earlier, an associate in an international health organization. She called her job "something boring, accounting in the pharmaceutical division," and although, she attempted to explain exactly - what it was that she did - Zack, also, found it boring.

Since she seemed almost as bored in the telling of it, he changed the subject, to ask if she enjoyed living in Paris. She confessed that she missed England, but not the weather. Paris, although, just as cold, was not as wet. Her three-year assignment would be up in the spring, and then, she would have to make a decision about returning to England. Without an extension on her contract, or the prospect of a new job, she would return home. It was the only logical thing to do.

Then, she asked Zack what he did for a living. He explained how he worked for the magazine of a travel company, writing articles about other cultures, as an incentive for people to travel internationally. His assignment was for only one year, although, he was hoping to extend his stay in Paris – if his editor thought his articles were worth it. Since everything was published online, it didn't matter so much where he lived. However, being in a foreign country, allowed him to write first-hand accounts, and having writers in the field made good sense from a marketing standpoint.

"So far, everything's going well," Zack said, referring to his assignment, but thinking that his time with Gwendolyn was also not going badly. She congratulated him on his initial success as a writer, and flattered, he gave her links to online sites, where she might read some of his articles. It was relaxing speaking in English, although, he felt illiterate, when listening to her polished British accent. Everything that came out of her mouth sounded brilliant. Why was that?

Gwendolyn did not bring up any of their neighbors in her conversation, and so, Zack felt uncomfortable cutting to the chase, to ask how well she knew the others. Then, she asked him, "How are you and the professor getting along?"

"Quite well," Zack said, confident that the professor would say the same, if asked.

"I heard him stop by your apartment at midnight, one night," she confessed. "You know, I hear everything that goes on above me."

No. Zack didn't know that. "Is my television or music too loud?" he asked, suddenly, concerned that this had been her real reason for the invitation to join her for coffee. Perhaps, this was how people in Paris aired their differences, settled their disagreements.

"No. Not at all," Gwendolyn reassured him. "I rather like the sound of someone above me. Since there is no one below me, it gives me some sense of security, knowing that if I were to scream loud enough – you might hear me and come to my rescue."

Zack was surprised to hear that Gwendolyn was afraid of living alone in Paris, in a building with a digicode, and a lock on her door. But, with all the strange comings and goings at the vacant apartment, he had to admit to his own fear. "Yes. I can understand. You can count on me," he said, hoping that if he screamed loud enough, that she, in turn, might come to his aid. "Let's have a signal."

"Yes," she said, eagerly. "Let's do."

"What do you prefer?" he asked. "A knock on the floor? Two thumps and a stomp?" He laughed.

"Two loud stomps from above," and I'll come running up the stairs, she promised.

"Ok," he replied, "Two loud thumps on your ceiling. Agreed?"

"Agreed," she said, then, laughed.

He liked her. She was plain, simple, straightforward, and had a wonderful sense of humor. Yes. He liked her, already. She had real friend potential, and he was sorry that she lived below him, rather than next door. He could imagine midnight glasses of wine with her, but he would have to settle for the ones with the old professor, Montague. However, now, he could picture Gwendolyn was right below him, listening through the airshaft to his late night conversations with the professor. It would make their discussions so much more interesting.

After they said their goodbyes, as she had shopping to do and he had none, he walked back to the apartment past Mme. Christy's flower shop. Daydreaming about Gwendolyn, he stopped to admire the changes in the window, noticing that inside, Madeleine was deep into conversation with a young man. The young man seemed frustrated, almost angry. She was calm, although, she had her arms crossed in a pose of defiance.

Zack felt embarrassed witnessing the scene, and stepped back from the window a distance, where he could still watch from behind a large bouquet of roses. The young man pounded his fist on the counter in front of Mme. Christy, who stood her ground without flinching. Instinct made Zack take a step forward towards the door, thinking that he should intervene, and protect her, but then, a man the size of an American refrigerator stepped out from a back room. In one fell swoop, he reached out with his large arm, and picked the young man up by the throat, pulling him helplessly across the counter. He was about to pound his fist into his face, when Mme. Christy said something, loudly, and the large man let the young man drop.

Zack was visibly shaken by what he had seen, and thought it best, if he quickly disappeared. Rather than cut a direct path to the apartment building, which was clearly seen from Mme. Christy's front shop window, Zack turned back in the direction of the café. About a block away, he met Gwendolyn returning with her shopping. He offered to carry her packages, and she, gratefully, allowed him to do so.

It was time to start asking questions, and if past experience had taught anything, it was that getting answers was an easier task if wine was involved. He took a chance and invited Gwendolyn to dinner.

To his relief, she said, "Yes. I would like that."

"About seven?" he asked.

"Yes," Gwendolyn agreed.

At six fifty-five, Zack was at her door and more than anxious to leave. Before showing up at Gwendolyn's apartment, he had watched from his window, as Mme. Christy locked up for the night. He watched her walk across the street to their apartment building, and then, he saw her leave, again, less than ten minutes later. What had happened in her shop? He wanted to follow her, to find out why the young man had been so angry? Who was he? And who was the man, who ran to her rescue? Was he just an employee, or was he something more, like a bodyguard? Maybe Gwendolyn would know.

Zack had continued thinking about the scenario as he showered and changed clothes for his evening out with Gwendolyn, and as soon as he could, he returned to the window to watch for Mme. Christy's return. By 6:50 p.m., she still had not returned, and obligated to meet Gwendolyn, he could wait no longer.

Gwendolyn must have been ready early because she answered the door after only one knock. Lesson Eight: Some women don't wait for two knocks at the door. Was it a British thing, or a Gwendolyn thing? He was trying to break his bad habit of generalizing about people, based upon nationality, as it always led to mistakes about the individual. But, his assignment in Europe was to study and write about people of different cultures, and unfortunately, that included women. However, what made women do what they do – had always been a mystery to him. Perhaps, Gwendolyn was hungry, and seven o'clock was late for her dinner hour. Perhaps, the British, traditionally, ate earlier. It could be something as simple as that.

They chatted about nothing in particular as they walked to a nearby restaurant, one Gwendolyn had chosen. Zack took the choice of location as evidence she was hungry, or needed a quick escape. He wasn't sure which it was. If things didn't go well with Zack, she could get home quickly. There would be no need for awkward small talk on the long walk home. Zack was hoping that her choice was based upon being hungry.

"I think you will enjoy the food, here," she said, as Zack opened the door to the restaurant for her.

"I'm pretty easy to please," Zack said, smiling. "Anything is better than my cooking." Gwendolyn laughed and this made Zack feel very comfortable. There was something warm and inviting about the woman, although, he had to admit that he felt no physical attraction to her. She was too plain to be considered anything other than average looking. Not beautiful. Not pretty. Not even cute. Just acceptable. All of her features matched. Her complexion was clear. Her eyes were a light color of grey, which never changed hues, not even on a bright sunny day. She was acceptably shorter than he was, but not squatty, and she had enough meat on her bones to be considered healthy, but not thin or fat, just average.

The most flattering thing, which he could tell her – and did over dinner, was that she had a wonderful sense of humor. To which, she answered, "Yes. So, I've been told." So she knew, he was surprised to learn, this time studying her face more closely, that she was not the greatest beauty. However, it did not seem to bother her. Rather, she was content to be exactly who she was, and Zack found this her second most attractive quality.

Gwendolyn was a realist, and this meant that there would be no game playing, if he were to pursue a friendship with her, or something more. This was refreshing. Soon, they were telling stories and laughing. Gwendolyn was intelligent, articulate, and kept Zack on his toes, discussing politics and news. Nearly four hours passed, before he realized the time of night. They had missed the light snow beginning to fall outside, a surprise for their walk home. Twice, when she started to lose her balance on the wet cobblestones, Zack offered Gwendolyn his hand, and she took it.

At Gwendolyn's door, Zack said a casual goodnight, and then, headed upstairs. Neither had expected a goodnight kiss, or even a handshake. It was as if they were already good friends, and this made Zack the happiest that he had been, since first arriving in Paris; first - because he now had a co-conspirator in the building, and secondly - because Gwendolyn had been so candid in explaining what was really going on. He had been so foolish to dramatize the obvious.

Thanks to Gwendolyn, he would sleep much better tonight knowing the truth.

Chapter 10

T he weather had opened up a bit, the skies were no longer grey, the wind had died down, and the booksellers along the Seine seemed happier. Zack took his coffee and walked from kiosk to kiosk, perusing the books and magazines from the 1950's and 60's, which all smelled of mold, and too many years in the rain.

He found a postcard, which his mother would like. It was of Charles Boyer and it looked as new as the day it was printed. Turning it over, Zack was disappointed to discover that it had been printed last year. He had hoped for a real souvenir of Paris's glorious past. However, she would appreciate any postcard from her son, since he had not sent her a real letter in over a month. She would be worried. The truth was he didn't know how to break the news to her. He wanted to stay in Paris.

It was premature to announce his intentions. What did he really know about Paris, other than what he had read? Not much, but there was something that spoke to him here, and it wasn't just the nagging voice in his head that guilt'ed him into sitting down at a keyboard, when he would rather be walking. Here, he was learning things about himself every day, and at a speed that escaped him in the States. Forced to interact with other people, despite his self-induced language handicap, he was growing – intellectually, socially, and maybe even spiritually. He couldn't imagine if he felt this way now, that he would feel any differently in a year.

But, it was too soon to tell his family that. His intentions to stay in touch with his family and friends had been sincere, but somehow, his time here in Paris had gone by so quickly that it became easy to lose track of time. Had it really been so long? Six weeks in the hotel, and how many months in the apartment? He had Mara to thank. She had made it too easy. All he had to do was deposit his monthly rent in a bank account down the street. How simple. She had told him, "I do not plan to return to Paris, so we do business this way. D'accord?" He said, "D'accord" (agreed), and it was done. Just like that!

Apparently, things had gone well for Mara and Phillipe in Avignon, and they had decided to set up house there, rather than come back to the big city. At least, that is what she told him in an email, and forbade him from telling the others. Perhaps, her boyfriend's parents had approved of her, and missing their son too much, allowed the young couple to move in with them in the south of France. Mara had emailed with three bits of news: the weather in the south was beautiful this time of year; her parents in Verdun still did not know that she had moved, so could he keep the charade going a bit longer; and oh, yes, she was pregnant!

Zack read that email twice, wondering at what point her parents would show up on his doorstep to visit their daughter. Would they think he was "the boyfriend," and not "the cousin?" And when Mara finally admitted that she was pregnant, or showed up on their doorstep with their new grandchild... would he be sought out and blamed? It seemed that Mara was living her life awfully loosely thought out. Did she not think of any of the consequences of her decisions?

Zack, by nature, detailed decisions to death, before he could act upon them. Paris had been the easiest decision he had ever made, and yet, he had agonized over it for three weeks, before telling his boss, "Yes. I will take the assignment." He, nearly, had lost out to another blogger, who was anxiously waiting to go overseas, and would have gone in a minute, if asked.

The other writer had been waiting for Zack to blink just once. Harrison's secretary had conveyed the behind-the-scenes drama to Zack in her email, congratulating him on his decision, and revealing the hidden competition for his new job. Whenever Zack did not feel like writing, whenever he was close to missing another deadline, he reminded himself of the other guy – still in New York – still waiting for his chance to move to Paris.

So, Mara was in Avignon. Zack was in Paris, and by all observations, no one had leased the apartment next door, which had been the catalyst for getting him into this building. The fact that an apartment could remain vacant in this part of Paris, for this long, was of great interest to Zack, and yet, none of the neighbors appeared nearly so concerned about it. That was why he had felt compelled to bring it up over dinner with Gwendolyn. Gratefully, she had been forthcoming with answers.

His dinners with Gwendolyn were becoming his pipeline to the others in the village, the name that Mara had given the collection of apartment dwellers. According to Gwendolyn, a couple from Italy had rented the apartment for a vacation home. She got her information from Marcel and Camille, who got their information from Mme. Durand, the concierge, who was the property owner's onsite representative.

Apparently, the knocking and hammering, which Zack had heard earlier in the autumn, was the installation of a new kitchen. The Italian couple wanted a more modern one. The wife had wanted the wallpaper stripped and replaced. Having seen the apartment, Zack could understand her decision. If he had rented the place, and had been given the option, the wallpaper would have been the first thing to go!

Gwendolyn's news about the remodeling, however, was amazing, considering that Claudine had implied that Zack could not change one nail hole, or repair one scratch on the floor. Perhaps, he had misunderstood her. Perhaps, the new residents had thrown enough money in the pot for the changes to be made.

Was it Claudine, who had rented the apartment to the Italian couple, or had the couple Zack had seen in the hallway been the Italians? Then, he remembered, that couple had spoken French, and he had detected no Italian accent. No. The handshake had meant nothing. They had not signed a lease.

Claudine had mentioned a third party, so there must have been a third real estate agent, who showed the place. Mara must have known when she practically accosted the apartment hunters in the hallway. Maybe the apartment hunters from Italy had gotten there first, and Mara was only being a good neighbor by defending their claim.

So, when would he meet the new residents? Christmas? New Year's? It seemed odd that neither, the husband or the wife had been to Paris to oversee the remodeling. How trusting. Gwendolyn didn't know. She had only spoken to the couple once, she said, before diving into her dessert.

Gwendolyn had been so relaxed in her explanation that it would have been difficult to believe she was hiding anything. Her manners were sophisticated, yet, they did not make Zack uncomfortable. Her

British accent made her appear refined, educated, and so knowledgeable about everything. How could he not believe her? If she had told him the world was ending, she could make it sound like an everyday occurrence, and not worrisome news.

Over dinner, they had discussed yet another protest, another labor strike somewhere in the world. She had used an expression, which he had not heard in years, "This too shall pass." From her lips, it sounded charming, and he had not noticed until that very moment, how very tempting her lips were – soft, moist, and very, very pink, although, she work no lipstick.

Gwendolyn had managed to fill in many of the gaps in Zack's education about this area of Paris, and about their neighbors. Whereas, Mara had been brief, when she first described the full-time residents, Gwendolyn was long-winded, revealing the minutest detail of the villagers' lives. She had let it slip that the professor had a habit of drinking late at night with whoever would allow him in. One night, it had been Gwendolyn, but she quickly learned, and had to teach him that her work schedule would not accommodate late nights.

He didn't visit her, again, although it had not harmed their friendship. Many residents had entertained him over the years, but in the past year, he had found Mara the most willing. The fact that Mara lived right across the hall made his choice easy because getting back to his apartment, after bingeing, was a seamless journey. No stairs to navigate. It helped, too, that Mara kept the same hours that he did, sleeping late in the day, and staying up all night. She had always frequented clubs that opened, when most people were going to bed, and came home, when most people were going to work.

When she tended bar at two different brasseries, one in the 4th, the Marais area, and the other in the Latin Quarter. If she came home early, before midnight, she would slip a cocktail serviette under Montague's door, letting him know it was ok to drop by. An invitation also meant that Phillipe hadn't followed her home. Montague's dislike of Phillipe was basic. The boyfriend cut into his time with Mara. Zack's eyebrows must have gone up on this news because Gwendolyn added, "Nothing like that. The professor is harmless... in that way."

Zack was not so certain. Based upon their conversations, Montague seemed anything, but harmless. However, Zack was looking at the situation through a young man's eyes. Any time alone with a woman held endless possibilities, especially, here in Paris. He wasn't being lecherous, just hopelessly romantic. His mind wandered as Gwendolyn continued.

The professor was semi-retired, lecturing only two days a week at the botanical gardens, and a school of horticulture on the outskirts of Paris. She was not certain of the exact location, but one of those days, he took the RER train. The concierge, Mme. Durand, allowed him to putter in the courtyard garden, which consisted mainly of potted plants and one scraggly tree specimen, which looked almost as old and bent as the professor. He had no family that she knew of, other than a nephew, who occasionally dropped by for Sunday drives in the country. The professor's eyesight was failing and he could no longer drive himself. He once told her that he blamed his deteriorating eyesight on chemicals, which had gotten into his eyes from one of the botanical labs, where he had worked. He seemed reluctant to admit that it might be old age.

Mme. Christy, Madeleine as Gwendolyn preferred to call her, was divorced, – not widowed as Mara had thought. Madeleine had confided in Gwendolyn that she was embarrassed that her husband had left her, and so she found it easier to say widowed, when asked by people she did not know well. As is often the case, Monsieur Christy had left Madeleine for another, younger, woman. Without regard for his wife's welfare, he moved with his new mistress to Nice, where he started another flower shop.

Justice came in less than two years, when the younger woman left Monsieur Christy for someone else, more affluent. But, by then, Mme. Christy's attorney had already made certain that her ex-husband would provide for his wife by giving her the Paris shop, free and clear of all debt. Gwendolyn told Zack that Mme. Christy made a fine living by Paris standards, although, Zack had no idea - what a fine living meant. What were standards for income in a city, where no one discussed salaries?

Zack asked if Mme. Christy had any... He searched awkwardly for the proper word. Did Mme. Christy see any...? He was still not able to come up with the word.

"Does she have any lovers?" Gwendolyn helped him out. "No. I have never seen anyone visit her apartment night, other than one or two of the other residents in the building."

Zack was not ready to admit to Gwendolyn, that he had been a visitor to Mme. Christy's...Madeleine's apartment. There was always the possibility, that he would be invited back, and Madeleine might want their relationship, whatever it became, kept quiet. Had Gwendolyn seen him coming or going from Mme. Christy's door? If she had, he would have to weigh his words, carefully.

"She seems like a pleasant person." He said, and then, added, "Her window displays are very elegant. Did you happen to see the white arrangement in the center, today?" Could Gwendolyn see through his smoke screen? Did she already know he had a bit of a crush on Madeleine? He continued talking about things, which he had no knowledge of – design techniques, use of colors. It was over-kill, but he seemed unable to stop. A guilty conscience did that to him. Should he tell Gwendolyn the truth?

Gwendolyn studied Zack's face on the last comment, before commenting. "Yes. They're lovely." She noticed that he seemed fixated on flower arranging. "So...you've been inside her shop?"

"No," Zack had to admit, now, embarrassed, that he had found no excuse to patronize one of the resident's businesses. It felt like an obligation, to support the other residents. In Paris, each building was a sort of village. He changed the subject, saying that he made a routine of buying meats and cheeses from the shops, where Albert and Arness worked, even though they did not own the shops. Of course, there was an incentive to do so. Albert and Arness had made a practice of giving all of their neighbors their best prices, often, free samples – little nibbles of the most delectable items on their shelves.

Gwendolyn liked Albert and Arness very much. As for their son, well, it was a different story. Gwendolyn liked Bog, Ivan and Berta's son, as did Zack, but like Zack, she did not care at all for Sébastien, Albert and Arness's son, who had made a nasty habit of chasing her cat up and down the hallway and stairs. Gwendolyn had told him, repeatedly, not to do this, yet, he continued. Eventually, she could no longer allow her cat out of the apartment, as the poor old feline was too traumatized by the child.

"Did you tell his parents?" Zack asked, trying to appear sympathetic.

"It would not change the child's nature," Gwendolyn answered, "and it would only damage our friendship. Sébastien will always be a little bastard," she said curtly. "It will take years for his parents to see it."

Bastard was the first crude word that Gwendolyn had used in front of him, and with her British accent, she had managed to make "little bastard" sound civilized. Yes. Zack agreed she was right. The child's nature was probably set for life. From little bastard, if Sébastien's actions in the gardens were any indication, he was moving up quickly to big bully, and then, one day, what? Career criminal?

"What do you think of the Polywogs?" Zack asked. "Do you visit with them much?" His question caused a burst of laughter. Then, he realized that she had probably never heard their last name pronounced quite like this. "Mara," he excused his error, "I didn't..."

"No, no," she said, interrupting him, and trying to calm herself, "it's perfect. I've had difficulty with the pronunciation for years. Polywog," she repeated. "Yes. I believe I shall start using it, as well - Ivan, Berta, and Bog Polywog." She sounded out there names, again. Then, another burst of laughter followed. Zack liked the sound of her laugh. "They would make great characters in a children's book. Don't you think?" She suggested.

Zack liked that she was always thinking ahead. He had come up with a similar idea for a book, wondering what the legal ramifications might be for using their names; or for making them the imaginary family, who lived in the Luxembourg Gardens in Paris. Perhaps, the Polywogs would go along with Gwendolyn's and his idea, if everyone could agree to share the royalties. Then, he wondered if he would have to cut Mara a portion of the royalties – as the name had been her invention.

"And Mara," Zack began. "What do you think of her?"

This was the first time that Gwendolyn paused before answering. At first, Zack did not know what to read into that. Perhaps, it was the way he had phrased the question. He was asking for Gwendolyn's personal opinion, not just idle facts about the girl's life. Perhaps, Gwendolyn did not want to say anything, for fear that she might contradict what Mara had already told Zack.

Perhaps, Gwendolyn knew something that she did not wish to share about Mara. All that he knew, so far, was that Mara enjoyed an active nightlife in Paris; that she had a boyfriend from Avignon; and she didn't mind drinking late at night with old men. So what more could it be?

Gwendolyn started slowly. "Mara is a very interesting girl, wouldn't you agree?" She was asking Zack to express his own feelings about Mara, before she revealed her own.

Zack said, flatly, "I know nothing about her, really, except that..." (Then, he remembered his agreement with Mara.) "...she is my cousin." He had almost blown their cover story. Then, he qualified that with, "...whom I never met, before coming to Paris. And now that I'm here, she spends so much time with her boyfriend..." (He momentarily forgot Phillipe's name.) "... I hardly see her."

"Yes, I noticed that she isn't home much," Gwendolyn said, seemingly satisfied with his answer.

Did Gwendolyn know the cousin story was a lie? Had Mara included her in her conspiracy? However, he couldn't break his agreement with Mara to find out. He had promised not to reveal their lie. No. He would have to wait, until Gwendolyn admitted that she knew if she knew. Then, Gwendolyn threw him a curve.

"Did you spend time with her parents last week, when they were in Paris?"

Mara's parents were in Paris?! Did she mean that Mara was in Paris, too? Zack's face must have revealed his surprise. "No, no," he answered. "I didn't." He could come up with no reasonable excuse why. Why wouldn't he want to meet his father's brother, his father's sister-in-law? (Think. Think. Think.) He made a mistake. He was about to further the lie without clearing it with Mara. "Our fathers ..." He could not look at Gwendolyn. "...Mara's and mine have not reconciled their differences. My uncle still blames my father for ... you know?" He didn't know, but he hoped that Gwendolyn did, and might fill in the blank.

"Oh," was all that she could respond.

Then, Zack realized that Gwendolyn must have met Mara's parents at the apartment building. How else could she have known that they were in Paris? "You saw them last week?" he ventured to ask, "Where?"

"Mara brought them by my office. They had a problem with their insurance and their agent in Verdun had died. I did what I could for them, but insurance is not my area of expertise. I gave them the name of one of my associates, and introduced them. Mara visited with me, while her parents met with their new agent. Then, the four of us had lunch together. I was surprised that you were not with them. But, as you say, if there are family differences... well..."

Mara seemed wavering, unconvinced, so Zack had to make up more to the story. "They were in love with the same woman."

"Ah," Gwendolyn said, knowingly. "I thought it might be something like that."

Bingo! Zack had hit the right button. Gwendolyn, it seemed, was a bit of a romantic. Saying that his pretend uncle and his pretend father had fallen in love with the same pretend woman had done the trick. Now, he was believable.

But, then, she started asking the questions for which he was unprepared. "Was that woman your mother?" She asked, unfettered by the boldness of the question.

He was caught in his own web, unable to disengage. He lowered his eyes to the table, hoping for an epiphany. None came. "Yes. My mother," he surrendered to her version of his lie. "So, you see, it's a bit of a ticklish situation for my uncle, who was never certain..."

(Oh, stop, please stop!), Zack told his imagination, but he was caught up in the momentum. The lie was taking on a life of its own. "He was never certain, whether or not he was my father... instead of my father, I mean. I mean... you understand, don't you?"

"You poor man," Gwendolyn said, nearly in tears, as she touched Zack's hand.

Zack looked directly into her eyes, trying desperately to hide his deception. Her eyes were beautiful, not at all average, as he had thought earlier. Yes. They were as pure as her thoughts. His eyes, on the other hand, were turning all shades of red, warning lights flashing that danger was near.

What would happen, if Mara had told Gwendolyn a different reason for their fathers' estrangement? Now, more than ever he needed to get in touch with Mara. Why hadn't she tried to call or email him – if she knew she was coming back to Paris with her parents? Did her parents know that their daughter was pregnant? That brought a worse problem into focus. What, if her parents thought he was the baby's father? He was living in their daughter's apartment, wasn't he?

Lost trying to devise an escape route, Zack appeared lost in thoughts about his uncle and his father. It only served to draw Gwendolyn in closer, seeing how torn up Zack was about his family situation. Zack had accomplished breaking through to her, finding her heart, but he had done so based entirely upon lies. No good could come from this. He, immediately, wanted to take back everything that he had said, but it was too late. He was in too deep. Because of his stupidity, his inability to keep to the script, "the cousin story" had acquired a new chapter, more to remember in the telling of it. Why couldn't he learn not to embellish?

"How is Mara?" he threw out, hoping that Gwendolyn might share a few truths – to balance out the lies.

"She's pregnant," Gwendolyn announced, quite cheerfully.

"So…She told you?" Zack said, as if it had been a well-guarded secret between cousins. He couldn't allow Gwendolyn to think that he never talked to Mara.

"Yes," Gwendolyn said. "It would have been a little difficult to hide." She indicated with her hand how much Mara's baby already showed.

"And how did my uncle take the news?" Zack asked.

"He seemed very pleased, indeed," she answered. "Of course, it is his first grandson, and that could have something to do with his enthusiasm."

"And Phillipe? Did Mara say much about his reaction?" Zack asked.

Gwendolyn's face fell. Something Zack had said, obviously, didn't sit well. "Mara didn't tell you?" she asked.

"No, what?" Zack responded.

"Phillipe left her." Then, she punctuated the sentence with "Bastard!" Gwendolyn, evidently, enjoyed saying that word.

Zack said what felt like the most appropriate response, repeating "Bastard!"

"Yes. My feeling exactly," Gwendolyn responded, approvingly. "And with the Christmas holidays nearly here." Then, "Why didn't Mara tell you?" she asked.

Rats! She wasn't going to let this go. "Probably because she knew how I would feel about it. I never liked Phillipe," Zack added, having never met the man.

"Nor did I," Gwendolyn added, satisfied that she and Zack were on the same page about this. "Thank Goodness, her parents were willing to take her in."

Yikes! Had he heard her correctly? If Mara's parents had taken her in, then, she would no longer need the apartment in Paris! He would be out in the streets, if the lie were no longer needed. He really had to get in touch with Mara. Tonight would not be too soon.

"Did Mara give you her new cell phone number?" Zack asked. "I lost it." (In fact, he had.)

Gwendolyn opened her purse and took out her cell phone. She found Mara's number in her call history, and wrote down the number for Zack. In fact, Mara had changed her cell number. No wonder she never returned his calls. He made up another lie. "She said Phillipe had broken her phone, and that she had to get a replacement, but would change the number. Now, it makes sense why. She probably didn't want Phillipe to know it." Had Mara changed it, so that Zack would not have it? He entertained the possibility a moment. No. Mara would not do that to him.

Gwendolyn wrote and said, "Yes. That's probably it." As she handed Zack the scrap of paper, she said, "Please don't tell her that I told you about Phillipe."

"No problem," Zack said. "I'll call her parents' number first." He lied, again. He didn't have her parents' number. The lies were flying off his tongue so quickly that it was as if he were writing a novel. He loved the creativity, but hated the ruse. One day, he would have to explain to Gwendolyn.

Looking at her face in the candlelight, he hoped that their new friendship would last longer than the lies. She was a wonderful, caring woman. He hoped that, when her assignment was up in Paris, she would stay. Maybe by then, he could figure out a way to explain, why he had such a problem telling her the truth.

With the news about Mara out of the way, Gwendolyn moved on to talking about the other residents in the building. Zack was interested, but now, he was watching the time on his watch, and wondering where Mara might be. Was she in Paris? Verdun? Or had she taken the train back to Avignon, to be with Phillipe? It took a few minutes for him to focus on the story Gwendolyn was telling.

Camille and Marcel, she said, were in the French Resistance movement, when they were only children. They had been recruited to carry messages between the various groups of underground fighters, and did so by placing small pieces of paper between the layers of leather in the soles of their shoes. Camille had come up with the idea of tying messages on ribbons, hidden in the braids of her hair.

Once, they were captured together and held in a barn outside of Paris for two weeks. Marcel was convinced that they would be killed because the Germans had run low on food and no longer wanted to feed the seven children being held. Marcel had been chosen the leader of the small pack of seven souls. It was his ingenuity, which devised the escape route out of the barn through a small hole in the tile roof. He had helped each of the children climb the rope, which they had tied together from scraps found in the barn. He was only eleven, but the oldest, and he was strong enough to hoist up the last two children with his sheer will and determination.

They stayed on the icy roof, clinging to it for dear life, while snow fell on top of them, providing camouflage from the soldiers down below. Eventually, the soldiers on the ground fell soundly asleep. Then, the small troop of children stealthily slid down the rope on the backside of the barn, and disappeared into the woods.

When they returned to Paris, courtesy of a local farmer and his wagon, they scattered, all except Marcel and Camille. Orphaned, they had nowhere to go, and no one to care for them. Their decision to stay together was a matter of self-preservation. Marcel felt Camille would never survive winter on the streets of Paris without him. Camille, although younger and smaller, thoughts were the same. Marcel needed her.

Marcel told the story with great pride every year at Christmas time. They had escaped on Christmas day, thanks to the Germans enjoying more beer than their usual ration, and needing extra hours to sleep it off. Camille was only eight years old at the time, but Marcel said, the moment he saw her, he knew that they would be married one day. Camille said, proudly, that Marcel had saved her life that day, and again, many times later. She failed to tell how her efforts had saved him.

Yes. Zack could see it clearly. Gwendolyn was a hopeless romantic - the worst kind; the kind that a mere mortal man, such as himself, would never be able to satisfy. His best effort to romance a woman, so far, had been to order two dozen red roses for a high school classmate on Long Island, who didn't like roses, and tossed them in his face on Valentine's Day. His second best effort was to buy a diamond ring for a girl at university without knowing what her feelings were for him. He mistakenly approached her publicly, only to be told "No," in front of his fraternity brothers, who had been recruited to sing during his proposal.

Past humiliations were still painful memories. How could he possibly fall for a woman like Gwendolyn, who had spent her entire life imagining the moment that a man might propose? No. The pedestal was too tall to climb. He would have to settle for being her friend, and nothing more, and so, he redirected the conversation. "What about the postman?"

"I do not know much about him," Gwendolyn had to confess. "He is a very private person, and after Camille and Marcel, he is our oldest resident," she added, then, corrected herself, "No. That's not true. By age, it is Marcel, Camille, the professor, Mme. Durand, the postman..." A person's age seemed terribly important to Gwendolyn.

Zack returned to his own thoughts during her tedious recitation. Zack forgot Mara for the moment. He was less concerned about the ages of everyone in the building, than he was about roles in the mystery. "What about the guy in 202?"

"He is a bit of a mystery," Gwendolyn said, leaning in across the table. "I think he works for a foreign government."

"Really?" Zack asked, now, completely intrigued. "You know, Mara thought so, too," he added. "Have any idea – which one?" he asked.

"Not a clue," Gwendolyn answered. "I cannot even place his accent. It's eastern European maybe, maybe former Soviet Union. I don't know. He never speaks more than a word or two to anyone in the building." She qualified her statement, by saying – "The others tell me, he never visits at the mailbox, or when they pass in the hall."

Then, she pushed up a sleeve of her jacket, and said, "He has a tattoo on his arm, about here, but I cannot see what it is. I've glanced at it twice, when he lifts his arm to open his mailbox. Marcel said he saw it once, too. We think he was in the military, but whose – we cannot say."

"Interesting," Zack acknowledged, "very intriguing."

"Yes. Isn't it?" Gwendolyn answered. "Did you ever see his face?"

"No," he answered, looking again at his watch. The evening was fast approaching midnight. They had spent the entire evening together, and what had begun as strangers had ended as friends. He was satisfied that nothing terrible was happening in the building, at least, nothing as dire as he had expected. Whatever mysteries were there –

were benign, and not nearly as frightening as his imagination had led him to believe.

Gwendolyn's gossip had answered many of his questions, and he could go to bed, knowing the villagers in his building much better. Even the fellow that everyone else thought was a spy didn't seem so scary. Zack had known many men like this one, having run into them in bars in New York. They were young and old warriors, who having returned from war, never wanted to talk about it, again.

"What's the spy's name?" Zack asked, getting his wallet out to pay for dinner, and noticing that Gwendolyn was not.

"Dmitry," Gwendolyn responded.

Zack laughed. "Of course," he answered. "Dmitry." He could not overlook the fact that Gwendolyn knew Dmitry by his first name. "Does he have a last name?" he asked.

"The name on his mailbox is Smith," she answered.

"Of course, it is," Zack laughed. "Dmitry Smith. Certainly, sounds like a spy to me."

"I thought so, too," Gwendolyn said, quite seriously.

Hers was a perfect match for Zack's imagination.

Chapter 11

C hristmas Day arrived in Paris with a dusting of light snow, and so Zack took an afternoon walk through the Luxembourg Gardens to watch the children delight in the gift. Life inside the apartment building continued as it had, but with each passing day, Zack felt a bit more of a resident, and less of a temporary visitor. Gifts of food were passed from neighbor to neighbor, and expensive brands of wine and chocolates were included as part of the celebration of the season. Zack delved into his savings to make certain his gift baskets matched the quality of those he was receiving.

The professor asked him if he would consider staying longer, now that Mara was pregnant and living with her boyfriend. This was the first time that Montague had confessed that he knew about Mara's pregnancy. Zack asked him, "Did Gwendolyn tell you?"

"No, Mara," the professor said, casually, as if Zack should have known that.

"Mara?" Zack responded without tempering his surprise.

"Doesn't she talk to you?" Montague asked, filling their glasses for the third time, "...when she visits?"

Zack was caught completely off guard. Mara was making regular visits to the other residents in the building? Why hadn't she called? Knocked? Emailed? He had been expecting an eviction notice every day, since first learning of her pregnancy. Should he admit that he hadn't seen or talked to Mara in person, since she moved out? Should he pretend the wine was making him stupid, forgetful... (which it was)? Should he come out and tell the professor the truth about their charade?

After all, Mara had not been very forthcoming about much of anything, since her departure. Now, he was learning that she was coming back to Paris, to the apartment building, without contacting him. Was she intentionally avoiding him? Didn't she want the packages, which were accumulating in the corner behind the armoire? He had given her his word, to honor their agreement. Didn't she owe him at least a visit, now and then? It seemed important, to continue to be "the cousin," but when was the ruse over?

Montague was staring at Zack, waiting for his answer.

"Mara knows that I do not like Phillipe," Zack began slowly, "and so, it has been a problem for us to talk much about the baby, and the changes in her life." This, Zack decided, was the right approach with the professor, who made no secret of his dislike of Phillipe.

Montague went off on a tangent of his own, unwittingly revealing some of the secrets that Mara had shared with him about Phillipe. This was perfect, as it might give Zack more information about her, but the professor wanted to talk about Phillipe, not Mara. Phillipe, he revealed, had been something of playboy in the south of France, acquiring a reputation for living off rich widows and divorcées, but he had gotten into some trouble with the police there. Montague did not know the extent of it.

"Passing bad checks," he suggested. Phillipe, by his own admission, had disappeared from the Alpes-Maritimes for a while, before coming to Paris, "Mara told me." Mara found the gigolo at an underground club, trying to hit on older, wealthier women. Mara had watched from behind the bar. When Phillipe's efforts had gone unrewarded, "She dragged the bastard home," Montague said, practically, spitting the words out with all the ire of a jilted lover.

Zack still wondered about the extent of the professor's relationship with the young French woman. Montague had never indicated that they were anything more than friends. However, there was a strong attachment, which suggested he might be in love with her.

"Did he move in with her, or did he keep a place of his own here in Paris?" Zack asked, already knowing the answer. Mara had told him, Phillipe kept a place with other friends.

"He had friends, other than Mara, who put up with him, but mostly he lived off his parents in Avignon. Mara said they sent him money." Montague took a swig of wine, slurping it as if his tongue had become too big for his mouth. He wiped his drool on his sleeve. "I hated him," he said, now, too drunk to weigh his words before speaking. "He also took money from her," he declared, incensed.

Zack admired Montague for a moment, thinking that the old

professor was being chivalrous about Mara's naivety, until he added, "money that I had given her!" It seemed that he was angrier about losing the money, which he had given Mara, rather than about Mara losing her own money. Perhaps, Mara had given him a bogus excuse as to why she needed the loan. Perhaps, Montague had felt taken in by the beautiful young woman, who was forced to find money for her gigolo boyfriend. Montague was too angry and too drunk to continue his thought.

Zack was keenly aware that Gwendolyn could hear their every word, and that the volume of Montague's words rose with his alcohol intake. He wanted to stomp on the floor, twice, only to see if she would come running to save him from his drunken guest. Would she? Or was she sitting there on the sofa, giggling, listening. He would have to call her, ask her dinner, so that they could compare notes. Perhaps, Gwendolyn knew why Mara was avoiding him.

The professor staggered home to his apartment next door about two o'clock in the morning, banging into the frame of Zack's doorway on his way out, and crashing into his own doorway on the way in. Zack thought that an apology to their neighbors on this floor and down below might be expected the next day.

However, Gwendolyn, whom he met on her return home from work the next day, said nothing about the drinking binge, although, she did accept his dinner invitation without hesitation. Neither, Albert or Arness, nor Madame Christy said a word about the late night rituals at Zack's apartment, which had become common knowledge. Zack had run into the three of them at the mailboxes, chatting about the weather in France. Zack found that the villagers discussed the weather a great deal, when not discussing the future of agriculture in various places in France, places with names he had yet to learn.

Once, in an effort to make conversation, and to improve his French, he had asked where such and such a place was located. "Near Avignon," Berta Polywog said, before Ivan nudged her hard. She looked at him, thinking that she had mispronounced it, but he appeared to be silently scolding her. Ivan's eyes got big and round, and then, hers mirrored his. Zack could not help, but notice. They made a quick departure on the excuse that they were late for work, huddling together, whispering in Polish.

Zack could not understand married people, especially those who kept such close tabs on each other's behavior. It was only another reason, why no one would want to marry him. He was incapable of conforming to a wife's idea of proper behavior, and would only grow to resent her nudges. While this time, it had been Ivan nudging Berta, twice before it had been Berta nudging Ivan. Evidently, Zack decided, when Polish, French, and English failed them – nudging sufficed.

In the park on a cold, but sunny Sunday, he had asked them a simple question. "How much does it cost to mail a package in France?" Both of their faces had gone completely white upon hearing his question.

Finally, Ivan asked, "Why are you mailing a package?"

Zack noted that there was always a bit of a pause before Ivan or Berta answered his questions, mostly because they were translating between three languages; Polish to French to answer his very poorly pronounced French questions, if they understood him the first time. When, they did not understand, they might ask him to repeat himself in English, just to clarify. This had become a normal pattern of communication, but his package question was followed by an unusually long pause of at least ten Mississippi's. This was a record. Zack also noted that Ivan had asked, "Why are you mailing a package?" not "Where?"

"I have some books to mail to my father's aunt," he answered, innocently, in English. "She's in Aix-en-Provence for the winter."

"Books," Berta interrupted, nudging Ivan, and looking quite frightened. "Booooks."

"Yes," Zack continued, struggling to find the right words in French. Ivan and Berta spoke French, much better than English. "Livres pour la tante de mon père. Elle est à Aix-en-Provence. Elle est un professor..."

"Ah, livres," Berta repeated, relaxing almost immediately. "Il veut dire livres, pas d'..." (He did mean to say books, not...)

This time, Ivan nudged Berta hard to get her to stop talking. It was the first time that Zack had seen them share the wide-eyed stare. He blamed his French. He really did intend to take lessons in the spring, he, apologetically, told them.

"You should ask the postman," Ivan said. "...at the post office," was his second suggestion, before clarifying. "Monsieur Le Postman does not deliver packages," he finished, as if the subject should be dropped.

"I just thought...maybe you mailed things from your job..."

Ivan gave Zack a wide-eyed look, as if to say, "When is the crazy American going to quit talking about this?" Zack finally got the message that he needed to move on with their conversation, to take it in a different direction, but he could think of nothing.

They sat in silence on the bench for a few moments longer, before Ivan asked, "Do you receive packages?" Berta leaned forward so that she could see around Ivan, in anticipation of Zack's response. Both Ivan and Berta appeared to be holding their breaths.

Zack looked at both of their faces, before answering, hesitantly, "Yes."

Berta sat back against the back of the bench and stared straight ahead. Ivan looked down, and took her hand in his, before speaking. "And do you open them?" he asked, nervously, as if he were expecting a disappointing answer to a very simple question.

Zack looked at both of his new friends, and laughed, "Yes. Don't you open gifts from your parents?"

Ivan and Berta turned to look at each other's face, then, blew out the breaths that they had been holding in – as they said, practically, hysterical, "Gifts?! Oui. Oui," they said in unison, "Les cadeaux de la famille."

Zack sat back this time and stared straight ahead. He had no idea what had just happened. They seemed to be communicating, but this was such an odd and labored exchange. It appeared that the business of sending and receiving packages in France was a tough topic to discuss. He thought, perhaps, he should have chosen a simpler subject, than today's delivery of his parents' belated Christmas gifts.

Berta asked, this time, "What was in your package?"

Zack smiled, "Money," he said, then, added, "and socks."

Ivan asked, "Money?"

Berta nudged Ivan hard. "And socks!" she said, almost scolding him for his errant thought about money that belonged to the American.

Ivan accepted his wife's warning, withdrew his curiosity, and repeated her words, "And socks!" Berta appeared perfectly delighted with Zack's answer. "Money and socks," She said softly, and Ivan looked at her, relieved that the conversation had ended so well.

A moment later, Zack announced, "Tomorrow is my birthday." He said it in a way that seemed almost anti-climatic to his previous announcement.

"Joyeux anniversaire!" Ivan offered. Berta repeated, "Joyeux anniversaire!"

At last, here was something, which they could discuss, openly, and without fear of hidden meanings. They liked Zack, despite his feeble attempts to speak to them in French, and their embarrassment to speak to him in English. However, neither Ivan nor Berta could be certain just how much Mara had been willing to tell her cousin about them... or the others in the building.

Had she explained to her cousin about the packages?

Chapter 12

T here was an odd coming and going from the apartment
building on Mondays, something more the usual start to the
workweek. Today, Zack had noticed the unusual activity of his
neighbors, right after the trash truck banged its way down
their street, and directly into his bed - or at least, it had sounded that
way. The disturbing sound of glass breaking and metal scraping was
exceptionally loud, and reminded him that he had slept with the
windows cracked open for fresh air. The slender opening had been just
wide enough to break the sound barrier, allowing the rumble of trash
trucks, and the sudden screech of their brakes, to reverberate off the
cobblestones down below.

Zack leapt from bed to close the windows only to catch an
unexpected glimpse of six of his neighbors, departing the building in
rapid succession. Gwendolyn was followed by Monsieur Le Postman,
who was followed by Ivan, Berta, and then, Arness and Albert. Oddly,
the six of them gathered in front of Mme. Christy's flower shop to stare
into the window, appearing fascinated by the flower arrangements that
they saw there.

Zack had seen some remarkable designs in the window of
Madeleine's flower shop, but he could not imagine what had caught the
eye of all six of his neighbors at once. Then, again, he rarely, ever, got
up this early. He stared a bit longer, convinced that Mme. Christy's
shop was not open yet for the day. He searched for the clock by his
bed, stumbling over his own feet in the process. It was 6:29 a.m.

By the time that he moved back to the window, the group had
disappeared. He thought that they had moved on, that is - until he
caught a glimpse of a hand in the flower shop window. It was removing
an arrangement! It appeared that Mme. Christy was already at work, as
her display window was being emptied at an amazing rate. One after
another, the beautiful bouquets disappeared, leaving the display case

completely empty. 6:30 a.m. and her day already underway.

He was about to return to bed with hopes of catching two more hours of sleep, when to his surprise the front door of the flower shop opened, and out poured all six of his neighbors, each carrying a large bouquet of flowers! Their collective image created a parade of flower arrangements, tall enough to hide their faces in the virtual garden, now moving down the street. Zack strained to see them as they separated at the corner, four turning one direction, and two in the other.

Zack fell back into bed, but his imagination would not allow him to sleep. What was it – a funeral? A wedding? Did they all routinely take flowers to their jobs on Mondays? Perhaps, because he was never up this early, he had missed this weekly ritual. Was today a French holiday; one, which he had missed reading about in his guidebooks, or failed to notice on his calendar? He pulled a guidebook to Paris out from under the nightstand and began flipping through the pages. Was there a chapter, which might enlighten him? Nothing grabbed his attention, and he was growing sleepier by the minute.

The book slipped out of his hand and hit the floor, momentarily, awakening him. Zack rolled over and blinked at the morning light coming in through the windows. It was getting light earlier and earlier each day. Was there a day set aside to celebrate winter? Officially, spring was still too far away. Everyone had grown tired of the past month of grey skies and bitterly cold wind. Only two days earlier, a welcome break had come with its blue skies, white puffy clouds, and the calm, which Mme. Durand declared, signaled spring would arrive early. However, Mme. Durand had said nothing about going out and buying flowers to celebrate.

He would ask someone, later... Zack closed his eyes and fell back to sleep with thoughts of dropping by Mme. Christy's for some fresh flowers for his apartment. Flowers would be nice... Flowers would smell nice... Madeleine smelled nice. Seeing Madeleine, again, would be...nice.

In his dreams, he watched the parade of flowers moving through the streets of Paris.

wendolyn had cancelled his latest dinner invitation, but at least, she had given him a believable excuse. "A broken tooth," she said. She would be at the dentist after work, and probably for at least two hours. She had been good enough to call him at lunchtime, telling him that he should make other plans. They could get together the next night, or the next, he suggested. His dance card was open, he had said, then, they both laughed. She had sounded as disappointed about cancelling their date, as he did, and this made him happy.

In the early part of the afternoon, he went out in search of something, which he could microwave for dinner, and to buy a cheap bottle of wine for Montague, whom he expected would come by later. Montague did not need a serviette under his door to know that he was welcome at Zack's door late at night, and this had made the old man very happy.

Zack noted that Montague did not care what he drank, as long as he did not have to pay for it. Zack did not mind the expense, as he had grown fond of the professor, and had learned a great deal from him, not the least of which was easy ways to improve his French. The professor, who had developed a method of remembering difficult words and phrases, shared it with the young American.

Zack talked of copyrighting the process, writing a book together, and recording a DVD. Montague found Zack's enthusiasm, refreshing. Zack had offered to be the professor's guinea pig and his ghostwriter, although, Montague would have to do the translations. For several nights in a row, they had talked of not much else.

Upon his return to the apartment, Zack found a note on his door. At first, he was hopeful that it was Gwendolyn, saying that her plans had changed, and that their dinner date was still on. Perhaps, the dentist had already fixed her tooth! But, opening the folded note, he immediately recognized that the handwriting was not Gwendolyn's. Instead, it was Mara's! It read:

Must see you A.S.A.P.
Meet me at Épicerie.

There was no date, no time, and no way of knowing how long ago Mara had left it, or if she would still be at the grocery store, if he went there. It was typical. Mara was such a foolish girl. He had been away for nearly two hours. Would Mara wait around the épicerie that long?

Zack hurried to put his boxed dinner away in the small refrigerator. There was not enough room, so he moved the carton of cream, which Mara had left for him months earlier, and which he had never bothered to throw it out. Now, checking the expiration date on the carton, he was about to become as foolish as Mara.

As he opened the small carton to pour its contents down the kitchen sink drain, the smell of rotten dairy permeated the room, causing him to gag. Yellowish-green lumps fell from the carton and covered the small drain, lying there, refusing to move. Zack held his nose with one hand and turned on the hot water with the other; hoping what looked like a life form from outer space would flow down the drain. Still, it refused, and so, he began pushing it in that direction with a spoon, and then, a knife, and then, Chinese chopsticks.

No amount of pushing, prodding, or poking would move the monster from the sink. It had become some sort of permanent glue, holding tight to the surface, and covering the drain opening. The sink began filling up with water. No. If his mistake was to go anywhere, it would have to be down the toilet bowl, but that would require disengaging the mass from the sink, first.

As Zack dug and scraped, the creature fought, sucking and hissing each time an air pocket was made, closing up immediately afterwards, holding on more tightly than ever. Zack cursed himself. It had been a stupid idea. Flushing it would have been a better plan to start, but even that was becoming impossible. He had managed to move the gunk to below the rim of the drain, and then it was too far down to retrieve a spoon, more cursing, and no amount of hot water seemed capable of dispensing it into the sewers of Paris.

In fact, in the end, he had to use a pan to bail and carry the water into the bathroom for disposal. "Rats!" Zack said, loudly. Gasping for fresh air, he went to the windows, and opened them as wide as he could, hoping that the odor would find its way out into the streets, before he got home. He looked up. No. No sign of rain clouds. He would just have to leave the windows open, while he went in search of Mara. He had wasted enough time. When he came back, he would call a plumber, maybe, Tito – if he could find him.

The épicerie was open and three or four people were inside shopping, when Zack arrived. Mara was nowhere to be seen. The man, whom he had learned from Gwendolyn, was Monsieur Épicier, was behind the counter. He owned the vacant apartment next to Mara's, she had explained, as well as most of the apartments in the building. He had acquired them, one by one over about twenty years. In addition, he owned several other Épiceries.

Zack had never spoken more than two words man-to-man, afraid that somehow he would still be mad at him for not signing Claudine's lease. He felt certain that Claudine had told Monsieur Épicier about the stupid American, who could not make a decision, even though his was one of the best apartments in all of Paris. Surely, if Monsieur Épicier knew that Zack was the stupid American, his money would be rejected, forcing him to walk much further to shop for groceries. Surely...

Zack was unable to finish his thought as Claudine walked in, and he was forced to dive behind a display case. He moved as she moved, mirroring her movements, and managing to remain hidden behind stacks of produce. From his advantage point, he could peek through holes in the melon display to watch and listen to Claudine's conversation without revealing himself to her.

She was as lovely as he remembered her to be, and it was the first time that Zack had seen Monsieur Épicier smile. The burly man came out from behind the counter and planted three big, wet kisses on Claudine's cheeks. She kissed him back, as if they were old friends. They spoke rapidly, too fast for Zack to catch all of their words. He heard something about money, and definitely, several times, the word "bail," which he had learned from Mara meant lease. Perhaps, there were other properties, which Claudine was managing for the man.

At one point, the man moved around the counter to retrieve a cigar box. From inside it, he retrieved a large old key, not unlike the one that Mara had given Zack. He handed it to Claudine, and Claudine handed over a large manila envelope. Probably, a signed lease, Zack decided. With their business concluded, Zack expected Claudine to leave, but instead, she stayed and chatted away, in a way so friendly, she seemed approachable. But, Zack knew better. Her warmth would not extend to him, should he make his presence known.

As he continued to watch, other shoppers maneuvered around him, looking at him suspiciously. He pretended to be examining the melons, picking one up to sniff it, and then, another and another. As this was how he shopped, by his nose, his behavior seemed quite normal to him. To the others, he looked like a bloodhound engaged in a search for a body.

Then, he saw Monsieur Épicier hand Claudine a white envelope so thick that it had been bound with a large red rubber band. It contained money, although, Zack could not see its contents clearly enough to answer "how much?" Thousands, he imagined, remembering the terms of the lease, which Claudine had presented to him. Claudine thanked the man, kissed him once on the cheek, and walked out of the shop. The man's face returned to its normal sour expression, the smile disappearing as if it had never been there.

Zack walked around the display and picked up a bottle of water. He was paying for it, when Mara walked in, and looked surprised to see him. She signaled for him to come outside.

"I've been here three times, looking for you!" she said, admonishing him for not being able to read her mind on when to be there. With that, she stepped outside.

He paid and stepped out, only to find her a half-block away, resting against the wall of a building, and smoking. Her pregnancy was in full-bloom, yet, she seemed unaware that her smoking might have any effect on her unborn child. In fact, she seemed unaware of her pregnancy, as she was dressed in the same black tights, boots, and short skirt that Zack had seen her wear months earlier. The only thing different was the extent to which her sweater was being stretched by larger breasts and an eight month fetus. The other change – she looked worried, very worried.

"Would you like to sit down?" Zack asked. "The apartment?" he asked, "or a café?"

"Not the apartment. Follow me," she said. "I know a place where we can talk."

Mara took Zack to a small café a fifteen-minute walk away from the neighborhood. It was a place in the basement of a building, where only the locals gathered. There was no sign on the door, no neon light, but rather, a small postcard-size note in one window, the only indication that it was any sort of business at all. The card said in hand-scrawled letters O.K.

Zack held open the door for Mara, who turned sideways to enter the dark entrance to the O.K. nightclub, which served only drinks, day or night. To her immediate right was a set of steep stairs, leading down into an even darker space. After his eyes had adjusted to the dark, Zack could see that there were six small tables, around an empty dance floor, and one large waiter. Other than that, there was no indication that this was a licensed establishment. The large stones in the wall seemed to say that this place, at some point in history, had been something more ominous in its original function. Prison, or worse, came to mind.

The air stunk of cigarette smoke, and Zack thought Mara could not have chosen a worse place for herself or her baby. It came as a surprise, that he was feeling protective of a person, who had yet to be born. It was a new and strange feeling. To his horror, Mara lit up another cigarette. He wanted to knock it out of her hands, but he didn't. It was her life to screw up. Still, he felt the baby needed someone to champion it. "Still smoking, I see," he said.

Mara ordered lemonade, saying that she had given up alcohol, during her pregnancy, and that had been difficult enough. This was little comfort, but it did relieve Zack of further worry about the effects of alcohol on an unborn child. At least, Mara was remotely aware of some health risks. He couldn't imagine that her mother hadn't already warned her about some of this. Why was he experiencing the need to parent Mara?

Then, Mara told him that she was no longer living with her parents, nor was she living with Phillipe. "I need my apartment back," she said.

"Ah," he said. "I see." (And there it was.) It was the worst news that he could hear, and yet, it was exactly, what he anticipated from the day, he moved in. Yes. He should have trusted his gut. He should have signed Claudine's lease. (He knew it. He knew it. He knew it.) Rats!

But, look at her. Eight months pregnant. It was obvious that she needed the apartment, more than he did. She needed her own space, a space she would soon be sharing with an infant. Yes. He knew that he would surrender to her request – without a fight. It was inevitable, and it was the noble thing to do, the only decent thing to do. He, also, didn't have a legal right to do anything, but surrender, and so, he said, "How soon?"

"Today," Mara said, looking up at him with large eyes and raised eyebrows, expecting resistance. "I have no place else to go," she threw in, after a long pause.

"Of course," Zack said, feeling that she needed reassurance, more than he needed a roof over his head. She had given him several months in the place of his dreams, at a price that had been more than fair. She had thrown in one free month, and although, he had spent most of that first month in bed – sick – it had cost him nothing. Well, almost nothing.

The money that he would have spent on rent for the first month, actually, went into the bank account of a local doctor and pharmacist. He told her the story of his bout with the flu. But, that too was ok. No. Mara did not have to worry. He would find another place, a hotel – if necessary. She could have her place back, today. Then, he asked, "Do you mind if I stay tonight? I can pack and be out in the morning."

Mara's face revealed her relief. "Of course, you can stay the night!" She was thrilled, not to have to battle for the place. "Stay two or three. Whatever you need until you find someplace else."

"Really?" Zack said, both surprised and relieved to hear that he was not being thrown out into the streets. He had already witnessed Mara's warrior skills once. That was enough. Should he push for more? After all, until the baby arrived and things got really chaotic, it might not be so bad having a roommate. He could sleep on the sofa. She could have her bed back. They both enjoyed staying up late, and sleeping in. It might work...for a while.

Montague would certainly be happy to have Mara next door. The lonely old professor would be thrilled to know that Phillipe was gone forever. Mara had launched into the story of how Phillipe had moved back to the south of France in pursuit of his former career. Zack knew that meant gigolo'ing, if that was a real word, or profession. The last thing, Mara heard about Phillipe was from one of his friends, who reported Phillipe was living with the widow of a wealthy landowner somewhere in the Gard region of France.

"I'm so sorry," Zack said, realizing that the pregnant pause in her story indicated an appropriate expression of pity was expected.

Mara seemed pleased that Zack was being so kind and sympathetic. He had learned a lot in her absence, for one, he was now able to embrace the rhythm of Parisian life, the ying-and-yang of complaining and listening, which that was so much a part of the French culture. Tell me how bad your life is going, and I will listen without offering help. Then, complain when you do not get enough offers of help, and I will listen. Then, I will offer my help, and you can complain about how inadequate it is, and how it came to you – too late. Ah. Yes. More wine?

Mara and Zack found their way back to the apartment building three hours later. A new agreement had been reached, and this one, unlike their earlier one, was forged with both of them stone sober. Zack could stay one more month for free, or until the baby arrived, whichever came first. Because he had told her the story of his first month in bed, coughing and walking through the maze of medical treatment in Paris, she had felt sorry for him. Zack had money, just no place to live. She had a place to live, and very little money. It seemed a perfect fix, at least, for the short term.

From Mara, Zack had learned that her parents were very disappointed in her lack of ambitions. They had expected Phillipe to marry her, and that she would be married, before the baby arrived. They were practicing Catholics, a minority in France, despite what other people claimed. None of this cafeteria-style Catholicism for them. They would not pick and choose their beliefs from their pew on Sundays, like many of the younger generation did.

There were enough bastards being born in France already. Their grandson would not become one of them. However, Phillipe had taken off, and Mara had not clung to him, convincing him to stay. Somehow, this all reflected badly on Mara's womanhood. Having a bastard grandson was Mara's fault in the eyes of her parents. They hadn't approved of Phillipe, but at least, he was a potential son-in-law. Who would take his place and raise this child now?

Mara was convinced that she needed no man to raise her son. In Paris, people understood such things. She would make it in the world on her own. As soon as the baby was out of her and in a day nursery, she would find work. Her old boss had already offered her a job, and at least, she didn't have the worry of paying for medical bills. The government of France would see to it that she and her child received health care.

Zack reassured Mara that during the next four weeks, he would make himself scarce. With the spring-like weather, he could work in the parks on good days, and on bad days, there were cafés. He did not need to be in the apartment except at night to sleep, if that was ok with her, and - of course, he would need to shower, occasionally. Mara said, sweetly, that he could come and go as much as he pleased.

In an especially emotional moment, she told him, he was one of the nicest people, whom she had ever met, then, without warning, began crying. She apologized for the tears, saying that it was the hormones talking. Zack put his arm around her shoulders as they walked slowly back to the apartment. Was this what the father of every pregnant daughter felt? He wanted to yell at her for being stupid enough to sleep with Phillipe, and yet, to protect and defend her in the same breath. The confusion made his head hurt.

As they came up the stairs, slowly (as Mara was not nearly as nimble as before), Gwendolyn opened her apartment door. She was caught off guard by the appearance of Mara and Zack together, but she recovered, quickly. "Mara!" Gwendolyn said with a forced smile on her face.

Mara stopped on the top stair, so that the two women could exchange kisses on the cheek. Gwendolyn looked over the shoulder of Mara and into the face of Zack. Zack shrugged, but did not say anything. Gwendolyn mouthed the words, "Call me later." Zack nodded, as Gwendolyn told Mara how happy she was that Mara was back. "We will have to have lunch – soon," she added, before letting go of her friend.

Mara and Zack stopped in front of their apartment door, as he searched for the large key, attached to a chain, hooked to the belt loop of his jeans.

Mara laughed, saying, "See – I knew you would have to get one," referring to the latchkey chain.

As Zack unlocked the door, Mara looked towards the professor's door. Zack noticed the question in her eyes, and reassured her. "He misses you, too," he said. "Talks about you all the time."

"Really?" Mara said, seeming surprised.

"Really," Zack confirmed. "He'll be coming over later. Then, you'll see for yourself."

Mara smiled. Inside the apartment, she was pleased to see that very little had changed, other than the color of the throw pillows. She waddled over to the sofa, and fell back against the cushions. She reclined as far back as her big belly would allow, before sliding into a horizontal position on her side. She closed her eyes as Zack searched in the kitchen for something to serve her.

He returned with a glass of orange juice and a glass of water, unable to decide which to offer Mara, but Mara had fallen asleep. Zack thought that she was beautiful with her rosy cheeks and fuller face. He also thought that the stress of the day, of meeting him, of finally finding herself back here, where even he could see that she belonged - exhausting. He covered her with the quilt, which she had left behind, and which he had rarely used because it was "too girlish." Then, he turned off the lamp, and sat down quietly in a chair across the room to watch her.

Nothing would be the same from this point on. Mara would be living here. Eventually, he would have to leave and live...where? The process of finding another apartment in Paris would begin, again. It might take a month, or more. It had taken more than six weeks to find this place. Could he find the courage to contact Claudine, again? Would she take his request seriously? Probably not. There were too many months left on his assignment in Paris to make renting a hotel room feasible. No. He would have to find another place to live. He got up, quietly, and wrote a note to Mara:

> Going out for dinner
> Be back late
> Help yourself
> to anything you find in the refrigerator.
> Zack

A moment later, Zack was standing at Gwendolyn's door, knocking softly. She was surprised to see him so soon, but pleased. "Dinner?" Zack asked.

"Good idea," was her response. "I'm positively starved."

Zack liked a woman, who wasn't afraid to admit when she was hungry. Gwendolyn, for all her poise and proper etiquette, could eat like a man. None of this bird food dieting for her, she had told Zack. The body needed to be fed and exercised just like that of any other species. Zack liked that about her too. She possessed a lot of commonsense, and what he needed more than anything else at the moment, was food and commonsense.

Over dinner, Zack explained what had happened, and that Mara was moving back in, and eventually, how he would be moving out. He was not bitter about the change, only concerned that everything was happening so quickly, he felt a little out of control.

"Control is an illusion," Gwendolyn said, succinctly. "Is there anything that I can do?"

Zack was surprised by her willingness to help. "No. Not really...not unless you know of a vacant apartment in the neighborhood with an incredibly reasonable rent. I can't afford much on my salary. Mara...I mean, my cousin, was very generous to let me stay in her apartment as long as she did. I knew it was temporary, just not – this temporary. You wouldn't happen to need a cousin," he teased, "would you?" Without waiting for her answer, he continued, "Unless, I find another long lost cousin in the next four weeks, I could be homeless."

"Be my cousin," Gwendolyn said, spontaneously.

The speed of her answer caught Zack by surprise, and he was not certain that he had heard her correctly. "Did I understand you, correctly?" he asked, looking deeply into her cool grey eyes.

"Move in with me. Be my cousin." This time, there was no hesitation in her voice, no room for misinterpretation.

"But, you hardly know me," Zack began.

"I know everything that I need to know," Gwendolyn replied with the confidence that Zack had already witnessed on evenings, when co-habitation was not the topic of their discussions.

Gwendolyn could see his trepidation, and felt the need for further explanation. "My work contract is expiring next month. The Paris division is not offering me another three years here in Paris. If I want to stay, I will have to tell London, officially, that I am quitting. You, moving in with me, would solve the most obvious problem."

Zack continued staring, speechless, so Gwendolyn continued. "Money for the rent," she said as if no explanation should have been necessary. "What did you think I meant?"

Zack was embarrassed to say what he was thinking - that a woman had just asked him to move in with her. He thought she wanted to take their friendship to a different level. Perhaps, he was hoping. "Nothing," he responded to her question. "I was just wondering how that might work," he hedged, "money-wise for both of us."

"Brilliantly," she said, "if you're asking me. I have some savings. You have monthly income. By you moving in, I will have time to look for a decent job, instead of grabbing at the first thing that comes along, in order to make my rent." She leaned in across the table to ask, "So...what do you say? Cousins?" Expecting him to agree, she held out her hand for him to shake.

Zack slowly took her hand, then, asked, "Do you want to tell my other cousin? Or should I?"

They walked back to the apartment, laughing all of the way, and remarkably, relaxed. Gwendolyn was relieved that her job at the pharmaceutical company was ending. It had been boring, she said, and she was more than ready for a change. There was nothing left for her, professionally, in London. She was eager to try something different, something totally unrelated to corporate life. Zack asked her what that might be, and she had no answer, except to say that when she found it – she would know it. Her eyes sparkled with the possibilities.

Zack did not go home to his apartment above Gwendolyn's that night; the apartment, which now held Mara and Mara's soon-to-be-born roommate. Instead, Gwendolyn fixed Zack a bed on her sofa. For a while, they were together, content to rest in each other's arms. But, about midnight, a sound familiar to Gwendolyn woke them.

Gwendolyn heard it first, and nudged Zack with a whispered, "Listen." It was the sound of an apartment door opening, followed by a surprised Montague, discovering that Mara had returned. Mara had let in the professor for a nightcap. As Zack and Gwendolyn lay there, listening to the professor and Mara's reunion, every word of it crisp and clear, Zack realized for the first time – just how much Gwendolyn already knew about him.

He turned on his side to look at her face. With the only light coming from the street lamp outside, her face looked pale blue, devoid of blood, a shade or two lighter than her eyes – which she slowly closed. Her brunette strands sparkled in the light, shiny, and soft to his touch as he ran his fingers gently through her hair. Gwendolyn murmured something, but he could not make out the words. He fell asleep, listening to Mara telling Montague her tale of woe, and Montague telling Mara that she had done the right thing by coming home.

Whether the professor spent the night with Mara, Zack could not say. When he returned to Mara's apartment in the morning, there were no clues as to what might have happened there during his absence. Everything was exactly as he had left it. Mara had already been out to buy croissants, and she had coffee ready and waiting for him in the kitchen. He wondered if she had heard him and Gwendolyn below with the same clarity, with which he had heard her and the professor. If she did, she did not mention it.

She did ask, however, "Why didn't you come home last night?"

"I thought you might need your privacy...your first night back in Paris, and all," he said.

It was a feeble excuse. Mara saw straight through it. "Girlfriend?" she asked, coyly. Zack's neck turned bright red, and then, his face, giving the truth away. Mara smiled. "I thought so."

There was no reason to postpone the inevitable. Zack explained, over croissants and coffee, he had worked out a different living arrangement, one, which would leave Mara free to enjoy her apartment alone for the month leading up to the arrival of her baby. He suggested that there would be many things for Mara to do, like finding a crib, stocking up baby supplies, etc. He reassured her, he would be happy to help her carry and assemble whatever it was that she might need.

Mara's eyes lit up with the prospect of creating a nursery within her apartment. She, genuinely, was touched by Zack's kind offer. She was also delighted that Zack had found a girlfriend, although, disappointed to learn that it was "the Brit" downstairs, as Mara called her. She thought Gwendolyn had always looked down upon her. Now that she was pregnant, Mara couldn't imagine that it improved Gwendolyn's opinion of her.

She blamed Gwendolyn's puritanical attitude on something, which she couldn't help because of her culture. The British held a different view on morality, marriage, children born out of wedlock. It wasn't Gwendolyn's fault that she hadn't received an enlightened education about these things. Mara sounded downright "snooty" describing

Gwendolyn, and it bothered Zack. His opinion was that Gwendolyn was anything, but puritanical. After all, she had asked him to move in, without benefit of marriage. Wasn't that enlightened?

Zack insisted that Mara was being too hard on Gwendolyn. Gwendolyn had always admired Mara's free spirit. In fact, he told Mara, Gwendolyn had said nothing but nice things about her. Mara looked at Zack, hard, really questioning his honesty.

He could tell she did not believe him, so he continued, sacrificing Gwendolyn's secret in the process. He said, "Gwendolyn wouldn't want me to tell anyone..." He had Mara's undivided attention, as he proceeded to tell Mara the secret. Gwendolyn would soon be out of work, and it would be she, who would need Mara's help. "Perhaps," he suggested, "you could help her find a job." He threw in for effect, "I would hate for her to get in trouble, you know, deported or something worse."

Mara liked the idea that for once, she was in a position of power, able to give advice to the Brit, rather than take it, as had always been the case before. Unemployment had a way of leveling the playing field, and lowering the noses of the players. His words had changed Mara's feelings about Gwendolyn, and this was Zack's whole purpose in revealing the change in Gwendolyn's circumstances.

He added that he would be paying half of Gwendolyn's rent, to help her out until she could secure a proper job and a decent salary. He could read the concern in Mara's eyes, and offered to pay half of Mara's rent, if that would help her with expenses for the baby. Mara was humbled by Zack's compassion and generosity. She really had not expected him to continue paying anything, as she had – in a sense – evicted him months ahead of their agreed upon schedule. No man, with the exception of the professor, had been so kind or so understanding. She said if he were willing to pay half, her parents would pay the rest, at least, until she was able to work, again.

Zack said that he was completely ok with the arrangement, and this time, they kissed cheeks to seal the deal. Mara was in tears, but then, everything these days made her cry. Her hormones were off the chart, causing her to dance one moment, and collapse in exhaustion the next. The doctor had said the baby was still four weeks away from making his entrance, but she felt like he could arrive any moment.

Zack asked where the birth was to take place, and Mara indicated a hospital not far away. Zack made Mara promise that she would call him the minute that she felt herself going into labor, so that he could call a taxi, and get her there in a timely fashion. He laughed, explaining that he had no experience with delivering babies, and didn't want to learn. Mara told him that the professor had made a similar offer, and that he shouldn't worry. Everything would go as planned. He wanted to believe her, but nothing in her life had gone as planned, so why should this chapter end any differently?

It was important that Mara and Gwendolyn did not exhibit any animosity towards each other. He cared about them both. As he spent the morning packing up his few belongings at Mara's place, in order to move to Gwendolyn's place, he revealed more than he should have. He revealed some of the things, which he had observed in her absence. Then, he talked about his suspicions, that something strange was going on in the building, but he hadn't discovered what it was – yet.

He told her about the succession of strangers, who had knocked on the apartment next door. He, also, described his evening alone with Mme. Christy. Mara became unusually quiet during his confessions, and when long silences followed his stories, it made him feel uncomfortable. His nature had always been to fill empty space by talking too much, telling more than was necessary. This time was no different.

When he had finished packing, and purging his idle thoughts, Mara said she was tired and sat down on the sofa, but it was so that she could think, rather than to rest. Zack was exactly what the others had suspected, a fouineur (a snoop). She had told the others that they were wrong about him. He was just an American writer. All writers were like him, observers. It didn't mean that he was dangerous. But, now, she wondered if they had been right about Zack, and she had been wrong.

Should she tell him everything, now? Would it make a difference? Would his generous offer, to pay half her rent, be withdrawn? Would he disappear as all the other men in her life had done at the first sign of trouble? Then, she remembered his email message about the packages. "Where are my packages?" she asked, then, quickly, corrected her words, "I mean my books."

Zack pointed to the armoire. "Behind there," he said, moving across the room to pull the armoire away from the wall, so that he could retrieve them for her. There had been eight at last count. The movement of the armoire caused the sound of a rip in the wood floors, and thought of the damage brought Zack to an abrupt stop. He looked down and felt sick. "I'm sooooo sorry," he apologized profusely. "I'll pay for that. You call someone to repair it, and I'll pay for every dime... I mean, Euro of it." He could only imagine, after what Claudine had told him about such things, that Mara might be furious with him.

Mara stood up to examine the scratch, waddled over, and then, shrugged, before moving to look behind the armoire. "Where are they?" she asked.

"Right there," Zack pointed, but then, looking at Mara's face, he realized that something was terribly wrong.

"Where?" Mara asked, again.

"There," Zack said, stepping around her to look for himself, and then, seeing nothing. There were no packages, not even one! He was overcome with confusion and fear. Someone had stolen them! How could they disappear like that? Who would have taken them? When? The questions were coming too fast and too furious for his head. He moved over to the sofa and slumped down on it, before lowering his face into his hands. "I had them," he said, looking up at Mara and hoping that she would believe him. "I did. I had them, right there," he said, pointing again to behind the armoire, "eight of them."

Mara joined him on the sofa, her face, turned suddenly pale. She breathed out slowly, before falling against him, to put her hand on his knee. Softly, but commandingly, she said in her near-warrior voice, "We have to find them. You have no idea how important they are."

By looking at her face, Zack had a pretty good idea. Then, it was his face, that went pale as he remembered, opening the windows to air out the apartment, after foolishly pouring the carton of cream down the drain. "Rats!" he said aloud. "I know how and I know when." Embarrassed, he explained about the cream, about the drain, about the windows, and then, asked what seemed like an odd question for the situation. "Do you have Tito's phone number?"

"Tito?" Mara said, surprised, and alarmed by Zack mentioning the man's name at a time like this. "What does he have to do with this?"

Zack said, "I think cleaning the drain will require the assistance of a plumber."

"Plumber?" Mara said, looking totally confused.

"Yes. You know..." He struggled to remember the French words, which Mara had used. "Entrepreneur de pompes funèbres?"

Mara thought Zack was so far off track as to be funny, and so, she began laughing, almost uncontrollably, her emotions fueled by her raging hormones. "You mean plombier, not undertaker," she clarified, then, burst into another round of laughter. "Tito was an undertaker, you know – the man, who prepares the body for burial? Not a plumber."

Zack stood up, suddenly, and asked again, "Not a plumber?"

"No, not a plumber," Mara confirmed.

"I really should sign up for French lessons," he murmured.

"A little late," Mara answered. "But, yes, you should."

"Then, who were all those people who came to his door, after he moved out?" Zack asked.

"Tito didn't move out," Mara answered. "I told you. He died."

"Died?!" Zack asked, excitedly. "You didn't say that he died. You said he was gone."

"Same thing," Mara said.

"No. Not the same thing," Zack insisted. "Did he die in the apartment?"

"Yes," Mara said, sadly remembering. "Montague found him in the closet. He had been dead three days, before the... you know. Before the smell..." She tried to stand. It took a moment to gain her balance. "Remember?" She asked, "I asked you, if Tito's work bothered you. I thought if you didn't mind living, where an undertaker had lived, you wouldn't mind living, where an undertaker had died. You said it did not bother you." She said defensively.

Zack stood up and began pacing. He was bothered by the idea that Tito had died, right next door. What did it mean? Why did the strangers keep coming to the apartment, if Tito was dead? Didn't they know? Didn't they read the papers? Claudine had not mentioned anything about a death in the apartment, and she had been meticulous about every detail. Nail holes in the walls, scratches in the floor, had each been so important to her. She failed to mention the body in the closet. How close had he come to finding it, instead of Montague? Why hadn't she mentioned the murder? Seems like a large detail to miss.

"Was it a... natural death?" he finally managed to get out.

"No," Mara said, quietly, "Murder." She watched Zack's eyes grew larger and rounder. "Necktie," she, crudely, mimicked a hanging.

The hole, the size of a man's fist in the back of the closet, now made sense. Tito had fought his attacker, fought death. Zack bit his lip, wondering what he was to do with this new information. Had one of the men, whom he had seen through the keyhole, been Tito's murderer? Were they coming back to find something they left behind? Perhaps, the murder weapon? Or a witness? Was that why Mara had been in such a hurry to leave? Had she seen something that she shouldn't have?

Should he reconsider his decision to move in with Gwendolyn, and just get the heck of Paris, before he joined Tito on the other side? Then, an even more fearful thought crossed his mind. Was Tito's murderer one of the other residents? Did one of them have a grudge to settle with the undertaker? What were all these packages about? Drugs? Counterfeit Euros? Jewels? Was Tito the ringleader of some sort of gang? Wouldn't that make Zack an accessory to their crimes? After all, he had willingly moved in, right next door to the murder scene. What jury would believe that he didn't know what was going on?

However, the truth was the truth. He didn't know what was going on. He didn't have a clue, but Mara did. "You need to tell me everything," he said, reaching out, and putting a tight hold on Mara's tiny arm. She started to pull away from his grip, as she had once too often been on the receiving end of a man's anger. Zack realized that his grip was too strong, and that he had caused Mara's unnecessary anxiety. "Sorry," he said, apologetically. "Really, Mara, this is serious business. You must tell me what's going on. I've been more than fair with you."

Fair, Mara understood. Zack was right. To secure and continue his goodwill, she would have to level with him. And so...her story began to unfold.

Zack listened closely, not wanting to miss any word, as his mistake, thinking Tito was a plumber had been huge, especially, now that he was in need of a real plumber.

The theft of her packages had changed everything, and Mara knew that the terms of their agreement no longer mattered. She explained to Zack, she would have to tell the others that he was not her cousin, but worse than that, she would have to admit she had lied to each of them.

It would be unforgiveable. Hers had been a selfish act, one that would have dire consequences, arrest, prison, or maybe even worse...eviction! As Mara confessed her sins to him, Zack listened carefully to every word, but none more so than her final condemnation, which chilled him to his marrow.

"You are now one of us."

⤳⳪ⳉ⳪⤳
Chapter 14
⤳⳪ⳉ⳪⤳

ara and Zack stood before Monsieur Le Postman's door, as Mara knocked lightly. From behind the door, a deep baritone voice yelled out, "Que voulez-vous?"

Mara leaned closer to the door, and said in a near whisper, "Napoléon est à Paris."

Immediately, the door was unlocked, but opened only a crack. Zack could see only the nose of Monsieur Le Postman, as the man whispered out, "C'est vrai?!" His voice seemed to break with disbelief in the asking, as if he were truly afraid.

Zack thought, "Afraid of Napoleon being in Paris?" Of course, Napoleon was in Paris, and buried, though, no longer much of a threat. Zack stood back, watched, and listened carefully. Napoléon was obviously code, but for what?

Mara bowed her head apologetically, unable to look Monsieur Le Postman in the eyes, answered, "Vrai. Il est de ma faute." (True. It is my fault.)

He opened the door a bit wider, and Zack could see the man's whole face up close for the first time. It was pockmarked and covered with black stubble. Obviously, this was not a workday, and he had not shaved to receive visitors.

Monsieur Le Postman had made a practice of moving quickly in and out of the building, never staying long to visit at the mailbox with the others. Zack knew nothing about him, except that he had been the only tenant, who had not dropped off some sort of welcome-to-the-building gift. Zack thought it was because the man was naturally, anti-social, or perhaps, didn't care for Americans. He had not taken the snub, personally, but from the sneer on the postman's face, as he examined Zack from head to toe, Zack may have been wrong. Perhaps, Monsieur Le Postman really didn't like Zack, and therefore, it was personal. His stare made Zack very uncomfortable, and Zack read into it a silent verdict. "This is your fault, foreigner."

From Mara's interaction with the man, it seemed clear that Monsieur Le Postman was the building's centurion. Her demeanor around him was that of a child, embarrassed to report to her parents that she had failed at school. She kept her head in a half-bowed position, and spoke only to answer his questions. Later, when they were alone again in her apartment, she would tell Zack that she had deferred to man's judgment on how the others should be told of her betrayal.

Monsieur Le Postman had told her, "Une heure. Nous nous réunissons à Marcel and Camille's appartement. Je vais le dire aux autres." (One hour. We meet at Marcel and Camille's apartment. I will tell the others.)

Solemnly, they returned to Mara's apartment, where they would await the hour of rendezvous. Zack wanted to be the one to tell Gwendolyn the truth, because his possessions were still in her apartment, and he feared she might throw everything out the window, upon hearing the news. Her new boyfriend was a fool!

Leaving the windows open to the thief had been his mistake, not Mara's. He had jeopardized the lives of everyone in the building because of a stupid mistake, pouring the cream down the drain and stinking up the place. Opening the windows, leaving them open for all of Paris to enter, was more than a mistake. It was criminal negligence.

Remarkably, Mara was not berating him, or burying him in guilt. Instead, she was claiming it all for herself. She should have never gotten involved with Phillipe, she said over, and over, again. "He was such a bum, such a gigolo. Montague tried to warn me. I should have listened. Now," she said, looking at her big belly, "Now, look at me."

She began crying and Zack did what any kind-hearted individual would do. He reached out, put a hand awkwardly on her back, and tapped. "There, there," he said, feeling totally ill equipped for this sort of sympathetic gesture. Mara surprised him by falling into his arms, and with her weight and girth, nearly knocked him over. Together, they fell backwards onto the sofa. Mara was nothing, if not a beehive of hormonal buzzing.

She rattled off in French a dozen or more reasons for why she should not have become involved with Phillipe. From what Zack could make of her words, now even more difficult than ever to understand, coming forth through blubbering sobs, Phillipe had been deeply engaged in crime, a crime that in France was so horrible as to become national news.

From their earlier conversation, Zack had assumed that everyone in the building was involved in some sort of crime – and each in varying degrees of participation. Tito had been the mastermind, and without his leadership, the operation was falling apart. They had tried to continue, but everything became impossible to manager without his leadership. They had tried.

The theft of Mara's packages was only the icing on the cake. By accepting Mara's invitation to live in her apartment and to masquerade as her cousin, Zack had become complicit in their crimes. Mara tried to deny it, but Zack said no court would believe that I had no knowledge of what was going on. If one of them went to prison, it was certain that they would all go, Zack concluded. This, Mara could not dispute. This was France, where justice was exacted equally among the perpetrators of any crime. So much for égalité and fraternité. After sentencing, he could say goodbye to liberté, too.

Zack paused on that thought for a moment. With the villagers gone, eleven apartments in the 6th Arrondissement would become available, all at the same time. Apartment hunters would be lined up around the block, if all of the villagers were all hauled off in chains on the same day. Imagine that! It was the dream of every real estate agent in Paris. An agent could retire permanently on eleven commissions for selling eleven apartments. He wondered, if he should tell Claudine about the possibility, or simply let her find out about it, by reading the newspapers – like everyone else.

His thoughts were disturbed by Mara's sobbing indictment of their neighbors. Zack learned that stolen items were being trafficked through Mme. Christy's flower shop, hidden in bouquets bound for restaurants, hotels, and Épiceries all over Paris, where they were exchanged for a remarkable amount of cash. But what? In his daydreaming, he had missed what it was that they were stealing and trafficking. Never more than now, did he wish he had listened in French class!

Mara continued talking and sobbing, saying that their return on their initial investments had been too tempting to resist. Greed! We were all too greedy! What had begun as a one-man operation with Tito had spread quickly to the professor, Mme. Christy, Albert, Arness, Ivan, Berta, Marcel and Camille, Monsieur Le Postman, and even (although, the last to be trusted) Mme. Durand, the concierge.

The only person in the building, who had not participated, nor was he asked, was Monsieur Le Spy. For obvious reasons, the others had practiced airtight discretion, whenever Dmitry was in the hallways. Thus, the code evolved. The discussions about weather and agriculture had held a myriad of coded clues, divulging when deliveries were due, or packages needed to be transported, and when flower arrangements needed to be picked up. Usually, it was on Mondays.

Zack thought, in hearing how the network carried out its crimes, that the system was brilliant, and might have survived detection for years – had he not been the stupid one. Whoever had the packages, Mara's packages, would be wise to their operation. All the thief had to do - was to un-wrap one package, and the evidence would be overwhelming, Mara told him.

There had to be something that Zack could do, something to undo the damage, and allow his neighbors to continue living the lives, which they had designed around their "investment income." Surely, there was something, he could do.

Then, he hit upon an idea! Yes. It was a little bit crazy, but it might work, if he could get everyone was onboard with the plan. Could he work out the details, before they met at Marcel and Camille's place? He checked his watch. Fifteen minutes remained, before they would all gather to discuss the problem. Yes. Maybe. Just maybe.

But first, he had to know exactly what it was that they were stealing. Drugs? Counterfeit Euros? Jewels? "What?" This time, he demanded that Mara tell him and in English, so that there would be no misunderstanding.

"No," Mara said, quite offended by his suggestions of drugs, or worse.

"We are not common criminals," she said, defiantly. "We are entrepreneurs!"

Ok. Zack thought. Honor among highwaymen. If she wanted to think it, they were the aristocracy of thieves. "Then – what do entrepreneurs in France steal?" Zack said, frustrated, thinking of all of the entrepreneurs on Wall Street, who had made fortunes stealing from their clients' portfolios.

"Truffles," Mara said, triumphantly, and with a great deal of pride. "We steal truffles."

Marcel opened the door into a living room filled with people. All of the residents, except Monsieur Le Spy, were there, and each fell silent as Mara and Zack entered the room. It was the first time that some had seen Mara so round and heavy with her pregnancy, but it was the American's presence in the room that stole the show. Eyes, which had fallen upon her belly, traveled up and over, staying fixed upon Zack's face.

Mme. Christy broke the ice, by coming forward, and putting her arm around Mara, to lead her to a chair, which Montague relinquished for his friend. Zack searched the room for Gwendolyn, who stood expressionless next to Monsieur Le Postman. She would not let their eyes meet. Later, she would tell Zack, she had been the first neighbor notified, and was afraid, if she looked at Zack, everyone else in the room would know that they had become more than neighbors. So far, no one other than Mara knew that they had become roommates, or that Zack had become her new cousin. She was not ready to share that news with the others.

Monsieur Le Postman, however, was aware that Gwendolyn and Zack had become "close" friends, and hearing his words had unnerved her, considerably. He had questioned her repeatedly about her loyalty to the group, imagining that Zack had already persuaded her to defect, to betray them. Perhaps, Mara's packages had not been stolen. He taunted her. Perhaps, she had given them to the American. She was, after all, Monsieur Le Postman had said, sneeringly, "British."

In relating the story, later, to Zack, Gwendolyn would confirm his earlier suspicions. Not every Frenchman had found closure on the Thirty-Year War between England and France. Gwendolyn had denied everything that Monsieur Le Postman spewed in his bitter accusations, everything, except her feelings for Zack. This revelation would leave Zack, wondering in the days that followed, just what it was that

Gwendolyn felt for him. In truth, this would become the scariest part of her story.

Camille offered Zack a glass of wine, and he took it, downing it almost immediately. It seemed to help, although, he noticed that not everyone was drinking. His next thought was that Camille had put some sort of drug in his drink to encourage the truth. After all, she had learned a great many interrogation techniques during WWII, hadn't she? Being in the French Resistance, even though she was a child, must have taught her ways to make enemies talk.

Soon, whether it was imagined or real, he found that he could not stop talking. The others had circled him, and the silence had to be filled. Did it not? They began asking a hundred different questions, and slowly, one-by-one, he answered them. Each of his answers had to be repeated in French, as each person translated his words differently, assuming his use of innuendo was intentional - to cover up the truth. He was an American, was he not? Americans were difficult to understand, so many different accents in one country, and always, they were very, very cunning. At least, they were in the movies. Zack was probably one of these.

Being a writer? Well, no doubt, that was his cover, a clever excuse for his surveillance of them. Was it not?

When Zack had difficulty understanding their questions, Gwendolyn did not step up and translate for him. He saw this as either her indictment of him, or her defection. What had happened to her feelings for him?

Surely, after all of his attempts to make friends with the villagers, someone would defend him, but if not Gwendolyn, then, who? Mara tried, but they shushed her, saying that she had profited by his presence in her apartment, and therefore, could not be trusted. Her defense of Zack would be worthless. Mara fell uncharacteristically quiet. In a corner of the room, she wept.

He was surprised to see that it was the professor, who stepped in after twenty minutes of a fierce and relentless interrogation, suggesting that Zack was stupid. Zack wanted to yell, "Finally! Someone gets me." Montague conjectured that Zack was a duped innocent, recruited by a silly girl, simply because he was in the right place at the right time. In the corner, Mara wept louder at the suggestion by her friends that she was "silly."

Montague did not let her emotions deter him. He said that Mara had no idea that she was compromising, or jeopardizing, their operation by inviting the young American into her apartment, and by doing so, inviting trouble into the village.

Zack agreed, jumping in to plead his innocence upon the professor defense of him.

Then, the others jumped in, saying, "We know about the two of you," meaning Montague and Mara. Now, it was the professor turn to fall silent.

Zack offered to show everyone his employment contract from the States, to prove he was a writer. He offered to show them the other apartments in the 6th and 5th Arrondissements, which he had previewed, and found too expensive, before accepting Mara's offer. He offered to show them his lease agreement on Tito's former apartment, which had really been his first choice, although – not now, not after learning the fate of its previous tenant. Zack thought the situation hopeless, as for every defense he offered, they countered with another suspicion about him.

Eventually, the group settled down, convinced that Zack was not the most immediate threat to their operation. No. There was even more of a problem to solve. It was the thief, who through a crime of convenience – an open window – had become the focus of their anger and their fears. If the thief attempted to sell the truffles, out right, without the distribution channels they had meticulously designed; or if he went to the police, well...it would be over for all of them. Wouldn't it?

This was a sobering possibility, which brought silence to the room. Wine glasses were refilled. The wait was painful, but the jury's summation was worth it. Zack heard himself being called clumsy, uninformed, and careless. He was a liability, but probably not to be punished. Mara should have told him sooner, what was in store for him, if he accepted her offer. With that, Zack was off the hook, and they turned their attention onto Mara.

Madeleine came to Mara's defense, almost simultaneously, along with the professor. In turns, they spoke of the punishment, which Mara had already suffered at the hands of her gigolo boyfriend, Phillipe. Neither, Madeleine or Montague, had thought him a suitable mate, and they had all been mistaken to have trusted him with the stolen truffle operation.

Phillipe's boasts, of knowing the right people in the south of France, who could replace Tito's truffle thieves, had proved too tempting. Certainly, he did have access to new sources of truffles by virtue of his location in the south of France. That much was true, but it had been no guarantee that he could get his hands on the treasures growing there.

Now, they wondered. Were the truffles, they were receiving, really coming off French truffle plantations? Or were they coming from China via the port of Marseilles? Yes. This was possible - Phillipe, over-charging them, and pocketing the difference. He was that sort of unscrupulous man.

The anguish of this thought was overwhelming. What, if they had been selling knock-off truffles to the great chefs of Paris? The shame, the crime - unthinkable!

If only Tito had not been killed, none of this would be happening, Mme. Durand lamented. "I should have changed the locks." Camille attempted to comfort the concierge. Even, Monsieur Le Postman seemed moved by her misplaced feeling of guilt. "Not your fault," he grunted.

When Tito supplied the truffles, (before Phillipe was pressed into serviced), there had been no trouble. Everyone profited. Their decisions, to turn a thought into a business, had brought financial stability to everyone in the village. They could relax, secure in the knowledge that whatever happened to the Euro, or the economy of the EU, they could rely upon their outside source of un-taxable income.

Tito's death had been more than unfortunate; it had nearly caused the collapse of the village economy. Why had Tito been killed? Zack dared to voice the bold question. Why had the police been so willing to drop the investigation so quickly? He followed the first question with an equally, alarming, second one.

It wasn't that they could accept the police's conclusion, it was an unsolvable crime, Albert said. They didn't want further intrusions into their personal lives. Keeping the investigation open would have meant - "borrowing trouble."

Ivan spoke up this time. What would happen, if the police, investigating Tito's murder, found out about their truffle smuggling operation? No. Poor Tito would have to "rest in peace."

"Or some other place," Berta added.

No one wanted to know where that other place was, but the thought of it brought another impenetrable silence. As they settled into chairs, on the sofa, and on the floor, to contemplate the fate of Tito, Camille passed around a tray of appetizers, and more wine. This time, everyone ate and drank, as they conversed quietly in French. Zack took a deep breath, and moved from the center of the room to a spot near the windows, which looked out upon a garden in the courtyard. It was the first time that he had seen the inner courtyard of the building. He was unaware that Gwendolyn had moved next to him.

"Well done," she murmured. It startled him. He studied her face. She was smiling, no longer cold and distant. "I knew you could do it," she added, quietly, before taking a sip of her wine. "Of course, it helps, too, that you're actually innocent."

Zack turned toward her, but kept his eyes on the others in the room, all of whom seemed distracted by their own discussions about what to do next. He sipped the wine this time, as his earlier gulp had gone directly to his head. "There's a difference between innocence and ignorance. I don't appreciate being kept in the dark, but I think I have a plan, which may help everyone," he said, "but I don't know how to present it to them. You know...with me being the new guy on the block, and all." He looked to Gwendolyn for guidance.

"Just blurt it out," Gwendolyn said. "We're bloody-well desperate...as you can see for yourself." She pointed to the group as she said it. "I think we'd listen to anyone at this point, if he could keep us out of prison."

"Ah...hemmm," Zack cleared his throat, and a few heads turned his direction. "I have...an idea." Now, more heads were turned, and the room was silent. No one was smiling, and this weakened his courage. Then, Zack realized that Monsieur Le Spy's apartment on the third floor was two stories up, but directly above Marcel and Camille's apartment. Did they share the small airshaft? He put a finger in front of his lips, indicating that everyone should be quiet, and then, pointed with the other hand to the ceiling.

Marcel knew what Zack was indicating. He walked over to the air register in the wall, unscrewed a copy of screws, and lifted off the cover. He stuck his hand inside and pulled out a large towel, which had been wadded up and stuck inside. "No problem," Marcel said. "You may speak freely here."

Zack relaxed and said in a normal voice, "I will take the blame for everything."

Gwendolyn nudged him, saying, "That's your plan?" She stepped one-step away from him, before adding, "We've already thought of that."

Zack blinked twice, looking at the face of the woman, whom he thought he knew. Her honesty was brutal. He continued, unsure if their plan was his plan. "I mean, if anyone – the police – or anyone comes looking for information, you can say that you know nothing. The only packages found, so far, were in Mara's apartment, but they arrived only after I moved in. Mara was already living away from Paris. All of this can be proved. The investigation will center on me, the American, whom none of you really knew. Correct?"

There were heads nodding in agreement. There were, also, a few murmurs, heads joining other heads in whispers, and then, a smile or two. They were considering reviewing and accepting Zack's plan. It would be much easier to blame him, if he were in on the plan, a willing fall guy. Zack could see it on their faces. It was coming together. Should he continue?

"Ok? (No objections so far?) "So, tell anyone who asks, the American had many visitors. You can say that you saw money change hands. It did. I paid for a pizza delivery one night. And, that you thought it was drug dealing, but you were too afraid to report it."

"And what will you do?" Montague asked, and in his voice, Zack thought there was real concern. "We can't let you go to prison in France. It's not like America."

Zack was touched, wanting to tell Montague that prison was prison regardless of country, but instead, continued. "I will disappear, move somewhere else in France," he offered. "If I have to, I will go back to the States and change my name. People do it all the time." Now, he was caught up in his own lie, imagining himself as a character in one of his favorite books. "Maybe Canada," he added.

He could live the rest of his life "on the lamb," moving from place to place, and writing about it under an assumed name. He could become famous, the famous American "truffle thief." It didn't have the panache of being a jewel thief, or a cat burglar, but there was something special about stealing truffles. Just talking about it made grown men, mostly chefs, cry.

The more he talked, the more the group got behind his plan. What did it matter to them, if the American took the fall for the rest of them? It was not as if Zack had ever been truly one of them. He was not French. He was not Polish. He was not even planning on staying in Paris more than a year. Hardly more than a tourist and there were millions of them. And, he had invested nothing. In fact, he was getting nothing out of this.

Hmmm?

Something changed in the room. Perhaps, it was the wine. Perhaps, it was the memory of other Americans, who had come to France to help the French, when they were in trouble. Those Americans, also, were getting nothing for their unselfish offer to help.

Hmmm?

There was no way of knowing why, but there was clearly a change in the emotional undertone of the words being spoken. It was palpable, flowing from one villager to another, until it had circled the room - twice. Zack thought his neighbors looked almost ashamed of their earlier dismissal of him. He had been no one, no one who mattered, then, all of a sudden, he mattered to them very much, and they could no longer disregard his feelings, or dispatch with the morning trash. Zack was a person, too.

They rallied in his favor. He had lived in the building long enough to have his feelings considered. It would be so easy to blame everything on him, but the fact, that he had been willing to take the fall for the whole village, well this...this made him a hero of sorts. Yes. They were ashamed. They proudly admitted their shame. They toasted their shame.

So, if Zack was not to become the sacrificial goat – then, what next? He had to spoil the moment by asking. Silence followed.

What would they do, or say, when the authorities came to take them all away? As surely, that would happen. It was only a matter of time. Marcel moved forward in the room, to lead the discussion, suggesting some of the tricks, which he and Camille had used to hide in Paris right under the Gestapo's noses, when they were children. He enjoyed the telling, as this was a rare occasion to have such a large audience. However, the stories were old and familiar to everyone in the room, except Zack, and none offered a suitable 21st century solution to the problem at hand. No one here was willing to give up his or her home in Paris to move permanently underground.

Zack was as fascinated with Marcel's recounts, as the others were bored by them. He would have loved, under other circumstances, to sit and take notes, but this was not the time. The others were, however, respectful of Marcel, and tolerated their boredom in silence, and with drink, already knowing the shelf life of the stories being told for the hundredth time.

After an hour, when Marcel, too, had tired of his stories, he left the room to use the W.C., and the professor stood up. It seemed to Zack that there existed a pecking order in the group, which was determined by age. If that were true, if each was entitled to take the floor for an hour, Zack quickly calculated that their time together would run well into the early morning.

Camille and Mme. Durand disappeared into the kitchen. They did not return, quickly, but soon, wonderful aromas filtered into the living room. It had been a brilliant move on the part of the women, as it speeded up the oral dissertations, and had the guests salivating in anticipation. Their thoughts of deceptions, plots, and devises were replaced with images of onion quiche, beef, and roasted potatoes. In less than an hour, the group was far too distracted by food to focus on any more conspiracy theories.

Gwendolyn and Madeleine retrieved from the tiny kitchen the two chairs there, to add to the table in the corner of the room, which at best could seat eight. As there more adults than chairs in the room, Zack, Gwendolyn and Madeleine offered to eat from the coffee table. Zack sat on the floor, allowing the two women to sit together on the small sofa. Ivan and Berta joined him on the floor, allowing the other guests to sit in proper chairs.

Each guest was asked to fill his plate in the kitchen and move to a suitable place to eat. Montague fixed a plate for Mara and took it to her, before serving himself. No one seemed to notice the kindness, except Zack and Gwendolyn, who gave each other a knowing wink. During dinner, Zack asked Ivan and Berta where little Bog was. Before either could answer, Arness said, from across the room, that her Sébastien and the Polywog's son, Bog, were staying together at a friend's house for the night.

"We thought it was best," Berta confirmed, and Gwendolyn

translated, "if they were not involved in our conversation."

Suggestions of discontinuing the truffle smuggling operation continued throughout the courses of salad, quiche, braised beef and roasted potatoes, served with green beans, cheese and fruit, and finally, a cherry tart. But when coffee and brandy followed, the idea of getting out of the truffle business had been dismissed because people were now admitting how much they needed, or wanted the extra income.

When everyone was nearly comatose from eating, the idea of stopping this seven-year transportation of truffles from the south to Paris was discounted entirely. Murmurs of "Who are we hurting?" surfaced.

Zack was surprised to learn that the reality, that truffle plantations were run by fellow French citizens, had escaped his Parisian neighbors. To them, this was a victimless crime. He wanted to say, "But wasn't Tito a victim?" Instead, he said, "but doesn't it take income away from the truffle farmers?"

Gwendolyn could read his mind, and answered, "Tito was probably killed by a woman. He had so many," she said, almost dismissively, leaving the question in Zack's mind that she might have been one of them. Then, she took on his verbal question. "Plantations grow so many truffles that they do not miss the ones we steal. Our 'harvesters' are very careful not to disturb large sections of ground."

Others in the room seconded her notion that Tito's murder had been one of passion, not one of vengeance, totally ignoring her assessment of the damage to truffle plantations. It was not any topic, which they wished to consider.

Zack wanted to ask, who the strangers at Tito's door had been, as they were all men, not women. Could they have been jilted gay lovers? Or, were they husbands looking for their adulterous wives? Perhaps, none of them had realized that Tito had already been eliminated by another, who shared their same anger.

Gwendolyn seemed to know what she was accusing Tito of doing, and that bothered Zack, greatly. Did that mean that she and Tito had a history of their own? Zack knew that question would have to wait until after dinner, when they were alone, again. How would she interpret his question? Would she think that he was jealous of a dead man? Was he? He wasn't certain. He was not one prone to jealousy.

Arness picked up where Gwendolyn had left off, saying that Tito, the undertaker, was quite the ladies' man. It seemed odd, but not impossible, that Tito had made the rounds of the building. Zack noticed a strange look in the eyes of each of the ladies in the room, when they mentioned his name. It was hard to believe that an undertaker could be that charismatic.

Then, another odd question crept into Zack's mind. Did the Italian couple, who were leasing Tito's apartment, not mind the history of the place? Or perhaps, like him, no one had bothered to tell them. He had to ask. "Do the Italians know Tito died in their apartment?"

Again, silence. But, then...a few coughs. A few smothered giggles.

"Italians?" Mara asked, totally out of the loop on this one.

"The Italian couple, who rented Tito's apartment?" Zack said, again, looking first at her and then, at the others, hoping someone else in the room would chime in with some answers.

"No one lives in Tito's apartment," Albert confessed.

"But, I've seen you, and you, and you..." Zack said, pointing to the professor, Madeleine, and Albert, "coming and going from there for months."

All three of them, along with others in the room, looked guilty, very guilty. It was Albert, who spoke up this time. "We needed a place to store the truffles, but not in any of our apartments. In case, the police found them, we could claim ignorance. Tito had stored them at the funeral home in caskets, until they needed to be moved around the city. But, with Tito dead, we had to change warehouse locations."

Madeleine explained that her flower shop had simply not been large enough to hide a storage operation, and there were other employees, who worked there to be considered. She didn't want more people involved. They might find the bags of truffles, and report her.

She had been willing to take small amounts with her to work, hide them in vases, and then, create the bouquets, which would be transported to restaurants and hotels by the other villagers. But, she wasn't willing to take any greater risks. As things were, her employees never questioned that she preferred to create the bouquets, personally. In fact, they were simply happy to work for such a successful florist. Hardly a day went by without a call from a restaurant or a hotel needing "Bouquets by Madame Christy" for weddings, funerals, anniversaries.

Madeleine insisted that she had wanted only to keep her business operating, and her employees, employed. She was not greedy, and she was not willing to take more risk than she already was, or to draw attention to herself. Her ex-husband was keeping too close an eye on the success of her shop, already. If she became too successful, he would become suspicious. Yes. The others had asked her to step in as the leader. With Tito gone, someone had to, but she had refused to accept any nomination.

So, they split up all of the work, which Tito had done as their leader. Instead of the stolen truffles being delivered to the funeral parlor, they were sent to the residents at the apartment building, disguised in small packages. To the post office, everyone in this building had become an avid reader, as the packages were always labeled "books." In a private joke, the villagers had begun referring to the vacant apartment as La Bibliothèque, rather than the truffle storeroom. Each week, packages were moved there, unpacked, and placed in flowerpots. The professor composted a special soil mixture, which ensured the best storage conditions for the truffles. To mask the smell, the hallway was regularly sprayed with an aerosol of cinnamon and nutmeg. That explained a lot of things.

"Then, no one lives in the apartment?" Zack asked, again.

"No one," Berta answered, "except for the man and his wife from Italy." She looked at Ivan, and then, at the others. No one was willing to continue the lie. It was silly to try, as Zack already knew too much. She looked down and dropped her hands in her lap.

Ivan came to her rescue. "It's ok. You can stop now." Embarrassed to admit his own role in the charade, he tried to make a joke of it, saying to Zack, "Perhaps, you could become their cousin. Do you speak Italian?" Some of the others snickered, but Zack had a look of confusion, so Ivan explained, "We made a copy of the lease, which you were supposed to sign, filled in fake names, and sent it to Monsieur Épicier with the deposit."

"Monsieur Épicier did not question the authenticity, as he was so happy to have the lease signed, and the deposit in cash. The Italian couple," Ivan continued, pointing at Montague, who took a bow for his excellent writing skills in Italian, "wrote a very nice letter to him, saying that they would always pay in cash. You know, this he could use to his advantage with the tax collectors – well... you know? He..." (searching for word) "...jumped at the chance."

"And who pays the rent?" Zack asked.

Several people answered, simultaneously, "We do."

Monsieur Le Postman spoke up for the first time. "I deliver it."

Zack could do the math. The monthly rent split between the villagers was reasonable insurance on keeping their secret – secret. This explained why, after the remodeling, he had never seen anyone come or go from the place, other than the other residents of the building. It also explained why he sneezed every time he passed the apartment, and craved cinnamon rolls. With his allergy to mushrooms, fungus, mold, and evidently, now, – truffles, it was a wonder he hadn't died of respiratory failure.

Keeping his windows opened a crack, even through the winter months, had saved his life. Living next door to the equivalent of a truffle plantation, also, explained why he had spent his first three weeks in bed, with an un-diagnosable ailment. How many people in the world were allergic to truffles?

Montague knew what Zack was thinking. "I had workmen put an air filtration system in La Bibliothèque."

"Thank you," Zack said, both surprised and grateful to his friend. "You probably saved my life."

"You're welcome," Montague said, humbly. "Sorry about the first month and all the noise. The first system didn't work properly, and we had to replace it."

That explained everything: the flu, three weeks in bed, the trips to the pharmacy, and the noise, starting and stopping, only to start up, again. But, moving out of the building, if not to Gwendolyn's, would be in his best interest. Could he sleep, knowing a truffle plantation was growing above his head at night?

Then, a thought surfaced that might put an end to his worries over truffles. Did he still have a bed at Gwendolyn's? Had her opinion of him changed with the evening's revelations? He had a few questions of his own, starting with Tito, the ladies' man. The evening had been a game-changer. That much was certain. Given the circumstances, which had brought them all together, it was remarkable that their conversations settled into a review of sports, the cost of good clean fish, and the prospect of rain for the weekend.

People casually shared their plans for the spring, as if no one expected to be spending it in prison. It seemed to Zack that no one was frantic about their impending arrest. In fact, the atmosphere had become rather jovial. Even the always-austere Monsieur Le Postman was smiling and clicking glasses with the others at the table.

Zack was taken aback by how welcoming the group had become, once his innocence had been established. Twice, they had asked his opinion, and once, he was asked about his plans for staying in Paris. His staying was now assumed, not questioned. Indeed, it appeared that he was now fully "acceptable" in their eyes, and if they were all to go down – they would be going down together with Zack in tow, whether or not he was willing.

Actually, after this great a meal, and so many glasses of wine that he had lost count, he would have followed the villagers, wherever they went. Twice, Gwendolyn had laid her hand on his thigh, as casually and as intimately, as if they were lovers. He thought it went unnoticed by the others because it happened underneath of the coffee table, but certainly, it had spiked Zack's interest in his new friend. There was a lot more to learn about Gwendolyn. For one, what had she found attractive about the undertaker, and why had she been so quick to discount the cause of his death?

Dressed casually in black jeans and a tight-fitting sweater, Gwendolyn had arrived for the evening's event, looking surprisingly sexy; a word that Zack would have never used to describe her daytime fashion. In the daytime, she dressed like a women trying to be a man. Perhaps, in her corporate world, it was a survival tactic. Although, she wore no makeup to work, tonight, her lips were painted a deep shade of pink, and her cheeks displayed a blush, missing from her normally unpainted face. Had she taken the time, to make-up her face for the villagers, or for him?

By midnight, the dishes had been washed and dried with the help of all the women present, except for Mara, whose larger-than-life presence in the kitchen made it impossible for the others to work. She retreated to the sofa and leaned against the professor, who smiled with the pride of an expectant father. The men ignored her presence, something that they did well, and she knew to keep her silence. She had started the trouble. It was best, if she didn't speak up, and remind them of the reason for their evening together.

Zack for the most part, merely, listened because his language skills were not strong enough yet, to participate fully. When asked a question, he would respond as best he could. The other men had asked if he had the telephone number of a French attorney, for when he would be arrested. The question caught him off guard.

Attorney? Yikes! This wasn't just a lie gone awry. This was scary stuff – the prospect of interrogation, jail, court – maybe even prison! Marcel saw the look on his face, and magnanimously offer, the name of his family attorney; someone he had known from "before." Zack imagined "before" meant from his French Resistance days. Zack thanked Marcel, copiously, and took down the information.

The meeting broke up at one o'clock, not because they had made any real plans on how to proceed from here, but because they were all too tired and too sleepy to move on with further discussion. There had been a basic agreement reached. They were all "In for a penny, in for a pound." No one was blameless. No one would be sacrificed. They would meet, again, at the end of the week, if nothing more threatening developed before then. Oh yes, and everyone was expected to bring a bottle of wine next time.

Kisses on cheeks ended the night.

Madeleine left, alone. Montague followed, helping Mara navigate the stairs. Zack and Gwendolyn stopped on the second floor and retired to her apartment. Ivan, Berta, Arness, and Albert did not seem surprised by some of the single residents, moving in the direction that recent developments in their romantic lives – demanded. Love was love, and love needed no explanation.

Mme. Durand, the concierge, remained at the bottom of the stairs with Monsieur Le Postman, and together, they watched and listened to the scenes being played out on the upper floors. Mme. Durand's face was exceedingly flushed, but whether it was the result of the wine, or the prospect of Monsieur Le Postman, spending the night, no one could be certain - certainly, not, Camille, who was watching through the keyhole.

"Viens te coucher, ma femme" (Come to bed, woman), Marcel chided. "C'est pas notre affaire" (It's none of our business)!

wendolyn agreed to meet Mara for lunch, so that the two women could do as Zack had suggested, "Help each other." Mara needed help for the basic things, standing up, choosing baby clothes, carrying shopping bags, etc. Gwendolyn needed to know which shops or cafés in the area might hire a British citizen, with a soon-to-expire work visa. Gwendolyn helped Mara pick out some cute and inexpensive clothes for a baby boy, while Mara instructed her on the ins and outs of getting paid "under the table" by potential employers.

She explained that there were plenty in Paris, seeking to avoid paying taxes to the government and benefits to employees. Gwendolyn would have to dress differently than she had been dressing for her office position, and she would have to know when, and where, to bring up the topic of job seeking. It did not take long for the détente, which Zack had been designing between the French and the British women to take hold. Both reported to him on what a good day they had enjoyed - together.

Zack had spent the day walking around Paris, contemplating the possibility of this being his last day of freedom. His rational side was telling him that he could run, perhaps, because back in the States it was Ground Hog Day. Everywhere he went, he could see his shadow. Six more weeks of something was certain, but he wondered if it was something as benign as bad weather. The words, "You'll need an attorney," still rang in his ears.

He could leave his new friends to fend for themselves, but his emotional side overrode this commonsense. Something had happened last night, which made escape impossible. He and Gwendolyn had made love for the first time, and he was fairly certain that this relationship had legs - longer than the ones, he had happily discovered under the blankets this morning. It had happened so naturally, so casually, as if they had both known this was where they were headed all along – no longer friends, but lovers.

The morning, as if celebrating this new chapter in their lives, had bloomed with bright sunlight, a warm breeze, and a feeling that all things were possible. Zack had completely lost sight of the fact – they could all be moments away from incarceration. In fact, the topic had not surfaced during a leisurely breakfast with Gwendolyn, chirping about the new job she hoped to have by month end. Neither did it surface in the shower, where they laughed about all the misconceptions, which they had, secretly, about each other.

He had imagined she would be prudish in bed, based upon how she normally dressed, and she had thought he would be too typically American (the definition of which she would explain in length later) - all talk and no action. He was delighted to find that "prudish" was the last word he would use to describe her. She had been, totally, uninhibited in bed. She laughed a bawdy sort of laugh, which he had never heard before. Yes. He could admit it. He had been completely wrong about her. She would admit, she had been mistaken about him, as well.

Mara dropped by the apartment, unannounced, but by then, Zack and Gwendolyn had dressed. Mara looked remarkably calm, cool and collected for a woman about to give birth – seemingly – any minute. Zack's greeting had become, "When are you going to have that baby?" Mara's response had become, "Never." What Zack really wanted to know was how the evening had ended for Mara and Montague, but his evening with Gwendolyn had taken precedence. He couldn't stop talking about what a wonderful woman, Gwendolyn was.

If Montague had spent the night with Mara, they had been exceedingly quiet, as Zack and Gwendolyn had not heard any noise or conversation from above. Then, again, Zack and Gwendolyn had been busy making some noise of their own. He was grateful that no one lived below Gwendolyn. Of course, Mara could have stayed at Montague's apartment. Either way, Zack had told Gwendolyn, "C'est pas notre affaire" (It's none of our business).

Zack walked to La Tour Montparnasse, and on through to La Gare Montparnasse. He caught himself looking at the departure board, imagining that he could board any of the hundred trains, which would be passing through the station today. In a matter of minutes, he could be gone – so far away that no one would know what had become of him. To say that it was not tempting would be a lie.

Then, he thought of Gwendolyn, and the others. No. Having a lover
and friends in Paris was too important to him. In New York, this would
have been a simple decision. Hadn't he already proved it, by leaving
that world behind, to come to Paris? No. He couldn't run away, no
matter how easy it was to do. The question was becoming, what would
he tell his family back in New York? What would they say when they
found out he had been arrested in Paris? ...That he was nothing more
than a common thief? Well, OK, maybe not that common.

Zack left the train station and backtracked to the Tour
Montparnasse stores, where he wandered around, looking first at baby
shops, and then, men's clothing. Perhaps, Gwendolyn had been right to
criticize his fashion sense. Perhaps, today would be a good day to
attempt the transition. If he was going to live in Paris, he needed to
look Parisian.

He stopped to sort through a stack of scarves, a good place to
start. An hour later, he left the shopping center, having purchased a
scarf, charcoal colored trousers, a black sweater, a hat, as well as a gift
for Mara's baby boy. Something about being so happy had loosened his
purse strings. Before, it had been about saving every Euro. Now, that
he was counting his remaining days of freedom, money did not seem so
important. Carrying the assortment of logo'd shopping bags back to
Gwendolyn's apartment, he felt Parisian.

As he turned a corner near his apartment building, he noticed
little Sébastien a few meters ahead. The little boy had a shopping bag
of his own, and seemed nervous, looking from side to side as he
walked. As far as Zack could remember, today was a school day. Why
wasn't the little bastard in school?

Arness had said that her son and little Bog Polywog would be
staying the night, perhaps, even a few days with friends. What was
Sébastien doing out on the streets of Paris, alone? Where was he
headed, looking so suspicious? And where was Bog? Ever the curious
sleuth, Zack decided to follow.

Sébastien turned on La Rue d'Assas, and then, into the first
opening large enough for him to crawl through into Le Jardin du
Luxembourg. Zack was too large to make the same entry into the
gardens, and with his cumbersome packages, he was reluctant to
follow. However, he did stay on the outside of the gardens, and he did

keep watch on where Sébastien was headed. At the first proper opening to the gardens, Zack hurried through and backtracked to pick up a view of Sébastien, stopping behind the beehives. Curious, Zack thought. What was the boy doing here?

Zack moved to behind a tree, where he could observe, but not be seen. It seemed doubtful, if Sébastien would see him at all, as the little boy was too intent upon whatever it was that he was doing. Zack watched as Sébastien turned the contents of the shopping bag upside down on the grass, and began digging with a little shovel better intended for use at the beach.

Sébastien dug and dug and dug, until Zack became so bored, he was about to leave. What did he care, if Sébastien wanted to play in the park, instead of go to school? This was a matter for his parents. What did he care if the little boy got stung by a million bees because he was stupid to choose this location? Little boys did stupid things, and he did not, particularly, like this little boy. Sébastien was mean, and mean little boys needed to, occasionally, learn their lessons the hard way.

But, just as Zack was about to turn away, he noticed something familiar lying on the ground next to Sébastien's shopping bag. It had previously been hidden by it. He could barely believe his eyes! One of Mara's packages! The little bastard had stolen the packages! He was the one! He was their thief!

Zack could hardly wait to tell Gwendolyn, and her old cat. The poor old feline's terrorist would be found out for the villain that he was, and, finally, punished. Good! Zack could not imagine that Arness and Albert could deny the nature of their child, in light of this news. Zack took out his cell phone, turned on the camera, and began recording the little criminal's activities. He made certain that a close-up of the package, displaying Mara's name was properly captured. There could be no doubt from these pictures. None at all. He had caught their little turncoat, and it would be a huge relief to the other villagers.

After he had finished burying his booty, Sébastien stood up, brushed the dirt off his knees, and wadded up the shopping bag. As he ran past the tree, behind which Zack had slid upon seeing Sébastien chosen escape route, the little boy laughed, tossed the wad of paper up in the air, and kicked it as far as it would fly. Then, he followed it, picked it up, again, and repeated his new game. This continued through the park, until he was out of sight, laughing and oblivious to the justice about to befall him.

Zack laughed, too. It would only be a matter of hours, before Arness and Albert would have their son in custody. "Let him enjoy his freedom."

Gwendolyn was already home, when Zack arrived, whistling. She was amused by his good humor, and assumed that it was because of the activities of last night. She remarked, "My goodness, someone is certainly in a good mood. I wonder why?" Then, she noticed all the purchases. "Did you win the lottery?" she asked.

"Something better," Zack answered, tossing the shopping bags on the bed. Gwendolyn immediately began unwrapping Zack's purchases, and admiring his choices. Zack sat down on the sofa, and began his story. He pulled out his cell phone to share the evidence. Gwendolyn suggested transferring it to her computer, so that they could burn a disc of it for the others to watch on a television. "Good idea," Zack said.

Gwendolyn was both surprised and delighted to learn that Sébastien had been the culprit, and not an outsider. It was as if a huge weight had been lifted from her shoulders. She immediately picked up the phone, and shared the good news with Monsieur Le Postman. Fortunately, he was home, and agreed to notify the other residents. A meeting tonight was in order. A movie was to be viewed, one worthy of a full house. He added, he would like to tell Arness and Albert in person, and so would call the others, after giving them the news at their shops. With that, he was off. Gwendolyn and Zack heard the front door slam within minutes of ending the call.

Zack wanted to be the one to tell Mara, as he felt that he owed it to her. After all, it had been his mistake, which had caused so much distress. He had been the one to leave the windows open. Gwendolyn insisted he not do it because there was a proper order to these things. Monsieur Le Postman was the village's chosen centurion. He announced all matters pertaining to all meetings. This should be his moment of glory, not Zack's, even though she promised to show Zack (later), just how very proud she was of him, for solving the mystery. This, he found too intriguing, and agreed to let the matter drop.

However, he convinced her that this seemed like the moment to celebrate, and since their desire for each other had only been discovered hours earlier, a repeat performance proved too tempting. As they were getting undressed, a rapid knocking at the door startled both of them. They acted as teenagers caught in the act, and hurriedly re-dressed, calling out to their unexpected visitor, "What?" simultaneously.

"C'est moi!" (It is me), the professor called out loudly. "Venez vite!" (Come quickly!)

Zack opened the door. The professor looked him up and down, silently, acknowledging his new role as Gwendolyn's lover. Gwendolyn appeared seconds later, behind Zack.

"Le bébé...il vient. It vient Maintenant!" (The baby...he comes. He comes Now!)

Gwendolyn ran past both Zack and Montague, taking two steps at a time to reach the third floor. She rushed inside the open door of Montague's apartment to find Mara lying on the floor, gasping for air, and rolling from side to side in pain. Gwendolyn dropped down along side of her. "À quelle distance sont les douleurs?" (How close are the pains?)

"Je ne sais pas. Je ne sais pas. Je ne sais pas." (I don't know.) Mara kept repeating, frightened, and barely able to speak.

"Restez calme. J'appelle l'ambulance" (Stay calm. I am calling the ambulance), Gwendolyn said in her most reassuring voice. Montague and Zack were entering the room, and Zack tossed Gwendolyn his cell phone upon hearing her words. Montague looked pale, and Zack thought his own heart was pounding too hard. He suggested that they both sit down. Montague chose to sit on the floor next to Mara, who looked at him with big round eyes, and began biting her lip. He stroked her brow, and whispered something in her ear in French, which Zack could not catch. It seemed to calm Mara, and for that, he was grateful.

It took approximately fifteen minutes for an ambulance and a doctor to arrive. Zack was surprised to learn that doctors made house calls, and that French citizens could expect it. Patients were stabilized at home, whenever possible, freeing up hospital rooms for the more seriously injured or ill. The system was not only efficient, but it made perfect sense financially. It also gave the patients what they needed in a more humane and expedient manner.

Since the medical team had arrived with lots of equipment, Zack moved out into the hallway to give them room. He joined Gwendolyn, and Montague, who was now wringing his hands with worry. Gwendolyn spoke to him, softly, in French, and it seemed to Zack, that no matter how compassionate her words, or how carefully selected, Montague could not be comforted. Zack realized just how much the old man loved Mara. With each of Mara's moans, Montague rubbed his forehead.

Mara moaned in a way that Zack had never before heard. She was like a wounded animal, writhing in pain, and rolling constantly from side to side. He hoped that the baby boy would decide he had waited long enough to enter the world, and simply pop out, allowing his mother some relief. But, it was not to be and so, the EMT team loaded Mara onto a medical sled, brought her down the stairs, and carried her out the front door.

In the street, people had gathered to watch their first-responding heroes in action. "Bébé!" someone said, loudly. A collective sigh of relief was followed by a cheer. It was a birth, not a death. "Félicitations!" (Congratulations!) Someone else yelled. "Je suis heureux que ce sera un garcon!" (I am glad that it will be a boy!) Another, "Un autre joueur de football pour la France!" (Another soccer player for France!)

Zack was amazed by reaction of the villagers from the other apartment buildings, who so generously lent support for Mara. It seemed apparent that not everyone knew her, but for this monumental event in her life, they all had joined to celebrate. Had it been a death, Zack wondered, if then, too, they would have gathered to mourn a stranger's passing. It was a scene, he would never forget. His next feature article would be about the health care system in Paris, and the benefits of living in villages, hidden within a metropolis.

Maurice Montague was born three hours later, with the assistance of a caesarian section. Mara survived, happy, but exhausted. Maurice was nearly ten pounds at birth, and this, more than anything else, had made necessary the surgical procedure. Mara was simply too tiny to deliver the little man on her own. Had the baby been smaller, there was no doubt that the doctor with the ambulance team could have safely delivered Maurice in the professor's apartment. Zack could not imagine that such things still happened in the 21st century, but Gwendolyn assured him that they did.

There would have been some karma, or spiritual justice served, if the baby had been born in the village. One soul, Tito's, had left, and another soul, Monty's, had arrived. But, it was enough to know that a baby would be coming home to the village, soon.

Montague had ridden to the hospital with Gwendolyn and Zack in a taxi. He had paced constantly during the medical procedure, certain that Mara would die. Gwendolyn and Zack had stayed right by his side, not certain if Montague might die from his own self-induced anxiety. When the doctor came out to speak to the "significant other," none of the three spoke, and so, Zack gave the professor a rightful shove, causing an awkward step forward.

The doctor had lived too long, and was too French, to assume anything. Montague was someone of importance, regardless of his age. From that point on, the professor was assumed to be the father, the grandfather, perhaps, even the boyfriend. As the doctor spoke, Montague listened, carefully, intrigued by the details, although, repeatedly interrupting to ask if Mara was truly OK. The doctor assured him that she was, as was the baby boy. He suggested that, in a few minutes, Montague could visit and see for himself that everything he said was true. Then, seeing Montague's condition, the doctor offered a sedative. Montague refused it.

In the background, Gwendolyn translated word for word so that Zack could follow the conversation. Despite his attempts to appear otherwise, he had been nearly as anxious as Montague, for the event to come to a successful conclusion. Gwendolyn could not help, but suspect that Zack harbored some feelings for Mara. She tried, subtly, to coax some confirmation from him, but Zack was too focused on the professor, and the situation at hand. Later, she would confront him on the matter, but now was not the time.

Despite her fears, Gwendolyn kept quiet all the way home, knowing that it would have been different, if Zack had been Mara's cousin. But, he was not, and that meant that anything could have happened in Mara's apartment, while he was living there. She entertained for a second, but then, dropped the idea that Zack could be the baby's natural father. Zack had never indicated that he and Mara had been anything other than friends.

She pushed the thought from her mind, long enough to ask the doctor, if she and Zack could also visit. It would depend upon Mara's level of fatigue, he said, suggesting that it might be better for them to return in the morning. They should allow "him" (pointing to Montague) to visit her, alone. Disappointed, they agreed.

Gwendolyn told Montague that they would wait for him in the

hospital cafeteria, and that he should take all the time that he wanted. He seemed grateful, but emotionally exhausted, kissing Gwendolyn on both cheeks, before taking Zack's hand to shake it repeatedly. Zack wondered how the professor would have survived the night, had they not been with him. The professor started to walk away, then, surprised them, by returning to give Zack a bear hug. Gwendolyn thought that she detected a tear in the old man's eyes.

They waited and watched as the professor followed the doctor down the hallway. There was a decidedly happy click to his heels, as he rushed to catch up. Whatever lay in store for Montague and Mara, it seemed all good, at least, for the professor. Zack hoped that Mara would feel the same way. Certainly, she had found a true and loyal friend in the old man. He wanted to believe that the young woman would appreciate how lucky she was to have him in her life.

Gwendolyn said that she hoped Mara's lack of maturity would not cause her to take the gift of Montague's friendship lightly, or the responsibilities of motherhood. Only time would tell, Zack responded, poetically. Mara's track record, up to now, had not been impressive, but then, she was so young. He remembered that his own history was much worse. It was easy to judge others, when one ignored his own mistakes. It seemed that Gwendolyn was being unduly hard on Mara, and when she refused to drop the subject, Zack did not find this to be one of Gwendolyn's finer moments.

Gwendolyn tugged at his arm. "Coffee?" she asked.

"Yes," Zack answered. It was going to be a long night.

Gwendolyn added, as enticement, "Later, we will go to the nursery to meet Maurice."

Zack corrected her, "Maurice Montague."

Gwendolyn said, "I prefer the name Monty. How about you?"

"Yes," Zack said, taking one more look down the hall at the professor, who was nearly out of sight. "Monty is an ok name."

"Can we talk, now?" Gwendolyn asked, wanting to change the subject to something more serious and closer to home. She wanted to talk about their relationship. It was her biological clock that was ticking, and if she were ever to have children, she had to have a cooperative partner. Zack was readily available for sex, but was he willing to take it to the next step? She had to find out.

"Talk about what?" Zack asked, totally unaware.

Chapter 17

L ittle Monty was nearly a week old, when he and mother Mara returned home from the hospital. The fat little bundle was recovering from a little jaundice, and Mara, from the caesarian. Their conditions did not prevent a parade of visitors from dropping by for the first two days. Zack and Gwendolyn had brought gifts, and left Mara and Monty in the capable hands of Montague, who had set up a temporary camp next to Mara's bed, so that he could assist her with lifting the baby during the night for breast feedings. Amazingly, for someone who had lived most of his life alone, he had become a natural in the new role of surrogate father.

Fulfilling Zack's hopes, Mara was more than grateful to Montague for his help, as her parents had put in only a temporary appearance, and were not expected to stay in Paris more than a day or two. Zack and Gwendolyn dropped by a second time, long enough to meet them. Mara did not ask them about Phillipe, and her parents did not offer any information as to his whereabouts.

Once they were back in her apartment, Gwendolyn felt compelled to mention the elephant in the room. Zack said that it was for the best, if Phillipe never became involved in his son's life. He had never liked the boyfriend, although, he had never met him. Based upon the professor's opinion, he never wanted to meet the bastard. Gwendolyn noted, during the past week, Zack had referred to Phillipe as the baby's father several times. She took this as good news, and was much relieved that Zack seemed content to let Montague do the parenting upstairs. Now, she and Zack were free to move forward in their relationship, without any unnecessary entanglements.

Sunday dawned with a grey overcast that hid the sun, making Zack think that it must be much earlier than the time on the alarm clock. He rolled over and saw that the other side of the bed was empty. Reaching out, he found the sheets cold. Gwendolyn must have gotten up early, he thought, yawning and stretching. Instead of getting up to join her, he pulled the covers closer around his neck, and listened for sounds of her movement in the apartment. Not eager to leave the warm side of the bed, he waited for the familiar sound of the coffee maker and the shower. He was just on the edge of REM sleep, when the apartment door opened. Popping directly up out of bed, and hitting cold air, he realized he was naked. He pulled a bed pillow over in front of him.

Gwendolyn laughed, heartily. "Well, good morning!" she chirped, happily, shaking the rain off her umbrella, and setting it in a wastebasket in the corner by the door. She set down her shopping bag to take off her rain slicker.

"Rain?" Zack asked, leaning over to look out the window.

"A bit. Nothing serious. Looks like it will be over by noon." Gwendolyn said, taking her bag to the kitchen to unload. She had picked up croissants, a baguette, a newspaper, and a bottle of orange juice. "Hungry?" she asked.

"Always," Zack said, reaching out to grab Gwendolyn's hand. "For you."

Gwendolyn put down the orange juice, and fell into bed, laughing. "I love you, Zack."

Yikes! The "L" word. Zack knew what should come next, especially after last night; especially after their hour-long discussion about his feelings for Mara, but he had not yet said, "I love you" to Gwen. Other than family, he had never said it to anyone, but his girlfriend at university, and then, it had ended badly. They had broken up within a matter of days. No. No good could come from saying the "L" word. He swore not to say it, again, until he knew for certain, and he was certain that day was not today.

The wait was monumental. The change on her face was heartbreaking, and so he found the courage to say what she expected, but which he did not feel. What was another lie, after so many? "I love you, too," he said, swallowing the words, and wishing that he had not been forced to say anything. Her sigh, the breath that she had been holding in, was heavy. She grabbed onto him, and held on as though she would never let go...ever. (Yikes!)

Then, something strange happened. Their lovemaking was wonderful, unexpected. He found himself enjoying a wild abandonment of all of the rules. Gwendolyn had become an entirely different woman. Wild. Wonderful. Was this the result of having heard the words, which he had withheld for years, while waiting for the right woman? Was this proof that Gwendolyn was that right woman? Maybe?

Much like the relationship, which was being tested upstairs between Mara and Montague, only time would tell about this one with Gwendolyn. If making love daily was part of the test, he could live with indecision a little bit longer. Gwendolyn seemed sure enough for both of them, and he had found her to be a woman, who was right about most things. Certainly, Gwendolyn had been right about Mara and Montague. She had assured him at the hospital that the two of them would work out whatever they needed in order to be happy.

It would take a few more days for Gwendolyn to confront him with her fears, but when she did, he would reassure her that he felt nothing more than friendship for Mara. Gratitude, really, he said. After all, Mara had taken him in while knowing very little about him. She had made a leap of faith; given him a chance to live in the neighborhood of his dreams; and even thrown in one-month free rent. Ok. So, maybe, Mara had been a little reckless in that regard, but hadn't she (Gwen) ever been reckless, when she was younger? No, he wasn't in love with Mara, insisting that she was not his type. Besides, they had only a few days together, before Mara had taken off with Phillipe.

Gwendolyn made the mistake of asking "what type" she was. Just like wanting him to say, "I love you," she had put him on the spot. He had not wanted to tell her the truth, especially, not the part about - how he hadn't found her at all attractive...at first; that it was only after they had shared a couple of dinners, and her sense of humor emerged, that he had found her to be his type. Nothing came out the way in which he intended.

She tried to see through his awkwardness and discomfort, to recapture the good she had seen in his compassionate heart, but under the circumstances, it was difficult for her not to be offended. Zack was not exactly the romantic type with whom she had envisioned sharing her life. But, yes, they did share a similar sense of humor. Was this enough?

"If this is how you feel about the people you love," she said, trying to express the whimsy, which he had said he admired, "I'd hate to hear what you think about the people you hate."

They both laughed, uncomfortably, and what came out of their mouths sounded more than odd. It was downright unnatural. Neither was fooled into thinking there was anything funny about Zack's explanation, or Gwendolyn's forced joke.

Zack felt the overwhelming need to apologize. "Hate is an awful strong word. Maybe, it's because I'm a writer, but I try to never use it." He was fidgeting. "Look," he started, "I like you a lot…"

Gwendolyn interrupted, "Like? When did love fall off the table?" She was, instantly, angry and hurt. "Or should I say…the bed?" She got up, crossed her arms, and paced, angrily.

Zack hadn't seen it coming, and he defended his words, "I do care about you Gwendolyn, but I hate using the word love because people throw it around like it means nothing. It means something to me, and I believe it means something to you. I believe you, when you say that you love me, but the truth of the matter is you haven't been around me long enough to be saying this. You don't know me, and I don't know you - really. If I did, I would have known that you had these feelings. You have to give me more time."

Gwendolyn did not respond. She lowered her face, staring at a scratch on the floor. Zack imagined that she was either, about to cry, or she was calculating the cost of the repair. He had been responsible for the damage, and certainly, this would influence the next words out of her mouth.

But, when she remained silent, he continued to fill the hollowness because it was his nature to do so. "I haven't been in a relationship for years. Maybe…" He thought it better not to discuss past relationships at a time like this. It was best. "Never one like this," he salvaged the moment. "You and I have known each other what? A few months at most? You have to give me time."

Gwendolyn, still fuming, was struggling to reconsider his words, but it was too late. Her mind was made up. "I can give you all the time you like, Zack - just not here, not sharing my apartment. I thought we had an understanding. Evidently, I was mistaken." She could no longer look at him, when she coldly announced, "You should pack, now."

And there is was - his eviction notice. He couldn't move back in with Mara, and now, Gwendolyn was throwing him out. Where next? He, too, was hurt, angry, but he had been willing to work through it with her. He had trusted Gwendolyn to be different from the other women he had met. But, no, she was just as unpredictable as were all of the others. Hers appeared to be a very short fuse. Funny. She had given him no clues, no warning shots. Was that a British thing? Or just a Gwendolyn thing?

Why couldn't women understand him? Why was the word love always getting in the way? It seemed that women heard only what they wanted to hear, and ignored the rest.

He packed quickly, certain of only one thing. Gwendolyn was not going to change her mind, at least, not any time soon, and not today. Passing the window, he pulled back the curtain and checked on the weather. The rain had stopped. He tried to hold onto one good thought, that if this was going happen, at least, she had thrown him out in the daylight, and on a day when the temperature was warm. If worse came to worse, he could sleep in the park. The nighttime temperature was above freezing. He wouldn't die, at least, not right away.

He looked around the apartment, shoved a few more things into his suitcase and an old backpack, and then, dug a pillowcase out of the dirty laundry.

Gwendolyn could not ignore his hurry. It only served to feed her frustration and anger. "Why don't you just leave and I can do that for you, later," she offered.

Women had thrown him out, before, but none had generously offered to pack his clothes. Should he trust her? "You know, I'll have to find a place to stay. Can I just leave this stuff in a corner for a while? You know...until I find something." Zack said, making an attempt to appear helpless. Perhaps, it would play upon her sympathies, and she would change her mind.

The expression on her face was not a happy one, but even she could see that this was happening all too fast for Zack to cope. He seized upon the fact that she was wavering. Maybe, she was not so certain that she wanted him to leave. "I promise, I'll find a place today, although, it will probably be a hotel."

He was waiting for a crack in her resolve, as he went to the bathroom to retrieve his toiletries. He tossed them into a side pocket of the backpack, before zipping it shut. As he put one arm through straps, it was obvious, that he was stalling. Inside the backpack was enough for one, maybe two nights, away from here. He waited. If she were going to cave, it would be now.

It was slow in coming, but finally, she said, "You can leave your things, but I don't want you - staying here tonight. There's no point in dragging this out."

"Done," he said with some finality, trying to sound in control, trying to show her that he could live without her. He headed for the door, knowing that he could live without her, but not without a roof over his head for long. "I'll be back, sometime around five o'clock. Just don't throw my stuff out in the hallway... or the street," he added, attempting a farewell laugh to keep things light.

She held open the door for him, and stood in the doorway, arms crossed, glaring at him as he passed. This time, she was not laughing.

Chapter 18

ack was leaving the apartment building as Monsieur Le Spy was entering. The chance meeting was a rare occurrence, as Monsieur Le Spy did not move about much in the daylight. In fact, since moving into the building several months earlier, Zack had never been within twenty feet of the man. This was his first chance to take a closer look at the man, whom all the neighbors assumed was into espionage.

It was also an opportunity for Monsieur Le Spy to assess the American, and so, it began. Silently, each man stopped to imprint a mental picture of the other. To outsiders, the encounter might have seemed normal, but to Zack it felt very, very strange. The other villagers had told him so little about Dmitry, and this left much to his imagination.

In that moment lasting only a few seconds, standing face-to-face, Zack noted that Monsieur Le Spy was taller and larger. He had black hair and deep blue eyes, but it was his face, that was most remarkable. He carried an old scar, one impossible to hide, which cut across the eyebrow of his right eye and trailed down a third of his cheek. It also appeared, whatever weapon had created the wound, had also removed a tiny portion of his right earlobe. The flap of flesh ended in a sharp point.

Monsieur Le Spy surveyed Zack's face, as if he, too, were recording every detail for a report, which he might file later.

With whom? With which government agency? Zack wondered.

Then, their eyes met, and neither man could look away. Monsieur Le Spy's expressionless face gave Zack the shivers.

The professor had learned to keep his head down around Monsieur Le Spy, and not to speak. Once, in the hallway in the dark, the foreigner had asked Montague a question, scaring him half to death, and the professor had reacted by faking deafness to avoid answering.

Zack asked the professor what the question was, and he answered, "Why does everyone here order so many books, when there are bookstores everywhere in Paris?"

(So, he had been right, Zack thought, to think book deliveries - odd - in a city like Paris.)

Madeleine, too, had been uncomfortable around Monsieur Le Spy. Her suggestion to Zack, in their first conversation at her apartment, was that he might wish to avoid the man, who lived above her, as that person was not particularly friendly. In her diplomatic way, she was telling Zack that Monsieur Le Spy was not one of them. Zack felt that at this moment, he understood exactly what Mara and Madeleine had been trying to tell him. Something about the man exuded danger.

Was it his cologne? Zack sneezed loudly and unexpectedly. The man took a step backwards. Zack, unlike the professor, could not pretend he was deaf. Even the birds, flying from the branches above his head, had heard his sneeze. Those flying by were knocked off course.

Monsieur Le Spy said, "Hello," in perfect English, stopping Zack's thoughts, and bringing his eyes up to meet another direct stare. The stranger's eyes were so deep a color of blue; they seemed limitless in their ability to see everything - clearly. The man wanted to engage Zack in conversation, and apparently, he was not about to move until Zack responded.

Zack studied the scar, which dominated his close-up view of the man's face, and nervously, he stuttered, "Hi."

"You are Zack," Monsieur Le Spy said, a statement, not a question.

It felt like the beginning of an interrogation, something along the lines of "Is that your car – illegally parked?" The memory from his New York days was suddenly vivid in his mind. He expected the next words to be, "Can I see your driver's license and your permit?" But, instead, Monsieur said, "Can I buy you a cup of coffee?"

Zack did not know what to say. His head was full of Gwendolyn, having just been kicked out of his only address in Paris. Having coffee with a man, who was not only a stranger, but a scary one, was not high on his list of priorities at the moment. Finding a place to rest his head before nightfall, was. Yet, he felt obligated. This man was also one of his neighbors, even if the others thought him capable of destroying the village. Zack owed it to Mara, to little Monty, to the professor, and

Madeleine, as well as the others, to find out what Monsieur Le Spy knew about them.

Was he really conducting espionage right under their noses? If so, how much had he learned about their secret truffle operation? If Zack had stumbled across it, quite by accident, surely someone as cunning and clever as an international spy had discovered it years ago. Maybe a better question would be "Why hadn't he reported it?" Perhaps, Zack could be the hero in this story, already, writing itself in his head. Perhaps, he could convince Monsieur Le Spy not to rat them out to the government, or to the police. Perhaps, Zack could find the words, which would fill the man's heart with compassion for the other people in the village, who had so far shown him none.

"Sure, OK." Zack said, attempting not to act intimidated.

Monsieur Le Spy smiled a cagey smile. Zack tried to read something into that, but the face was still too new, too foreign to decipher. They walked side-by-side down the street toward a familiar neighborhood café. Was this the place, where the man always drank his Sunday morning coffee, and why was it, that he had never seen him there?

Monsieur Le Spy entered, signaled to the waiter, who seemed to know him, confirming Zack's suspicions. Zack followed him to a booth in the back corner, where his intriguing host could watch every corner of the room, in addition to the foot traffic outside on the sidewalk. A mirror to his left gave him the added advantage of seeing anyone, who might be walking toward him from behind the bar. A perfect place for a covert surveillance, Zack noted. The scene was exactly as he would have written it, if he wrote spy novels.

The waiter brought two cups of black coffee without being given the order by either man. A moment later, he came back with a plate of pastries. Zack wondered how the waiter knew that they took their coffee black. He, himself, had been in this particular café maybe six times, total. Maybe, the waiter had just gotten lucky. Or maybe, the waiter was psychic. Or maybe, the waiter just didn't care. All of his customers got coffee – black. If they didn't like it, they could leave. The only person, whom he seemed focused on pleasing, was Monsieur Le Spy.

Monsieur Le Spy stirred his coffee, although, he had added nothing to it. Zack couldn't take his eyes off the peculiar action, which caused his imagination to kick into high gear. What if, the waiter was a collaborator? What if, Monsieur had arranged for the waiter to put a drug in Zack's coffee? Was that why no cream or sugar had been offered? Did they want nothing to dilute the poison? Zack was not so anxious now to take a drink. He waited to see if his host would drink, first. But, that would not prove anything, he realized, and pushed his cup away a few inches.

"You do not like coffee?" Monsieur Le Spy asked, raising his hand to get the waiter's attention. "I will order you tea," he offered.

"No. No," Zack said. "Coffee is fine. I'm just not especially thirsty at the moment. Too much coffee already this morning," he added, an excuse, so as to spare his host's feelings. Just because he was a spy, it was no reason to be rude.

"Oh," was the man's response, sounding somewhat disappointed. Then, he offered, "Pastry?"

Zack thought. Yes, there's a drug in the coffee - definitely. Look at his face. Look at how disappointed he is. He was hoping to make me talk, but I will fool him, by going on the attack. "So, how long have you lived in Paris?" Good leading question, Zack, he told himself. Better than being on the defense. He, hungrily, eyed the pastries, while waiting for his answer. They looked delicious, and he was ever so tempted.

"Ten years," Monsieur Le Spy replied, without dropping a beat. "And you?"

A volley, quickly, fired back, Zack noted. Good shot. "Less than a year," Zack answered. "What do you do?" Wow. He amazed himself with a direct hit. Did he really expect the man to tell him the truth; to admit – "Yes, I'm a spy, and I've been spying on you and everyone else in this building. Nice work, but the pay if not so good."

"I'm an inspector," he said, without drama and without expectation of a favorable reaction.

The speed of his answer caught Zack off guard. "Inspector?" he repeated, then, asked, "a police inspector?"

This brought a smile to the man's face. "You might say that," he answered, now, being more cautious. He took a sip of coffee. Zack watched, as if expecting there to be a chemical reaction. Nothing happened. However, the smile had fueled Zack's suspicions. Monsieur Le Spy would tell him a little, but not enough to satisfy his curiosity, an obvious ploy to feed him only the answers that he wanted Zack to have, and to encourage Zack to give up more information. Well, it was working. "You married?" Zack asked.

"No," Monsieur said, with a finality that declared that some topics were off limits.

Zack said, as a friendly gesture, "Me neither..." Thinking of Gwendolyn for a split second, he added, "I may be off women forever." His wording was not well thought out, and evoked an image, which made Monsieur laugh, spontaneously, spitting out his coffee.

Drying himself off with his napkin, he was still laughing, when he replied, "Yes. I know what you mean." He lifted his hand to ask the waiter for more coffee. The waiter walked over, and Monsieur said, "Bring a fresh cup for my friend here. His coffee has gotten cold. Mine, as well." With that, the waiter took their cups away.

Zack was surprised. The laughter had changed the expression on Monsieur Le Spy's face, making it seem far less frightening. "Thank you," he said, first to Monsieur, and then, to the waiter, who was long gone. Could he have been wrong? Was there really nothing at all frightening about this man? Was he simply another foreigner, trying to find his place in Paris? Were they really so very different?

"What do you do for a living?" Monsieur asked Zack.

"I write," Zack answered.

"Write what?" He asked.

"Travel related articles for an online magazine," Zack answered.

"Oh," Monsieur responded, giving no indication if he was impressed, or uninterested. But, then, he said something, which Zack found profoundly curious. "I wrote," he said. "Perhaps, you've read something of mine."

"If I knew your name..." Zack said, not certain, if he should be embarrassed for not knowing his neighbor's name, after nearly a year of living in the same building.

"Dmitry," the man said, "but I wrote under a different name. Perhaps, you've heard the name Granville...Granville DeMonnay?"

Zack was stunned. He had read DeMonnay at university. It had been required reading. The man was a genius. A DeMonnay could keep him up all night, and had on several occasions. Once he had you hooked, you were hooked. A string of books, hit after hit, over several years, and then, suddenly nothing - had sparks rumors that

DeMonnay had died. Zack told Dmitry so, again, making the man laugh.

"Yes," he said, "I have read many reports of my demise. It seems a shame, that one day they will all be proved wrong. Such a disappointment for them, he joked. Such vivid imaginations, my readers have." Then, he added with a decidedly sad tone, "So ready to throw me in the ground." He punctuated his words with a deep sigh.

Zack was acting like an enamored schoolgirl, sitting on the edge of his chair, crossing one leg, and then, the other, as he eagerly hung onto Dmitry's every word. The moment was real, overflowing with emotion. He was here, in Paris, with one of his literary heroes, and the man was buying him a cup of coffee! It was as if he was someone deserving of breathing the same air. (Wow.) He felt that it should be the other way around. He should be buying Dmitry champagne. Wasn't that what DeMonnay's heroes in all of his books drank?

With the ice broken, they talked for hours. By afternoon, they had shared coffee, breakfast, and a dozen of Zack's ideas for new books by his favorite author. Dmitry had listened, politely, but in the end, insisted that his novelist days were over. As they were standing up to leave, Dmitry said, casually, that he was quite happy to be an anonymous inspector in Paris. Zack had forgotten about his new friend's profession, as he had been too wrapped up in the previous one, which the author had abandoned.

"What is it that you inspect?" Zack asked.

"Restaurants," Dmitry answered.

"Really?" Zack asked with his mind racing ahead. It explained a lot of things; why the waiter already knew what Dmitry wanted, before he sat down; why the service they received had been so conscientious; and why they had been allowed to sit at the best table in the place. Hanging out with Dmitry could have all sorts of benefits in Paris.

Zack imagined the two of them, dining in all the best places, discussing bestsellers, and becoming the best of friends. If only, he could convince the other residents that Dmitry was not a real threat to their secret operation. But, the truffle operation had never been brought up, by either of them, and so, there was no way of telling whose side Dmitry would take – that of the truffle thieves, or that of the government. Dare he tell Dmitry about his neighbors? No. He could not. Maybe the other villagers were being paranoid. Maybe their secret was safe.

Then, Dmitry surprised Zack with another invitation. "Would you like to join me on today's inspection?"

Had the invitation come from anyone else, it would have sounded boring. Inspect kitchens in Paris? Eat the food? Yes! Sample the pastries? Of course! Imbibe a new vintage? You bet! But, inspect refrigerators, meat lockers...dirty garbage cans? No thanks. However, Zack could not resist an offer to spend more time with the famous, reclusive author. He would have accepted an invitation to accompany the great Granville DeMonnay to the garbage dump to count rats. They started walking in the direction of the Métro.

"Which arrondissement?" Zack asked, casually

"Sixteenth," Dmitry answered.

"Wow." Zack replied. It was where rich people dined.

"Yes...wow," Dmitry noted. "You wouldn't believe their kitchens." He coughed a deep hoarse cough. "Then, again, that's a matter for the health department. I only inspect their food." He coughed again, then, apologized. "Allergies," he explained. "Always bad in the spring."

"Mine, too," Zack said, delighted that they shared a common malady. "Mostly mold and pollen, but also some other things. Like, for instance, I can't eat mushrooms," he added. "Imagine that, being in Paris, and not able to eat a mushroom quiche, or a mushroom omelet. Sad... really." Zack kept walking.

Dmitry stopped and looked at Zack. "Do you sneeze in your apartment?"

(Ooops!) Zack had almost let the cat out of the bag. "Ah...yeah, sometimes," he admitted. "I had a plumbing problem," he offered as the reason, "and mold on the bathroom floor." Then, as if that were not enough, he added, "and in the kitchen." He waited to see if Dmitry had accepted his cover up.

Dmitry studied Zack's face, as if Dmitry was weighing the truthfulness of Zack's words. There was an uncomfortable silence, before Dmitry shrugged. "Yes, maybe that's it. I had a leak last year, too. The tourists in the attic left the shower on too long. It happens."

It seemed that the moment of danger had passed, and so Zack relaxed until he heard, "It seems worse at home than anywhere else I go." Zack gulped hard, just as Dmitry moved on to another subject. "But, you can eat onions. Right?"

"Yes," Zack said, "Thank goodness."

"Yes. Thank goodness," Dmitry agreed. "In France, you would die, if you could not eat onions."

"Garlic, too," Zack said, happy to discuss anything else. "I mean, I can eat garlic, radishes..." Zack listed an entire grocery list of vegetables, before he could stop talking. A guilty conscience did that to him.

By dinnertime, he and Dmitry, truly, had become buddies, able to laugh at just about anything. He had asked a million questions about a million things, and Dmitry had been patient with him. Almost all were about the books, which Granville DeMonnay had written.

However, Dmitry's priorities were different, and he was far more interested in talking about the two restaurants, which he had just inspected on their busiest day of the week. Owners had nearly wet their pants, when they saw him coming in the front door. No one even bothered to ask who Zack was, or why he was accompanying Dmitry.

Everywhere they went, people cooperated, visibly afraid that one wrong move might result in the restaurant being shut down. All feared their place of work might acquire the dreaded notice posted on the door, the equivalent of a "Do Not Eat Here Ever Again!" billboard. Zack was duly impressed with the power that Dmitry could wield just by his presence at the door. Restaurant owners, apparently, had recognized him from previous inspections.

Of course, too, it helped that Dmitry looked like a thug from a 1940's Hollywood film, and not the run-of-the-mill product inspector. The scar across his cheek, his thick black hair and eyebrows, and the black raincoat added to his sinister demeanor. It was not his fault he looked like the quintessential bad guy. Then, again, maybe that was the reason the French government had hired him, over one of their countrymen. With Dmitry's appearance and deep baritone voice, no one was going to refuse him entry. No one.

Zack, by contrast, in his jeans and grey university tee shirt, looked like a lost concert groupie, someone hanging around backstage, waiting to be told where to stand and what to do. He wished that he, too, had Dmitry's affect on strangers. Watching his hero had instilled both admiration and envy. He loved the way Dmitry's very presence in a doorway could clear a path across the room. Twice, waiters had fallen over each other to get out of his way.

Even in the 16ᵗʰ Arrondissement, where money could buy influence, grown men trembled before the product inspector. It was awesome to watch. When his work was done, Dmitry turned to Zack, and chirped cheerfully, "Dinner?" How could he refuse? For Zack, it had been the most exciting day of his life, the equivalent of hanging out with Hemingway. Dmitry led them to a small café, around the corner from the last restaurant inspection, saying - this was a place where he ate regularly. Zack noted that it lacked the pretense and décor of the last place, but offered instead, a warm, family atmosphere.

Inside, there were only four other people having an early dinner. Strangely – no one attempted to dive under tables to get out of Dmitry's way, nor did they act in any other way intimidated. A man in the kitchen looked out, waved, but there was no bowing, no groveling as Zack had witnessed earlier in the other restaurants. This place specialized in Russian cuisine. Dmitry commented that the cooking was almost as good as his mother's.

After a plate of appetizers had arrived and disappeared, Zack had to agree. It was about the best food that he had eaten, ever, in Paris. If what was to follow was anything like the first course, he anticipated this was going to be a great meal.

"So, then," Zack said, "You are Russian? Like your biography reads?"

"Yes," Dmitry answered. "Are you surprised?"

"Yes and no. I mean, your book covers said, where you were born, but you do not have much of a Russian accent," Zack said. "Your English is perfect."

"I studied your American language," Dmitry answered. This time he spoke with a heavy Russian accent, to amuse Zack.

Zack laughed. "Yes. It's not quite the Queen's English is it? What other languages do speak?"

Dmitry ordered a vodka and ice, before continuing. "You?" he offered a glass. Zack shook his head. Dmitry continued, "I studied five languages, but now, I use only one. French. However, I enjoy speaking American with you. You give me practice. How many languages do you speak? I hear you speak French, but you are not very good. Why?" he asked.

Zack could not lie. "Too lazy to take lessons," he admitted, a bit embarrassed. "I studied Spanish, but only so I can order Mexican food."

Dmitry shook his head, then, laughed. "You come to a country to live, but you do not study the language. So typical. Yes. You should not be so lazy. French is a good language to know. We use it a lot in former Soviet Union, almost as much as Russian." He threw back another glass of vodka, draining the glass.

Zack was fascinated with every aspect of Dmitry's life. He was flattered that the man, who had been a stranger less than a day earlier, was now so open, and so gregarious. His thoughts wandered. Gwendolyn would not believe...

"Oh, No!" Zack said, jumping up, panicked. He had forgotten about Gwendolyn, and about finding a place to live. Yikes! "I have to go. I'm sorry...I"

"Go where, my friend?" Dmitry said, interrupting, and confused by Zack's sudden change. "Sit. Dinner is coming."

"My stuff is at Gwendolyn's place," he said. "If I'm not back there by five o'clock..."

Dmitry reached up and grabbed Zack's wrist. "Sit down, my friend," he said, pulling Zack back into his chair, and then, calmly, tapping his watch. "It's six o'clock." Seeing the look on Zack's face, he added with a calm and reassuring manner, "Your Gwendolyn will not throw your things in the street. Trust me. I know women."

Zack slumped, looking sheepishly embarrassed. "How did you know?" Had Dmitry heard him asking Gwendolyn not to throw his things out? Had Dmitry been spying on them from his apartment down the hall? Or through the keyhole? Or from an air duct?

"I know a lot of things," Dmitry said, almost smugly, touching the side of his nose. "I know more than you think I know." Dmitry signaled the waiter for a second glass. When it arrived, he filled it with vodka, and shoved it across the table at Zack. "Sit. Drink." Dmitry insisted, "You have all the time in the world, my friend."

Sure. Why wouldn't Dmitry have spied on his neighbors? Zack did. It did not make him a spy – nosy, maybe. Rude, sure. But, not a spy. Slowly, Zack slunk down even further, and stared into his glass of vodka, unsure whether or not he should drink it.

Dmitry showed him his wristwatch, again, confirming that it was after six o'clock. "Too late for your woman," he laughed. "But for us, the night is young!"

This time, it was Zack, who threw back the entire glass of vodka. Gwendolyn was already furious. Zack coughed, unused to the taste of vodka. Dmitry laughed, clicking his glass against Zack's. "Za vas!" was quickly followed by, "So...now, we talk."

The evening went by quickly. Four rounds of vodkas were intermixed with four courses of Russian food. Zack could not remember when he had eaten so well, or so much. But, of course, Zack, whose limit was two glasses of wine, could not remember very much at all. The liquor had worked its magic on his head, leaving him no idea of what had escaped his lips. Had any of it made sense?

In the morning, he was still dressed, but he was lying on a wood floor, which he did not recognize. He had vague memories of the taxi ride back to the apartment building, but no memory of crawling up the stairs from the first floor to the third. His eyeballs, actually, hurt. Even, his eyelashes hurt. Was that possible? And there was that decidedly acrid odor to his breath. Somehow, his teeth had grown fur. Yes. His tongue ran back and forth over them, confirming it..

When he could open his eyes, they were focused on two naked big toes, standing at attention only inches away from his head, and he was fairly certain that they were not his. Worse still was their odor, which increased with his awareness of what they were, and where he was. Pushing himself up on his elbows, his field of vision widened to include the rest of the body lying on the floor. Dmitry was on his back, snoring at a volume level that could have awakened the dead for about three blocks.

Zack's head was about to explode from the concussion of each breath that Dmitry took, and the strange animal sounds, which followed. Zack tried to stand, but found his first attempt unsuccessful. Another attempt had him grabbing onto a chair with one hand, and pushing up from the floor with the other. Eventually, he wobbled into a tentatively vertical stance, but the room was spinning wildly, and the net impact of his effort was to wish for the floor, again.

The change in altitude also made him aware that the contents of his stomach did not appreciate being disturbed. Zack looked around for a solution to the problem. Finding the toilet was not difficult, nor was falling down on his knees. However, avoiding vomit on the floor of a stranger's bathroom was. After three rounds of purging the best meal in all of Paris, and resting his head on the toilet rim, he remembered that he and Dmitry were no longer strangers.

What they had become, based upon the past few hours, was brothers in a weirdly, wonderful fraternity. The evening had turned into some sort of hazing exercise. Had Dmitry, intentionally, gotten him drunk? What would be the point? Dmitry was still passed out, evidence that he had gotten equally wasted. Zack worried, if earlier, he might have purged something more deadly, like the villagers' secret. Perhaps, he had spilled his guts about them with the same generous spirit, dispatching what was left of his dinner. The thought only made Zack want to vomit more.

How could he betray his new friends? How could he have been so careless? Zack's stomach took over, causing him to wretch, until his mind could not concentrate on anything else. Between bouts of dry heaves, he glanced back into the room to check on Dmitry, but his host was still out cold, and apparently, no amount of noise was going to disturb him. Zack washed up; first, himself, and then, the bathroom. It was the least that he could do. He also found aspirin, and swallowed two, before returning to lie on the sofa.

The apartment was eerily quiet, causing him to stare intently at Dmitry on the floor, first - to make certain that he was still breathing, and then, to make certain that he was not awake. Zack wanted a moment to search the apartment. He had to find something, which could verify Dmitry's identity. He wanted, desperately, to believe that Dmitry was, indeed, Granville DeMonnay, but there was that lingering doubt. Dmitry had been convincing, but Zack could not believe his good fortune in finding the reclusive author. There had to be something here, a passport, a driver's license, something remaining from his previous life. A school yearbook? Something...

Zack stood up, steadied his balance on an earth still off its axis, and took a few soft steps in the direction of Dmitry's nightstand. The picture of a beautiful woman was set next to lamp. Zack picked it up, and read on the bottom right hand side:

"Love, Always, Yvonne."

The woman was dressed like a movie star, and it would not have surprised Zack, if the picture had come with the frame. The photograph was too professionally produced. Then, again, Dmitry was a very interesting man. Who was he to say that the Russian did not know women, who were movie stars? Even if it were a studio shot, she might have given it to Dmitry, after a night of passion. Zack's imagination engaged. Dmitry had a rough-cut sort of sexiness about him. He could see that some women would find that attractive.

Putting down the framed photograph, he knocked a pair of reading glasses off the edge of the nightstand. Miraculously, he reached out and caught them in mid air. Dmitry snorted, but was otherwise, unaware. Zack folded the glasses, before setting them down. Slowly, he slid open the drawer in the nightstand. It made the slightest squeak as it opened, causing him to glance back at Dmitry. Something inside the drawer caught, preventing it from sliding out further. Zack quietly struggled with it.

Of course, he could not close it, again. Leaving it in the half-open position would only condemn him as a thief, if Dmitry were to see it. In his attempt to return things back to normal, to hide his sin, every sound seemed magnified a hundred times. His headache was raging. Three more tries and the drawer shut with a decidedly loud POP. Dmitry mumbled something, and attempted to sit up.

Zack froze, scared half to death. Then, just as suddenly, Dmitry fell back with the force of a dead man. His head hit the floor so hard that Zack suspected Dmitry had knocked himself out. Zack walked over and stood above him, searching for signs of life and for signs of blood, afraid that his skull was cracked. Dmitry was breathing heavy, and there was no visible damage. Soon, his heavy breathing was replaced with loud snoring.

Now, the growls and snorts became comforting signs that Zack could resume his search, uninterrupted. He let his eyes conduct a quieter search, and he was rewarded, by spotting an envelope on the mantel. On closer examination, he could see that it was addressed to Dmitry. The return address was the surprise. It was from a B. Pennington in Long Beach, New York. The letter was twenty-years old!

For Dmitry to have kept a letter this long, and to have given it a prominent place on his mantel, it had to have great meaning. A long lost love? Zack was dying to open it and read it. He glanced back over his shoulder at the slumbering wooly mammoth on the floor, then, reached for the envelope. He had the two-page, handwritten letter out of the envelope, when Dmitry mumbled, "Where? Where is she?"

Dmitry was sitting up and rubbing his eyes. His thick black hair stood nearly straight up.

Zack hurriedly put the letter and envelope inside his shirt, before turning around to face his accuser. "She?" Zack asked, attempting to look innocent.

At the sound of Zack's voice, his head swiveled around, "Who?" he started to say, "Who are you?" but then, settled for, "Oh...you." He struggled to his feet, and Zack felt compelled to move over and assist him.

A blurry-eyed Dmitry stared at Zack's face, before accepting his hand. "Zack? Za?" he said, his accent now, clearly Russian.

Zack answered, "Yes. Zack," as he helped Dmitry to a temporary vertical position, before the half- sleep man stumbled toward the sofa, and fell onto it. He would try, again, later. Zack remained standing, wondering how in the world he was going to put the letter back into the envelope, and set it on the mantel without Dmitry's knowledge. "I guess we both had a little too much to drink last night," he said, forcing a laugh.

Dmitry rubbed his eyes, again, and then, scratched his whole face. With his eyes closed, his tongue appeared to be taking an inventory of his teeth. Then, he opened his eyes wide to look around the apartment. Zack eyes followed Dmitry's around the room, as he hoped that his host was not taking another inventory of the apartment. Perhaps, Dmitry had awakened, expecting to see that he had been robbed. Overnight guests had to be a rarity for this man.

Zack tried to imagine what Dmitry was seeing. Everything would look in order, at least, from this level. However, once Dmitry stood up, the missing letter would be obvious. He needed a diversion. "I could make us some coffee," Zack offered. "That is... if you have coffee."

"Hmmm." Dmitry yawned, pointing to a cabinet next to the sink. The coffee maker was set just below it. "You make. I sit. Ok?"

"Good idea," Zack said. Perhaps, making coffee would distract Dmitry's attention for a few minutes, and certainly, Dmitry did not appear capable of doing much more than just sitting at this point. Somehow, Zack would have to replace the envelope on the mantel, before he left the apartment. Surely, Dmitry would have to take a piss at some point. "Cups?" Zack asked. Dmitry pointed to another cabinet on the other side of the little efficiency kitchen. Zack found three, two small and one large. Giving Dmitry the larger one was a calculated choice. More coffee - greater affect on the bladder. At some point, the equation would tip in Zack's favor.

While waiting for the coffee to brew, Zack came back and sat on the floor, directly across from Dmitry, keeping his eyes focused on this side of the room, and away from the fireplace. "That was quite an evening," Zack said, hoping that Dmitry would want to discuss some of it, especially since, there was very little of it that Zack could remember past the main dish. Then, a sliver of a memory surfaced...a piece of chocolate cake, but that was about it. "Great dessert," he said, hoping it would inspire conversation.

Dmitry ran his tongue over his teeth, and swallowed a belch. "You drink like a woman." He thumped himself on the chest. "Not like me."

Zack grinned, not knowing what that expression meant, "Yeah, I guess I do. You, however, drink like a..." Zack could not risk insulting his host, by choosing the wrong word.

Dmitry grunted something that sounded like a laugh. "You were going to say Russian bear. People think all Russian bears drink too much," he added, "So do I, but I never saw a bear drink like you." He yawned and stretched. "Why do people say that? Russian bear." It was a question without an answer, so none was expected.

Zack saw that Dmitry was looking around the room, and so he, immediately, got up to get the coffee – afraid of what might follow, afraid that he might hear, "Where's my letter?" As he was pouring the coffee, he almost dropped the larger cup, when he heard...

"Where is..." Dmitry paused, and Zack froze. "...the woman?"

"Woman?" Zack asked, spinning around, confused. He spilled the coffee and had to set the two cups down to clean up his mess.

"The big woman with the big..." Dmitry was holding his hands out in front of his chest, indicating large breasts. "You know the one who followed us home?" He continued looking around the apartment, as if he expected her to jump out from behind a chair.

Zack walked over and handed Dmitry the large cup, before returning to his spot on the floor with his smaller one. "I don't remember any woman. Then, again, I don't remember how we got home."

Dmitry took a long sip of very hot coffee, which seemed to have no effect on his senses, then, leaned forward to speak to Zack in more of a whisper. "I think she stalks me," he said.

"Why?" Zack said, totally confused.

"I don't know," he said, shrugging. "Maybe she loves me," Dmitry confessed, but seeing Zack's face, he laughed. "Women. Who knows?"

Zack had no idea what had happened last night. There could have been an entire contingent of women, following them home, and he would not have been aware of it. Short of a lost weekend at a fraternity party, he had never been so drunk in all his life. "Oh," was all that he could say, as this was the first that he had heard of the woman. Or, if Dmitry had told him about her, the story was long forgotten. "Why would she do that?" Zack asked, again.

"Women," Dmitry said. "Why do any - do what they do?" He took a long slow drink of coffee this time. "I make water, now." With that, he jumped up from the sofa with the energy of a much younger man. It seemed that the coffee had done its trick.

Zack breathed a sigh of relief as the door on the W.C. closed. He jumped up, drew the letter and envelope out of his shirt, and put the letter back in the envelope. Just as quickly, he set it back on the mantel. He tried to appear cool, but he was sweating profusely as he moved back into his position on the floor, waiting, expecting Dmitry to reappear any moment.

But, when it became obvious, that Dmitry was not coming back soon, Zack's curiosity got the better of him. He popped up, and with two long steps, had the envelope in his hand. Nervously, he pulled the sides apart, and peered inside. He could read the first line of the letter. There it was, the confirmation that he needed.

The letter began, "Darling Dmitry, or should I say Granville? Thank you for an evening that I will..." He could see no further, but it was enough. His host was exactly who he had said he was, the great, Russian novelist, who had disappeared off the face of the earth twenty years earlier.

(Wow.) It was true.

Zack put the envelope back in place, and walked to the kitchen to refill his coffee cup, before returning to his place on the floor, content to have spent the night in the presence of literary greatness. Suddenly, Dmitry's feet were not so smelly, his snoring not so loud or annoying. No. Zack was in the presence of greatness, and with greatness came respect and forgiveness of sins, large and small. Zack breathed it all in, filling his lungs with historic reverence. Granville DeMonnay lived here in the disguise of a man, called Dmitry, his stand-in, his stunt double. With every snort and snore that Dmitry breathed out, Zack was breathing in Granville's DeMonnay's breath.

(Wow.)

Perhaps, this is how he would have felt, if he had met Hemingway in Paris all those many years before. Dmitry was no Hemingway, but then, Hemingway was no Dmitry. Zack began a conversation in his head between the literary giants, imagining what they might have discussed over Vodka and Pampushki. With Hemingway's love of potatoes, the two writers might have become great friends here in Paris. But, in some crazy twist of fate, Zack was being given that esteemed honor.

Dmitry stayed in the W.C. so long that Zack remembered that his own morning needs had not yet been met. He got up, stood on one foot, and then, the other. He moved to the window to admire the courtyard, which he had rarely seen. As the sprinkler for the flowers popped on, its subliminal message made him wish he were still welcome at Mara's, at Montague's, or even at Gwendolyn's – at least, long enough to use one of their toilets.

Guilt, also, kicked in. What had Gwendolyn thought, when he did not returned to her apartment as promised? Had she worried? Had it only fueled her anger? Would she take him back? They had made a connection. She had said, that she loved him, didn't she? And what did she know about love that he didn't? Didn't love mean forgiving people, when they screwed up?

His thoughts were interrupted by the flush, and a more pressing question. Could he make it to the bathroom in time? He muttered, "Excuse me," as he rushed passed Dmitry, and shut the door. Once inside, he realized that he really should have asked permission, but there are some things in life, which cannot wait for permission. This was one of them. It was so much easier to ask for forgiveness, than permission. Besides, he had already territorialized the bathroom in ways that he did not wish Dmitry to know. In real ways, he had created an intimate relationship with the space, earlier.

When he emerged, rested and relaxed, Dmitry was sitting on the sofa. His head was back against the cushions, and his eyes were closed. A half-drunk cup of coffee hung from his fingers, in a precarious position, short of spilling onto the sofa. Zack walked over softly and removed the cup, taking it back to the kitchen. He placed his cup, alongside of Dmitry's, in the sink, making a slight "ding."

"You leaving?" startled him. Dmitry was awake, again.

"Yeah," Zack said, looking around for his backpack, which had miraculously made it to Dmitry's place last night, although, he could not remember how. Zack picked it up and slung it onto one shoulder. "I should be going. Gotta find a place to live. Remember? I promised Gwendolyn that I would... yesterday." He looked embarrassed.

"Thanks for dinner," he said, heading towards the door. He stuck out his hand for Dmitry to shake as he passed the sofa. "I really enjoyed meeting you." Dmitry leaned forward, took Zack's hand, and shook it once, before falling back against the cushions. Neither man seemed to know how to express his feelings. Zack had enjoyed one of the best days, and possibly, nights of his life - if only, he could remember more of it, and it demanded a greater expression of gratitude. "Thanks, too, for letting me crash here last night," he added.

"Where will you go?" Dmitry asked.

"Don't know yet," Zack said. "A hotel, probably...until another apartment comes along." He looked at Dmitry, and realized that he really had no plan. Nothing. He was as worthless and as ill prepared for living in the real world, as Gwendolyn had declared in her fit of anger. He was condemned to live day-to-day, hoping for the best, and relying on the kindness of others. "Blanche Dubois had better survival skills than you!" She spit out the perfect ending to her tirade.

Gwendolyn wasn't the only one. His boss, Harrison, shared a similar opinion, and this would only make it harder to explain to him, why he had moved, especially, after bragging about the great place he had found, just down the street from other great writers. Harrison's comment was, "Good. Maybe some of it will rub off on you. You can use all the help you can get." Zack was working on his latest excuse for missing another deadline, when he heard...

"You can stay here," Dmitry said, somewhat hesitantly, "Until you find home," he qualified the offer. Fatigued, his accent had returned. "You can sleep on sofa," he said, patting it. "Ok. Not bed, but ok. Sometimes, I sleep here." Then, thinking that he might be sending the wrong signals, "But I have bed there," he added. "You – here. Me – there." It seemed important that they were both clear on the terms of his invitation.

Zack laughed. "And where would the woman with the large...." (Zack indicated breasts) "sleep?"

"You can have her!" Dmitry laughed. "She scares me."

They both laughed as Zack tossed his backpack on the floor, and sat down. "Thank you," he said in his most genuine voice.

"Looking for an apartment in Paris scares me."

ಶಿಂ೭ಾ
Chapter 19
ಶಿಂ೭ಾ

Hunger drew them out of Dmitry's cave, but the outside world was a bit too bright and loud for their ears. Silently, side-by-side, they walked back to the café, where Dmitry had led Zack for coffee. With a nod to the waiter, two black coffees magically appeared at the corner table. Having grown comfortable with each other's company, neither man felt obliged to speak - a welcomed silence for both.

Selfishly, Zack was breathing easier, knowing for the moment, he had a roof over his head. There seemed far less likelihood that a man, especially one who understood women the way that Dmitry did, would throw him out as quickly as Gwendolyn had. Dmitry had a long history with difficult women, and that offered the possibility of a sympathetic ear. Zack had spent the evening, listening to Dmitry's tales of woe and woman. These, amazingly, he could remember.

There had been Dominique, the French acrobat; Lorraine, the German diplomat; Katrya, the marine biologist; and of course, Varushka, who (Dmitry was convinced) was still stalking him, (although, he had not seen her in the daylight in years). It seemed to him that she slept in the daytime, only appearing in the shadows of his nights. The thought had occurred to Zack that Varushka was more of an apparition, perhaps, even a warm memory, than a threat. Zack had never found a woman quite like that, yet, but he had read about them. They stole your heart, and then, your soul, and somewhere in between – your sanity.

Dmitry had not, yet, revealed why he stopped writing, or why he had dropped out of sight for more than twenty years, but he did share a few details of his personal life. It included more than the long list of women, whom he had left alongside the road on his journey. Why the Russian had chosen him to hear these things was still a mystery.

He had not lied to Dmitry about being a writer. Shouldn't Dmitry be suspicious of another writer's motives, especially one still seeking fame and fortune for himself? Did Dmitry trust his stories would not be stolen or published by his young friend? Why? What made Zack so different? He was no one, really; nothing more than an internet blogger without much of a track record. Why would Dmitry trust that Zack would not tell the world, Granville DeMonnay was alive, reveal where he was living, or give away his alias?

By most media standards, this was a major scoop, one demanding a great deal of reward money. Dmitry already knew what Zack was getting paid for his Paris assignment. Yes, it was a faux pas in France to reveal your salary, but Dmitry had asked, and Zack had answered, seeing no reason to withhold the information. Dmitry had said, simply, "Hmmm. So little?" So, based upon that, Dmitry had to know that a chance to sell the "I found Granville DeMonnay" story represented big bucks to Zack.

Why wouldn't the young writer run with the story? Zack's curiosity demanded that he wait for the reason. Perhaps, in time, Dmitry would tell his whole story, not just throw him bits and pieces. Perhaps, (Zack fantasized), Dmitry would authorize him to write his long-awaited biography, a story sure to blow the lid off the twenty-year mystery. Zack already had a few titles in mind. *Alive and Well in a Paris Kitchen* was one. *On the Town with Granville* was another.

Of course, he would have to stop drinking to the point of amnesia, if he were to write anything at all. His memory was not that good, when he was sober. If he had to follow Dmitry around town every night, matching him drink for drink, he didn't have a hope of putting pen to paper.

Zack plunged into the biography, taking shape in his head. How would he begin Dmitry's story? How could he dramatize what he already knew? So far, his story was not especially mind-blowing, with the exception of the exotic women Dmitry had bedded. His last ten years had pretty much followed the course of an ordinary life.

As for his early years, the young Dmitry had not been a very good student. As was true of many geniuses, he had failed in the one area, where he would later excel – literature. In his motherland, where he had spent his youth, his self-worth had been gauged by his strength and achievements in sports. He had always been strong, able to lift an opponent twice his size, up and over his head, before slamming him down on a canvas. Wrestling had been his best sport.

However, the young Dmitry had been, also, an exceptional chess player, which made for a natural conflict. He called it mind over matter. As a boy, he was forced to balance his time between physical and mental tests, forced to decide, which would be more important later in life. He wanted the immediate validation that all young men wanted, and needed.

His wrestling coaches wanted him to train for the Olympics. His chess coach told him that he could become the best chess player in the world. Both told him that every match mattered, and no opponent was to be too easily dismissed.

"What did you do?" Zack had asked.

"Abandon both." He answered, flatly.

Zack noticed there was no apparent regret or sadness. "But, why?" Zack had to pursue it because he had never been that good at one thing, much less two. So, it was difficult to understand why anyone would walk away from becoming the best at something.

His best was, at best, only average.

Dmitry explained that he always had been plagued with self-doubt, especially, when faced with choices, and especially, when under pressure from others. Both of Dmitry's coaches disagreed. His record demonstrated that he had made splendid choices in competitions, almost always winning. But, the pressure was too much.

Dmitry spoke to Zack of the mental anguish, which he had experienced, silently. When too many people told him, what to do with his life, he panicked. He did not want to disappoint anyone. With a wrestling match and a chess match on the same day, he said, it became a simple choice. "I was only fifteen, when..." Dmitry continued, "I ... disappeared."

It was the most revealing chapter in Dmitry's saga, and Zack viewed it as the beginning of a lifelong pattern. When Granville DeMonnay's books became too popular, and he - too famous, it was easy to see that the pressure had become too much for Dmitry. Just as before, the boy – still inside the man – panicked. Dmitry dropped out of sight, dragging Granville DeMonnay, the author, with him.

As a boy of fifteen, Dmitry, had dropped out of everything that he could, school, home, but even that did not give him enough space and freedom. Soon, afterwards, he left Russia, which was not an easy task in those days. Lying about his name and age, he signed on as crew for a cargo vessel. In a place he had never been, somewhere near Finland, he made a decision that would change his life forever. Anticipating that he would be found out and shipped home, he jumped ship - literally.

"My real name is not Dmitry," Dmitry confessed. He could not look at Zack, when he confessed it.

"Wow," was all that Zack could say. Not only was Granville DeMonnay not Dmitry, Dmitry was not Granville, and to make things even more confusing - Dmitry was not even Dmitry. It was very intriguing. "Your real name?" Zack ventured.

"No, my young friend," Dmitry looked up and smiled, wagging his finger to make his point, "some things remain a secret. It is best."

"Then, why tell me?" Zack said, gathering up the courage to question his part in this unfolding mystery.

"I like you," Dmitry said, without emotion. "I have watched you for some time, with your little notebooks, and your writing alone in the park. I see you, trying to make yourself like the others. You try so hard to be Parisian, but I can see you wear your heart outside your shirt."

"You mean – on my sleeve," Zack corrected him, then, thought, "What an idiot I am! Correcting a famous writer?"

"Is ok," Dmitry said, seeing Zack's distress. "Yes. Heart on sleeve. You are correct. I was not good student."

Then, the real meaning of his words sunk in and Zack was stunned. The Russian had been watching him. Who else had Dmitry been watching in the building? What else had he learned? Did he know about his neighbors' truffle smuggling? He liked Dmitry, but he also liked his new friends in their village, and felt protective of them. He had to find out how much Dmitry knew, what he had heard, and especially, how much he had reported to the government.

After all, in his new life, Dmitry was a food inspector. He had to make routine reports to the government about anything affecting France's food supply. If he had observed illegal activities in restaurants, he was obligated to put that in his reports. Wasn't he?

Dmitry had been working in the business for ten years. Who better than him – knew what restaurants bought, and from whom? Had he been in some of the restaurants that were receiving the stolen booty? Did he examine every delivery? Was there a little truffle-sniffing dog in his government office, jerking at his leash for an opportunity like this?

Or was the threat even closer to home? Had Dmitry been watching the parade of bouquets, flowing daily from Mme. Christy's shop to restaurants and hotels all over Paris? How could he not see it? It happened every Monday morning. Ok. His apartment faced the courtyard, not the street. But, he must have observed something. Did he not have a keyhole with a direct view to the stairway?

Zack was a novice and already aware of far too much. No. Dmitry had to know more, much more. Zack was certain of it. The real question was, "Why hadn't Dmitry turned his neighbors over to the police?"

Rats! This was another mess. If Zack were to keep a roof over his head, he would have to keep his mouth shut about everything... and everyone. He could not reveal what he knew about the truffle smuggling to Dmitry, and he could not reveal what he knew about Dmitry to the truffle smugglers. It was a trap. Everywhere he turned, he seemed to fall further and further inside the web of lies.

"You watched me?" Zack said, hoping Dmitry would reveal more without being asked.

"I know you. I was not so very different from you...when I began writing. I, too, sat and observed people. I made my little notes," he said, "I kept a piece of paper, always, in my pocket here, here, and there," he said, mimicking Zack. "You do the same." He laughed. "I see you," he repeated, seeming to enjoy the discomfort it was creating for his guest.

"Yes," Zack said. "I'd be lost without them. I have a terrible memory," he admitted.

"So, get out your little notebook," Dmitry instructed him. "I have a story to tell you."

Zack was thrilled. Was Dmitry asking him what he imagined? Was Dmitry asking him to ghost write a new novel? (Wow. Wow.) It was all that Zack could imagine and hope for, a chance to work with the great Granville DeMonnay. He didn't even care if his name was on the cover, or in the credits. Just the experience of working with the man would be enough. (Take that!) Zack mumbled to his university English professor, the man who had said – "You'll never be a writer."

Zack unzipped his backpack and retrieved a tiny notebook, which up to now had been filled with notes for travel articles. Today, he would be graduating from internet travel blogs to writing a great novel. Today, he had a tutor, the best in the business. He sat down, pad and pencil in hand, and leaned forward, ready to capture Dmitry's every word.

Dmitry smiled, before beginning, slowly. "I, Granville DeMonnay, do solemnly swear this to be my last will and testament."

Zack gulped.

Chapter 20

wendolyn was closing her apartment door at the same time that Zack was opening Dmitry's. It was impossible for them not to meet. Zack could not close the door and pretend that he hadn't seen her. The expression on Gwendolyn's face was beyond surprise, and she was uncharacteristically speechless.

He stuttered out an amateurish attempt at being casual. "Oh...hello," he said, as if he hadn't been missing in action for three days; as if there had been no promise to pick up his belongings; and as if he had not heard her say, "Get out of my life." He saw that she was dressed in one of her conservative business suits, and toted a briefcase, instead of a purse.

She stared, wide-eyed past him, expecting to see Monsieur Le Spy standing behind him, but there was no one in the apartment, other than Zack.

Zack waited for her to say something, but she seemed frozen in place. "I guess I should explain," he began.

Gwendolyn watched as Zack closed the apartment door behind him, and took two steps in her direction. Still, she had nothing to say. Her face was laced with questions, like – "What were you doing in the spy's apartment?" or "Where have you been for three days?" But, she said nothing. Instead, Gwendolyn looked Zack up and down, which caused Zack to remember that he was still in the same clothes that he had been wearing when Gwendolyn tossed him out. She must be wondering about that, Zack told himself.

But, no, Gwendolyn was wondering how in the world Zack had made contact with Dmitry – when no one else in the building had managed to enter the spy's private world. What did this say about Zack? Had Zack been Dmitry's co-conspirator all along? Had he used his excuse of being a writer, to spy and gather information about the rest of them? Were he and Dmitry planning to rat them out to the police? Had Zack slept with her, just to get information?

Zack felt compelled to say something. "Job interview?"

Gwendolyn looked down, and suddenly, remembered where she was going. "Yes. Job interview," she repeated, nearly robotically. "Job interview." She glanced at her watch, and it created a time dilemma. She was late. Could she delay further, if her cooperation with Zack made the courts more lenient in their judgment of her? The job interview could wait a little longer. "Your stuff is right here," she offered, too cheerfully to be believed. "I can get it for you." She gave him no chance to refuse, setting down her briefcase, and unlocking the door before Zack could even respond.

Her overly friendly demeanor baffled him, but he was not about to refuse the opportunity to get his belongings out of her apartment. If their history was any indication, she could change her mind, quickly. He followed her to her door, but did not enter, waiting instead - until he saw, that she was having trouble carrying everything. "Here," he said, "Let me give you a hand." As he took his things from Gwendolyn, she stared at him as if he were a complete stranger.

Back in her normal conservative mode of fashion, without makeup, Zack could see that she looked like the Gwendolyn, whom he had first met. There was no physical attraction whatsoever. Without her sense of humor showing, he wondered how they had ever transitioned to lovers.

He thanked her for keeping an eye on his stuff, as he stepped out into the hallway. She could barely speak, uttering a simple, "Of course. No problem." It was evident that she could not wait to get away from him. Upon seeing Zack pull a key to Dmitry's apartment out of his pocket, she practically ran down the stairs. No doubt, she would share what she had just seen with the others. Zack had not been merely visiting Dmitry, which would have been enough of a scandal. No! He, actually, was staying in Monsieur Le Spy's apartment!

Zack unlocked the door and put his things inside, before setting off for the day. Dmitry had left hours earlier, explaining that he was obligated to inspect three restaurants, and this would take him through the dinner hour. He would meet Zack, later, that night for drinks, or if Zack preferred, for gelato. "Your decision," Dmitry had said on his way out the door. "I do not drink every night," he added, as if Zack needed the reassurance. "Some nights, I eat only."

"Good idea," Zack said. "I write better – sober."

"I think better – drunk," Dmitry teased. "Maybe we make compromise." He laughed, heartily.

Zack liked the sound of Dmitry's voice, especially, his laughter. The man laughed the way he lived – at full throttle. He had been so wrong about Monsieur Le Spy, as Mara had nicknamed him. The man was actually a pussycat, although a gregarious one, but not at all frightening, when you got to know him. However, he could not share what he had learned with Gwendolyn, not with Mara, not even with the professor. They would have to continue thinking that Dmitry was a spy, or whatever else they wanted to think of the man. Apparently, Dmitry preferred it that way.

Dmitry had enjoyed anonymity for twenty years, the last ten of it here in Paris. He did not want anything to change about his lifestyle. That, however, did not stop him from wanting his story told. He had confided in Zack that his greatest fear was that he might die without anyone knowing the truth. So, he had watched Zack, to see if he might be the one, the man capable of telling his story, while keeping his secret. His autobiography could not be published until he was dead. That was the deal. If Zack could live with their agreement, to forego his own fame by not publishing until that fated day, then – Dmitry would tell him everything.

"Everything?" Zack asked, disbelieving his good fortune.

"Everything," Dmitry confirmed, but added as a reminder, "I might live a hundred years. I might outlive you."

Zack thought about that last sentence. He was young and healthy, at least twenty years younger. What were the chances? No. This was too good an offer, a once in a lifetime gift. Of course, he would agree. What fool wouldn't? "I'm willing to take that chance," he told Dmitry. He might have to wait some years for his moment in the sun, but it would be worth it. He would wait here in Paris, with Dmitry, hoping that the day would never come, but knowing that when it did, there would be champagne corks popping everywhere. The world would know that Granville DeMonnay had lived a long and wonderful life, playing out a marvelous joke on his most loyal readers.

Zack headed off for the park with his notebook in his shirt pocket, instead of his sleeve, the place where Dmitry had declared he wore his heart. He wanted to reread his notes on Granville DeMonnay. Only he would know that every word was true. Even if the notebook were stolen, no one would assume that these few coded words were anything more than academic research on a novelist long thought dead.

Prospects for his future - made Zack smile. Monsieur Le Spy, the great Granville DeMonnay, had confided in him, not anyone else. Him. It was as if Hemingway had said, "Zack, my boy. You're an OK egg. Now, pull up a chair, and let's talk."

Mme. Christy was coming out of the front door of her flower shop, as Zack was leaving the apartment building. He did what he always did, and waved. She lifted her hand, but he could see it in her face. Gwendolyn had gotten to her, and Madeleine stared at him as if seeing him for the first time. Zack smiled. It was strangely pleasurable, knowing that the others found him intriguing – perhaps, even a little dangerous - now that he had made friends with the one person in the building, whom they did not trust. Before, he imagined that they had found him boring. Suddenly, things had changed in his favor. Dmitry was the game changer.

That said, however, he did not want his new friends to distrust him, to freeze him out. No, somehow, he would have to fix this. Instead of heading for the park right away, he made a detour across the street. Madeleine seemed startled by his change of direction.

"Bonjour, Zack," she said, maintaining the air of friendship.

"Bonjour, Madame," Zack said. "Beautiful day, isn't it?"

"Yes. Beautiful," she said. "You look very happy today. Sleep well?"

"Yes," Zack said. "Very well." He liked this charade. Perhaps, he would continue it for a while, before telling her that Dmitry was no one to fear. Perhaps, he could leave it at that, and tell her nothing more.

They stood looking up at the sky, unable to make the change from the weather to another subject. Finally, Madeleine said, "I have to go inside. Flowers to arrange and deliver. You know?" She said, hoping that he would not bring up the truffles, which she had spent most of the morning stuffing into vases.

"Oh, yes. Of course," he said. "You have deliveries to make. I forgot," he added, as if what he knew about the truffle operation had completely skipped his mind. "I have writing to do. Deadlines, you know." He said, tapping on the notebook in his shirt pocket. He waited for her response.

"Of course," she said, bending over and pretending to clean the leaves from a pot of begonias on the sidewalk.

He moved on down the sidewalk in the direction of the Luxembourg Gardens, knowing full well that she was watching his back every step of the way. No doubt, she would tell the others, like Gwendolyn had told her. By night, everyone in the building would know that Zack was still living there, but this time, he had become the Russian's American "cousin."

He laughed at the thought. If he kept this up, by the end of his year in Paris, he could be related to everyone in the building, and the landlord would be none the wiser. All anyone outside of a private village saw of him was going in and coming out of the front door of the building. Where he slept at night, and in whose apartment, was only a matter for the villagers to decide. Already, he had been passed around three times, and his mailbox no longer had a number on it. Mara had seen to that change, thinking that he would want his own private box, now that he was no longer her cousin.

When Zack returned home several hours later, he was surprised to be met on the sidewalk by two American tourists, obviously moving into the apartment building. They announced, without being asked, that they were in Paris for two weeks, having rented the little holiday apartment in the attic for a ridiculous amount of money. They laughed at themselves for being so foolish, but could not hide that they were thrilled to be in Paris. Zack could relate.

The holiday apartment renters were a retired couple, in their mid-fifties, from California. Bill had been part of the dot.com generation, lucky enough to get out of the industry, while there was still money in his retirement account. Dorothy had been a legal secretary, and able to parlay twelve years of overtime into adequate retirement savings. Together, they had visited fourteen countries in six months. Paris was their last stop, they said, before they would be heading back to Napa.

Zack was surprised that holding a conversation in English was so satisfying. It was, also, the first time that he had started a conversation in French, only to transition to English. He was thinking now in French first, English second. To converse with Bill and Dorothy, he had to reverse this thinking process. What a surprise! Maybe taking a few French classes was a good idea, after all. He would look into it, when he wasn't so busy.

The Americans had brought with them to Paris - Pickles, a snarling, little rat-terrier. They had hidden him in a scarf-covered handbag, in case any of the neighbors might object to their traveling companion. Pickles made it known, immediately, that he objected to Zack. He expressed his discontent in staccato bursts of rapid barks, capable of piercing one's ears.

"He does not bark at night," Dorothy said in defense of their beloved pet. Bill confirmed it, afraid that two weeks with a dog in the building, might be a problem for Zack, or their other new neighbors.

Zack knew that a barking dog would be the least of the villagers' worries. He worried that the tourists would become too nosy. Strangers in the building for the next two weeks could only complicate the moving of truffles in and out of Tito's apartment. Anyone living in the attic would have to pass that particular apartment on the third floor. Anyone coming in and out of the truffle storage room might be seen.

They would have to come up with a system of signals. For two weeks, every movement would have to be carefully calculated, based upon the tourists' schedule. Zack wanted to ask Montague, "How were these matters handled in the past?" Did they simply ignore summer visitors? Or did they engage them in conversation to steer their activities away from the building at certain hours, when the truffles needed to be moved?

Zack walked into the building with the tourists, followed them up to the third floor, and directed them towards the attic stairway. He continued to listen to them, as they climbed the last, steep flight of stairs to the attic level. Their conversation consisted of a discussion on how to operate properly the key in the lock, and then, Dorothy's complaint that the ad didn't mention the lack of an elevator. Bill told her that they were lucky to find any place in Paris to rent, and that she should stop complaining all the time. Elevators were an American invention. Dorothy retorted that at these prices, the place should at least have an elevator.

Zack muffled a laugh, when he overheard her say, "Well, it better have a bathtub." Gwendolyn had already told him that the small studio barely had room for a toilet. The shower was improvised, next to it, providing about enough room for the dog. He had not heard the dog bark, not even once on the way to the attic, and so, he hoped that the wife's comment about Pickles sleeping through the night was correct.

Monty's crying in the middle of the night was enough noise. It had taken a few nights, but he had learned to adjust to it. After all, a baby, who would be living his whole life here, was to be tolerated by the other villagers. But, a yippy little dog, brought in by tourists, was another thing. Perhaps, the landlord hadn't known about the dog, when the tourists rented the attic. Zack suspected, probably, not. If he needed something to blackmail the visitors into silence – this was probably it.

He knocked on Montague's door. But, it was Mara's door, which opened. Montague was standing there, holding the baby in one arm. "Zack!" he said, as if they were long-lost friends. "Come in! Come in!" he said. Zack was surprised by the professor's cheerfulness in seeing him, and his lack of apprehension. Obviously, neither Gwendolyn, nor Madeleine had gotten to Montague with the news of his possible betrayal.

The professor put the half-asleep baby into the bassinet, secured Monty's ringed nipple in place, and chirped, "Beautiful boy. Sit. Can I get you something to drink?"

Zack sat down, and answered, "No, thanks. Where's Mara?"

"She went out. Gwendolyn called her with an invitation to meet for lunch. I insisted that she go. She hasn't been out, without him," (pointing to the baby) "since coming home from the hospital. It's good for the women to talk."

That was not what Zack was thinking. "In that case, I only have a few minute, but you and I need to talk."

Montague leaned in to listen, a response to the serious look on Zack's face. Zack told him that in the next few hours, perhaps...minutes, if Gwendolyn were quick about delivering her news...his friend would hear something that would upset him. He might hear that Zack had moved in with Monsieur Le Spy, but the professor was not to be concerned. Zack would not reveal anything that he knew about his neighbors. Their secret truffle operation would remain secret. What they did with their lives, how they chose to make a living... well, it was none of his business. He thought, he was doing the right thing by telling Montague this, but the result was not what he expected.

"None of your business?" Montague shouted a bit too loud for the baby. Monty cried, and instinctively, Montague picked him up to comfort him, before continuing. With the baby in his arms, Montague admonished Zack. "Of course, this is your business. You know. Therefore, you are one of us. You cannot go back to being...an outsider.

If you were to reveal anything to anyone, it would be.... indefensible!"

Again, his voice was too loud, and Monty cried.

"A secret is a secret," Zack whispered, so as not to disturb the baby. "But, really, I have nothing to do with...you know...truffle smuggling. I wouldn't know a truffle if I saw one, unless...it made me sneeze. I came here looking for an apartment. Tito just happened to die at the right time...No, I mean, the wrong time." Zack was stumbling all over himself, trying to extricate himself from the truffle smugglers, but also, from looking like a traitor.

His intent was to reassure Montague, to convince him that he would keep their secret. Montague was capable of convincing the others. "I need you to tell the others that it's OK. I'm cool with what is going on. And they can trust me. I know what I'm doing." Then, Zack told him that Dmitry was actually a very nice guy. "I like the man. He's not a policeman. He's not what you and the others think."

"A spy?" Montague said the word, flatly, definitively. He was visibly upset with Zack. "He's not one of us." Montague insisted.

"Because he's Russian?" Zack asked, innocently.

"Russian? You think that this has anything at all to do with where a person is born?" Montague sniffed, as if the mere hint of that sort of prejudice was insulting. "None of us care about this. We accepted you, didn't we? And you're an American!"

The way that Montague said it, implied that somehow Americans were lower on the list, than Russians were, in their potential for acceptance into French society. It was a curious note, which Zack would have recorded, if the moment had not been so precariously emotional for both of them. Maybe, it was because (as Dmitry had chastised him), Russians had taken the time to learn French, and learn it well, whereas Zack had not.

"Would you feel better about Dmitry, if he knew the truth?" Zack asked, again, ignorantly innocent of the implication.

Montague's eyebrows shot straight up. "Are you crazy?" he asked. "Tell Dmitry? Mon Dieu! The man is a restaurant inspector! Have you lost your mind?"

"Food inspector," Zack corrected the professor, who made no visible note of the difference. Zack could see that this was getting him nowhere, and Mara would be back soon with Gwendolyn's side of his story. Between the two women, they would find some way to make him out the bad guy. Women had a knack at doing that. Nothing was worse, than a woman scorned, unless it was two women – miffed.

From his reaction, Zack could see that Montague would be onboard with the women's opinion of their upstart American neighbor, who was too stupid to know he was messing with danger. In Mara and Gwendolyn's eyes, (for good reason), men could not be trusted. He had lived up to every fear that they had about men. He had broken promises, broken hearts, and so far, had not apologized for either. This one had betrayed them, just as they had anticipated. He had been selfish, and yes, arrogant. He had allowed his personal interests to take priority over the needs of his friends.

Now, he was only minutes away from losing his closest ally in the building, if he could not convince Montague, that none of it was true. He was not a traitor to the rest of them. What could he, possibly, say that would make the old professor believe him? What words would make him believe that he would do everything possible to protect the village? What would assure them, Dmitry could be trusted, if they decided to include him in their secret? Nothing, he could think of at this moment.

"You just have to trust me," he said, in desperation. There was simply nothing else to say. Dmitry had sworn him to secrecy with a shared vow of loyalty. Protect Dmitry, and he would get to write the man's story. Dmitry held not only Zack's financial future in his hands, but also his place in literary history.

Dmitry had said most of the people in Paris knew only that he was an inspector. Some did not even know - of what? "He works for the government," they might say. He preferred it that way. His ten years of anonymity in Paris had been his happiest. Here, he lived the life of a common man. That was precious to him, and Zack had to protect Dmitry, too.

Zack wanted to become famous; Dmitry wanted to remain unknown. The villagers feared becoming notorious. This was a difficult tightrope to walk for a young man, who knew nothing about the laws of France, the unwritten rules of a French village, or what constituted treason among friends.

Not only did Zack's friendship with Dmitry depend upon his ability to keep secrets, but also, his future as Dmitry's biographer. However, the future of the other villagers depended upon his resolve to keep their secrets, too. Could he walk this tightrope without falling? Why did he, always, have to be in the middle? Must he be the villain for one, in order to be the hero for the other? It wasn't fair.

"You should go," Montague said, with the baby once again asleep in his arms. "Mara will be back soon. I will tell her you stopped by. You have given me much to think about."

Zack could see that this was painful for the old man. He was wavering, and Zack hoped it was because Montague liked the young writer. "Can we have a drink tonight? You know, like old times?" Zack asked. "I could knock on your door around midnight."

"No. Not tonight," Montague said.

"Ok. When?" Zack persisted.

"Not tonight. I need time to think."

Gwendolyn had said much the same thing, when Zack had withdrawn his declaration of love. Did no one trust him? "Ok," Zack surrendered, as he stepped into the hallway. "Please don't worry about this. I promise, I won't say anything to anyone. Please. Tell the others." He looked directly into the old professor's eyes, when he said it. "I won't betray them. I won't betray you. I am your friend. You know that." Zack looked first at the baby, and then, at Montague, hoping it would be a reminder of their shared experience at the hospital.

Montague wanted to believe Zack. He liked the young American, but this was so much to trust to someone so young, so un-French, and so unlikely to keep his mouth shut – after one glass of wine. Zack could not hold his drink, not like a Frenchman, not even like an American. Montague wondered how in the world Zack had survived university life.

Should he ignore what he had already witnessed? During their late night drinking sessions, Zack talked nonstop. He had heard it all – the miserable relationship that Zack had with one woman for eight months, the near-miss engagement to another. Zack whined about not finding his place in the world; the reasons for coming to Paris in search of inspiration; and why he thought Gwendolyn was "sort of" interesting. No, Montague concluded. Zack was not one to be trusted. It was not the young man's fault, he was just young, and undisciplined - but that did not lessen the risk to the rest of them. Zack might jeopardize everything that they had worked seven long years to gain.

"You must go," Montague said, this time with regret. He would miss his late nights with Zack, but found comfort in thoughts of Mara and the baby. His life was fuller now. Perhaps, he would not need the midnight talks, as much as now. Zack would have to find someone else to listen to his miseries; tap someone else for inspiration for his stories. He felt compelled to add, "I'm sorry."

"Me, too," Zack said, standing in the doorway, and looking up at the old man, who had become so important in his life. He bit his lip, so not to cry. It was as if he were being blackballed from a secret fraternity. Had everyone else voted? Was there no one left, who would defend him? It seemed not. He turned, dejected, rejected, and uncertain of the path he would take from here.

Downstairs, there was Dmitry's apartment, but without Dmitry there, it was only another place to sit and stare. "No," he mumbled, as he passed the second floor on his way to the front door. There, he encountered only silent stares from Mme. Durand, Arness, and Berta. These women had been told. That much was obvious, but told by whom? Zack muttered a polite "Excusez-moi," and moved out the front door and into the streets, not sure of his destination.

Mme. Durand stood in the open door for a moment, watching to see which direction Zack walked, before returning to the other women. Zack did not have to turn around to know that they were huddled up, discussing what to do about the American. Somewhere else in Paris, Ivan would be calling Albert at work. They would discuss how to proceed, now, that Zack had chosen to remain an outsider. How soon should they expect the police to come storming into the building? Would it be better to take the women and children to the country to stay with relatives?

Zack imagined that the village, inside the wonderful building, in the perfect Paris neighborhood, might become a ghost town. Having once produced the equivalent of a gold rush, the illegal operation would be shut down, and the gold reserves moved. One by one, the villagers would disappear, not unlike Dmitry from Russia, and then...where would he go, when there was no longer a need for "the cousin?"

∞ↃↃ⇐⟐∞
Chapter 21
∞ↃↃ⇐⟐∞

M onsieur Zahhk," Bog said, touching Zack's sleeve as he sat, head bowed, on the park bench.

Zack had not seen the young boy approaching slowly from behind, nor see him stop at the edge of the bench to observe quietly his American friend. "Oh," Zack said, startled. He had been so lost in thought that the world around him had ceased to exist for the past hour and a half. "Bog. How are you, buddy?"

"What is buddy?" Bog asked, innocently, in his still newly acquired English.

"Friend. It means friend," Zack said as Bog smiled.

"Friend," Bog repeated, as he did with almost everything that Zack said. It was how he learned. "Friend. You mean ami?"

"Oui," Zack answered. "We are friends, aren't we?" he asked, not sure if Bog had been told anything of Zack's changing status in his village.

"Mais, oui!" (but, of course), Bog answered, cheerfully.

"You're probably my last friend," Zack said, glumly.

"Why sad?" Bog asked, confused by his friend's expression and words. Bog climbed up on the bench, and sat down. He reached up, placing a hand up as high as he could reach on Zack's shoulder. His friend needed comforting, and this was what he had seen his father do, when someone needed another person to listen. "Tell me," he said, and waited patiently.

Zack looked down at the little face, which held so much warmth in its innocence. How could he explain things to little Bog, in a way that would make sense to a child? Bog continued to smile and wait, as if there was nothing more important in the world - than this moment, and his friend, Zack. Zack broke into an unexpected smile. Children could cut through all of the nonsense and break problems down to their smallest common denominator.

What was wrong? Zack had never felt emotionally invested in anything before - as much as he was at this very moment. He needed to protect his friends, all of them. He really had grown to love each and every person in the village. It had not mattered, that they were different, older, younger, richer, poorer, smarter, dumber, better spoken, or silent. Each had his or her place in his life in Paris, and in his heart. Unfortunately, each had a secret to keep.

Never before, had he been trusted with so much responsibility. He was afraid he would let them done, just as they suspected he might. He did not want any of them to hate him. He wanted his place in the village and in their lives. He did not want to be exiled. He did not want his trustworthiness – doubted. It hurt. It hurt in a way, he had never experienced before, and he wanted the pain to go away.

"I like you, Monsieur Zahhk," little Bog finally said, as if he had been waiting for just such a moment to say it.

Zack leaned over, and put an arm around Bog, to tell him, "I like you, too, Bog. Let's go home. Your parents will be worried about where you are."

"OK!" Bog said, now content that his mission had been accomplished.

"Where are they?" Zack asked, casually, knowing that Bog rarely came to the park alone, and that surely, someone must be looking for him.

"Over there!" Bog pointed.

And there they were, Ivan and Berta, standing patiently in the shadows of the trees. They had been watching from a safe distance, but Zack had no idea why. As Zack and Bog approached, they both smiled. Tears filled Zack's eyes, as the warmth of their smiles filled his heart. Somehow, they had found it possible to trust their hearts. Zack was still their friend. Did the other villagers feel the same way?

"I found him, Mommy," little Bog said, happily taking his mother's hand.

"I see that," Berta said. "Come, we all go home, now." She turned, with her son in tow, and started walking back across the Luxembourg Gardens toward their neighborhood. Ivan stayed behind in an obvious ploy to speak to Zack, alone. Zack saw that there was more to be said and waited. "Przyjedziemy w jednej chwili" (We will come in a moment)

Ivan called out to his wife. "Ok?" he turned to ask of Zack.

"Of course," Zack, eagerly, agreed.

Ivan led Zack away in a different direction, further into the park, where there were less people. He stopped in the shadow of another tree. Zack waited to hear the verdict, which his jury of peers in the village, apparently, had given Ivan to deliver. Ivan reached out and placed a hand on Zack shoulder, grasping it tightly in his grip. Zack could feel the years of hard work, which endowed the hand with great strength. His bones ached under the force, but he did not dare move.

"You will not tell our secret to anyone," Ivan declared in a statement, not a threat. It was the confirmation of a decision reached by a majority of his neighbors.

Zack could not immediately respond. His mind was working overtime, asking too many questions. Would he ever know who had agreed, and who among them had objected? Were there others, who had abstained from voting? He searched Ivan's face, which provided no answers. Ivan was still smiling, as if he were expecting more of a response, but was willing to wait. When Zack felt Ivan's grip on his shoulder, finally, relax a little, he slumped. Relieved, he uttered, "Thank God," said, as much as a prayer of thanksgiving, as it was a reaction.

"Tak," Ivan agreed. "Thank God."

Zack wondered, "Who would have delivered the verdict had it gone the other way?" The postman? Marcel? Madeleine? Mara? - Who had been the one guilty of introducing him to the village? Or would he have been silently escorted from the building by all of them, collectively glaring, to oversee his belongings being thrown into the streets, and him, along with the luggage? That was the outcome, he had expected, but he could not be more grateful that his expectations were wrong. No doubt, there were other things, about which he had been wrong, as well. He was more than happy to accept punishment for his arrogance, as long as it did not include eviction.

"We go home, now," Ivan said, "and then, you move out of Dmitry's apartment."

Zack froze in mid-step. "Move out of Dmitry's?" he heard repeated in his head.

"That is a condition?" he asked.

"Yes," Ivan stopped, now frowning. "Is problem for you?"

"I will be the one to tell him?" Zack asked, afraid that there were other conditions to meet, other actions being taken behind his back, which might jeopardize his new relationship with his literary hero. Even as they were speaking, he worried that Dmitry was finding out things in a way, which might cause him to question Zack's loyalty. Had the villagers knocked on Dmitry's door, and demanded that the village wizard release his magical hold on Zack?

Zack was more anxious than ever to get back to the apartment. He looked at his watch. Yes. Dmitry might be returning home from work. He stared at Ivan, hopeful that his friend would accept his counter-proposal.

"Ok. You tell him, but you tell him tonight." Ivan left no room for negotiation.

"Ok," Zack agreed. "I will move out. I will tell him tonight." Zack took a step or two, but Ivan did not move. "What?"

"You tell him tonight and you move out tonight." Ivan said, unsure if Zack understood the importance of timing.

"Yes. Yes. I understand. I move out tonight." Zack said, forgetting in his eagerness to agree, that he had nowhere else to go. It was the start of tourist season, and a hotel room would be hard to find on such short notice.

Ivan seemed accepting of Zack's last response, and they walked back towards their neighborhood. Although, the closer they got to their street, Ivan had trouble, keeping pace with Zack. Zack it seemed was very anxious to speak to Dmitry, or perhaps, (Ivan hoped) Zack was eager to move out of Monsieur Le Spy's apartment. It would be best, best for Zack, best for everyone. Ivan was sure that, now, there would be no more trouble.

"After you talk with your..." (He did not want to think that Zack and Dmitry had become friends) "...him... you knock on my door." Ivan said, as if he could only now reveal the rest of Zack's instructions. "You tell me, it's done. You understand?" he asked, quite serious in his delivery of the message. This was not a request. It was a further condition.

Zack reluctantly agreed, "Ok. It might be late," he added. "Dmitry is working late." (That was not entirely a lie.)

Ivan smiled a knowing smile. Zack was buying time. "I will stay up late, tonight," he said, reassuringly. "Do not knock too loudly. Bog will be asleep."

Zack nodded.

They shook hands, to seal the agreement, and parted in the lobby, as Ivan had made the excuse he needed to check his mailbox. Zack walked slowly up the stairs to the third floor, but as he put the key into Dmitry's lock, he heard a door open downstairs on the first floor. No doubt, Ivan was reporting to someone – probably, Monsieur Le Postman.

Monsieur Le Postman would have to report to everyone else – what Zack's response had been to their message, the one that they had decided Ivan was best suited for delivering. Zack smiled. They had been correct about Ivan, but it was actually little Bog, who had eased the pain and fear of abandonment, and the little boy had needed no coaxing from anyone to do that. It had come natural to his innocent little heart.

Zack fumbled for the light inside Dmitry's apartment. He had become so accustomed, to the one inside the door at Mara and Montague's, it seemed odd that there was none in the same location at Dmitry's place. Eventually, he located it, but not until after he had knocked something over on the floor. He held his breath, expecting to hear the inevitable breaking of glass. Looking over the edge of the small table stacked with books, he saw a ceramic vase, fortunately still intact, rolling from side to side on the carpet. A small bouquet of flowers was scattered, and water began soaking into the rug.

As Zack ran to the kitchen to grab paper towels to clean up the mess, he knew he had been very lucky. Two more inches to the right, and the vase would have been smashed to bits on the hard wood floor. He dried the rug as much as he could, picked up the vase, and sat it upright on the floor. An odd sound caught his attention. Inside was a small package, wrapped securely in a plastic bag to protect it from the water. Zack's immediate thought was "drugs!" Why else would someone...?

Then, he thought of Madeleine and the truffles she hid her bouquets. Should he assume that Dmitry already knew about her? Had he found truffles in one of her flower bouquets, during one of his restaurant inspections, and brought them home? For what purpose? To blackmail the others, when the time was right?

Zack hurriedly cleaned up the mess he had made, thinking all the while that there was a greater mess to sort out. At any moment, Dmitry could walk in the door, and then, Zack would have to confront him. But, it was too late. Even as he was attempting to add water to the poorly rearranged flowers in the kitchen, the doorknob was turning.

Zack turned to face Dmitry, and the look that met him said it all. The small package, still in its wet plastic bag, lay on the floor, next to the wet spot on the rug. Dmitry slowly closed the door behind him, and stood stoically in front of it, a veritable bulwark of human flesh. "You've been a busy boy," Dmitry said, arms crossed.

Zack apologized profusely and held the vase out to Dmitry as some sort of peace offering. The flowers (many broken) hung, pathetically, in dying clumps over the edges of the container. Dmitry's eyebrows went up in response to what he saw. Zack remained in the kitchen as Dmitry refused to give up his place in front of the door. There appeared to be an unspoken standoff. Dmitry's eyes scanned the room, as if anticipating he would discover further damage. When he was certain that this was the extent of Zack's destruction, he moved near to the small table, which had held the vase, and put down his keys. Zack assumed that Dmitry was sending him a silent message, and so, in response, produced Dmitry's apartment key from his pants pocket. He held it out. With the vase of broken flowers in one hand, and the apartment key in the other, Zack's image made Dmitry smile, and then, burst into laughter. Zack was caught off guard, and confused. Then, Dmitry said, "Did you look like this, when Gwendolyn threw you out? Flowers in one hand and your manhood in the other?"

Zack looked down at himself, and then, up at Dmitry. "Yes."

Dmitry laughed louder this time. "Sit down, my friend. Accidents happen."

Zack blew out the breath he had been holding, before moving slowly, carefully, this time. He placed the vase of flowers on the coffee table, where he was less likely to knock it off.

Dmitry watched. "Yes. I like them there. Is better."

Zack, still tentative about his guest status, sat down on the edge of the sofa, and ignored the package on the floor, as did Dmitry for the moment. Dmitry walked around the room, before choosing a chair across from Zack. The package was still in Dmitry's peripheral vision, but for Zack to see it, he would have to turn his head. Zack was certain that he would not be the first to bring up the elephant in the room. The little box could remain there all night, as far as he was concerned. How far was Dmitry willing to go in denying that it existed?

"Where did you go today?" Zack chose to ask, as if this was to be a casual conversation.

"The 8th," Dmitry said. "Beautiful restaurants. Wonderful menus. Great chefs. You would like," he added, readjusting his weight awkwardly in the chair built for smaller people. "Maybe one day, we go there together."

Dmitry had slipped into a colloquial Russian speech pattern, what Zack would come to know as Dmitry's "at home voice." Zack wondered if it was the result of fatigue, or was being done for effect, a conscious choice to intimidate him. If, it was being done innocently and not maliciously, the net effect was the same - fear. Zack had watched too many movies about the cold war era, not to imagine that he was about to be interrogated.

The timing of Dmitry's entrance had been too serendipitous. Everything about this moment seemed too scripted - the lighting, one lamp above his head, and Dmitry, sitting across from him in the dark. The shadows in the corners of the room seemed to hold their own secrets. Were his words being recorded, his image being filmed? Where was the camera? He searched the dark over Dmitry's shoulders for any indication of a hidden lens.

"What did you do, today?" Dmitry asked in a similarly casual fashion.

"Not much," Zack began. "Went to the park. Wrote." Talking too much, again, he added, "Thought about going to a movie."

"Did you?"

"No." Zack slumped. Ok. He might as well get into this business of moving out. It was going to happen with, or without, Dmitry's approval. He might as well get on with breaking the news. "I think I should leave. Find my own place."

Dmitry smiled, weighing his words, carefully, before responding. "It was only a vase and it did not break," he offered, knowing that the vase was not the reason Zack was moving. "No big thing." He paused. "Is there something that I've done, something that I've said?"

Zack was confused. He had expected Dmitry to be up and out of his chair by now, eagerly holding open the door for his departure.

"Perhaps, you are worried about something else. Shall we talk about it?" Dmitry suggested. "Perhaps, you would like a drink, first?"

Dmitry had done it. He had done it, just as Gwendolyn had. He had put Zack on the spot. It seemed, too, that Dmitry was enjoying it, almost as much as Gwendolyn had. So, leaving Dmitry was going to be just as difficult as leaving Gwendolyn. He couldn't blame it on his inability to understand the French, the British, or the Russian cultures. Breaking someone's heart was just messy business, and it didn't matter, where any of the hearts were born.

He hadn't prepared for this. Yes, a drink would help. But, why wasn't Dmitry already inebriated? By this time in the evening, normally he would be. Had he changed his routine, not gone to a brasserie after work? Had he followed Zack to the park? Had he seen him return with Ivan? Had he overheard Ivan relaying the demands of the other villagers?

Dmitry's face told him nothing. Monsieur Le Spy had become an expert of disguise. Zack looked deeper for some sign from Granville DeMonnay, whom he knew lived somewhere below the surface. But, Granville was not at home. He would have to deal with Dmitry. Why did this conversation have to take place, when they were both stone sober?

To make the situation worse, the rain began to pound the windows with large pellets. The sound startled both of the men into looking that direction. "I was going to suggest that we go out for a drink," Zack said. "But, now..."

Dmitry took the cue, and rose to retrieve a bottle of wine. "We stay in tonight," Dmitry said with finality. "It's best," he said, uncorking the wine, "Unless you have somewhere to go?"

Zack was really squirming, now. "I do have somewhere to go, but not yet. We can have a glass of wine, together, and talk first."

"You break up with me?" Dmitry said, laughing, and handing Zack a glass, before sitting down.

"No. No." Zack said, uncomfortable with the choice of words. "It's just that I work best when I live alone. You understand. You were a..." Zack had made a stupid choice, starting to say, "You were a writer," reflecting upon Dmitry's past in a negative way. Dmitry was still a writer, just one – temporary out of the office. Zack regretted his words, and did not attempt to continue.

Dmitry observed his friend's discomfort, debating whether, or not, it was time to let him off the hook. Obviously, the little package on the floor was not much of a concern, if Zack had not immediately brought it up, had not questioned him as to why he had hidden it in the vase. Maybe Zack could be trusted with more of the truth. "You know boy called Sébastien? Lives downstairs?" Dmitry pointed towards the front door.

By directing Zack's eyes in that direction, it made it impossible for either of them to ignore the object on the floor. Dmitry chose this moment, to pretend it was the first time that he had seen it. "What's this?" he said with false surprise, before getting up and bending over to pick up the wet plastic bag. "Yours?" he asked, holding it out to Zack.

This was a chance to see what was inside! Should he take it? (No, stupid.) Dmitry was playing him. (No, don't bite.) If he said "Yes" he would be portrayed a thief. If he said "No," what? He might never know what was inside. Did he owe it to the others to say, "Yes, it's mine." Grab their missing package, and run! (Stop!) Leave it alone. He's holding out bait.

"No," Zack chose to be honest. "I think it fell out of the vase."

Dmitry took the plastic bag to the kitchen, dried it, opened it, and withdrew its prize. A small, brown paper wrapped box sat in his hand. There was no writing on it, no stamp, nothing. It did not match the one missing from Mara's apartment.

(Whew!) Zack felt relieved. So Dmitry hadn't found the missing package from Mara's stash of truffles...books.

Dmitry brought it back over to where Zack was seated, and placed it in front of him on the coffee table. Zack stared at it a little too long, and Dmitry, watching his face as he sat down, took another long sip of wine, and savored the taste on the back of his throat. "Is there anything that you would like to tell me?" he asked.

"About what?" Zack asked, looking up and trying to appear as innocent as he possibly could.

"About that," Dmitry said, tilting his head towards the box, which seemed to grow larger and larger with Zack's pretense.

"Don't know what you mean," Zack said. He was not about to give up his friends, even though it might mean giving up this budding friendship with Dmitry. It would break his heart to lose this opportunity to write the famous author's biography, but losing the trust of so many others meant more. If he had doubted it, Bog had driven the point home. Zack needed a sense of belonging to something greater than himself. He needed a village and a place to call home, more than he needed fame and fortune. It had been a hard lesson to learn, but at this very moment, he was certain.

"Never saw it before," Zack said, and then, Zack decided to do something, which he had never had the courage to do, before. He decided to challenge Dmitry. "You into drugs?"

The unexpected remark caught Dmitry off guard. "Me?" He sat back in his chair. "You crazy?" He held up the wine bottle. "I like wine." He poured himself another glass, but did not do the same for Zack. "You like drugs?"

Zack could smell success. The match had begun. Whether it was a mental match of wrestling or chess, they were engaged. He had just tossed Dmitry and Dmitry had not expected it. "Me? No, I get sick taking an aspirin. But, you have to admit – it's a little suspicious," he said, nodding toward the box. "Everyone has his own poison, right?" Zack tried to sound relaxed and casual with his remarks, and so, leaned forward to take a drink from his near empty glass. "I can't judge you. I was young once." He laughed. "Maybe you're going through a second childhood."

Dmitry didn't know where Zack was headed with this. "Open it," he insisted.

Zack sat back, thinking game on. "It's not mine to open – unless, of course, you're making it a gift." Zack reached for it, only to see Dmitry snatch it back with lightening speed.

"No," Dmitry said. "Not gift for you. Gift for me."

Zack smiled a slow knowing smile. He was ahead. Your move, Dmitry.

Dmitry took another drink, still holding onto the small box. Zack got up and retrieved the bottle. He topped off Dmitry's glass first, and then, refilled his. Dmitry watched him out of the corner of his eye as Zack took the bottle back to the kitchen, rather than leave it on the coffee table. It seemed that his guest was buying time, a ploy to make Dmitry nervous. Dmitry did not want to admit that it was working.

Did Zack really believe that there were illegal drugs in the box? This was not going as he had planned. He wanted Zack to admit what he knew about the smuggling that was going on in the building. Dmitry had suspected it for months, but he needed more proof. The small box of truffles had been, indeed, a gift to Dmitry, but one that came to him

from a restaurant chef, who revealed that the truffles came to him each
week from a flower shop. He would not reveal the name of the flower
shop or how the truffles had been purchased. He feared losing his job,
and so Dmitry agreed to keep the secret.

What Dmitry needed was an eyewitness, who would be willing to
confess under pressure. He suspected that other restaurants were
receiving the same deliveries, but he had no proof, so far. He had
suspected for some time that Mme. Christy's shop was involved.

Dmitry was certain that Zack was the key to solving the mystery.
He needed to know what Zack knew, as he had spotted Zack leaving
Madeleine's apartment on at least one occasion, and hanging around
her flower shop on another. He had tried to approach the beautiful
woman, but had failed. She made it obvious, on Dmitry's first attempt
at conversation, that she did not like him. Yet, in Dmitry's mind, she
had never given him a chance. Yet, she had invited into her apartment,
the young American.

The other villagers would not tell him anything. That much was
certain. For whatever their reasons, they did not talk to him. But, Zack
was different. Zack was an outsider, like himself, and yet, Zack had
been permitted inside their inner circle. The lucky, young American
had already cohabited with two of the females in the building. Yes. If
anyone knew what was going on in the building, it would be Zack, and
if anyone were going to share what he knew with Dmitry, it would be
Zack.

Zack sat down, and launched into the conversation, which was his
purpose in being there. "I have to find a place to live," he said. "Would
you know of any apartments in the area? I figure you must know about
everyone in the neighborhood by now... I mean, after ten years of living
in Paris."

Dmitry studied Zack's face and body movements. The American
was either incredibly stupid, or incredibly clever. Which was it? Then,
Zack's words surprised him, helping him to decide - it was the latter.
Zack was a clever boy, even if he was being played by the villagers as
their pawn.

"Did you know Tito well?" Zack asked.

"Tito?" Dmitry asked, no longer attempting to hide his surprise.
"Why do you ask?"

"I saw similar boxes at Tito's place." Zack was lying, a calculated risk to make Dmitry reveal what he knew about the truffle smuggling. "It was when I was looking for an apartment. You remember? His apartment was vacant for a while...before the couple from Italy took it?"

Dmitry struggled to believe Zack. "Italy?" What was a dead man doing with boxes in his apartment? What was Zack babbling about? Tito was dead. If it had been a suicide, would he have left evidence lying around? And if he had been murdered, as the police suspected, wouldn't the murderer have taken the treasures for himself? No. Zack was making this up, but why, and how could he prove it?

"Books," Dmitry said, dryly.

"Books?" Zack said, as if he wasn't aware of any of the deliveries, he had witnessed.

"Tito liked to read."

Yes. It had been the pat answer, probably, overheard by Dmitry - every time a delivery had been made to the Polywogs, to Gwendolyn, to Madeleine, and to Arness and Albert on the floor below. OK. He had overheard it at least a dozen times, across the hall at Mara's and Montague's apartments, too. "Your books are here," the deliveryman would knock and say, before leaving the packages at the door. But, that alone did not mean that Dmitry knew what was in the boxes, unless...

Zack wondered. Had it been Dmitry, rather than Sébastien, who had stolen Mara's packages from his apartment? Were the two of them in a conspiracy of their own design? Looking at Dmitry, it seemed more likely that Sébastien had been the one, who might fit through the tall, thin windows. And, it would take quite an acrobat to accomplish the feat of climbing around on the roof, especially, in broad daylight. Was Sébastien that talented? Wasn't it one of Dmitry's ex-girlfriends, who had been acrobat? Maybe she taught the author a few tricks of her own.

Zack glanced at Dmitry's box. It was much smaller than the books, which he had been receiving. Madeleine delivered the truffles inside her vases, by putting smaller amounts of truffles inside waterproof boxes. How many truffles could fit in such a small box? At €3000 per kilo, a person wouldn't need many. Was Dmitry's small box – one of Madeleine's? Zack had never seen one before, and couldn't be certain.

"You could move upstairs," Dmitry suggested, catching Zack

caught up in a daydream of cat burglars, truffles, and the places, where Dmitry might, or not fit.

"Upstairs where?" Zack asked, intrigued. "That's for tourists."

"There are two attic apartments," Dmitry said. "You didn't know?"

"No," Zack said.

Dmitry explained that there were two, very small attic spaces, which had been converted into holiday rentals. One was rarely rented because it was too small, and only suitable for one person, but both were available for short-term rental. As Zack was only planning to stay in Paris until his contract expired in a few months, Dmitry suggested that the smaller space might work. It was for selfish reasons, why Dmitry wanted to keep Zack close by. He needed to keep an eye on the young writer, who knew too much about Granville DeMonnay.

"I could ask Monsieur Épicier for you, if that would make it easier," Dmitry offered.

"Yes!" Zack said, enthusiastically, without concern for seeing the place first. The space, regardless of its size, would solve so many problems. It did not demand that he become anyone else's cousin. He could remain in the village, without obligation. "The grocer owns this place, too?" Zack asked.

"He owns most of the apartments in this building," Dmitry answered, before going on to describe the place. There was a single bed, a sink, and a toilet, but no shower, no kitchenette, but a hot pot for making coffee, and a small refrigerator. "It has a nice, big window, which opens to the street," Dmitry added. "But, it is so high, the noise below is not a problem, and the light is very good."

Zack had other priorities. "Does the plumbing work?" he asked.

Dmitry confirmed that it had, the last time that he had been in the apartment. Of course, that had been a month ago. Zack did not question why Dmitry would know the toilet flushed, or why he had been in the apartment. Instead, he said, "Yes. Of course, I want it! It's a brilliant idea!" He could not think past the convenience of its location. He would need only to move his things up a couple of flights of stairs, rather than across town to a cheap hotel.

"Good!" Dmitry said. "I talk to Monsieur Épicier in the morning. Now, we drink." With that, he lifted his glass in a toast, "Za vas!"

Zack lifted his glass, "Za vas!"

"Tonight," Dmitry said, "You sleep on sofa."

"Thanks," Zack said, before remembering his promise to Ivan, his vow to tell him the deed was done. However, it wasn't done – entirely. He could not move out of Dmitry's place, until morning. Would Ivan give him grief about the delay? "I have to go out for a few moments," he said, apologizing. He was already anticipating Ivan's reaction, and practicing how he would present his argument for staying at Dmitry's one more night. It was just one night. How could that matter so much? Another twelve hours. Zack picked up his backpack to find his wallet. "I'll be right back. Can I bring you anything?" It was important for Dmitry to think that he was leaving the building, rather than knocking on a nearby door.

"No," Dmitry said. "We have everything we need right here."

"Not quite," Zack said, getting up and walking to the door. "Be right back."

Dmitry smiled, still holding the small box in his hand, and knowing that he had won. This little American pawn had no idea which game was being played. Little did he know that Dmitry had always preferred chess, over-wrestling, but he was prepared for either challenge, whichever was necessary to win.

Chapter 22

T here is a problem," Albert began, embarrassed to admit to those gathered that his son was, once again, at fault for creating chaos in the village. It was only the latest in a series of emergency meetings, but it was Sébastien's errant behavior, that had become the focus of this one. The boy had not been able to lead his father to all eight packages, which he had randomly buried in the Luxembourg Gardens. Each had been buried separately over a period of two days in a deliberate attempt to extend what he called a game of "pirate."

He proudly told of hiding his treasure, delighted that neither pirate, nor grownup, could find it, the last of his ill-gotten booty. What Sébastien's alter ego, his black-bearded little heart, had succeeded in doing was to strike fear into the hearts and minds of the villagers. Without that last package, they were doomed. How could one small, mischievous boy do so much damage?

It had never occurred to Sébastien that taking the boxes was the equivalent of stealing. He had grown up for seven years, watching boxes come and go, come and go. Boxes seemed to belong to everyone in the village. Why not him? He was just playing a game. His game. His rules. Wasn't that what the adults were doing?

The question brought silence in a room full of jaw-dropping adults, who had no proper response. In some cruel way, the boy was, absolutely, correct. He could tell from their faces that he had won this silly game.

"I thought so," the boy said, glibly. "Your game. Your rules."

Of course, he had no idea what he meant by that, but he could smell their criminal intent, as it was so similar to his own deviant nature. He had observed their conspiracy, their secrecy in practice. Gwendolyn's "little bastard" had been watching through his keyhole, just as others in the building had been watching through theirs. By his apprenticeship, he had learned from the best, and therefore, beat them at their own game.

"Where is the eighth package buried?" Monsieur Le Postman insisted that Sébastien confess.

Embarrassed and frustrated, Albert told the others about the hours, which he had spent retracing his son's steps. The boy had led him to seven of the boxes. Two were completely water logged, having been buried too close to the gardens' sprinklers. The air filled with laments. Thousands of Euros – lost! Albert, quickly, reported that five were still intact, and perfectly fine, as he hoped this would appease them.

"That's some compensation, isn't it?" Berta asked, wanting to support Arness and Albert in their plight.

As much as they cajoled, pled, and threatened, the boy could not remember "exactly" where he had buried the eighth package. It had been a long day for a little boy, and digging was hard work. For certain, he said, it was inside the park, but he had no idea – where. He was telling the truth. It, also, had been a long, long time ago. Still, they continued in their attempts to jar his memory, even to the extent of bribing him, but, clearly, the game was over. They, reluctantly, had to accept that Sébastien didn't remember. Short of hiring a truffle-sniffing dog, there was little likelihood, that the eighth treasure would ever be found.

"Should that news comfort us?" Monsieur Le Postman asked, rudely, revealing his utter frustration, being placed at the mercy of a mere child.

Zack sat in the corner, keenly aware of his own complicity in the crime. Leaving his windows open, to a child with acrobatic skills was unthinkable, and nearly, unforgiveable – although, each person in the room had told Zack – "It was not your fault. You did not know." When Albert and Arness were not around, they would add, "You do not know the little bastard, the way we do."

Evidently, before Zack moved in, there had been a meeting in the village to confront Arness and Albert about their son, who worst crime – up to that point - had been to break the lights in the hallway by throwing his soccer ball at them. Madeleine had nearly killed herself falling down the stairs in the dark. That had been enough of a reason for a village meeting to be called. Everyone loved Madeleine, and almost, no one – with the exception of his parents - loved Sébastien. As he was hearing the story unfolding for the third or fourth time, Zack found it hard to believe that so much should be blamed on one child. He, himself, had not been a prize, when he was growing up. He could relate too easily to the culprit in this story, recalling that an open window was only an invitation to a child with a full imagination.

No. This had been Zack's fault. It could have been just as easily an adult bandit, who saw an opportunity. Zack started to say something, to defend Sébastien, but he was cut short by Mme. Durand, the concierge, who did not want to hear anything more that Zack might have to say. She was still irritated that Monsieur Épicier had called her about someone renting the smallest apartment in the attic. She fumed about climbing all those stairs, when her knees hurt her so badly, to make the bed and clean the bathroom - only to find out that the tenant was none other than Zack! It had been a week ago, but she was still pissed off about it.

Zack thanked her, again, for her efforts, but to no avail. She was certain that she was not appreciated, and bathed herself in misery. The others had come to accept her negative demeanor, and to remain unaffected by it, but Zack felt guilty, which was the concierge's desired objective. Her complaints, however, did not taint his joy, for having found a spot in the village. He had fallen in love with the space on first sight.

Yes. It was small, but reflected exactly what he had expected, before coming to Paris. Novels were filled with descriptions of tiny artist garrets, very much like this one. There was no kitchen, only a small refrigerator, but really – what else did he need? A folding cutting board was hinged to the wall above the refrigerator, and it fell down to serve as a small dining table. There was small three-legged stool, which provided seating, when it wasn't being used for a lamp table next to the bed.

In the corner, stood a small lipless sink, and above it, instead of a mirror, a shelf had been placed for the barest of essentials: soap, toothbrush, or razor. He shaved in front of a mirror by the front door. A narrow closet, to the side of the sink, held a toilet. As for a shower, well, there was none, but he had learned in the past few days – just how easy it was to bathe in a sink with a washcloth. "Kind'a like camping." he had admitted to Dmitry. By the second day, he had devised a clothesline out of several wire clothes hangers, and dangled it from the ceiling, so that underwear and towels could dry above the sink.

A week earlier, true to his word, Dmitry had gotten up early to meet Monsieur Épicier on his way into work. Less than a half-hour later, Dmitry returned with the key to lead Zack up the stairs to the fourth and final floor, for a preview of the place. He had told the landlord that Zack was an American student in Paris to study for six months, and by that, had successfully reduced the rent. Tourists would have been forced to pay twice as much, he boasted to Zack of his negotiating skills.

Zack thanked Dmitry over and over for suggesting the place, and for acting as his agent in negotiations. Dmitry answered, "It's what friends do for friends, right?" Zack liked that Dmitry considered them friends because Dmitry was straightforward and righteous in his convictions. He had the knack of cutting through much of the noise in Zack's head. Thanks to Dmitry, he was beginning to see the world differently.

Strangely, for a man of few words, Dmitry could speak volumes. Perhaps, this was because the words he used were always chosen, carefully. Zack was not about to walk away from the chance to learn from the master. This sort of apprenticeship was priceless. Somehow, he would learn to walk the tightrope between apartments, between secrets, between friends. He had to. His new life in Paris was too precious not to, and he was not about to risk exile from the village, or worse, lose Dmitry's friendship.

Madeleine stood up and proposed that operations be suspended until the last package could be located. They had plenty of money saved up for a moment like this. There was no real reason to continue, if the risk was proving too great. Then, she revealed, for her the risk had become too great. Without placing blame, she said, the others were putting her in a precarious situation. She blamed only the circumstances. Albert and Arness, who already felt terrible, felt worse. Madeleine did not have to point any fingers. This was all, their son's fault.

No one in the room could argue that Madeleine's role was not a crucial part, nor argue that she risked the greatest exposure. Her shop would be closed down, her legal income lost, if their illegal operation was discovered. Yes. A vote should be taken. That much was agreed.

Gwendolyn raised her hand, to be recognized by Monsieur Le Postman, who acted as parliamentarian. He nodded, and she stood. "Are you saying suspended for a few days, or a few weeks?" She sat down to await her answer.

Madeleine, who had never sat down, turned toward Gwendolyn. "We vote on that, too. Who is in favor of shutting down for one month?" She asked, but no one's hand was lifted. "A month?" she asked, looking from face to face. It was obvious that none of them had gone a month without the extra income. A month? Really? The possibility passed silently from one to another to another. A month? Really?

Madeleine had her answer. "Ok. Two weeks? Can we stop for two weeks?" One hand, that of the professor went up. Mara's followed. Slowly, one-by-one, each of the others followed suit.

Monsieur Le Postman said, "We have a consensus. It is agreed. Two weeks it is."

Marcel spoke next, attempting to make it sound festive. "Everyone - take a holiday! Two weeks. Then, we meet again to discuss the future."

With that, Camille got up, and Madeleine followed her to the kitchen. No meeting would end without food and drinks. To do otherwise would be uncivilized. As the other villagers moved their chairs back into proper places in the room, Arness and Berta retrieved plates and napkins for everyone. Ivan and Monsieur Le Postman uncorked a few bottles of wine, leaving Albert alone, hands in his lap, with head down. He was still grappling with his perceived failure as a father, when Zack sat down next to him. Zack felt his pain, a strange and totally new emotion for a childless man.

"Buy you a drink?" Zack asked.

Albert replied, "A drink would not help." He continued hanging his head.

"How about a walk?" Zack said, looking around the room to see that the others were very involved in their individual tasks. "Would they miss us, do you think?"

Albert's eyes lit up with the prospect of getting out from under the spotlight. "I go to buy cigarettes," he called out over his shoulder to Arness as he got up, and headed for the door, not leaving time, or room for objections. "Come Zack," he added, louder, "I want to show you where to buy that screwdriver."

"Screw..." Zack could not get the question out of his mouth, as Albert was ten steps ahead. Zack followed. "Oh, yeah," he said, closing the door behind them.

When they were safely outside, Albert stood upright, filled his lungs with fresh air, and looked at least five years younger. "Merci," he said. "You saved me."

"Not really," Zack said. "I needed some fresh air, too. They get a little intense, sometimes."

"Sometimes?" Albert remarked. "Always," he said, finding Zack's observation too much of an understatement. "My son is a monster."

Zack could not respond without hurting Albert's feelings by agreeing with him, and so, they walked silently side-by-side in the direction of the grocery store, and then, into the neighborhood, where more shops brought out more people. In a crowd, Albert felt more relaxed and comfortable talking openly about his problems. "He is such a different child from the one we were expecting. He does things that I do not understand. Where does he get such ideas? I never...as a child, would have such an idea as to sneak into my neighbor's house."

Albert took a deep breath, and sighed. "My father would have killed me dead...right there. Yet, I...I cannot strike the boy." He took another step and turned around to confront Zack. "Should I?" he asked, expecting an answer.

Zack was unprepared, taken aback by the question. "You're asking me? I have no children. How would I know?" he sputtered out.

"Ah," Albert said, turning around, and falling back into a comfortable stride. Then, after another few steps, "No wife?"

"No," Zack answered.

"Ever?" Albert persisted. "You did not have one in America?"

"No, never," Zack admitted, feeling that perhaps, he was making himself even more of an outsider.

"You lucky, lucky man," Albert said, stopping in front of the hardware store. "Now, we buy you a screwdriver." Seeing Zack's face, he explained, "Not because you need one, but because we must. I told the wife."

Zack added, "And cigarettes."

"Yes. Quite right," Albert said, thanking him for remembering the lie.

Zack and Albert returned to the meeting, where there was still food and wine, and no one the wiser for their lie. They had returned home with cigarettes and a new screwdriver, which was more a trophy, than a tool. It would set on Zack's nightstand, a reminder of his newest friendship. Only Zack and Albert would know, sometimes, men lie to get fresh air and to find space to share life's burdens.

Zack had given Albert no advice on how to parent a misbehaving child, or how to handle a wife's expectations, as he would have been an ass to do so, but somehow, Albert had returned a better man. Somehow, the company of the young American had made him feel younger, more energized, and stronger in his convictions. Perhaps, it had been the very last thing, which Zack had said to him, before he turned the doorknob.

"He will grow out of it." Zack had said, adding, "I did."

Ivan had the floor after dinner, explaining that he and Albert would pass the word along to the Épiceries and restaurants that there would be a two-week moratorium on truffle deliveries. Madeleine said she would notify the hotels. Monsieur Le Postman said he would notify the "book" deliveryman. Mara said she would call Phillipe's friends in the south of France, adding tentatively, "If I can't find Phillipe." This led to a long discussion, as to why Mara should not bother to call Phillipe, or his friends, and why Phillipe's friends should be replaced.

"Phillipe cannot be trusted," Marcel said. "We will not bother him." Mara knew that was the end of the subject. She would not attempt to contact Phillipe, nor would anyone else in the room. When Marcel spoke, the matter was closed. Marcel, always, got the final vote. Zack, and the professor, were both thinking, "Not that Phillipe ever could be trusted." They silently applauded Marcel for his decision.

Mara got up to leave, giving the excuse that the girl, who was babysitting Monty, had to go to school. Everyone said that he or she understood. However, everyone knew she had left because of her embarrassment, the fact that she had brought up Phillipe. After she had left, Phillipe was given a proper roasting. The word "bastard" was tossed about as if it was confetti. Unanimously, they voted to dispense with their suppliers, agreed that their interests were best served by paying off any outstanding debts to Phillipe's friends. They wanted to be done with this trio of petty thieves, once and for all.

Albert leaned over and quietly explained to Zack that Phillipe had been a mistake, a desperate attempt to find suppliers, to replace Tito's equally despicable and unreliable group of bandits.

In Mara's absence, the professor found the courage to bring up an idea, which had been brewing on a back burner for months. "What if we no longer needed them?" he threw out, only to have his words met with mutters of derision and huffs of disdain.

A low rumble of voices caused Marcel to interrupt. "No longer need the thieves, or the truffles?" he asked, which gave the professor, the respect he deserved as a long-standing member of the group. "Are you suggesting that we stop operations all together...forever?"

The mutters and huffs became un-muffled growls of disbelief. Was Marcel suggesting "C'est fini?" It was over? "Impossible!" The day that they had not wanted to imagine was finally here? "Sacré bleu!" Why hadn't someone said something sooner? "Je ne suis pas prêt!" No one was prepared for this. Could it be true?

It took a few minutes for everyone to calm down long enough to listen, to what Montague had been trying to explain, over their emotional outbursts. "What if, I told you," he began, slowly, "that I have developed a truffle by other legal means? What if, I said, I have produced a better, far superior truffle to any of those, which we risked life and limb to obtain illegally?"

"Impossible! Ah, Oh, Aw, Ooh," Disbelief swept the room. Zack did not participate, confused as to why this should not be good news. At one point, it felt as if all of the air had been sucked out of the room. Seconds later, a collective breath out - nearly took the lace curtains off the windows. (Wow.) This must be a momentous thing, he observed.

The others completely ignored Zack, far too intent upon discussing, "Was it possible? Could this be patented? Could the professor's discovery be protected? How did it happen? Tell us everything. Could this be a grand, unprecedented moment in history? Should they call the press corps?"

Silence.

Or should this become the most safely guarded secret in the world?

Silence.

Then, reality set in. Had the professor really said - what they thought they heard? Had he managed to counterfeit the greatest treasure in the world? Was this not culinary sacrilege? Was this not blasphemy of the highest order? Man, attempting to recreate, what only God could create? For Heavens' sake, man, we're talking truffles here!

Silence.

Zack sat very, very still, studying the expressions on the faces of the other villagers. Each was lost in his or her private thoughts. Montague, too, sat silent, waiting for his long-anticipated praise. Surely, what he had done was a good thing, was it not? He had no doubts, having already treaded heavily through all of the possible objections.

To Zack, it appeared that the others were just beginning that long journey. He ached for his friend, who had spent his life in an attempt of the impossible, to recreate the perfect truffle, only to have his moment in the sun, teeter back and forth on the nervous twitches of his friends' lips. Finally, Zack could wait no longer. It was not his place to say anything, but Montague was in need of a champion. "I think it's a brilliant idea. Yep. Bloody brilliant. No more worries. Solves all our problems."

Heads turned one-by-one to stare at Zack with disbelief. Who was the American to say anything about anything, and certainly, about something so inherently sacred to the French? But, before the silent accusation could find verbal expression, Madeleine jumped up. "I agree with Zahhk," she said. "This idea would solve all our problems. No more hiding. No more payoffs to petty thieves. No more sleepless nights. We do exactly what we have been doing – but now, we do it, legally."

Silence.

It was the first time that Madeleine had admitted that she had embraced such worries. To the others, she had always appeared so stoic, so committed, and so calm – even after the divorce, when the fate of the flower shop was in question. Mme. Christy's confession gave the others permission to reveal their own concerns. The small hole in the dyke, which she had punched with her pinkie, quickly, turned into a floodgate. One by one, the villagers admitted to the stress they had experienced. They were not criminals by nature. The smuggling had caused them great concern, and many sleepless nights. Soon, the victims of their own crime were talking over top of one another, eager to share the extent of their damaged minds, bodies, and souls.

Zack observed, fascinated that the collective purging of sins was having such a bonding effect upon the group. He assessed that none of them, by nature, truly possessed a criminal disposition, or a felonious heart. Their goal had been only a way to pay off a few debts, perhaps, accumulate a little nest egg for retirement. Each had been happy to parlay the expertise, which he or she possessed into something, which in a collective way would benefit the village. That was all. This was nothing new, Marcel insisted. It had been done for centuries, in places much smaller than Paris. Was it such a crime? Each contributing so that all could survive? How was this different from the post-war, when everyone had to pitch in to rebuild Paris?

"Exactly!" Zack confirmed, seizing upon the moment. Their philosophy was correct, their lack of criminal intent dead on, and their innocence equally defensible. "The important thing now," he said, as much for his own self-interest as theirs, "the really important thing is to stop, right now, before the authorities get involved. This is a golden opportunity. Close down the operation, and clean up the loose ends as soon as possible. Tell those guys...I mean, your suppliers in the south of France that you've gone bankrupt, if you have to. Tell them the police have been snooping around here, or whatever it takes to shut them up and keep them out of Paris."

He had their undivided attention, and that appeared to be a surprise to everyone in the room. Zack was demonstrating new abilities, leadership skills, which they had not before seen or appreciated. Could it be? Was Zack the best project coordinator since Tito? Tito had always been able to work the room, build consensus where none existed. Strangely, Zack possessed this same talent.

Zack felt the change of ions in the air. Sometime, during his spontaneous outburst, a charge of electricity had arced from his body to theirs. Its sparks had warmed the atmosphere. He could feel it, if he had not already seen it in their eyes. Yes. Even Monsieur Le Postman was smiling. His face was sending a message. The young American was right. This was a golden opportunity.

The rest of the evening was spent discussing the professor's explanation of his scientific project, which had been ongoing for twenty-years in the backroom of his botanical lab on the outskirts of Paris. It had only been in the last few weeks, he revealed, that everything had come together in such a brilliant resolution of data. At first, even he could not believe it. However, the data didn't lie, and the truth was staring him in the face. He had been growing his own truffles for seven years, but these latest ones were perfection...better, he admitted, than the ones stolen in the last harvest!

Toast after toast to his success passed around the room. He was heralded as a 21st Century Einstein. Emc2 might equal relativity, but Emc8 = Truffles. Masses of truffles! All he had to do was discover the missing ingredient, and that was "love." Male truffles liked to reproduce with female truffles, and why wouldn't they? They're French!

Once Montague could not bear any more praise, he used the excuse to check on Mara and Monty, to make his departure. He said, upon taking his leave, "The rest of you may decide how to clean up the operation. Let me know, what will be my part in the process."

No, no, said the others, insisting that the professor had already done enough. He should concentrate on his discovery, and how best to protect it. They would shut down everything else; move everything from the vacant apartment; finish delivering the last of the truffles stored; and it would be done.

Montague thanked them, adding that he was feeling a little fatigue. "Probably, too much wine," he added. It was the first time, that Zack had heard him mention the amount of alcohol, he had imbibed. It should have been a warning.

Marcel and Camille discussed where they might go after the truffle operation shut down. They had talked for years of a small farm near the water in the area of Deauville. This came as a surprise to the others, who could not imagine Paris without them. "It is time," Marcel said, content that they had arrived at that age in life, when change was welcomed. "The city has become too much for us. We need to rest quietly in the mornings, and to walk in the evenings," he added, "without dodging automobiles and dog poop!"

"Hmmm," was all any of the others could rally in response. Albert and Arness, Ivan and Berta, were all too young to imagine their lives away from Paris, away from schools, doctors, noise, and they were too young to envy the joys of retirement. Monsieur Le Postman was, admittedly, envious, although still a few years away from executing his own retirement plan. His was to move to the southwestern coast of France, nearer to the beaches, which winter rarely visited.

Mme. Durand said that she would never leave Paris, because she loved the activity, and yes, even the noise. An alarm clock was not even needed, she boasted. "The garbage man wakes me up!" The others laughed. "I mean...his truck wakes me up," she clarified, blushing from embarrassment.

Madeleine reminisced about her previous life as a married woman of leisure, wishing that she could trade her flower shop for one luxurious day of sleeping late. Camille insisted that Madeleine should meet her friend, Monsieur G., who was only recently widowed. "He's rich." Camille teased. Madeleine kindly resisted Camille's matchmaking.

Zack wondered if Madeleine had a lover, hidden somewhere else in Paris. She was such a beautiful woman, who didn't deserve to spend his middle years without love, or a man to share her bed. She could easily have had any man, whom she wanted. The question was "Did she want one?" Then, he remembered. Her words had revealed only that she lamented the loss of leisure, not the loss of a husband.

The only person, who had been especially quiet throughout the evening, was Gwendolyn, and Zack was afraid to ask her, "Why?" Their short-lived relationship did not need to become a topic open to discussion. No one in the room was ignorant of what Gwendolyn had described to Mara as an ill-fated love affair. Montague had told Zack that much of Mara and Gwendolyn's luncheon conversation.

Zack told Montague that, characterizing what he and Gwendolyn had shared as a love affair, was exaggerating. They were friends, who made the simple mistake of having sex too soon. Surely, the professor could understand, Zack suggested, wishing immediately that he could take back his words. The look of shock on the professor's face revealed too much.

Gwendolyn stood up and retrieved her purse, a signal that she was leaving. Zack watched her make a concerted effort not to look in his direction. She made up the excuse that she had to be at her new job early in the morning. It was a casual announcement, confirming that she had successfully found work.

Mme. Durand was the first to ask, "Doing what?" She needed to know that all of her tenants were capable of paying their rent. That was her job.

"Accounting...another pharmaceutical company," Gwendolyn said, exhibiting no enthusiasm at all, for what she viewed as a burden. "I'll be an accounting clerk, until I die," she sighed, then, realized how dramatic she had sounded, when the others laughed at her. Zack did not understand. Wouldn't having a new job, so soon after leaving another, be a good thing? Gwendolyn was a complicated woman. Zack felt guilty to admit that he was happy to see her leave early.

Ivan slid over, into the chair next to Zack. "So," he began, "When do you think you and Gwendolyn will..." (He searched for the correct idiomatic American phrase.) "...move over this mountain in the street?" He was close. "Bump in the road," Zack corrected, but Ivan's words were closer to the truth. What stood between them was a high mountain, not a speed bump. He could not imagine ever being close to Gwendolyn, again; at least, not in the way Ivan was suggesting. "And the answer is - probably never," Zack added, and shrugged. "Women. What can you do?"

Ivan said, "That is too bad."

Albert came over to them, sat down, and soon, the other men followed. The women gathered in the kitchen to help Camille with clean up. All of the conversations evolved into unemotional discussions about neighborhood issues, the changing prices of food, weather, children, schools, and Zack dissolved more and more into the background.

Without a wife or children, without a basic knowledge of local history, without the necessary native French instincts to understand what was right, and what was wrong, with current trends, he could not comment. It was good, however, to be included with the other men, as if one day, (given enough time); he might have something worthy to add to their conversation. They did ask, however, how certain issues were resolved in the United States. That led to a series of very short answers, as Zack attempted to explain how neighborhood associations and local governments were organized on Long Island. Zack did not burden his new friends with how well, or how badly, the system worked because some words were not, yet, in his French vocabulary.

Zack was the last to leave because his new apartment in the attic had no air conditioning. With summer approaching, it took longer each day for the small space to cool down. When only he, Marcel, and Camille were left, he said, "Merci," and "A Bientôt," and started towards the door. Marcel said, "Stay a while." Marcel had never asked him to engage in a one-on-one conversation. That implied there was something important for them to discuss.

"Ah...Ok," Zack said, smiling, but hesitant. He was not about to turn down the most important man in the village, but what could he want to discuss? Zack's mind raced to grab onto a subject that Marcel might enjoy. He needed a topic for a new feature article for New York, and if Marcel were willing, perhaps, the French Resistance Movement might be just the ticket. Marcel, however, had other things on his mind - Dmitry, for one.

Marcel led him to a small library in the rear of the apartment. There was room for one large chair and one small chair, but not much more. Three of the four walls were covered in books, and a tall window filled the fourth. A large grey cat, who had never made his presence known during any of the meetings, got up, stretched, and left the room.

"Sit, please," Marcel said, pointing to the smaller of the two chairs. Camille appeared at the door about that time, and Zack realized that Marcel was offering him what was obviously Camille's chair. "No, please," Zack said, offering the chair to Camille.

"I am tired," she said, smiling. "I believe...if you will excuse me...it is my bedtime."

With that, she set down a tray with two cups, and a hot pot of something, which smelled Heavenly, next to her husband. She bent over and kissed him on his head. They murmured to her each other, softly, and although, Zack did not understand what was said, it was a touching and intimate moment to witness. Zack waited, until Camille had left the room, before he sat down. Marcel noticed.

"I like you Zack," Marcel said.

"Thank you," Zack said. "I like you, too, Sir." He felt that should add the "Sir." It seemed natural and fitting, as Marcel was at least as old as Zack's grandfather, and most likely, older. That alone demanded a certain degree of respect.

"You may call me Marcel," he replied, impressed with Zack's politeness, but wanting them to talk on a more personal level. "...and I shall call you Zack," he added with a wink. He turned, still sitting in his chair, to pour from the hot pot, but it was an awkward movement, and apparently, uncomfortable. Zack saw how difficult it was for him, and got up.

"May I do that for you?" he offered.

"Yes, thank you," Marcel said. As he watched Zack pour, they both sniffed in the sweet dark chocolate aroma. "I like hot chocolate at night. It helps me sleep."

"Me, too," Zack said, remembering cold winter nights, and his childhood. He handed a cup to Marcel, and returned to Camille's chair. It was a wonderful room. The chairs had been placed near the window, with two antique lamps at the perfect heights and angles for reading. He could imagine the lovely old couple, sitting here together, reading on cold winter days and long summer nights. In the corner, there was an old phonograph, with a column of LP's stacked underneath. The cover of the top album displayed a jazz trio.

Marcel was content to sip chocolate for a moment, before launching into the subject at hand. He had agreed to be one to discuss with Zack the subject of - What was to become of the young American, if he continued his friendship with the Russian spy?

Marcel would have to break the news to Zack, that Ivan's report had left some doubt in their minds. Ivan had reported that Zack came to his door, but it had been very, very late in the night, and the news was not good. He had awakened Ivan, who had purposely slept in a chair by the door, waiting for him – only to disappoint him, by announcing - he would not be moving out of Dmitry's apartment until the next morning.

First, this violated Zack's agreement to leave immediately. Secondly, Dmitry had gone to, and interceded on Zack's behalf, negotiating a lower rent for the holiday apartment in the attic. The Russian would not have done this, had he not had an ulterior motive.

"Can we call him by his name?" Zack asked, hoping that it was not too much of an affront to his host. "His name is Dmitry. I don't like referring to him as 'the Russian,' anymore than I would like to be referred to as 'the American.' I know that's who and what we are, but it's kind'a...condescending."

Marcel paused to consider Zack's words. Zack feared that he had offended the senior, whose generation seemed to divide everyone in the world by nationality first, and their names second. Zack hated these kinds of designations, as he had seen them used so often in the States. There, people were Canadians, Mexicans, African-Americans, Native-Americans, and so on. He thought categorizing people, de-humanized them, and only made it easier for some people to discount the feelings of an individual, because he or she fit in a different category.

"D'accord," Marcel said. "You are quite right. My grandson tells me this same thing. You, young people, are very smart."

Zack smiled, not because Marcel thought his generation was very smart, but because by phrasing his statement...You, young people...he had once again categorize a group of people. Old habits were hard to break. "I'm sorry. I interrupted you. You were saying something about Dmitry?"

Marcel wanted to know directly from Zack what he thought Dmitry's motive was. Zack said that he hoped Dmitry had helped with the apartment because he liked Zack. He had no idea why the man would like him, other than, they both played chess. Marcel paused, once again, to ponder the explanation, and because his hot chocolate was getting cold.

Zack's had been a spontaneous lie. Yes. Dmitry loved chess, and yes, he was a champion, but they had never played, at least, not on a chessboard. Mentally...perhaps. However, Zack was a novice at the game, only having played a little at university, but then, not at all since graduation. Dmitry would have found him a pitiful opponent. But, better than any other excuse, at the moment, this one did seem plausible – if not probable.

In terms, which the old warrior Marcel could understand, Russian and American chess players had been doing battle for half a century or more. On that basis, it was an understandable competition between Dmitry and Zack, and one, which did not need to base itself on friendship. In fact, it would become a better matchup, if the opponents were natural enemies. Marcel continued to weigh Zack's answer.

"You like chess?" he said.

"Yes. Crazy about it," he said. Then, he could not let the lie rest in peace. Taking a sip of (now cold) hot chocolate, he had to add, "I'm surprised that Gwendolyn didn't tell you."

("Stupid. Stupid. Stupid.") A voice in Zack's head shouted, as he waited for the inevitable.

"How about a game tonight?" Marcel offered, pulling on a drawer of the table next to him, so that Zack could see the many chess pieces hiding inside. "The board is next to Camille's chair." He pushed his ottoman with his foot in Zack's direction. "We put the board here."

Zack was had, fairly and squarely, and there would be no denial in the world good enough to pass muster with this old French Resistance fighter. It was as if Marcel had been on guard duty, and had shouted,

"Password!" Zack had shouted, "Chess." It wasn't the correct password.

Perhaps, Zack should have shouted, "Fool!" Instead, he yawned, and opted for a more appropriate response. He glanced at his watch, for greater effect. "It's pretty late," he said. "I don't know about you, but I'm pretty tired. Maybe tomorrow night?"

Marcel smiled. OK. So Zack was buying time. That, too, was OK. No one's life was held in the balance, tonight. Whether Zack confessed, what he knew about Dmitry now, or tomorrow night, it did not matter. The message had been delivered. Zack was not getting off the hook so easily, just because he had moved into the attic. No longer pretending to be someone's cousin, did not mean the entire village was not watching him. It would be nearly impossible for him to enter Dmitry's apartment without someone reporting it.

"So how do you find Dmitry's company?" Marcel asked.

"Fine. He's a very interesting man," Zack said, wishing that he hadn't said it. A question had to follow the idea of him being "interesting."

"Yes. I've always thought so," Marcel said.

It was not what Zack had expected. "I've always thought so?" What could Marcel possibly mean by that? How much did he already know about Dmitry? "Oh, so you have played him at chess?" Zack said, attempting to sound innocent, and ignorant of Dmitry's spy reputation.

Marcel scrunched his nose and twisted his lips. "No, but we've had some – to use your word, interesting chats in the hallway. I heard others in the neighborhood say that he is an inspector, something to do with restaurants. A man's business is his own, so I do not know if this is true."

"Yes. You are correct." Zack said, "It is true." Marcel knew, at least, what it was that Dmitry did for a living. Surely, this knowledge proved that Dmitry was not the spy that others had accused him of being. "He invited me to accompany him to a couple of his restaurant inspections."

Marcel's eyebrows rose. "And did you accept the invitation?" He asked, intensely curious.

An explanation was needed. "I wrote a very good magazine article about the experience for my employer in New York," Zack offered. Marcel's eyebrows settled back into their normal positions. "Would you like to see a copy?" Zack asked.

Marcel said, "No. No, thank you." He was less certain than ever – what to make of the young man. "Do you write about 'everything' you experience in Paris?" He wanted to ask, "Do you write about everyone in Paris?", but he could not.

"If I find someone willing to talk about his or her job, then, yes. I write about that experience." The time to turn the conversation around was now. "I would love to write an article about you and your experiences during the war...if you would agree."

Marcel wavered, flattered, but cautious. He loved to tell his stories, which were in rote memory after all these many years, but was this only a ploy by the young man to distract him from the business at hand? Was there nothing more to this man, than searches for stories? Was he another one of a thousand writers, who appeared on doorsteps all over the 6th Arrondissement, hoping to become famous?

Marcel finally decided that the only weapon he needed, to keep this hungry hound at bay, was stories, and after all these years, he had an arsenal that could keep Zack occupied for months. By then, this messy business of truffle smuggling would be only a faded memory. He would have no trouble keeping the little snoop under wraps until then. Marcel began with the first Christmas. Zack put down his cup, and pulled out his notebook.

Black King's Knight to White Queen's Bishop.

Lesson Nine: Sincere flattery is more valuable than stolen truffles.

even birds sat on the windowsill of the attic apartment window, and side-by-side in a row, quietly, stared at Zack. It was their shadow, which he saw, first. They were large and looming across his white sheet; seven dark shadows twenty times larger than life. He blinked several times. Was he still dreaming? What manner of creature were these?

Then, he looked up and squinted into the sunlight. Seven pigeons, silhouetted against a bright yellow sun, almost perfectly centered in the opening, began cooing and cheeping at once. His head hurt a little from the wine, but more from the unexpected chorus at the foot of his bed. With his attempt to sit up, they all flew away at once, leaving a flurry of feathers behind.

Zack fell back down and closed his eyes. It was easy to understand why the birds liked his window. This apartment was like a nest for bird and beast, alike, cozy, and warm. The sheets still held his body heat, making it easy to slide back into the most inviting spot. It was Sunday. The streets below were quiet. All was right with the world.

Until this morning, he had been unsure of many things, but after last night, he was certain that things would work out...for him, for his friends, for the future that he hoped would include Paris for many years to come. This was his niche, the one he had been looking for – for so many years. This was it. Everything about it felt right. Even the woman, who had just dumped him, didn't care that he was still in the building. There was an unspoken détente. In fact, it was as if they had never slept together, the memory of it - erased. She was back to being Gwendolyn, and he was back to being Zack, both unattached, and still looking for love.

Mara had the professor, and together, they shared little Monty. In addition, the professor had his experiments, which were going to make him rich, and everyone else – richer. Mara was more content than ever, and Monty was thriving. She no longer cared if Phillipe claimed the boy as his own. She preferred, as did all of the villagers, that Phillipe stay away.

Montague had begun taking Mara and Monty to the park on Sundays, and it seemed to Zack that the old professor walked better. Perhaps, even his eyesight, had improved – now, that he was living a younger man's life. Sometimes, Montague's new family crossed paths with Ivan, Berta, and Bog. Although, Zack played the unfamiliar and awkward role of "uncle," Sundays with his friends in the park ensured that he and little Bog would remain "buddies."

By allowing Zack to share their son, Ivan and Berta were compensating Zack for missing out on his nephew's life in the States. Both boys were about the same age. When Bog discovered something new, Zack realized that his nephew was discovering something similar on his side of the Atlantic. This brought Zack and his sister closer. When she wrote about her child, Zack could relate, writing back about little Bog and Sundays in the Luxembourg Gardens.

Marcel taught Zack about what things concerned older French citizens, such as Marcel and Camille, who were planning their retirement on the coast. How did social security here work? How did health benefits for the elderly work? Were there French rest homes for the aged? He had never bothered to discuss these topics with his grandparents. Now, he wished that he had. A dozen new ideas for feature articles surfaced.

Even though Monsieur Le Postman was still years away from retirement, the man could see the finish line in the not-too-far distance. He told Zack, in a rare and candid moment, when no one else was around, that he did not want to die alone. Zack, in a spontaneous moment of thoughtless compassion, told Monsieur Le Postman that Mme. Durand had been waiting, breathlessly, to offer a remedy, and she was only across the hall. The look in the man's eyes had been incredulous, but priceless. Zack had to repeat what he had said, in English, before he could be certain of what he heard. Mme. Durand had feelings for him?

Mme. Durand had accepted that Zack would become something more than a casual visitor to their village, and so, had not held him in much regard. However, now, knowing that she would have to see him every day for the foreseeable future, she had softened her attitude toward him. Once the postman began to visit her for purposes, other than village business, she wanted to thank someone – not knowing that it was Zack, who had delivered her long-held fantasy. Zack imagined that, if she found out, Mme. Durand would want to thank him; perhaps, even apologize for how she had treated him. He smiled in his near sleep, thinking about it.

Albert had accepted Zack, even though Zack's friendship with Arness was still tenuous. Since Zack preferred no relationship with little Sébastien, (lest something else turn up missing), keeping a civilized distance from the boy and his mother was best for everyone. He and Albert could enjoy their "guy time," when Zack could stop by, and ask Albert for advice, in a devised ploy to get Albert out of the house. Albert could knock on Zack's attic door and seek counsel, but mostly to inquire, if being a bachelor was as great as he remembered.

Zack had made one decision after the last meeting, and that was that he would invite Madeleine to dinner. It would not be a casual trip down the street to a neighborhood café, but rather a proper invitation to a nice restaurant, maybe the one in the 16th, which he and Dmitry had visited. Madeleine deserved to be treated with respect, to be convinced that beauty and sexuality did not disappear with age. She deserved more than she was getting out of life. Perhaps, a closer friendship was possible. It was worth a try.

With that, Zack fell back into a heavy, deep sleep. He did not hear the police knocking on the front door of the building, or the scurry of feet on the second and third floors. Instead, it would be the solid sound of one loud KNOCK on his door, which would startle him from his bed, and the voices that followed.

"Police! Ouvrez la porte!"

The smallest of the three police officers wanted to know who he was, and how long he had been renting the apartment. Truthfully, he could say that he had only been in the apartment less than a month. There was no lease to indicate anything different. "Tourist?" they asked. "Student?" "Writer," he would answer. Their eyes would roll. The policeman, who had hung back in the hallway, would mutter, "Ils sont tous les écrivains" (They're all writers), referring to all Americans living in attic apartments in Paris.

The entire interrogation took less than five minutes, during which time, he had to produce his passport. They passed it around so that all three police officers could briefly flip through its pages. "American," the first said, handing it to the second. One noticed that Zack had arrived months earlier, according to the date stamped by immigration authorities. "Where have you been staying?" the first officer asked, when alerted to the discrepancy. "Before here?"

"A hotel," he said, then, offered to get the receipts. It was almost true, but not entirely. The police had more, pressing things to do, than to watch him as he dug through his luggage for hotel receipts.

"Which hotel?" the lead interrogator asked.

Zack told them the name, watched as another officer scribble it down, and prayed that no one would actually call the hotel. If they did, they would learn that he had moved out after six weeks, and there were several months missing in his nearly yearlong stay in Paris, when he had not revealed – where he had slept, or with whom.

"Have you seen anything suspicious," he continued, "since you moved into this building?"

Truthfully, Zack could say, "No." All of the suspicious stuff, which he had witnessed, had happened long before he moved into the attic. These past few days had been incredibly normal, if the he did not mention anything - about shutting down the illegal truffle smuggling operation; the professor's discovery that was going to rock the western world, and send chefs with their meat cleavers, screaming all the way back to culinary school. But, "No," other than those things – "No, nothing," Zack answered.

The police thanked Zack, and then, did something Zack found amazing. They apologized for disturbing him, hoping that he could get back to sleep. Imagine that! He had pictured himself being dragged, kicking, and screaming, down the stairs in cuffs. He had pictured being thrown into French prison and not surviving the night. Instead, the police had said, "Have a nice day," and in English!

Zack's legs were shaking by the time he had secured the lock on the door. He wobbled his way over to the bed and sat down, unable to control his knees knocking. The physical reaction surprised him. This had been too real to be a dream, but the scene held a surrealistic quality. Then, he heard the police knock on the door of the holiday rental next door. He crept across the floor, afraid to trust his legs. He crouched as close to the wall as he could, to hear their responses.

The police officers' interview with the American couple went as quickly as his. He heard the same courtesies being extended to this couple. "Have a nice day!" was followed by heavy footsteps on the stairs. Since this was the end of the tourists' two-week stay in Paris, it didn't surprise Zack - that when the police had gone - the next sound he heard was of the Americans hurriedly packing. Apparently, they couldn't wait to get home, and tell their friends what had happened to them in France.

Zack couldn't wait to talk to the other villagers, but whom should he visit, first, after the police were gone? Had the American tourists been the last on their list to interview? Perhaps, it would be best, if he stayed out of the building for the rest of the day, in case they returned. He and the others could always compare notes later. With that decided, he went to the window to locate where the police cars were parked. He could not see much of anything. The roof of the third story, just below his window, was designed in such a way it hid a direct view of the street below. He could capture only a bit of Mme. Christy's shop canopy, and only the top third of her display window.

No. He would have to go downstairs to learn anything more, and visit Madame's flower shop. He could always use the excuse of buying flowers for the apartment, (if the police were present), and if they weren't, he would ask Madeleine, directly, what was happening. Since she had admitted that she had the most to lose, he could count on her honesty. Who had called the police? Who had betrayed the group? He also wanted to tell her, himself, that it wasn't him.

He hurried to dress, certain that a meeting would be called sooner rather than later. He needed to know when and where, before searching for Dmitry. He felt certain that Dmitry would know how to handle the French police. After all, Dmitry worked for the government. Surely, he had contacts, people who would know how to find out what was behind the police showing up at the building. What was it that they suspected? Dmitry had to know someone in the government, whom he could call. Zack was counting on it.

The building, which only minutes earlier had seemed filled with activity, was now eerily quiet. Not a footstep, not a banging water pipe, not even a baby's cry broke the silence as Zack descended the stairs, and waited near the mailboxes. Minutes went by and no one appeared to be at home. Nothing, not a radio, not a television was to be heard. Either everyone had left on the heels of the police, or they were all lying low, holding their breaths – collectively.

Zack did not want to be the first one to cause any of them more distress by knocking on a door, so he left a note in the postman's mailbox. It read:

"Sorti. Être de retour à 14:00. Veuillez donner des conseils sur heure et lieu de la réunion. Laissez la note sous ma porte. (Gone out. Be back at 2 p.m. Advise on time and place of meeting. Leave note under my door.) Zack."

After the visit by the police, the meeting could not take place in the apartment building, but Zack had no idea, where else they might gather - privately. This was not a discussion to be held in a café, or within earshot of an off-duty policeman. The flower shop, perhaps? It was his next stop. However, he stepped across the street only to discover the "Closed" sign in Mme. Christy's shop window. The first clue, that something was terribly wrong, came from the bouquets in the window. They were the same ones from the previous day.

Zack knew that Mme. Christy emptied the display case every night, before closing the shop. He walked by every morning to admire her new creations. The blue hydrangeas from yesterday were still there, and this was a serious indication that Madame had veered from her normal routine. What had happened? Madeleine never took a day off, except Christmas day. The closed sign indicated that Madeleine had either, not yet opened for the day, or had closed immediately upon hearing the news about the police across the street at the apartments.

Zack put his hand up to block the sun, and peered into the shop window. There were no lights on and no sign of movement. Strange, he thought, too strange. Madeleine opened at 10:00 a.m. on Sundays, and it was already half past.

He turned back to look back at the apartment building, hoping that signs of life from one of the windows would comfort him, telling him that he was not alone. However, it felt very much like he was the last man standing. Where had everyone else gone? The curtains were drawn in Mara's apartment on the third floor; so, too, in the vacant apartment next to hers. Gwendolyn's drapes were open, but he knew she went to church on Sundays, and was likely already singing in a church pew. If someone had called or texted her about the police raid, probably, she was on her knees praying.

The Polywogs' drapes were open, but as Zack watched for at least five minutes, there was no movement in their front room. This, too, was strange. Their Sunday mornings were spent at home, sleeping late, reading newspapers, and playing with Bog. Zack knew their routine because he had spent many Sunday afternoons with the Polywogs at the park. He wondered if he should have left them a separate note, apologizing for missing today's picnic. Should he call? No. The phone ringing might be just as frightening as a knock on the door.

That left only Mme. Durand's window just above the street level. On the first floor and with the word "Concierge" emblazoned on her apartment door, she must have been the first to hear from the police. No doubt, her apartment had been first on their list, and their knock would have been so loud, that it could have awakened the dead, (but not Zack in the attic). How had Mme. Durand reacted to the news that the police wanted to question everyone in the building? What had she told them about the Americans in the attic? Surely, she had thrown him under the bus with the other tourists. It was not as if he were truly a resident, truly one of them.

The villagers, whose apartments looked out upon the courtyard, must have been the ones most caught off guard by the unexpected visit from the police. Peacefully, on this quiet Sunday morning, they would have been sipping coffee, reading papers, listening to the radio, but not anticipating what was coming next. They could not have seen the police cars parked in the middle of the street outside. Zack could not prevent the question from surfacing, again, and again. What had each of them told the police about him? Had anyone broken down, and confessed?

Getting away from the building, in case the police came back, seemed like the most rational thing to do. He wasn't running away, he kept telling himself. This wasn't about self-preservation. He simply didn't want to contribute to the problem, by saying the wrong thing at the wrong moment. He needed time to think this through – thoroughly. Zack viewed his role in the drama - as that of a scout, a person assigned to reconnaissance duty. He would bring back every bit of information that he could, in order to save the village. It was the least that he could do, but first, he would have to find Dmitry.

Zack's first stop was the neighborhood café, where Dmitry had taken him, and not just because Zack was hungry (which he was), but because Dmitry had mentioned going there on Sunday mornings. Zack was disappointed to find Dmitry's corner empty. The waiter recognized Zack and offered him black coffee, but Zack said, "No. Have you seen Dmitry?" By doing so, he had put the man on the spot, and the waiter was not one to give out information easily, and certainly, not about the man with the power to close his café. Eventually, he weighed the question, and finding it innocuous, answered, "Not today."

Zack was growing nauseous, not certain if it was hunger, or fear. Did it really matter if his search continued immediately, or resumed ten minutes from now? He chose to stay and eat, convinced that Dmitry might still show up, even though the time of day suggested that Dmitry had been up and gone for hours. He was probably walking in the 14th, Zack imagined, as Dmitry told him he preferred Parc Montsouris to the Luxembourg Gardens, especially on Sundays. "Fewer tourists," he had explained.

Zack had not yet been there, and so, had no idea where to begin looking for Dmitry in the 14th. Instead, after breakfast, he returned to the Luxembourg Gardens. If all were normal, Ivan, Berta, and little Bog would be there. This would be a good sign.

Zack found them, just as he had hoped, near the pond and fountain. Little Bog was preparing to float the boat, which he and his father had built together. Berta was on a bench not far away. Ivan was distracted, standing over little Bog to supervise the launch, as Zack walked up behind him, scaring him half to death by saying, "Sorry I'm late." Bent forward, Ivan jumped at the sound of Zack's voice, nearly falling into the water. "Sorry," Zack apologized, grabbing Ivan's arm to rescue him from taking the plunge. Berta gasped, but Bog thought it was hysterically funny.

"Where were you?" Ivan whispered, his tone of angst palpable. "What did you tell the police?"

"I told them nothing," Zack whispered back. "It went pretty well, I think. They only wanted to know how long I had been living there, and if I had seen anything suspicious. How about you? What did they ask you?"

"The same. We told them we hadn't seen anything. We pulled the immigrant routine. You know. We speak Polish. We cannot understand the questions. Can you repeat them, please? They were frustrated with us, muttering that we should learn French, if we plan to stay here. You know. You're an immigrant."

Zack was surprised that Ivan considered them equals in this regard, but yes, it was true. The police had muttered something similar about learning the language to him. However, because he had been in the holiday rental apartment in the attic, they had been more polite about it. Perhaps, they were more courteous to tourists, whose money was important to the Paris economy. Ivan and his family, on the other hand, were taking jobs away from French citizens, while enjoying the social benefits that accompanied employment in France. Perhaps, the police felt justified in a harsher treatment of those they (personally, if not professionally) considered "interlopers."

Zack listened as Ivan repeated the police officers' questions. The interrogation of the Polywogs had taken longer, about twenty minutes. They were asked to produce their passports, their work visas, and Bog's birth certificate. As if that was not enough, the police demanded to see Ivan and Berta's marriage certificate. Apparently, having children out of wedlock was acceptable for thousands of French citizens, but not so for immigrants.

Berta had viewed this as harassment, and she took offense at the implication that little Bog was illegitimate. Fortunately, Ivan said, she kept her tongue, until after they had left. The experience had hurt her impression of Paris, and damaged her respect for the French police. Before this, she had thought France welcomed immigrants. Now, she could see that it was no different here, than any place else.

Zack tried to filter the experience for Berta, saying that - had they lived in New York, they could have expected the same treatment, the same questions, and probably, to be asked for their documents.

Ivan said, "Yes. That is what my cousin told her. She called him in New Jersey and asked him if we should move there."

"She is that upset?" Zack asked, surprised by the uncharacteristic reaction from Berta. He had always thought she was the most gentile natured of his new neighbors.

"She frightens easily," Ivan confessed. "Everything here frightens her. She was getting better, until this happened. I hope this will not make her want to move back to Poland."

"Would you do that?" Zack asked.

"I would not, but I have a wife, who misses her family, and scares like a rabbit. I do not miss anything, and my family visits us here. Hers does not." Ivan explained. "They do not have much money, and like Berta, everything different frightens them. Would you believe it? They think Berta is the brave one. Imagine that."

Ivan and Zack stared at Berta a moment. She seemed terribly distracted, not even aware that little Bog had gone off on his own somewhere. Ivan, however, had Bog under his radar, keeping a watchful eye, but from a distance, so that the boy would learn to be brave away from his parents.

Ivan continued with the rest of his story. After the police had finished interviewing everyone, and they had left the building, Ivan had gone to Marcel and Camille's apartment to check on them. He felt that this older couple, more than the others in the building, might have experienced more stress. Ivan explained, saying that while migrating from Eastern Europe to Western Europe, he and Berta had similar experiences with the police. Everywhere they stayed more than a month, authorities became overly curious. If they stayed more than 90 days anywhere, immigration officials demanded to know their intentions.

Ivan revealed that Camille was not in the best of health, and he worried that her heart might have been affected by the confrontation. It was the first that Zack had heard of any heart problems. Ivan reassured him that Marcel and Camille were fine, when he left them. The drama, however, had fueled a short conversation about Marcel's plan to move them to the coast. Ivan said that Marcel is committed to getting Camille out of Paris, and into some "healthy sea air, and the sooner, the better."

Had Ivan talked to any of the others? Zack wanted to know.

"In person, only Albert," Ivan confirmed. Gwendolyn had not been at home, as Zack had suspected. Mara had called Ivan, just before he and Berta left for the park with Bog. She reported that she and the professor were in the hallway on the third floor, about to put the baby in the stroller for a walk, when the police arrived. They laid the baby on the floor and used the stroller to transfer quickly all of their boxes of truffles (books) from their two apartments across the hall and into the vacant apartment. By the time that the police worked their way to the third floor, Mara and Montague had the baby back in the stroller and were on their way down as the police were on their way up.

"And Madeleine?" Zack asked.

"She was already at work," Ivan said, not knowing that Zack had found her shop closed. Zack recounted his search for Madeleine, and Ivan was as dumbfounded as Zack to hear that Madeleine's shop was closed on a Sunday, and that she was nowhere to be found. Ivan had no new ideas on where she went, when she was not working, because she was always working.

"I walked the neighborhood, looked in the cafés, and even the grocery stores. I couldn't see her anywhere," Zack said, before asking, "What about the vacant apartment?"

"Mara told the police that the Italian couple had been there, recently, but that they had gone home to Italy. The police seemed disappointed."

"Only disappointed?" Zack asked.

"Her words, not mine," Ivan answered. "Yes. She definitely said disappointed." He glanced over at Berta, who seemed even more distracted. Her head was down, staring at her hands, which she kept wringing. "Berta is quite worried. She would like to go back to Poland for a while to visit, but she does not want to violate her work visa, or risk another visit from the police. She worries about deportation."

Zack's heart ached for the woman, who feared losing everything, she and Ivan had gained by moving to Paris. Remaining a member of the village was important to her, but there were tears in her eyes. She regretted getting involved in truffle smuggling; that the temptation of getting rich quick had proved too irresistible. Berta had been nothing but kind to him, since his arrival in France. Like the others, her imagination had exceeded her reach. Was he not guilty of the same thing? "Gotta go," Zack announced, suddenly.

"So soon?" Ivan said, surprised. "We brought enough food," he offered, thinking that it might be the reason Zack was leaving before they ate together. This was a Sunday afternoon tradition, one that they had shared for months. "Please stay."

"Sorry," Zack said. "I need to conduct a little investigation of my own."

"I don't understand," were all the words Ivan could get out, before Zack took off toward their neighborhood at a fast walk, and then, a full run.

He was headed for the flower shop, but this time, he swung

around the block to find the alley and the delivery entrance. Rapid, loud knocks on the back door of the shop brought no one. Rats! He was counting on someone being inside. Deliveries of flowers came on Sunday afternoons, he remembered from his evening with Gwendolyn. She had revealed that Madeleine worked on Sundays, taking deliveries, so that the shop had plenty of fresh flowers on Monday mornings. It had just occurred to him that she would have to be there to sign for the deliveries because they were scheduled months in advance. An unexpected visit from the police was not going to stop the delivery schedule.

She had said it only a few nights earlier. "I will lose everything - my savings, my shop, my reputation." Zack couldn't let that happen, and so knocked, again, but lightly this time, so as not to frighten her. Then, impatience took over, and he knocked louder, adding, "C'est moi...Zahhk...I mean, Zack."

This time, he heard her voice from behind the door. "Vous êtes seul?" (You are alone?)

"Yes," he answered. "Please let me in."

Quickly, the door opened, and he slipped inside. She looked exhausted, standing in front of him in her dirty work clothes. A clink, lock, bolt behind him signaled that Madeleine was not alone in the shop. He turned suddenly, frightened that someone else was in the room with them. Was it friend or foe? He found himself staring into the chest of a man, who was twice his size. It was the same man, whom he had seen months earlier, defending Mme. Christy against a younger man, who had dared to threaten her. As Zack eyes traveled up the chest, he could see from the expression on his face that the man was not convinced that Zack was not a threat.

"Il ne menace. Il est mon ami" (He is no menace. He is my friend.) Mme. Christy told her employee, who was, once again, acting as her body guard. Reluctantly, the man moved away and returned to unpacking flowers, which had been delivered only moments before Zack's arrival. "Claude is very loyal," Madeleine said to Zack.

"I can see that," Zack said, still a bit undone by the close encounter. "Can we talk privately," he asked.

"You can say whatever you like in front of Claude," Madeleine assured him. Claude smiled in response to her words, making it obvious that Claude understood English as well as French. This was not reassuring to Zack, who had hoped for some privacy. Madeleine must have read his mind for she offered, "Coffee?" Looking around, Zack could see no coffee available in this room. With Claude's back to them, Madeleine winked, and nodded toward the next room. Zack caught on and replied, "Yes. Please."

They moved into the next room, a small one, overly filled with old office furniture, and centered by a desk stacked high with papers. It was Madeleine's home away from home. A cat sat in the middle of the desk, oblivious to the disorder his presence made. As he climbed down from the desk, half of a stack of papers flew off in various directions, falling to the floor. Madeleine bent down, petting the old cat on his way past her. "Monsieur Oscar," she said, "Monsieur Zahhk," as if Zack needed to be introduced to the cat. The cat took one look at Zack, and with a flip of his tail, left the room.

"Sit," she insisted, although there was no place free of paperwork, as all chairs were performing double duty, filled with florist supplies and garden catalogs. "You decide where," she said, laughing at her organizational skills. "I will get us coffee." With that, she disappeared, leaving Zack to readjust a few things in order to find an edge to sit down. She returned a few moments later, carrying two cups. "Black?"

"Yes," Zack said, accepting the coffee. "You remembered."

"Yes. I try," she said. "These days, I think my memory is not so good." Her chair was the only one available. Erasing the image of her normally elegant body language, she slumped down. Her face looked older, as if she might have been working all night. Zack made the unconscionable mistake of mentioning it, not knowing that a woman does not like to be reminded that fatigue shows on her face like a billboard advertisement. He meant only to show concern for her welfare. "Yes, I know," she acknowledged, sadly, ignoring his ignorance. "I have not slept well in many weeks. We really must end this...charade soon."

"We will," Zack reassured her. "Were you home when the police arrived?"

"No. Here," she said. "Mme. Durand called me. I turned off the lights and put out the sign immediately."

"So, then, they have not questioned you? Do you think that they will come here, next?"

"Probably," Madeleine said, flipping casually through a calendar on her desk. It displayed pictures of beautiful beaches on the southern coast of France. "I was thinking of going on holiday this year. You know," she turned her attention to Zack's face, "I never take a holiday."

"Yes, I know," Zack said. "Sounds like a good idea to me. Are you packed?" he teased, "We could leave this afternoon."

She laughed. "Yes. Sounds like a good idea to me, too."

"Is the professor correct...about growing a new truffle in his laboratory? I mean, I know nothing about these things, but would it be possible...in your estimation?" Zack really wanted to know.

"You thought it was a brilliant idea," she teased him about his defense of Montague's proposal. "Don't you remember? I thought you knew." She could see the red beginning at Zack's collar line, and traveling up his face. She had caught him. He had had no idea if the professor's idea was good or bad. He had taken advantage of a serendipitous moment, to jump on the promotional bandwagon. In truth, Zack had seen the professor announcement as a welcomed escape route, a way to save his own skin. If the villagers were no longer engaging in illegal activity, then, he had no secrets to protect from anyone.

Well, that is, with the exception of Dmitry's, but that was a whole 'nother story – one waiting to be written.

Yes. Madeleine was partially correct. His presence in the village, and what he knew about the villagers, would no longer present a threat to anyone, but more than that, he would be able to visit freely Dmitry – with or without permission from the others. And, although, they had no inkling of his motives, his long-term hope was to integrate Dmitry into the general population of the village. No one, living there as long as Dmitry had, should be made to feel an outsider. Not even, Monsieur Le Spy.

She let him off the hook, too tired to play the game. "Truffles have always been expensive because they could not be reproduced, not like other mushrooms and fungus. Montague has discovered something, which proves what other scientists have only speculated. Truffles enjoy sex just as much as... well, just like human beings...although Gwendolyn would probably disagree. She might say that truffles need to fall in love, first, in order to reproduce."

Zack's face told Madeleine, what she already knew about him and Gwendolyn, and more specifically, about their difference of opinions on sex and love.

"As a woman gets older," Madeleine said, coyly, "she knows the difference plainly. Gwendolyn will learn, too. Give her time." Madeleine took a long sip of now cold coffee. "But, we were talking about truffles. Yes. To answer your question, Montague has done it. I am convinced, and although, I am neither, a botanist or a scientist, I believe him. He has never been one to exaggerate the truth."

Zack could disagree. Evidently, Madeleine had never been privy to Montague's late night rants and incantations after a bottle or two of good Bordeaux. Zack could give her a few examples of his hyperboles, but this was not the time. Perhaps, when it came to science, the good professor knew where to draw the line on truth and lies. "Well, then, what can I do to help? You, obviously, have all the manpower you need," he said, referring to Claude. "There must be something I can do to speed up the cleanup."

Madeleine sighed, looked across her desk at the stack of paperwork, and asked, "Are you any good at bookkeeping?"

Now, it was Zack's turn to sigh, "Not as good as Gwendolyn."

Madeleine picked up the phone and offered it to Zack. "Do you want to call her, or should I?"

"Unless you want her to hang up, it would be best – if you called," Zack answered.

Zack stood up to go, just as Madeleine dialed. "Where will you go now?" Madeleine asked, waiting for Gwendolyn to pick up.

"I have to find someone," he said.

"Dmitry?" Madeleine asked. Zack froze. Why had she assumed that? What did Madeleine know about Dmitry? "I saw him return home about twenty minutes ago, when I was in the front of the shop," she explained.

Zack was now anxious to get back to the apartment building, and apparently, this showed.

Gwendolyn answered, and Madeleine said, "Un moment, s'il vous plaît." Turning to Zack, she said, quite seriously, "Do not tell the others about Dmitry. Not yet. It is too soon. Do not let them see you at his apartment. Arrange to meet him elsewhere." Zack was stunned. Did Madeleine know as much about him and Dmitry, as she did about him and Gwendolyn? Were there no secrets in the village? But, more importantly, what was she not saying? "You must trust me on this,

Zahhk," she added, before speaking to Gwendolyn. "Gwen, are you free this afternoon?"

Zack walked a few blocks, before returning to the apartment building. There was a lot to consider, the strange conversation with Madeleine, the police interviews with all of the villagers, Berta's fear of deportation, and what he was going to say to Dmitry about all of this? Could he even get a message to Dmitry without being observed by the others? Was Madeleine saying that someone had reported his comings and goings from Dmitry's apartment? Could he attempt to visit Dmitry ever again, without someone spying on him, and reporting back to the others? Probably not. Women. Rats! Why did they always have to complicate things?

On his way into the apartment building, he met the American tourists on their way out. With luggage in hand, they seemed in even more of a hurry. Zack could see a taxi was waiting, and so, did not delay them. In passing, he did wish them a safe trip home, but regretted that they blew past him so quickly, that he could not ask them about their encounter with the French police. They smiled, broadly, waving from the taxi, which left him in a cloud of dust.

He felt that he owed these Americans some sort of an apology for his adopted country's rude disturbance on a peaceful Sunday morning. Their last morning in Paris had been ruined, and he did not want the encounter with the police to leave a bitter taste in their mouths, or to ruin what had been, according to them, a wonderful trip to Europe. No doubt, the interrogation would be the last thing that they would remember, and probably, the first thing, that they would tell their relatives back in the States. Somehow, it would convince other Americans not to come to Paris. Would this be a good thing, or a bad thing?

Another idea for an article was forming in his mind, as he climbed the stairs past the second floor, where the two families, Gwendolyn, and Madeleine lived; and on past the third floor, where Mara, the professor, Dmitry, and the make-believe Italian couple lived; to his safe haven in the sky. He passed no one on the ascent, finding the building as quiet upon his return as it had been on his departure. The only difference was the unusually heavy aroma of cinnamon and nutmeg, which seemed to permeate the air on every floor. There was also an unusual draft of air blowing down through the stairwell of the third floor, and it appeared to be flowing down from the attic level.

Oh, no! Had he left his windows open, again! He ran. The source was apparent. The American couple had vacated their holiday rental in such a hurry that they had left the door wide open. Zack discovered that it was their window left open this time, not his. "Thank goodness," he muttered, unable to embrace any more guilt for Sébastien or Dmitry's adventures, or for his own negligence.

It was his first chance to see the place, and so he entered, motivated by opportunity, and uninhibited by the lack of eyewitnesses. He was surprised to find that the holiday apartment was just about everything that his small place was not. The layout and the décor were a mirror image of his apartment, but this one was much larger – as if every dimension of his place had been duplicated, but then, expanded by a full two meters. This made him envious, especially, when he saw the full size bed. He was not discouraged by the condition of the apartment, knowing that its former occupants had left in such a hurry.

The bed linens had been left in a jumbled mess. He peeked inside the bathroom only to discover that it, too, was a mess. Wet towels still lay on the floor of the shower. This apartment had a real shower! He ignored that Mme. Durand had not been upstairs, yet, to clean. Perhaps, she was not aware that the tourists had left, as the door key lay on the edge of the bathroom sink, either, forgotten or intentional left behind, additional evidence that the tourists had left in a hurry.

His jealousy, over the luxurious space, which the tourists had enjoyed without his knowledge, grew. With each new discovery, his satisfaction with his little nest next door began to fade. This unit had a microwave and a hot pot. His did not. This place proudly displayed on the wall across from the bed, a flat screen television. Below it was an internet connection and a telephone! His apartment did not even have a transistor radio, much less a telephone.

He wondered. Could Dmitry re-negotiate with the landlord on his behalf, so that he could switch apartments for the remaining three months? The impromptu tour had convinced Zack that it was worth a try, although, he doubted it could be rented for the same amount of money. What did a little more space and a few luxuries matter? He was already paying a ridiculously low price for what was advertised as a holiday rental. It was adequate for his needs, but his imagination would not let the idea drop. He took one long last look at the apartment with his hand on the doorknob, realizing that he was practically salivating at the prospect of moving in, when he remembered his real purpose in being there. He walked back across the room, closed the window, was about to close the door, when something stopped him in his tracks.

His apartment and this one were identically decorated, right down to the color of the bed linens and towels. What was missing? It had been a passing glance, a clue almost ignored. In his apartment, there was a mirror next to the entry. It was the only mirror in the place, and one he used every day when shaving. It was ornate, very gold, and very, very old. Below it stood a tiny antique table, hardly large enough to hold a wallet, a set of keys, and can of shaving cream, but equally as ornate as the mirror.

In the abandoned tourist apartment, the evidence spoke louder. A ringed shadow on the wall, faded, but quite apparent, memorialized the place, where the gilded mirror had hung. The precious antique was gone! Stolen! So, too, the antique table! Yikes!

Zack looked around the apartment, looking for more missing items. What he found, instead, was a mound of dirty clothes, stuffed in a large plastic trash bag, and hidden beneath the bed. The conclusion was simple. The tourists had filled their suitcases with souvenirs, but unwilling to settle for ashtrays, they boldly had pilfered larger, more valuable treasures. Quite possibly, these souvenirs of Paris were sixteenth century, and better suited for museums.

It seemed obvious to Zack that the American couple knew immediately what riches they had found. Did they think the exorbitant rent entitled them to take home whatever they liked? Or, had they been career thieves, poised, waiting for just such opportunities? Had the pictures of the apartment, posted on the internet, been too enticing? Had they come here, specifically, to steal the antiques?

Zack had to report this to Mme. Durand. He ran down the stairs, not checking his own apartment, too concerned that the tourists would get away with the landlord's possessions. If they called the police, now, there was a chance the tourists could be stopped at the airport, before they got on their flight home.

His repeated knocks on Mme. Durand's door brought not only Mme. Durand to the door, but also Marcel and Monsieur Le Postman into the hallway. Whether they were expecting an encore performance by the police, or something worse, both men had arrived prepared to do battle. Marcel held a rolling pin, and Monsieur Le Postman, a hockey stick. With one look at Zack, both visibly relaxed.

Then, Zack said, what they did not want to hear. "We've been robbed!" His choice of words revealed just how invested he had become in the welfare of the village. "We," he had said, not you.

They, of course, thought he meant robbed of the truffle stash, and reacted accordingly. Monsieur Le Postman took two steps at a time on his rush to the third floor. Despite his age, Marcel was not far behind. Zack helped Mme. Durand navigate the stairs at a much slower pace, but one remarkably fast, even for her. Upon reaching the third floor, Monsieur Le Postman and Marcel detoured toward the vacant apartment, while Zack and Mme. Durand continued upwards towards the top floor.

"Hey!" Zack shouted over his shoulder to the two men. "Up here."

Marcel and Monsieur Le Postman were confused, looking first at the undisturbed door of the vacant apartment door; then, at each other. They shrugged, before continuing up the stairs behind Zack and Mme. Durand at a slower pace this time. Upon reaching the attic floor, Zack went ahead and pushed open the unlocked door of the holiday rental. "See!" he said, pointing at the wall.

Immediately, it was clear to all four. The apartment had been robbed. They saw the shadowy remains on the wall and floor. Zack pulled the trash bag out from under the bed and placed it on top, opening it wide for all to see. "See!" he said, again. "They must have filled their suitcases with the mirror and the table." Mme. Durand put her hand in front of her mouth in disbelief. Never before had such a thing happened. Certainly, not on her watch.

Marcel and Monsieur Le Postman were suddenly panicked, each looking at the trash bag full of dirty clothes, and then, at each other. Simultaneously, they rushed for the stairs. Zack was left, standing alone in the middle of the vacant holiday rental. He had no idea what was going on. He saw the top of Marcel's head disappear on the third floor landing, from which there came a collective "Gasp!" Was it possible? Could it be?

By the time, Zack reached the third floor, a crowd had gathered in the hallway and on the stairs. His knocking at Mme. Durand's door had started the alarm, but it was the town crier calling out, "Thief!

Thief! Stop!" that the villagers had heard. Mme. Durand had called out, fleeing down the stairs without stopping on the third. She was on her way to call the police, when Albert caught her and stopped her.

Turning her around, he said, "No police," he said. "Not yet."

The villagers had listened against their front doors, or through unstuffed air vents, when Zack first announced the robbery. They followed their audio assessments with visual ones conducted through keyholes. Soon, sock-footed feet had slip softly across hallways, and up the stairs. A consensus had been reached. A public investigation was warranted.

Without his knowledge, nearly every soul in the village had inched his or her way up the stairs to listen to everything, Zack revealed in the holiday apartment. Then, in a flurry, they had scattered, as quickly as they had assembled, leaving Marcel and Monsieur Le Postman to scout out the rest of the danger for them. As Marcel and Monsieur Le Postman had rushed to the third floor, and Mme. Durand had come screaming down the stairs, the villagers returned to provide backup.

Zack had been stunned to find himself in the midst of a village throng. Camille, Ivan, Berta, Bog, Albert, Arness, Sébastien, Mara, Montague, with Mme. Durand providing the caboose to their train, they were there. Gwendolyn had accepted a different kind of hazardous duty across the street in Madeleine's flower shop. With them gone, the only villager missing was, of course, Dmitry. Zack found this profoundly curious because Madeleine had just told him, Dmitry had returned home.

If Dmitry was, indeed, home, he was lying very, very low. Perhaps, he was even watching through his key hole. In a way, Zack hoped that he was. If he learned of the truffle operation now, and confronted them, it would let Zack off the hook forever. No one could accuse him of betrayal. How could Dmitry not be watching? He would have to be deaf not to have heard so many sets of feet rushing up and down the stairs.

The villagers were breathless, not from the ascent or descent, but from the suspense of waiting for Monsieur Le Postman, who was fumbling with the key to the vacant apartment. When he finally succeeded in unlocking the door, the entire entourage pushed in, forcing him into the room. Zack followed, unable to resist the temptation to see what his imagination had painted as a very dangerous place. After all, Tito had died here.

Inside, a cacophony of voices expressed shock, simultaneously, in French and Polish. He could not understand what was being said. "Robbed," Mara said, loudly, translating. "We've been robbed!" Indeed, there was nothing in the room, except empty flowerpots. Brown paper wrappers, the kind that had graced the outside of dozens and dozens of book deliveries, were wadded up in little balls, thrown in every corner of the room.

Zack took another look, and one last deep breath, before collapsing under the weight of uncontrollable sneezes. His lungs were overloaded with allergens, and his head spun. The floor dropped out from under his feet, he was seconds from passing out. Montague caught him, pushed him out the door, and into the hallway. "Come with me," he said, continuing to push Zack across the hall in front of him. Ivan jumped in to help steady Zack.

Montague kicked open his front door in time for Zack to fall across the threshold. Montague and Ivan picked him up, and managed to get him to the sofa, where he dropped half on, half off. Zack struggled to breathe. His sneezing quickly exhausted the air in his lungs, but fresh air from the hallway had helped keep him conscious.

Montague rushed to his bathroom cabinet, and returned with an asthma inhaler. "Here," he shoved it into Ivan's hand. Zack had never used an inhaler before, and so looked confused. "Like this," the professor demonstrated, showing both of the men. Ivan handed the inhaler to Zack. Zack tried a couple of times, before getting it right. A moment or two later, he did feel better, and leaned back against the sofa cushions, relieved to be alive and breathing. The sneezing subsided, as well. Montague had saved his life. Or so, it seemed.

"What was that?" Zack asked.

"You said it yourself. You are highly allergic to fungus, apparently, to truffles, as well. You are too allergic to be living near this room. I think you should consider moving, at least, until we can clean out the apartment."

"I'd say someone else just did that for you." Zack wanted to laugh, but could not. "The American tourists?" he asked, knowing that his guess was probably dead on.

Montague nodded his head, "Yes. I would guess so. Maybe the police knew more about these people than we did. Maybe they were the ones suspected of being thieves. Maybe the police wanted nothing from us, but information about them."

"Will Mme. Durand report the robbery to the police?" Zack asked.

"Yes, but not until we have this apartment completely clean. No sign of truffles must remain. The police might want to see every apartment, next time, whether or not the tenants are home. They can do that, if there is enough evidence to support that sort of investigation."

"Yikes!" Zack said.

"Yes, Yikes," Montague said, mimicking Zack's American accent.

Across the hall, an impromptu meeting had been called. Zack was unable to attend for obvious reasons, and Monsieur Le Postman offered to bring him, as well as Mara and Madeleine, the details of any decisions reached. Later, Zack would learn that a cleanup crew had been designated, which would include Albert and Ivan and their wives. When that was done, Monsieur Le Postman would bring in repairmen, to put the apartment back into its original condition, appropriate for renting to a real tenant, not an imaginary one. When that was done, Marcel, Camille, and Mme. Durand would talk to the landlord about the robbery, making it seem like the American tourists had just left, (not weeks earlier), and reporting that the robbery had just happened. They would pay the rent on the holiday apartment from the village's coffers, so that the landlord would not know any differently.

Bog and Sébastien wanted to stay and help, but their parents would send them away for a short vacation in the country with Albert's brother's family. Both boys, having seen empty flowerpots and containers, would ask too many questions. They would be told to keep their mouths shut about the "flower" garden growing in the vacant apartment, as it was a surprise for Mme. Christy, whose birthday was next month. The little boys liked Mme. Christy, almost as much as they liked secrets, so it was easy to believe the lie. But, little boys had short memories, and they might say something at the wrong time. It was best if they were not in Paris, when the police came back to investigate.

Mara and Montague were given the task of locating a proper tenant for the apartment, so that when the imaginary Italian couple gave their thirty day notice to vacate, there would be another tenant lined up to move in. This would relieve the village of the obligation to pay rent. Montague's new breed of truffles could not be stored in an apartment, where the temperature could not be constantly monitored. Therefore, the need to keep the warehouse space no longer existed. This was a huge relief for everyone.

Zack climbed slowly up to his tiny attic apartment, his lungs tired; his mind still spinning, an attempt to process what had happened on this strange Sunday. It was getting dark outside, and he had consumed nothing more than a croissant and coffee all day. Just as strangely, he was not hungry. Something about coughing up his lungs and sneezing out his brains had produced this effect.

He looked once, in passing, at the still open door next to his, then, unlocked his and disappeared behind it. He did not even bother to turn on a light. This place had become a sanctuary, away from the madness of the village, and the darkness made his nest feel even more secure. What had he gotten himself into – here in Paris? He fell into bed, exhausted, totally ignoring the two notes lying on the floor: one from Monsieur Le Postman, regarding the proposed meeting place and time, the other was from Dmitry. It would be morning before Zack would discover them.

ack awoke before dawn, a rare event. He allowed his eyes a moment to adjust to the darkness, and his mind, to the idea that it was still night. A cool breeze was blowing in through the open window, as he stumbled out of bed to close it. The clear sky and morning stars were mesmerizing, the silence, too. Then, in the distance, a siren broke the serenity. In a matter of seconds, two cars raced through the street below, followed by a policeman. A light on the top floor of a building on the next block popped on. Zack stood there, watching as the city of Paris woke up. He had never experienced this before, and it was fascinating.

He would have continued to observe, but nature directed his attention elsewhere. He left the window open, as his body had adjusted to the cooler temperature in the room. Upon his return from the W.C., the morning light from the window fell across the wooden floor, to reflect off the two white pieces of paper lying there. Zack reached down and picked them up. Dmitry's was read first; then, the one from Monsieur Le Postman.

Dmitry's read:

Tomorrow, we eat together.
Same place 16th. 18:00.

"Yes," Zack said, relieved that Dmitry understood just how difficult it had become to knock on his door. Dmitry, ever the outsider, had not expected Zack to do the impossible. Zack sat down on the edge of the bed to watch the night become the day, wishing that he did not have to wait another twelve hours to see Dmitry, to ask him what he made of the police's visit, and if he knew about both robberies.

As he lay there, a scurrying outside his door startled him. He could see movement beneath the door, then, another note! He jumped up and grabbed what revealed the delicate handwriting of a female. Quickly, he unbolted the door, startling Gwendolyn, who had just turned toward the stairs in the darkened hallway. Zack was almost as surprised to see her, as she was to see him.

"Cripes! You scared me," she said. "I thought you'd be asleep."

"You would think so, but not today," he answered. "You on your way to work?" he asked, although the answer was obvious. Gwendolyn was dressed in one of three navy blue suits, which flaunted the monotony of her style. In her left hand was her purse, and over her left shoulder was a strap, attached to her computer case. Her hair was pulled straight back from her face, and it was slicked down with hair gel. She wore no makeup, other than a light pink lipstick. This was the Gwendolyn, whom he remembered from their first meeting. No flash. No sparkle.

Perhaps, her style reflected, also, that nothing had changed in her personal life, but the address of where she worked. Probably, she preferred it that way, Zack thought, looking at her with no passion whatsoever. A woman, showing up at a man's door this time of day, could be issuing an invitation, and should be inciting some sort of romantic response. Not Gwendolyn. Whatever was in her note, still unread, was incapable of eliciting a spontaneous tryst.

"Did you read it?" Gwendolyn asked, looking at the note still in Zack's hand.

"No," he answered. "What does it say?"

"You should read it, later, after I'm gone," Gwendolyn said, and started towards the stairs. "I'll be late." With that, she was gone.

"Wait!" Zack called after her, but she was deliberately ignoring him. "Let it be," the voice in his head chided, and so, he did. It was dark and cold in the stairwell, and there was not enough light to read anything. He returned to the warmth of his apartment. Inside, the room was bathed in morning light, although the sun was still hidden below the rooftops of Paris. He moved to the window, and opened Gwendolyn's note. It read:

"I miss you. When can we talk?
Gwendolyn."

That was it? That was the big message? I miss you? When can we talk? "Well, five minutes ago would have worked fine for me," Zack said aloud, frustrated. Women! He wadded up the note, and tossed it out the window, watching it bounce down four stories. Geez! Why couldn't she have just said it?

No. Not Gwendolyn. She had to stay in character, that cold, "I know what I'm doing," stiff-upper-lip Brit. Hadn't she learned anything from watching French women? Hadn't she learned anything by living in Paris? Zack pulled his hands through his hair, and continued staring out the window. And what was it that she expected him to do? Go running after her? Women!

Dmitry would know what to do. Certainly, Granville DeMonnay would have known how to rewrite this love affair. He had written some of the best love scenes ever read. Maybe what Zack needed to do was to introduce Gwendolyn to Granville – not the man, but his books. Maybe a trip to the bookstore would do the trick. Yes. That sounded reasonable. If Gwendolyn didn't know what a woman was expected to do, after reading one of Granville DeMonnay's novels, then there was no hope for her. It was worth a try.

Resolved to find one of Dmitry's books in English, somewhere in Paris, Zack set about to shave and start his day. Below him on the streets of Paris, men and women were getting on with the business of living their lives. Some were merely winging it, empowered by love, inspired by Paris, and fueled by their imaginations. Somewhere, there were those reckless Frenchmen, who desired sleeping in, making love and enjoying a second cup of coffee - before going to work. And for these brave hearts, there was always enough time. The world could wait.

Today, Zack could not. There were problems to solve, answers to find, a village to save, and women to... well, there were women. That was enough to keep any man busy.

Zack stopped by Dmitry's breakfast café for black coffee and a quick chat with the waiter. "No, again," he said, "Monsieur Dmitry has not been here today." It did not prevent Zack from lingering over a second cup of coffee and a second croissant. If anyone would understand, it would be Dmitry.

Zack took out his notebook, to refresh his memory on the exact location of the restaurant, where he would be meeting Dmitry for dinner. He saw his notes from his first week in Paris, and re-read them. So much had changed in his life. Nothing had unfolded as he had expected, but yet his life was better, fuller. No two days were the same; each bringing a new problem to solve, a new drama to witness. He had experienced more in nine short months, than he had in the previous nine years. Soon, he would have to make a decision to go home, or stay. Like Gwendolyn's employment, his contract came with an expiration date. So, too, his work visa.

Zack walked through the streets of the 6th, the 7th, and then, the 16th, looking in every bookstore along the way. He found only one of Dmitry's...Granville's novels. It had ragged edges and was missing the back cover. It also looked as if a glass of wine had been spilled on it, about half way through the last chapter. This novel was one of Granville's sadder ones, and no doubt, the reader had been crying through the ending. Zack could picture it, the hand that reached for tissues, and carelessly, knocked over the glass of Syrah. He put the book down. Gwendolyn deserved a less cherished copy of his hero's work. Whoever had owned this copy had practically loved it to death.

In the 16th, he thought that he had spotted Dmitry near the entrance to one of the restaurants, which they had visited weeks earlier. A closer study of the man revealed it not to be Dmitry. Zack was disappointed, as there were still a couple of empty hours to kill, before their rendezvous at the Russian café. He started to wander with no particular destination. If he got lost, he figured he could catch a taxi to the restaurant.

When the street split in two directions, he was faced with a choice. The street on the left looked familiar, too familiar, and then, he remembered. Two or so more blocks, and this street would cross the street, where Claudine's office was located. He had only walked it once, embarrassed that his staged chance encounter with the woman had gone so badly. Dare he try it, again? He wanted to turn around, but something inside told him to forge ahead. He had no commonsense, not when it came to beautiful women.

Three storefronts away from Claudine's real estate agency, Zack could see the lights were on. That side of the street was in shadow, but a definite bluish-white light fell from the windows across the sidewalk. That meant someone was in, but it didn't guarantee that it was her, Zack reassured himself, urging himself to proceed. Walking past was not a crime, the voice in his head said, unemotionally. He listened and continued, but just as he reached the edge of the window glass, he stopped, feet frozen.

There were pictures covering the glass, photographs of available properties for sale and lease. He forced his feet to inch over, slowly, in front of one, in hopes that he could glance quickly around it. Her desk was about ten feet back on the right-hand side. It would take no more than a second to verify if she was sitting there. Do it! Do it! The voice in his head kept yelling. What have you got to lose?

Ok. Head up, look quick. Head back. Yes. His heart skipped a beat. She was there. Now what? He could not stand there forever. Then, the unfortunate happened. A voice, and not the one in his head, asked, "Puis-je vous aider, Monsieur? Location ou achat?" (May I help you, Sir? Leasing or buying?) The young face was not that of Claudine.

Relieved, but feeling compelled to answer, he said, "En considérant seulement" (Looking only). He hoped that Claudine was not inside listening, perhaps, recognizing his poorly executed French. One glance between advertisements confirmed that she was still on the phone. The helpful agent disappeared back inside, and Zack turned back the way he had come.

He had walked only twenty steps down the block, when Claudine called after him, "Monsieur, Puis-je vous aider?" She was not about to give up as easily as her young assistant. A looker was always a potential buyer.

Zack did not know what to do. It was definitely Claudine's voice calling after him. If he turned around, and she saw him, would she call the police? "Stalker!" He imagined, based upon their last encounter, she would. If he didn't turn around, and kept walking, would she chase after him? Even Claudine had her limits. Surely, she would not embarrass herself in this way, chasing a potential client down the streets of the 16th.

To keep walking was the easier of the two choices, and so he did, but began picking up the pace with each step. By the time that he reached the next intersection, he was running, not even certain if anyone was following. Zack thought about what he was doing. It had been stupid. He had been running, not from Claudine, but from his past, and so...he stopped.

Beautiful women did not run after him. Women like Gwendolyn did, women who were as unsure of themselves as he was. Why couldn't he find one of these women to marry? Then, they could muddle through their self-doubts – together. Why did he always set his sights on the unobtainable? If he didn't figure it out soon, there was a great possibility that he would be spending the rest of his life alone...like...like Monsieur Le Postman ...and (He hated to say it,) ...like his hero, Dmitry. Is that what he wanted? To spend the rest of his life like a recluse?

If he listened long enough to Albert, maybe even to Ivan, he might think it best. Certainly, they had complained enough about their wives to make him question, if marriage was worth it. Marriage did not guarantee that he would get laid any more, as a husband, than he did as a boyfriend. There were the headaches, the periods, the attitudes, the lack of enthusiasm, the "you pissed me off again, you stupid man" moments, which he never quite understood. Perhaps, it was best that he remain single, and ok, maybe a little lonely...but at least, unencumbered. No one else's sanity depended upon his.

He walked slower, now, that an encounter with Claudine was out of the picture, and with an hour left to kill before meeting Dmitry. Remarkably, a bookstore appeared two doors away from the Russian café. It was one, which he had somehow missed, when he was here before. Inside, a stylishly dressed young man about twenty offered to help him. A quick scan of his online catalog revealed that there were two Granville DeMonnay novels in stock. He mounted a ladder, which reached a shallow mezzanine, disappeared for all of ten seconds, and returned with both books in hand. It was an amazing bit of luck. Rather than attempt any more decisions, Zack bought both, and resolved to read one, while waiting for Dmitry at the restaurant.

Inside, the restaurant was dark, and it took several minutes for Zack's eyes to adjust, even after he was led to the table set aside for Dmitry. Yes. Even here, there was one. All Zack had said was, "I am meeting a friend, Dmitry..." and before he had finished saying his name, a waiter had stood more erect and bowed. " Yes, Sir, this way."

Amazing.

In the corner, where they had sat before, Zack settled in. He asked, "What do you recommend for a cocktail?" The waiter brought him a Dmitry style aperitif; vodka over crushed ice with a twist of lemon. It was not Zack's drink of choice, but he did not want to tell the waiter. Instead, he thanked him for the excellent recommendation. The waiter smiled and bowed. Being a friend of Dmitry's, apparently, had many benefits. Not the least of which was courtesy.

Zack read and read and read. A second glass of vodka magically appeared, with fresh ice and fresh lemon, even though, he had barely touched the first. Reading DeMonnay was a bit of nirvana; and the nostalgia from his university years was not wasted, enveloping him as he dissolved into the stories, becoming one with the main character. DeMonnay's work had always had this effect upon him. This was what had captured his imagination as a younger man, and had inspired him to write.

In reading DeMonnay's words, his talented twists of a plot, his mind seemed clearer, more focused, and his path more set. He was exactly where he needed to be. He was meant to be in Paris at this point in his life. This was what he had dreamed about since childhood. This was what he had daydreamed about from his desk in New York.

Sure. Dmitry was important to him, a catalyst for moving forward. Writing Dmitry's biography...well, that would be wonderful, but that was still many years away. The epiphany was that Zack was capable of writing his own novels, his own stories, not just travel logs, not just features for an online magazine. He was wasting his time with that. Like DeMonnay's hero in his books loved to say, "The future is for cowards. Today is mine!"

He had decided. When his contract expired in three months, he would not return to the States. He would stay. It was set in stone... and for once, it was chiseled there by him, alone. No one was going to decide his future, or even the next moment of his life. He laid down the book and picked up the vodka. Whether he succeeded or failed, he had to do what he had come to Paris to do...meet his destiny head-on. He would become from this day forward - a novelist. "Za Vas!" he said to no one else in the room.

Dmitry's body filled the doorway. His shadow fell across half the room, and in that moment, he appeared - a giant of a man. Granville DeMonnay certainly was, Zack thought, watching Dmitry's every step toward him. How had Dmitry managed to morph into at least two distinct personalities? There had to be just as much of Granville inside of him, as there was this man, he had chosen to name Dmitry. But, who was he really? Would there come a day when Zack would find the heart of this man; when Dmitry trusted him enough to reveal his real identity?

Granville's main characters were popular, not only for their mental superiority over their enemies, but because of their physical attributes. None was too tall, too thin, too short, too fat, too bald, or too pale. Zack had grown up wanting to be any of them. The fact, that Granville knew what words to put in his characters' mouths to seduce women, had also influenced Zack's life. However, those same words from his mouth never produced the desired results. Perhaps, Dmitry could teach him how to become believable, not just on the written page, but also in the bedroom.

Dmitry was smiling as he approached. The waiter, anticipating Dmitry's order, followed with a vodka bottle, crushed ice, and a bowl of lemons. Dmitry slid into the booth, his strong cologne preceding him. He had sweated through his shirt, and chest hair was visible beneath the wet areas. His breath spoke of garlic, onion, and Burgundy. A whiff spoke to Zack of a free lunch at one of the best restaurants in Paris. Yes. Dmitry's job definitely had its perks.

Tonight, there would be another story, a tale of what lay behind the swinging doors of a famous kitchen. Any other day, Zack would have been happy to hear it, but, there was a more serious matter to discuss. Zack waited for Dmitry to settle down.

As the waiter moved away, Dmitry pulled his shirt out and away from his body, an attempt to cool down. "I rush," he said.

"You did not have to," Zack said, tapping the two books lying on the table. "I had good company." Dmitry saw the titles, and smiled, broadly. Zack added, "I thought Gwendolyn might enjoy reading them."

"Women do not appreciate them the way that men do," he said. "I learned that a long time ago." Zack was visibly disappointed. "Do not worry," Dmitry said. "You will find your woman someday, but trust me, it is not Gwendolyn. You two are fire and water."

Zack wanted to defend his friendship with Gwendolyn. "But, she possesses a great sense of humor, and we laugh." Then, he remembered the times when they didn't. Dmitry could be right. Certainly, if anyone understood anything about women, he did. Perhaps, Zack should pay more attention to the fact that Dmitry had chosen to remain a bachelor. There was probably a good reason why.

"My grandmother made me laugh," Dmitry said, looking around the restaurant at the other people. "It did not make me want to marry her." He took a sip, before beginning, again. "So, what did the police ask you?"

"So, you know about their visit?" Zack asked.

"Of course," Dmitry sniffed. "I know everything that happens." Then, he laughed a belly laugh. "You believe me?"

"Of course," Zack answered, taking a sip of vodka, attempting to mirror Dmitry. It was nothing more than hero worship. He had even begun to sit like Dmitry with shoulders slightly arched forward, head hung, so that his eyes had to peer upwards to see anything. It sent the message that anyone approaching might be interrupting serious conversation. Zack had witnessed the effect that it had on waiters. Dmitry's body language spoke almost as loudly as Granville's words.

"They questioned everyone in the building." Then, Zack said, out of context. "Geez, Dmitry. They were right next door...the thieves," he clarified. He ran his hands through his hair. "I even told them goodbye as they got in the taxi! I could have stopped them right there and then. How could I have been so stupid? ...so unaware of what was happening right next door?"

Dmitry reached over and touched Zack lightly on his arm to get his attention, as Zack was lost in his thoughts. "Take it easy, my friend. You are not Nigel." It was a reference to one of Dmitry's characters, who had a sixth sense about danger, and always managed to foil his enemies. "If it makes you feel better, I did not know they were thieves. I, too, believed they were nothing more than tourists, and I have endured, for ten years, tourists in the attic."

Zack found his choice of the word "endured" interesting, and his attempt to comfort – touching. Dmitry could have laughed, or worse; he could have condemned Zack for not preventing the theft. "Were they really valuable antiques?" he asked, knowing nothing about these things.

"To the landlord, priceless," Dmitry answered. "They belonged to his family. Mme. Durand told him not to put heirlooms in the holiday rentals, but he refused to spend his money on new furniture, and so, well, he took the risk. I, too, told him it was a mistake, but Monsieur Épicier is a stubborn man."

Zack listened, surprised, that Dmitry spoke of Mme. Durand and Monsieur Épicier so casually, as if he interacted with them on a routine basis. The impression, which the other residents had given him about

Dmitry, was that Dmitry did not interact with anyone in the building. But, Dmitry spoke of Mme. Durand, as if he and she spoke, regularly. Which was it? Who was telling him the truth?

"How well do you know Mme. Durand?" Zack asked, no longer afraid to speak his thoughts aloud around Dmitry.

"I've lived in the building for ten years," he said, again. "I know her as much as she will allow anyone to know her."

"Right," Zack said. "I understand. She is not an easy one."

Dmitry said. "It is her choice. Respect it," he added, as if Zack needed further warning. Mara had said much the same thing to him months earlier. "When she wants to become your friend - Run!" Dmitry said, chuckling. This was a story for another day. It was time to get down to business. "You can visit me at my apartment, if you come from the roof." Dmitry said.

Zack laughed. "Roof? What? You want me to become a cat burglar?"

Dmitry laughed. "How do you think the little bastard got into your apartment?" Zack's expression told Dmitry what Zack did not know. Zack was too busy wondering, if Dmitry knew what was in the packages of "books." He must. He said he knew everything, Zack reminded himself. Zack answered, "Albert and Arness said he climbs trees. I guess, I thought it was not much different."

"You give the boy too much credit, although, I admit he is clever, but not in a good way. No. There is a fire escape. You have not seen it?" Dmitry asked, surprised how unaware Zack was, even though had had lived in the building for nearly a year. "No one showed you...in case of fire?"

"No," Zack admitted. "I never got an instruction manual from Mme. Durand."

"Under the telephone in your apartment," Dmitry said.

"I don't have a telephone in my apartment," Zack said.

"NO!?" Dmitry said, shocked. "I must talk to Monsieur Épicier."

"No, no," Zack said. He didn't want the landlord to raise his rent over the simple addition of a telephone. Zack could manage without one, although, it would have been nice, if someone had shown him how to get out of the building in an emergency. "Where?" He asked, referring to the fire escape.

"Next time you look out your window, you know, the small one in the W.C., look down." Dmitry continued, "It looks like a ladder, but is fire escape. Be careful!" he added. "It is steep climb until you get to third floor."

His words smacked of first-hand experience, but how could a man his size fit through such a small window? For that matter, how was he supposed to get up to the window to escape? He would have to stand on the back of the toilet, not just on its lid. Then, what? Was he to hoist himself up, and possibly fall out the window, landing four stories below, IF he didn't find the ladder? Zack imagined in emergencies miracles happened. However, he could not imagine using the window in the W.C., or the ladder in what would be a near vertical drop. And certainly, he was not going to use it to visit his friend, Dmitry. No. There had to be another way.

And suddenly, there was. "Or you could use secret pathway," Dmitry said.

"Secret pathway?" Zack was engaged. He loved a mystery.

"From the apartment, where tourists stay, not yours," he qualified, "there is a small door. You did not see it? No one does. This small door enters the attic. I can come and go from the attic to my apartment without anyone seeing me. Also, I can go from my apartment to the fire escape, and from there, anywhere in Paris, without using the front door."

"Really?!" Zack said, fascinated with Dmitry's knowledge of the building. "How did you discover this?"

Dmitry smiled, and put his finger up alongside his nose. "Spies do not share their secrets."

"Got it," Zack said. "You know everything." He laughed. "You know something, Dmitry? You are not so very different from Nigel."

Dmitry roared. "Thank you! I like my character. One day, I would like to become Nigel. Beautiful women came to his door every night."

Zack smiled. "Yes, I remember."

"Where else could a person go from inside the attic?" Zack asked.

"There are panels in the ceilings of all of the apartments on the third floor. Did you not notice this, when you lived with Mara?" Dmitry asked.

"No! Where?" Zack found this very exciting.

"In the professor's apartment, it is above the front door; in Mara's, the same, but in mine, it is above the sink."

"The sink?" Zack said, trying to remember, if he had ever noticed anything unusual about the kitchen ceiling tiles of Dmitry's apartment.

"Yes. I will show you," he said, "and then, you visit me without the others seeing you. OK?"

"Yes, please, show me," Zack said, enthusiastically. Then, another thought struck him. "Could we visit Tito's apartment this way, also?"

"In the vacant apartment, the kitchen has been removed." Dmitry said, "A big drop to the floor, but quite easy to come and go," he said in a strange way. "I can show you, if you need to know this for yourself."

"Have you visited the other apartments in this way?" Zack had to ask. How many times had Dmitry spied on his neighbors? For that matter, how many times had Dmitry spied on Zack in Mara's apartment? How many conversations had he heard? What else? This was creepy.

"No!" Dmitry defended himself against what he could see Zack was thinking. "I am no peeping Bob," he said.

"Tom," Zack said, making the same mistake, again, correcting the great writer. "It's Peeping Tom, not... Never mind. Sorry."

"Yes. Quite right. Peeing Tom," Dmitry said.

"No, not peein... Never mind," Zack said. He took a long sip of vodka, thinking it might help ease the worry, growing in his head. "I would hate to think that you heard everything I said to Mara, Montague, or..." (He was thinking more of what Dmitry might have seen.) "I mean, it would have been nice, if you told people, when you dropped in on them...or rather, when you were hanging around in their ceilings." It sounded almost like a reprimand, and that was not his intention.

Dmitry grew silent, as if his feelings had been hurt. He looked down at his glass, and stirred it, although, there was nothing to mix. Zack noticed that he did the same thing with his black coffee every time they had met for breakfast. The waiter brought the first course, and after a cursory "Merci," they began eating, not speaking, and this made Zack worry. Had he offended Dmitry? Zack bent down to sniff his food, before picking up his knife and fork.

Without warning, Dmitry stabbed his appetizer forcibly with his fork and left it there, boing'ing back and forth, like a piano tuning fork. "Why do you do that?" he demanded. "It makes me crazy!"

Zack sat back. "Sorry. Habit, I guess."

"Well, stop it! Stop it when you eat with me." It was a command, not a suggestion.

"Ok," Zack said, slinking backwards from the table, embarrassed others nearby had heard Dmitry. Slouching at least six inches shorter, he timidly dug into the food, and did not look up, again, until he was finished. Dmitry went back to eating and he, too, was silent. It was not until the waiter cleared their dishes away that Zack was able to say anything. "Sorry. I didn't realize it bothered you so much."

"No," Dmitry interrupted, "Ok, maybe, it does bother me, but that is not the problem." Zack leaned in to hear better, as the restaurant was becoming noisy. "I try to do right thing, and always, I am bad guy." Dmitry seemed truly hurt. "Why?" He pounded his fist on the table. "Why do they hate me so much?" He asked with eyes big, round, and childlike.

"No one hates you," Zack tried to sound convincing. It didn't work.

Dmitry, in a softer voice this time, revealed that he had always felt different from the others. It did not matter how long he had lived in the building, the others had treated him as an outsider from his first day in the village. He compared it to how he felt as a child in school. He was always different, so much stronger, than the others, that they shunned him.

Zack listened, before suggesting. "If they hated you, and I'm not saying that they did, it was probably because you were so much smarter than them. Maybe it's the same here in Paris. Maybe people know you can 'out-think' them, and it puts them off."

"Off what?" Dmitry asked, not able to follow every nuance.

"Maybe they feel inferior," Zack said.

"Maybe it is my job?" Dmitry asked.

"Maybe. I mean look around. You sneeze and three waiters come running."

Dmitry laughed. "Yes, I know. Personally, between you and me...I like that."

Zack laughed, "Yes. I know."

Zack told Dmitry that he had felt very much the outsider, until he began making the needs of others in the village, more important than his own needs, like becoming Mara's cousin. He related the whole story of that escapade. He told Dmitry it had been, after the others realized he was not so selfish, that he was accepted by them.

"But, how did you do that?" Dmitry asked. "How did you make them know this about you? How did you make them like you?"

Zack could not explain without revealing his role in covering up the truffle smuggling operation, and so, he shrugged. "I'm not sure. It just happened."

"See," Dmitry said, convinced that it was something more. "I don't think they like me and that they will never like me, so forget it!" He said, downing the last of his drink. "I don't care! I don't need them. I don't need anyone!"

Zack knew in his heart that Dmitry did not mean it. It was the false bravado of a little boy on the school grounds, not a man of Dmitry's size and stature. If only Dmitry would allow Zack to tell the others, to reveal that they had a great author in their presence, it would change everything. He suggested it, but Dmitry was adamant about protecting his privacy and anonymity. Dmitry would not allow Zack to tell them anything. Anything! He insisted.

If they could not accept him as he was, a simple food inspector, than he did not want their friendship. He was not Granville DeMonnay, he insisted. Granville was dead. "Sometimes," he said in a near whisper, "I wish I were."

Zack was stunned by the revelation. But there was more.

"The only reason, you are here –is because you think I am Granville," Dmitry said, wanting Zack to refute the statement, but afraid that he would not.

"Dmitry," Zack began, quietly, looking around at others seated nearby. "I like you, and if Granville DeMonnay never wrote another word, I would still like you. You're my friend."

Dmitry's eyes filled with tears. "Really? We're friends?"

"Yes," Zack said, reaching over and placing a hand on Dmitry's shoulders. With that, he lifted his glass, "Za Vas!"

Dmitry lifted his glass, clicked it carefully against Zack's, and chimed in, "Za Vas!"

They fell silent, again. Neither seemed able to bridge the growing gap, too intent upon processing what had just happened. Zack was imagining Dmitry crawling around that attic, spying on everyone. Dmitry was weighing how much to reveal to the young writer, whose imagination matched his. This was dangerous territory.

Perhaps, more of the truth would put them on an equal footing.

Dmitry played with the idea in his head, but decided it could wait until after dessert. It was difficult to eat and talk of such serious things. The dessert was hot and the vodka was cold. What else could be more important at the moment? Zack started to lean into his food, a habit, before sniffing, but this time, he drew back and did not. For Dmitry, that was a small victory.

"Do you miss Varushka?" Zack said, unexpectedly, as the last dish had been removed.

"Varushka?!" Dmitry said. "What makes you say such things?"

"Sorry," Zack backed off. "Just curious." He had hoped that they might be able to talk about something they both enjoyed - women. Varushka was supposed to be a lead into the conversation he really wanted to have with Dmitry, a conversation ending with Dmitry's advice about women. Obviously, it had been a mistake. Varushka was off limits. Analyzing his relationship with Gwendolyn, and enlisting Dmitry's help to decipher what she meant by "I miss you," apparently, would have to wait until another day.

But, Dmitry's insight surprised Zack. "You have problem with woman?" Dmitry asked, sitting back, and patting his stomach. Zack stared because Dmitry always did this. Was his habit of smelling food any more irritating than Dmitry patting his stomach? Dmitry sensed what Zack was thinking, and immediately stopped. "Which woman?" He asked, as if there could be possibly more than one.

"I have no woman," Zack began, "I..."

Dmitry interrupted. "I see your problem." He laughed.

Zack did not. "Ok. Got me," he admitted. "Gwendolyn thinks she misses me. What does that mean?"

"Your Gwendolyn has had no man in three years...except you," he added, as if Zack should already know it. "She is thirty-six years old and wants baby. They all want babies at that age," he said with the confidence of a pop psychologist. "Or they want a..." (a hesitant pause) "You say boy toy?" he asked.

"Yes. Boy toy," Zack helped with the American expression, before protesting, "I'm not a boy toy." Then, it hit him, Gwendolyn's age! "Did you say thirty-six? Really? I thought, twenty-nine, maybe."

Dmitry laughed. "How old are you? Twelve?"

"Twenty-five," Zack answered.

"Really. You act twelve. Twenty-five? I have shoes older than you!"

The thought made him pause a moment before continuing. He studied Zack's face, while rubbing his own stubbly chin. Yes. Zack looked twenty-five, and he had forgotten how young that was in terms of experience with women. "You do have problem with women, if you cannot tell how old they are. This is very big problem. I will tell you," he said, enjoying his role as mentor. He signaled to the waiter for an after dinner liqueur, then, turned to Zack.

He lectured, dividing a woman's life into decades, as unemotionally, as if he were dissecting a frog in biology class. Despite being a confirmed bachelor, Dmitry prided himself on being something of an expert on this subject. Zack would have preferred the bawdier stories, which might have been the source of Dmitry's knowledge, but Dmitry kept his dissertation on this more academic level. In the end, Zack felt that he had been immersed in a course to learn a subject, which previously had not existed. Women 101. How many men knew what Dmitry knew? Not many, he bet.

Zack dropped his head down on the table, when Dmitry had finished.

Dmitry placed a hand on his shoulder. "I know," he said, "You had no idea, correct?"

Zack answered, "None whatsoever. Who knew? It's like I've been speaking Greek and women have been speaking Latin. No wonder we could never understand each other."

Dmitry laughed. "Good analogy. May I use it?"

"Be my guest." Zack assumed that at this point, the bill would be paid, and they would saunter back to the 6th Arrondissement. It was an unusually warm night and the skies were clear. He had no one waiting for him, and was fairly certain the same could be said for Dmitry. Dmitry, however, had other ideas, and led Zack to an underground nightclub already in full swing – somewhere between the 7th and the 6th. He had never been there before, but evidently, this was another one of Dmitry's hangouts. The bouncer at the door knew him, immediately, and spoke to him in Russian. Dmitry tipped him, generously, as they passed others still waiting in line to get in.

"You will like this place," Dmitry said, confident that all Zack needed was exposure to his style of Parisian nightlife, and not another evening cloistered in his attic apartment. If the young writer had problems with women, perhaps, he had simply not met the right kind of women. Indeed, inside, there were plenty of beautiful women, and no shortage of "types." They were every size, shape, age, and nationality. The percentage of women to men also seemed tipped in his favor.

Dmitry waved to a tall woman, with short Merlot-colored hair, who spotted him from across the room. She introduced herself to Zack as Delphine, but no introduction seemed necessary for Dmitry to squire her away. They explained that they were old friends, as Dmitry began towing her back across the room to a group of three women and two men, waving to join them. Dmitry whispered something in her ear, and she laughed. Then, over her shoulder, she called back to Zack, "GO! Find yourself a woman!" Laughing, she pointed to the opposite corner of the room, where a younger group of women had gathered.

Zack felt awkward in this crowd, and abandoned. He had not been invited to join Dmitry's group of friends. Around him, he could hear several different languages, none of which he spoke, and this made him even more reticent to mingle. He was looking across the room at Dmitry, now huddled up with his friends, and the center of attention. He was telling a story.

Zack was lamenting the loss of an invitation, when a voice behind him said, "You new in town, Mister?" The accent was decidedly familiar, and Zack spun around to take in the face of a fellow Long Islander. "Tina," the woman with the short dark hair said, smiling. "Garden City. You?"

"My disguise didn't work?" he asked, laughing. "Long Beach." Zack found the sound of English, or as Dmitry would distinguish as 'American,' to be exactly the medicine, he needed. Until this moment, he had not realized how very homesick he was. "Zack," he said, and offered his hand for a handshake.

"Hope you don't mind," she said, taking a sip of her drink, "I was eavesdropping on you and your friends. I thought I detected a New Yorker in the crowd." Without dropping a beat, she added, "Great music, huh?"

"Yeah," he said. "You here on vacation?" He found it a relief, not to have to think about his words, or whether or not, he was pronouncing them correctly. With this fellow New Yorker, he could talk in abbreviated sentences, or practically in code. She would understand him.

"No. Student. Sorbonne," she explained. "Semester abroad. You know. See the world. It was this," she teased, "or join the navy."

And so, Dmitry had been correct. This was all he needed, a night with a sympathetic female, who could relate to his dilemma. They spent the rest of the night (what was left of it) dancing, talking, drinking a little, but not too much. They commiserated about things no one, but a fellow American, a fellow New Yorker might notice in Paris.

He did not feel quite so alone, and he had completely forgotten about Dmitry, when he asked Tina, if he could see her, again.

She said, "Yes. I'd like that."

Dmitry watched from across the room, where his friend Delphine was keeping him entertained. Zack had not seen her hand, rubbing Dmitry in all the right ways. He also missed seeing Dmitry pass her money under the table. When Delphine led Dmitry upstairs for a half-hour, Zack failed to miss that, too. He was too busy looking into the eyes of a beautiful Long Island girl, who thought he was about the funniest guy she had met in a long, long time.

Zack would not have understood that a man like Dmitry might prefer to pay for sex, rather than fall in love; or that, Dmitry had asked Delphine to set Zack up with someone for the night. However, Dmitry understood that Zack was the kind of man, who needed encouragement, and a visiting American college student was a perfect choice. He thanked Delphine by slipping her an additional hundred Euros, when the club closed.

Zack told Tina goodbye on the street in front of the club. She caught a taxi with two other friends, whom Zack had not met, before this very short hello and goodbye. He watched the taxi leave, and Dmitry watched the expression on his face. Yes. It seemed that all had gone exactly as expected. Zack thanked Dmitry for bringing him to the club. Dmitry said it had been only an introduction. After this, it would be up to Zack to find his own women.

The two men sauntered home through the streets of Paris, in the tender light of dawn. To anyone passing, they were two buddies, content with life, and pleased with the way their night had ended; and indeed, they were. Dmitry had gotten laid in a private room upstairs in the nightclub, and Zack had learned that there were women, living outside of his small little village in the 6th. He had even gotten the phone number of one, who would be in Paris for three more months.

Unlike Gwendolyn, this one had no hidden agenda. Tina was in

Paris to have a good time, and this made it much easier for Zack to face the future. Gwendolyn could miss him all she liked, especially, now that Dmitry had explained that she had always been like a deer hunter. For the past few years, Gwendolyn had set her guns on finding a perspective mate, a father for her yet-to-be-conceived child; but not necessarily, a husband.

Tina, on the other hand, was only nineteen, and ready to explore the world. According to Dmitry's chart, settling down with a husband or a baby was the last thing on Tina's mind. This young woman knew that she had only a few years to kick up her heels. She wasn't about to waste a single one of them.

Zack thanked Dmitry over and over, again, for explaining just how close he had come to getting hit with the "I want a baby, and I want it, now!" bullet, which – as Dmitry pointed out – "brings down smarter men than you." The last thing he needed was a pregnant girlfriend. Yes. He was grateful to Dmitry.

Strangely, this new information brought sympathy for Mara's boyfriend, Phillipe. Then, he remembered that Mara was not even twenty-one. No. Her pregnancy had been an accident, or divine intervention, or something else – like stupidity for failing to find a condom. Somehow, she did not fit neatly into Dmitry's devised pigeonhole. Zack mentioned it to Dmitry, who answered, "It's not a perfect science."

As they reached the borders of their neighborhood, Zack asked, again, what he had wanted to ask earlier, "So...Do you know what's going on in the building?" It was a pregnant question, and unlike Gwendolyn, he had his target. His desire to end this charade was greater, now that the future looked brighter, and he felt braver. Something about spending the night in the arms of a beautiful did that to a man.

Dmitry looked at him with that, "Do I have to tell you, again, that I know everything that happens?"

Ok. Go for it, the voice in his head, commanded. "Then, why haven't you told the police?" Zack said, afraid that even the mere mention of notifying the authorities might encourage Dmitry to do just that - rat out the entire village.

"What they do is their business. I do not make it mine. They chose not to include me. I respect that. Neither do I...want them in my business." His look was a serious one, no longer of a blurry-eyed reveler. "It's that simple. Understood?"

For him, there was nothing more to discuss, but Zack could not drop it. "Why don't you simply tell them that?" His desire, for Dmitry and the others to get along, was too great to ignore. Dmitry would enjoy the dinners, which he had been privileged to enjoy at Marcel and Camille's place. Dmitry would enjoy Sundays in the park with Bog and the Polywogs. Perhaps, Dmitry would even enjoy a drink with Madeleine, occasionally. They were close to the same age, and Dmitry had revealed that women of her decade enjoyed sex without regret.

And more importantly, if Dmitry had no plans to tell the authorities, then, the others had no reason to feel threatened by him, or to exclude him. Zack waited, unwilling to walk on without an answer. "Well?" he said, unable to wait any longer.

"What are you? The U.N.?" Dmitry asked, sounding a little perturbed. "You have to go around the world making peace?"

Zack laughed. It was a good analogy. "I just want everyone to get along."

Dmitry debated in his mind, if he should ask the next question. Zack looked up at how the light played on the rooftops at this early hour as they sauntered toward home. Dmitry kicked a small glass bottle off the sidewalk, and into the gutter.

"Why don't they like me?" he asked. It sounded like something a child would ask. One look, however, warned Zack not to laugh. Dmitry was completely serious. He could not understand what he had done, or said that made the others exclude him.

"Frankly, you frighten them," Zack said, in his uncensored honesty. "Hell, you frighten me," he clarified, "the first time I saw you, I mean."

"I can't help the way I look," Dmitry said, both hurt and angry. "Angry chef," he said, running a finger down the center of his scar. "I should have ducked."

"Forgive me," Zack said, "I should have said your job frightens them."

"My job!?" Dmitry said, not believing Zack. "Why?"

Zack had caught himself in his own trap. Why would their neighbors care what Dmitry did for a living, unless it in some way jeopardized their own income. Yikes! He had really done it this time.

(Think. Think.) What did Dmitry's job, inspecting food in restaurants, have to do with a botanist, a florist, a pharmaceutical accountant, two old retired French Resistance fighters, a postman ...? (Think. Think.) "I don't know," he lied.

Dmitry rescued him from a new web of deceit, before it smothered him completely. "Is it because of the truffles?" he asked, flatly.

Zack coughed, overcome by hearing the word "truffles" aloud. The word, deliciously dangerous, had been only been whispered for months.

"Ah," Dmitry said, quietly, "I see."

Zack opened his mouth, but was seized by another fit of coughing.

"No, no," Dmitry said, putting up his hand in front of Zack's face, "No more lies. Don't tell me. I imagine that they have sworn you to secrecy." The look on Zack's face said it all. "I know what to do about this," Dmitry said, as he hurried toward their street.

Zack fell in behind him, still, coughing. "Wait!"

Dmitry would not stop until a few minutes later, when their apartment building was coming in view. "It is best if you go in, alone. We cannot be seen together. I will come home later. You go, now."

Zack hesitated, before leaving Dmitry. "We should talk about this," he said. "What do you plan on doing?"

Dmitry, in that commanding way that left no room for argument, said, "That is my business, not yours. You go home. Pretend nothing is different. Ok. Now, go."

Zack did as he was told, but with the uncomfortable knowledge that everything was different, and certain that he had no clue as to - what was about to happen. As he reached the front door, even the doorknob felt different in his hand. Should he warn the village? But, if he did, what was the danger?

Looking back down the sidewalk, he could no longer see Dmitry. What was Monsieur Le Spy up to? His nickname never fit him more than now. Dmitry had been spying on the village for years. But, how could Dmitry know everything, yet, had no idea why the others were afraid of him? How could someone so smart be so stupid? And stubborn!

Upstairs, secure in his attic nest, Zack took off his jacket and slipped the two books out of its pockets. Would he give them to Gwendolyn, even though, he knew so much more about her now? No.

She did not need any encouragement, and besides, according to Dmitry, she would not appreciate the writing. His books were written for men. Thank goodness, Dmitry had told him, before he made another mistake with Gwendolyn. Zack did not need any further romantic entanglements with her, especially, not now – now that he had met Tina.

He fell into bed fully dressed, thinking of the lovely American student, who lived not so very far away in the 5th. She, also, did not live so far away from his home on Long Island. This held all kinds of possibilities. They had agreed to meet the next weekend at another club, this one in the Latin Quarter. As he fell asleep, he didn't need Granville DeMonnay's help to write this love scene.

ome quick!" he heard Mara shouting at the top of her lungs. "Come quick, everyone!"

Zack awoke with a start. He looked at the clock. He had been asleep for hours, and yet, it was still middle of the day. He had been on his stomach, and so pushed up and off the bed. Looking down and seeing that he was still dressed, he ran out the door. "What?" he called out to Mara, without seeing her. Coming down the stairs, he could see that the door to the vacant apartment stood wide open.

Mara was hung over the railing, calling to someone below, "Call the ambulance!"

Zack could hear the scrambling of feet.

"I have already called. They are coming!" Monsieur Le Postman was calling back up to her.

By then, Marcel and Mme. Durand were in a competition to see who could hobble up the stairs the fastest. Ivan, Berta, Albert, and Arness were gone, at work, and so too, Madeleine, leaving only the oldest and youngest villagers to deal with the emergency. Zack feared from the sound of Mara's terror that something had happened to little Monty. Mara grabbed Zack's hand as soon as she saw him, and practically, dragged him into the vacant apartment. There on the floor lay Montague, a lifeless figure, and on the tables, which had been empty only hours before, lay a hundred different size shopping bags full of truffles!

He knelt down next to Montague, felt for a heartbeat, and then, laid his cheek next to his nose and mouth to feel for breathing. He reassured Mara that Montague was not dead. He was unconscious, but not dead. About the time that the senior villagers reached the doorway, Montague was coming to, moving slightly, and mumbling "truffles." Zack heard their gasps over his shoulder, and feared that upon seeing the truffles returned, all the villagers would be dropping like flies. He stood up, as Mara knelt down next to Montague to cradle his head in her hands. She whispered, "You will be alright, Monty."

Camille, having been the last to arrive, had grabbed her heart upon seeing the magical return of their truffle stash. Her gasp had startled Marcel, who turned, steadied her, and led her to the only place to sit in the apartment, the toilet. "Breathe," he instructed her as is she needed to be reminded. "Stop it! You old fool," she said, "I'm perfectly fine!" She continued in old age to be ever the tough little warrior, refusing to stay where he had put her. "Where did they come from?" she demanded, walking back into the main room, and thinking that she had missed an important part of the conversation.

"I have no idea," Marcel said, still full of wonder and amazement.

Monsieur Le Postman was deep in contemplation, but it was obvious that he was just as stumped. "Why would the thieves bring them back?" he asked. "It makes no sense." Then, he remembered his position in the village, and turned to leave. "I will let the others know." If he could not figure it out, perhaps, one of the others could. A meeting would need to be called. His problem was getting the others to leave their jobs early. This matter could not wait, until tomorrow.

Mara was having difficulty getting Montague to his feet, and Zack reached down to assist. "Shouldn't you lie down, until the ambulance gets here?" He suggested.

"Ambulance?" Montague said, alarmed. "Get me out of here. They cannot see this!" he said, panicking.

Zack and Mara helped Montague back to his apartment. There was a goose egg size bump growing on the back of his head, and medical attention was a prudent idea under the circumstances. Montague was not a young man.

Mme. Durand said that she would lock the door. With that, Marcel and Camille made their way back downstairs, just as the paramedics were making their way up. "In there," Mme. Durand pointed to Montague's apartment. There had been enough excitement for her for one day, and these young professionals were completely capable of handling an old man with a bump on his head. "Fell down," she said to them as they passed her on the stairs. As if they needed an explanation for the call, she added, "Old men fall down all the time."

Zack waited outside in the hallway with Mara, as the small

apartment did not lend itself well to four adults, much less six. Then, he experienced the first of six sneezing attacks, one right after another. Mara slipped past the EMTs to retrieve the atomizer for Zack from Montague's medicine cabinet.

Montague's examination did not take long, and although, he was already complaining of a headache, the decision was made not to take him to the hospital. One of the EMTs stepped into the hallway in the middle of Zack's third or fourth sneezing attack, to ask if he wanted medical attention. Zack held up the asthma inhaler, and shook his head, "No."

"Allergies," Mara explained for him.

Montague was told (as was Mara after she asked the EMTs about his condition) that he should remain awake the rest of the day. They were both told what signs to look for – if there was a concussion. Mara complained to Zack that Montague should have been taken to the hospital, regardless of his opposition to the idea. She and Montague argued until the professor reminded her that his head already hurt. Then, and only then, did she soften.

Zack walked upstairs to his attic apartment and opened the door to find Dmitry sitting on the bed. "Close the door," Dmitry said, seeing the look of surprise on Zack's face. Zack complied, before whispering, "What are you doing here? How did you get in?"

Dmitry was covered in dirt and cobwebs, and his very presence in the room made Zack begin sneezing. What he had been doing no longer needed any explanation. "You?" he spit out between sneezes. "Moment," he said, digging in the drawer of his nightstand. Montague had convinced him to buy an asthma inhaler of his own, if he insisted on staying in the building. Two sprays later Zack was able to converse. "Let me see if I get this right? You stole the truffles? Then, you put them back? Why?"

"I wanted to help," he said, confused. "Aren't they happy?"

Zack sat down on the bed to catch his breath. He had been in the room with the truffles too long. Dmitry went to the window and opened it wider. "You want a drink of water, or something?" he offered.

"No, no," Zack wheezed out. "I want answers. Grab that chair," he said, pointing to an old wooden one used only as a place to hang clothes.

Dmitry complied, not willing to leave his friend, who appeared to need him. "I can tell the ambulance not to leave, yet, if you want to go to hospital." His concern was real.

"No, no," Zack said, better able to breathe. It just takes a few minutes to kick in. "But, it would be better, if you kept your distance. You have truffles, or something all over you."

Dmitry had not thought of that, and so, immediately, began shedding his clothes. He was down to his underwear, before Zack could stop him. He ignored Zack, rolled his clothes up in a bundle, and tossed them out the window. Zack's eyes grew big. How was he going to get Dmitry out of his apartment, if he was half-naked? Dmitry sat down on the chair, and Zack tried averting his eyes, as Dmitry began his explanation.

Dmitry had overheard the aftermath of the villagers meetings, but because he was not privy to all of the information, and evidently, not all of the decisions, he acted upon what he knew. He thought everyone wanted the operation shut down, and so, he did what would help them best, in his estimation. He got rid of the truffles. Well, actually, he moved them out of sight and into the attic above the vacant apartment. He did it, while the police were there, interrogating the other residents.

But, when he found out that the police were not there about the truffles, he planned to move everything back as it was. However, everyone had rushed into the apartment so quickly that he had barely enough time to climb back into the attic. After the robbery was discovered in the holiday rental, things sort of got out of hand. Everyone assumed that it was the American tourists, who stole the truffles.

"So, why put them back?" Zack asked.

"Because they weren't mine. I was just trying to protect them..." He hesitated to say it, but then, finished, "I didn't do it for me. I did it for them. I thought..."

"Thought?" Zack asked. "Don't you know everything about everything?" he said, frustrated with his friend. "You know, they'll just have to get rid of them, again."

"Yes. Now, I know that. But, maybe this time, I can help...the right way. I have connections, you know, kitchens all over Paris."

Zack thought about that for a moment. Wow. There was an idea. Dmitry could be the new salesman for the... (Stop it! Stop it!) "I think the connections that you have, and which they need, are in the government. They need to know why the police were here in the first place. The police couldn't have known about the missing antiques. It had to be something else. Can you find out what? We need to know - if the police know - about the truffles."

"What am I supposed to ask? Seen any stolen truffles, recently?" Dmitry said, irritated with Zack's naivety.

"No, I don't suppose you could do that," Zack said, seriously contemplating the possibility. They talked for another half hour, before a knock at the door interrupted them. Zack called out, "Yes? Who is it?" Dmitry was already in the W.C., standing on the toilet, and about to hoist himself out the window, before Zack motioned him to come back in.

"Gwendolyn," she answered.

"Gwen, this isn't a good time to talk," Zack said.

"I don't want to talk. I wanted to tell you that the paramedics took Montague to the hospital. They decided it was his heart, not his head," she said.

With that, Zack opened the door wide enough to slip out into the hallway to ask, where Montague had been taken, and how long he might be there. When he stepped back inside his apartment, a moment later, Dmitry was gone. Zack ran to the window, half-expecting him to be dangling from the ladder, or splattered on the ground below. But, Dmitry was nowhere to be found. Zack looked for sliding panels, and miniature doorways in his ceiling and walls, but came away even more confused. Dmitry had disappeared into thin air. Stranger than fiction, he said aloud, sitting back down on his bed to rest.

Gwendolyn had said that Montague had been taken to the hospital for observation. His heart rhythms were unusual, and the paramedics didn't want to take any chances. Mara had asked her to watch the baby, while she accompanied Montague in the ambulance. Gwendolyn had been delighted for the chance to play surrogate mother to the infant.

Zack saw her eyes sparkle, and this only reinforced his decision to keep his distance from her. She was fertile and feverish, neither a particularly sexy improvement over the old Gwendolyn. He wished she would appear, as he could use someone with a sense of humor to help him sort out the chaos going on around him.

Dmitry had meant to be helpful. Instead, he had only frightened the other villagers, who could not imagine anyone – other than the American tourists – stealing their booty from the vacant apartment. If the Americans tried to sell the truffles, it would only mean one thing, getting caught. Getting caught meant confessing. Confessing would lead the police right back into the heart of the village, and they would all be taken away to jail.

Finding the truffles returned only quadrupled the problem because now someone other than the Americans were involved. But who? Was it the police setting them up for a fall? They all wanted to hide under their beds and would have, but Montague's fall and trip to the hospital had prevented it.

No. Now, they would have to call an emergency meeting without him. Monsieur Le Postman appeared at Zack's door, less than ten minutes after Gwendolyn departed. "Downstairs. Marcel and Camille's. Now," he commanded. Zack stopped on the third floor, but Monsieur Le Postman walked down another flight to Madeleine's door. Madeleine, having just returned from work, was putting her key in the door. Zack started to listen, but thought it better to see, if Dmitry had returned to his apartment.

On the third floor, there was no light coming from beneath Dmitry's door. He wondered. Where in the world was the half-naked Dmitry hiding? He leaned into the door, hoping to hear movement inside. Nothing. Rats!

Monsieur Le Postman and Madeleine were standing at the bottom of the stairs, and so, he quickly, ran to the stairs, not wanting to be caught anywhere near Dmitry's door. As he hit the landing, he thought he heard an odd sound, something along the order of a window slamming. He hoped his friend had landed safely on his home planet. The last thing this place needed was a half-naked cat burglar, hanging from the roof.

Marcel and Camille apologized for not having a dinner prepared. Food was the least of anyone's worries. Gwendolyn and Madeleine sat with Berta and Arness. Gwendolyn had Monty on her lap, and the women had circled around her, to coach her on what to do with an infant. Camille had managed to find something to put in the baby's bottle, and it was keeping Monty fairly content. Ivan, Albert, and Monsieur Le Postman had gathered in the furthest corner of the room to discuss something too frightening to discuss in front of the women.

What would happen to the children, if they all went to prison?

Zack couldn't decide which group would be the most welcoming. It was then, that Marcel made the decision for him, by taking him by the arm and leading him into the library. "What?" Zack said, anticipating a favor.

"You need to recruit Dmitry. We need his help and we need it, now," he said. "Can you find him?"

Of all the favors in the world, finding Dmitry might be the hardest thing that Marcel could have asked him to do. He had no idea where the man could be. Inside? Outside? Hanging from a gargoyle? However, in the end, Zack could not refuse the old man, whose grip on his arm seemed more to steady himself, than it was to impress his point upon his young friend. "Ok," Zack agreed. "Should I leave now?"

"Yes," Marcel said. "Bring him here when you find him. Tell him... Tell him whatever you have to, to get him to agree." Then, he leaned in and whispered, "I'm counting on you, boy."

It was World War II all over, again, and Marcel was asking Zack to carry a message across enemy lines. He would have to risk his life in the process, but there was no one else, whom Marcel would trust with this mission. Zack understood at that moment, what it must have been like for Marcel, the boy, and Camille, the child.

"I won't let you down," Zack reassured the old warrior.

Zack walked back into the living room, and murmured something on his way out. Hardly anyone noticed. They were all too absorbed in their own dramas to appreciate the one about to take place outside. Zack went directly up the stairs and to Dmitry's apartment. He knocked loudly, and as he anticipated, rallied no response.

"Dmitry!" he called out. "It's Zack. I have to talk to you! Open up!" Still no response. "Come on," he said louder this time. "I'm not kidding. We have to talk. No more games."

If Dmitry was in there, he wasn't coming out any time soon. Zack no longer had his key, and so, he bent down, and looked through the keyhole. There was nothing to see. Dmitry had placed something in the keyhole to prevent two-way viewing. "Rats!" Zack said, stomping up the stairs to his apartment. He had thought, just maybe, Dmitry might have returned. He went to the window, leaned out as far as he could, hoping to see, at least, Dmitry's clothes laying on the roof below, but there was nothing there. So, he grabbed his wallet, his cell phone, and his jacket. It was going to be a long night.

Zack followed the route, which he had Dmitry had taken home from the nightclub. Along the way, he stopped in various restaurants to ask if anyone had seen his friend. No one had. The nightclub was not opened, yet, for business, but Zack managed to get a woman on the first floor to call downstairs, so that Zack could talk to the club manager. He told him that it was very important to get in touch with Dmitry. The manager could offer no suggestions, except he did give Zack, Delphine's telephone number, after Zack was able to describe her to him. The manager must have figured that if Zack could describe her that accurately - right down to the mole on her shoulder - he had to be one of her customers.

Zack was about to give up, when he arrived at the Russian café in the 16th only to find Dmitry's table vacant. The waiter tapped Zack on the shoulder, on his way out, and whispered, "He's in the W.C." Zack's face lit up. He waited outside of the W.C. There was no way that Dmitry was going to disappear again. Not tonight. Dmitry came face-to-face with Zack, in a way that no man wishes to meet his friend. He was zipping up his trousers. Zack had to apologize, backing up, quickly.

"What are you doing here?" Dmitry asked, and not in a particularly, welcoming manner.

Zack took Dmitry by the arm. "They need you and they need you, now. Come on."

"I haven't eaten dinner," Dmitry protested.

Zack was already pulling him toward the door, and it was not an easy task. "There isn't time. You wanted them to like you... well, this is your chance. Forget about dinner. I'll buy you dinner afterwards." Zack was not going to relinquish his grasp.

"Ok. Ok." Dmitry said, "But you do not tell them anything about me. Agreed?"

"Agreed," Zack said. "This isn't about you. It's about them. Understand?" Zack was irritated with the man, who thought the world should both ignore him, yet, praise him for his famous past life. "They don't care about your past. They only care about their children's future. If you don't help them, they'll probably all go to prison. You understand?" Zack was thinking that Granville DeMonnay would understand. He understood what it took to be a hero. "Well, Dmitry... or whatever your name is, here's your chance to be a hero. You going to help them? Or are you going to stay here and have dinner?"

"I go with you," Dmitry said, quietly, somewhat embarrassed that his ego had gotten in the way. "I was only trying to help."

Zack let go of his arm, and headed towards the door, "Well, maybe you should explain that to the people, who matter."

Dmitry took one longing look over his shoulder as the waiter was about to bring his dinner to the table. He said to put it on his tab, and he would be back tomorrow night. The waiter glared at Zack, knowing somehow this was his fault. Zack knew that the waiter was right in more ways than he could possibly imagine.

Since moving to France, Zack had gotten very little correct. In his friend Dmitry's eyes, missing one of the best meals in all of Paris was unforgivable. There were times when putting down your pen to pick up your fork was worth the diversion. Putting down a fork to follow Zack to confront the villagers, who had never made him feel welcome? Well, this was a serious risk. Dmitry had never been asked to trust anyone so much as Zack.

There was no time to saunter. The occasion demanded a taxi, and so, with one hand tightly attached to Dmitry's arm, Zack raised the other. Within seconds, a taxi screeched to a stop in front of them. Inside, Dmitry was beginning another protest, saying that their neighbors would only hate him more, if he failed in helping them. Before, he had been trying to help on his own. That was different. If he had failed then, no one would be the wiser. No. He insisted, Zack was treading, where he shouldn't be treading.

"The French are not like us," Dmitry announced, only to have the driver jerk his head around at the perceived insult. Dmitry shut up. Zack shot him a look, as if to say, "Are you nuts?" The last thing they needed was for the taxi driver to throw them out. Marcel and the others were waiting. Zack glanced as his watch. Traffic was terrible, and they were crawling, compared to the people on foot, zipping past. Perhaps, being thrown out to walk would not be such a bad thing.

Then, the driver – perhaps, because he had grown tired of their conversation – or because he read Zack's mind, found an opening and went for it. Jerking the vehicle to the right, and then back to the left, he managed to navigate around the delay, a minor fender-bender. They arrived home a few minutes later. Zack got out first and paid the driver. Dmitry was slow to move, a ploy to buy a little more time. Zack looked over the roof of the taxi at him, wondering if he was going to bolt.

Dmitry had complained that he did not like the idea of standing in a room full of people, who had ignored him for nearly ten years. "A lion's den," he had called it in the taxi. "Why are you throwing me to the lions?" he asked Zack.

Zack said, "It's just the opposite. They're the ones, expecting to get eaten alive, and they don't even know by whom. The police? The American tourists? Some goons from the south of France, who haven't been paid by a dead man? You? They have no idea that you were the one moving the truffles in and out. You have to explain that, and help them figure out the rest. They're looking for a defender."

"I can't be that." Zack surrendered to his ineffectual status as an outsider. "I don't understand how things work here in Paris. You may not be French, but you know people in the government. You can advise these people. Trust me, Dmitry. They don't know you...like I do. I know you're a..." He hesitated to say it, pussycat, because he didn't know how Dmitry would feel about the characterization. "Stop acting like such a bully. It really doesn't help."

Dmitry was surprised. He had gotten use to people thinking the worst of him, based upon his looks, and his accent, and yes...ok, his attitude. But, this gave him space, mentally and physically. Other people moved out his way, and after all these years, admittedly, he had begun to expect it. He liked it that way.

Zack was saying, "Cool it. Don't come on so strong with these people, and maybe, just maybe, they will like you...because they'll see the Dmitry that I've come to know." Was Zack right? Dmitry's palms were sweating as he pulled on the handle of the front door, and Zack punched in the digicode.

Marcel and the others were still there, still waiting. The only one, who didn't appear nervous, when Zack entered with Dmitry right behind him, was Monty, the baby, who had fallen asleep. Gwendolyn picked him up and carried him to Camille and Marcel's bedroom. No one spoke, while she was doing this, afraid to wake the infant, but more afraid to say anything in front of Monsieur Le Spy.

"I believe everyone knows everyone?" Zack said, waiting for someone to offer Dmitry a chair. Zack looked at Ivan for help, and Ivan complied by getting up and offering his chair.

Dmitry shook his head, then, after a look from Zack, said, "Thank you, No. I prefer to stand."

It seemed that everyone was waiting for Gwendolyn to return before speaking. A soft knock at the door, behind Zack, caused him to move. It was Mara returning from the hospital with news about Montague. That pushed Dmitry's entrance down the list of priorities for the moment. "How is he?" Zack was the first to ask.

"Resting," Mara said. "He said to tell everyone that he's sorry that he can't be here, to help you sort things out."

"And?" Marcel asked.

"He'll be home sometime, tomorrow, after they run a few more tests. His doctor thinks that everything looks good so far. It was just a sudden reaction to something. Of course," Mara said, looking around the room, and then, suddenly, seeing Dmitry for the first time, "Oh!" she said.

"It's ok, Mara," Marcel said. "I invited Dmitry to the meeting." This seemed to bother the others, who had spent Zack's absence talking about Marcel's decision to invite Dmitry. From what Zack could observe, the vote had been split down the middle on whether, or not, it had been a good idea. "Dmitry can help us," Marcel continued, looking directly into Dmitry's face, "if he chooses to."

It was time for Dmitry to make his intentions known. "I moved the truffles into the attic, when I heard the police. I thought they would find them, and..."

There were expressions of surprise. Monsieur Le Postman was the first to interrupt. "Why would you do that for us?" He could not believe that Dmitry's motives were altruistic. "Were you planning to blackmail us, later?"

"Hmmmph," Dmitry said, and turned toward the door to leave. Zack slid in front of it to stop him. "I told you," Dmitry muttered, pushing Zack aside.

"You gonna give up that easy?" Zack said, confronting Dmitry with little more than eight inches between their faces. "I would have guessed you were braver than that." Dmitry grew red, either - from anger or embarrassment. Zack was not certain which, but his words had their effect. Dmitry turned back toward the crowded room of faces, still waiting for his answer. "I thought I could help. You do not need to know why, but No!" looking fiercely at Monsieur Le Postman, "I do not need your money. I have my own, thank you!"

Monsieur Le Postman backed off, partially because he did not want to fight the man in a room full of women, in case he lost, also, because Marcel had reached out to touch his arm. The signal was clear. "Not in my house." He would respect another man's home, or leave. "Ok, then, why?" Monsieur Le Postman persisted.

"I told you, Monsieur," Dmitry said, adding that the subject was ended.

Marcel intervened. "Dmitry, we are happy to have you in our home. Camille, please bring our friend something to drink. Would you prefer wine or vodka?" he asked.

Dmitry looked to see if the others were drinking. They were, but none had anything other than a wine glass in his or her hand. "Wine, please," he said, trying to be agreeable.

Marcel looked at Camille, and said, "Bring both. I believe I would prefer vodka." Then, he looked back at Dmitry, and the two men smiled. "Perhaps, later, when our business is finished, you would honor me with a game of chess."

Dmitry's eyes lit up. "Yes. I would like that very much."

Ivan, now, spoke. "Please take my chair," and this time he was insistent.

Dmitry moved to that side of the room, and sat down, happy that it was the furthest away from Monsieur Le Postman. The others never took their eyes off him, as if he were about to do something quite unexpected. When he sat, he crossed his arms, and stared past them, and then, only then, did they begin to relax.

Arness was the next to ask, "You moved the truffles? Where?"

"The attic," he said, pointing upwards.

Arness, Berta, and Madeleine said collectively, "There's an attic?!"

No one knew. No one had known in all the years they had lived there. Mme. Durand admitted that she did not know, but then, she rarely went past the second floor. It was just too difficult with her poor knees. Camille, if she knew, did not acknowledge it. Ivan and Albert discussed the possibility of an attic, once, based upon the structure of the building, but they had gotten lost in the engineering details of such a space. Gwendolyn and Mara remained silent, intent upon watching Dmitry, whom neither trusted.

Dmitry surprised them, by saying quite casually, "Sébastien

knew."

"He did?" Albert said. "How do you know that?"

"He was the one to show it to me," Dmitry said, as if the boy's father needed to pay more attention to what his son did. "So, he did not show you?" Seeing the look on Albert's face, he answered his own question. "No, I guess he did not."

Ivan asked, "Does Bog know about the attic?" He was afraid that Sébastien might have recruited Bog for some sort of mischief.

"You would have to ask Sébastien," Dmitry said, already bored with the conversation.

Arness and Albert had their heads together, whispering about what was going to happen to their son, when he returned from the country. Ivan and Berta, too, were wondering aloud just how much Bog knew, and why he hadn't told them. He was such an honest little boy.

Madeleine, who had been staring overhead for some time, and suspecting that the roof extended partially over her apartment, and therefore, perhaps, the attic, too, had to ask, "How far does it reach?"

Dmitry smiled. "I do not spy on my neighbors, if that is what you wish to ask."

Silence. It was, of course, what everyone had been thinking. Monsieur Le Spy was, indeed, a spy. But, then, so was Sébastien, the little bastard. What had this eight-year child seen, or heard? They were all embarrassed, as well as a little irritated. Albert and Arness seemed to withdraw, shrinking their presence in the room.

"It is large enough for me to stand above the third floor apartments. That is how I was able to work so quickly to remove the truffles from Tito's apartment. I tied a rope to the rafters and lowered myself down, then, tied a basket to another to make as few trips as possible. You have been very busy..." he stopped, not certain how to describe his neighbors. He wanted to call them what they were – thieves, but in their presence, and more importantly, in front of Zack – he did not wish to offend them.

"If I had known that putting the truffles back would cause the professor to drop dead," he said, without thinking how his words would affect Mara, who gasped at the idea of Montague lying dead, "I would not have done it."

Zack had been standing behind Dmitry, and gave him a sudden thump on the back of his head, which caused him to reconsider his words. In response, he flinched and looked over at Mara, "Sorry."

"He's going to be ok," Mara said in response, as if she needed to hear it, more than the others in the room.

Gwendolyn patted Mara's hand. "Of course, he is," she said, glaring at Dmitry, as if he had been a crass old fool to have planted any different idea.

Camille had passed around the wine bottles, before bringing out a tray with several empty glasses, and a bottle of Russian vodka. Dmitry saw the label and was, immediately, distracted from the conversation. Marcel read his look, poured two glasses of vodka, and handed him one. Holding his up to the others in the room, Dmitry said, "Za Vas!" The others were not so rude as to avoid a toast with Dmitry. "A votre santé!" they said, holding up their wine glasses. Dmitry's glass was empty in one swallow. Marcel refilled it without being asked.

"I made a phone call," Dmitry revealed, having not shared the news with Zack. "A friend in the police department." Now, he had everyone's undivided attention. "Tito's estate is being contested by two women."

The sounds in the room were in response to the news of only two women. The comments were that it would be a miracle, if there were only two. Tito had been something of a ladies' man. Who knew that undertakers could attract women like flies?

The remodeling of Tito's apartment had been paid for, not by the landlord, but by one of Tito's women, Dmitry continued. The police had a theory she had paid for the remodeling to hide her crime. A second woman was accusing the first woman of stealing valuable paintings off Tito's walls, as soon as she discovered him dead.

Zack remembered the shadows left on the faded walls. Behind, where the paintings had hung, the wallpaper had been brighter, more vibrant. Evidently, a post-mortem inventory of his possessions revealed the missing artwork. Although, Tito's family had removed his belongings, some paintings were, indeed, missing. The police were not the only ones interested. There was the insurance company, and of course, the courts, as the French government had a vested interest in the taxes, still owed on Tito's estate. Someone was going to pay them. The question was who? The police were investigating the possibility that someone inside the building, someone close to Tito, was a thief.

Yikes! Zack thought upon hearing the story. The villagers had picked the worst possible apartment in the building for hiding stolen truffles. The police might have looked for stolen artwork in all of the apartments, and found so much more.

Silence.

Dmitry got up, asked where the W.C. was located, and left the room. The buzz began with him out of the room. What to do? What to do? The truffles were back in the apartment, and there was no guarantee that the police would not return at any moment. The obvious thing to do, they decided in his absence, was to follow Dmitry back up into the attic and repeat the process of towing basket load after load back up there. With Albert and Ivan volunteering upon Dmitry's return, Zack thought it might not take long at all. He, too, volunteered to help.

Dmitry turned to look at him, "Are you crazy? I almost killed one man today. I do not wish to kill two. You stay here, where you can breathe, and blow your nose, you silly man."

Gwendolyn and Mara were surprised that Dmitry knew so much about Zack, that he cared that Zack was allergic to the truffles. How long had Zack really known Dmitry? What was he not telling the others? Zack turned to find both women staring at him, biting their lips, so not to speak. "What?" he asked.

"Nothing," they said, simultaneously.

Marcel looked tired. His glass of vodka was still half-full, and Zack suspected that Marcel did not really care for vodka. Why he kept a bottle in the house was a wonder. Zack sat down next to him, and picked up the bottle to examine the label. "I sent Camille out for it," he admitted. "I thought our guest might enjoy something familiar."

"Good idea," Zack said. Gwendolyn and Mara got up to check on the baby. Camille and Madeleine had retired to the kitchen to speak in private. The idea of someone hanging about in the attic had unnerved Madeleine, and she sought the advice of an older woman to calm her angst, before she said something that she might regret later. For the moment, they needed Dmitry cooperation. A single woman's outrage would only alienate him.

Mme. Durand chose to move over next to Zack, so that she could hear what they were discussing. Zack looked at her twice, unable to read the expression on her face. Mme. Durand was always more reserve around Marcel and Camille, deferring to them in a way that she never did around the younger residents. "He always pays his rent before it is due," she said, in defense of Dmitry. It seemed that anyone was ok in her book, as long as he paid his rent. Because he paid early, he was even higher on her list. Zack did not know what to say in response to her comment.

"It would appear that we have had two different sets of thieves in the building," Marcel said, "Tito's women and the American tourists. Let's hope that's all."

Mme. Durand's expression changed. "Are you accusing me of something?" she said, defensively. "I run a good building. I take care of business. I am honest. You know that. You see how I am; how it is!"

"Yes. Mme. Durand," Marcel said in a way that was both calming and reassuring. "This has nothing to do with you. Although, changing the digicode and putting new locks on Tito's apartment would be a prudent thing to do. Can you take care of this for us?"

It was apparent that Mme. Durand did not care for any assignments. Everything was a burden, even the mere thought of walking two blocks to the locksmith. "I suppose that I could find time on Tuesday," she offered, reluctantly.

"Please," he said, "for me, find time, tomorrow."

There was nothing anyone could do, when Marcel asked a favor. He was the village mayor. What he said as a request was really a command, and so, Mme. Durand just nodded.

"Thank you," he said. "Would you do me another favor? Would you go into the kitchen and ask Camille if she remembered to take her heart medicine today?"

Camille was eager to get up, before another assignment came her way. In truth, Marcel wanted time alone with Zack, and he had seen Camille take her medicine earlier in the day. "You believe Dmitry is sincere in wanting to help us?"

"I do," Zack replied without hesitation. "He has his faults, as we all do, but he's a good man. A better man than you might realize, but I'm hopeful, in time, everyone will come to appreciate the man as I have."

"During the war, I made the mistake of trusting one too many people. I was young and I did not know better. I was almost killed, but worse, Camille was almost killed. I do not wish to make the same mistake, again."

Zack could see that the old man did not wish to cause his old wife, with her old heart, any more stress. He wanted only to move to the sea, to live out whatever days they had left, together, and in peace. He leaned in, so that no one else could hear, and said, "I promise you. Everything will work out. You will be fishing off your back porch by summer."

That made Marcel smile. "You are a very good chess player, my friend."

That made Zack smile. He reached for a glass, and asked, "Mind if I pour?"

"Be my guest," Marcel said.

With that, Zack poured himself a glass of vodka, held it up in a toast to Marcel, and said, "Za vas!"

Monsieur Le Postman, who had followed Dmitry and the others, not to help in removing the truffles, but rather to investigate the attic, returned alone.

"It is done," he announced.

ack moved into the larger attic apartment, thrilled to have both the added space and amenities. There were two concessions required: additional rent, which was not enough to squelch the deal, and the other, occasional visits from the other villagers curious to see the attic for themselves. The best and safest entry was through the tiny door in the wall of Zack's new apartment. Guarding it made Zack feel important, but not as a centurion.

That job belonged to Monsieur Le Postman, who like Marcel pressed Mme. Durand to change not only the digicode, but all of the locks in the building. He offered to drive her to the locksmith, and back home. Who was to say that former residents had not had keys made? The comings and goings of strangers to Tito's door, as reported by Zack, had been proof enough. Delighted, Mme. Durand accepted Monsieur Le Postman's kind offer.

When Tito's apartment had been thoroughly cleaned, the repairmen came and installed the new kitchen, which had been missing for months. Each of the other villagers contributed something to the furnishing of the vacant apartment, a bed, a chair: and so, it very quickly became what it had been portrayed to be, the apartment of the Italian couple, who did not exist. The timing of its completion could not have been better because the police arrived on the following Monday, demanding a key to the vacant apartment from Mme. Durand.

She led them up the stairs, confident that they would find nothing out of the ordinary. Nearly every keyhole was filled with an eyeball, behind every door waited a coupled ear, as the arrival of the police needed no announcement. The village had been expecting the visit. Dmitry's friend at police headquarters had called on Sunday afternoon to warn him, and then, he not Monsieur Le Postman, contacted the others in the village. Zack, later, educated his friend about the breach in protocol. If he did not want to make an enemy of Monsieur Le Postman, he would have to follow the rules of the village. Respect the position, if not the person.

On Tuesday night, Dmitry attended the meeting of the villagers, this one held at a neighborhood restaurant in his honor. The others felt that he had been the key to their survival, and such heroism should not go unacknowledged. It was also the first time that Montague had felt well enough to socialize, since returning home from the hospital. The evening was one of great celebration. Zack sat alone and wished that he could have invited Tina, but was happy to enjoy the fruit of his labor. Détente had been established. The entire village had turned out. No longer was any one of them - an outsider.

Dmitry made a point of sitting next to Madeleine, and although initially she seemed uncomfortable, by the second round of drinks, all that had changed. Dmitry was capable of charming women, when he put his mind to it, and this night it appeared that his purpose was to charm Madeleine into a late night tryst. Later, his disappointment over her refusal would be tempered with an invitation from Marcel to play chess.

Zack would leave Marcel and Dmitry huddled over the chessboard, to join Tina at, yet, another underground jazz club. He delighted in the fact, that the two men were so engaged they hardly noticed his departure. Peace had returned to the village.

Montague returned to the botanical lab on the outskirts of Paris, and made arrangements to have his experiments patented and copyrighted, so that thieves of a different kind could not rob him of his life's work. Carefully, the new variety of truffle was integrated into the genuine articles, in a test to see, if anyone could tell the difference. It became quickly apparent that the professor's truffles, grown in a lab, were as good, if not better than the ones growing below ground in the south of France.

Because Montague could produce only a small amount of the new hybrid truffles, the prices remained high for the old homegrown type. The two, the old and the new, continued to be delivered to area hotels and restaurants, but no longer in bouquets of flowers. Mme. Christy had begged to be released from her role as courier. Dmitry was delivering them to restaurants, in packages marked "books," as his route expanded to include these new locations. The thought of getting caught did not worry him and, instead, brought new excitement to a job, which had grown boring. This had become a game, and Dmitry was very good at playing games. Monsieur Le Spy's offer to do this for the village served him well.

Marcel and Camille began keeping Tuesday evenings open for Dmitry to come by for dinner, and afterwards, there was always the possibility of a game of chess. Ivan and Berta invited Dmitry to join them for Sunday picnics in the park. Albert and Arness provided him with all the meats and cheese he could possibly consume, and Dmitry could consume a great deal.

Dmitry offered another favor to the village. He volunteered to teach their little bastard the proper techniques of wrestling, suggesting that it might teach the boy self-discipline.

Even Madeleine had warmed up to Dmitry, agreeing to meet him once a week for drinks at his favorite Russian café. Somehow, Monsieur Le Spy's charm had broken through her defenses. Proof lay in the fact that she had begun wearing her hair down, a sure sign that she was ready to be appreciated for woman she was, rather than as Madame Christy, the florist. Perhaps, it was his dangerous persona, which she found so attractive. Perhaps, it was because she, like Zack, realized that the big Russian bear was nothing more than a pussycat at heart.

Whatever Madeleine's reasons, it did not matter. What mattered was Zack's friend and hero was no longer alone, and now, when he and Dmitry met to work on the biography of Granville DeMonnay, the first chapter no longer began with the great man's last will and testament. Both, Dmitry and Granville, had much happier lives. Writing a final chapter was never, again, mentioned.

Monsieur Le Postman began bringing Mme. Durand more than the mail, and no one seemed the wiser for it, except Zack who had caught him slipping out of her apartment early one morning, half-dressed. Nothing was said. It was as if it had never happened. However, after that, the postman was much friendlier whenever the two men met.

Montague had felt compelled to fix the problem, which both of the remaining unattached women, Mara and Gwendolyn, shared. He invited his nephew to join them for a dinner in the city, with the hope that a proper father for Mara's baby might be found, now that Phillipe was permanently out of the picture. Word arrived from Phillipe's parents in the form of a certified letter that their son had been killed in a sports car, belonging to a woman twice his age. The accident had occurred somewhere near Monte Carlo. With the letter, they had included a check for one-half of Phillipe's life insurance. It seemed that his parents felt responsible for the baby that their son had never claimed.

Dinner went well, but Montague's nephew found Gwendolyn, not Mara, more to his liking. It was not long before Gwendolyn had her sights set on seducing the man. The nephew, who was only a year younger, was kind, intelligent, and secure in his job, which was almost as boring as Gwendolyn's.

Montague told Zack over late night drinks that he was happy that the nephew had not chosen Mara, as he and she had a "comfortable arrangement," despite the difference in their ages. Zack would not ask; Montague would not offer an explanation of what comfortable meant. In time, Monty would grow up with plenty of male role models. The men of the village would be generous with their time, knowing that there were more important things in life, than knowing who your father was.

In time, the vacant apartment would be rented to another married couple, who sought Paris for a permanent home. They were from the Netherlands, and for a while, Jan and Hans would be considered outsiders. It would take a few months for them to understand the rules of the village, to pay homage to the mayor and his wife, and to give respect to the centurion, who would issue the first invitation to join the others for dinner. They would come to appreciate the meats and the cheeses, the trips to the park, the stories of WWII, and the sense of belonging to a village in the middle of a city as big as Paris.

In time, Zack would return to New York and to Long Island, to search for a young woman, he had met in Paris years earlier. Tina was his Varushka, and like Varushka had done to Dmitry, Tina had left Paris, taking with her – Zack's heart, soul, and yes, a bit of his sanity. His time in Paris would never be forgotten, or the lessons that he learned there. His articles would be collected and published in a book, which would provide his entry into that sacred inner circle of serious writers. Lesson Ten: Life was meant to be a mystery.

Thankfully, it would be years, before the biography of Granville

DeMonnay would be ready for publication, but that was just fine with Zack, because it meant his friend, Dmitry, was alive and well, and living in Paris.

Packed, ready to depart Paris, Zack stood on the sidewalk for one last, long look at the place, which had changed his life forever. Movement up above caught his attention, as a sign appeared in the attic window. This time, it was not upside down.

Paris
6th Arr.
Appartement Louer

/ / /

If you enjoyed this book,
Please, share the title with your friends.

Merci for your purchase!

Peggy Kopman-Owens

Books and Series by Peggy Kopman-Owens:

SEVEN PARIS MYSTERIES SERIES:

THE PROMISE, Ypóschesi
...
THE SEASONS IN THE GARDEN
Les Saisons dans Le Jardin
...
GAMAN, The Japanese Art of Patience
...
THE CLUE, L' Indice
...
TOO RICH FOR RAIN
...
UNDERGROUND, L'autre Métro
...
NEVER CHANGE, Montmartre

MRS. DUCHESNEY MYSTERIES SERIES:

A JAZZ CLUB IN PARIS
Mrs. Duchesney's Mystery at Caveau des Trésors
...
AN ODD BOUQUET FROM PARIS
Mrs. Duchesney's Mystery in the Flower Market
...
UNDER A PARIS SKY
Mrs. Duchesney's Mystery on the Rooftops

...

A BANK IN PARIS
Mrs. Duchesney's Mystery along the Seine

...

A LETTER FROM PARIS
Mrs. Duchesney's Mystery in the Stamp Market

...

A KEY TO PARIS
Mrs. Duchesney's Mystery in Parc Montsouris

...

FRANCESCA'S STORY - The Interview

...

LOUIE'S STORY - The Interview

...

The Education of Francine Robinsworth Duchesney
A SUMMER ABROAD

SIMON PENNINGTON MYSTERIES:

OUT of TIME in PARIS

...

FOUND & LOST in PARIS

...

WAITING in PARIS

Single Mysteries:

THE MIST OF MONTMARTRE

...

PARIS, APARTMENT FOR RENT

...

LATE PASSENGER, A NonStop Mystery

...

QUOTES
The Wit & Wisdom of Paris Sleuths

Books co-authored with Michael D. Owens:

A Special Talent in a Place Called HEAVEN

...

WINDWARD HOME

...

SEVEN SHORT STORIES FOR STAGE

Merci!

Ingram Content Group UK Ltd.
Milton Keynes UK
UKHW011822170323
418736UK00001B/22

9 798215 355824